George Wilkins

The Growth of the Homeric Poems

George Wilkins

The Growth of the Homeric Poems

ISBN/EAN: 9783337397814

Printed in Europe, USA, Canada, Australia, Japan

Cover: Foto ©Andreas Hilbeck / pixelio.de

More available books at **www.hansebooks.com**

DUBLIN UNIVERSITY PRESS SERIES.

THE GROWTH

OF

THE HOMERIC POEMS:

A DISCUSSION OF

THEIR ORIGIN AND AUTHORSHIP.

BY

GEORGE WILKINS, M.A.,

LATE SCHOLAR, TRINITY COLLEGE, DUBLIN;
ASSISTANT MASTER, HIGH SCHOOL, DUBLIN.

DUBLIN: HODGES, FIGGIS, & CO., GRAFTON-STREET.
LONDON: LONGMANS, GREEN, & CO.

1885.

PREFACE.

TO present to English readers the main results of German criticism of the Homeric Poems, so far as it is sound and trustworthy, is the object of this book. The very latest publications of the Press of Germany have been consulted, so as to collect, up to date, the materials for forming a judgment.

I have to tender my acknowledgments and thanks to the BOARD of TRINITY COLLEGE for accepting the book for their Series, and to Professor MAHAFFY for many valuable suggestions while the sheets were passing through the Press; also to Canon THORNHILL for his assistance in revising proofs.

GEORGE WILKINS.

TRINITY COLLEGE, DUBLIN,
Sept. 4th, 1885.

CONTENTS.

b

ERRATA.

Line 11, page 95, *for* contest *read* contrast.
Line 10, page 121, *omit* τοὶ δ' οὔτε πάλιν οἶκόνδε ἀρίστους εἶσε λόχον.

GROWTH OF THE HOMERIC POEMS.

N O apology is needed for the publication of a work in English dealing with the Homeric question. Seneca thought life was too short to consider it, but found plenty of time for other things better neglected ; since his day, however, the world has had over a thousand years to ponder the problem, and for the last century, at least, European scholars have essayed its solution with more or less success. The literature of the question in Germany has become quite an ocean in its extent ; in England not much has been done, principally owing to a foolish prejudice that it is wanton impiety to subject Homeric poetry to a critical examination—

‘We do it wrong, being so majestical, to offer it the show of violence’.

But was it impiety in Newton to resolve the sunlight into its elements, and to explain the cause and nature of the rainbow ?

B

I think anyone who has literary perception sufficiently
fine to have really felt the completeness which characterizes
a perfect work of art—the achievement of a single artist—
an ode of Pindar, or a play of Sophocles, cannot fail to see
that the Iliad and Odyssey are not sufficiently 'at one' with
themselves or with each other to be the work of a single
mind.

English scholars, who often care for little besides the
beauty of the episodes in the poems, will not take the
trouble of acquainting themselves with a study which they
think as unprofitable as unpalatable—a kind of Intellectual
Sauerkraut, which none but Germans can appreciate; and
readers, who are unable to examine the Greek for themselves, perceive such a general similarity in the style and
subject of the poems, that they rest quite satisfied in opinions which seem as incorrect as though one should think
the 'Book of Common Prayer' or the 'Psalms of David'
were the work of a single author.*

Even granting that the poems were the work of one
man, would it not be an interesting and profitable study
to try to trace the development of his mind and art; for
poems of such extent grow up gradually, receiving constant
additions from the poet himself, if from no other, and may
therefore well show indications of differing moods and differing powers, and thus afford tangible basis for an hypothesis as to their evolution.

Few, however, have inclination for such a study, which
in this country is decidedly unpopular. Most real lovers

* Cf. Professor Mahaffy's ' History of Greek Literature ', vol. i. p. 69.

of poetry look upon it with aversion, while another class, pledging themselves to an admiration of the poems that is almost aggressive, cannot tolerate for an instant that 'bold, bad man' the critic. These remind one of the lovers of the picturesque in Heine's poem—

'Philister in Sontagsröcklein
　　Spazieren durch Wald und Flur;
Sie jauchzen, sie hüpfen wie Böcklein,
　　Begrüssen die schöne Natur.

'Betrachten mit blinzelnden Augen,
　　Wie alles romantisch blüht;
Mit langen Ohren saugen
　　Sie ein der Spatzen Lied.'

And it is for such as these that those epideictic essays are written, in which the essayist points out the exceeding beauty of Homer, as who should exhibit the sun by the light of a candle. Therefore, when some German critic who has long contemplated the brightness of that glory, and like an astronomer, has long been familiar with its sun-spots, comes forward with an hypothesis to explain them, the good souls, who were it not for the candle would never have known there was any sun at all, cry out as though it were about to be destroyed.

The sooner we get to feel that 'Homer' is but a convenient 'label' to mark certain books upon our shelves the better. Of Homer the man we know and can know nothing beyond his work, that is, beyond the origination and partial development of the Iliad, and perhaps of the Odyssey. If we erect to him a shrine, a 'Ομήρειον, as did the

Smyrnaeans, it must bear the inscription, 'To the Unknown Bard'. Of course nothing is easier than to yield to
the soft allurement of those graceful stories which the Greek
mind, beyond all others, could invent to make up for deficiency of facts about the poets :—'the blind old man of
Scio's rocky isle'; Anacreon and the grape-stone; Ibycus
and the cranes; Arion and the dolphins; the Athenians
purchasing their freedom by reciting passages from the
plays of Euripides, and returning home to thank the poet.
Who can forget the thousand and one lovely stories which
charmed our boyhood, but which to the adult mind, seek-
ing for truth, are mocking mirages, which make us call to
mind the words of Pindar—

> ἦ θαυμάτα πολλά, καί πού τι καὶ βροτῶν
> φάτιν ὑπὲρ τὸν ἀλαθῆ λόγον
> δεδαιδαλμένοι ψεύδεσι ποικίλοις
> ἐξαπατῶντι μῦθοι.

I.

We have told the reader he will find here an agnostic standpoint with regard to Homer: he will therefore probably lose patience when we proceed to discuss the poetry and poets who preceded the Unknown Bard; but as he has no doubt often quoted the words of Horace, 'Vixere fortes ante Agamemnona', so let him bear with our 'quid pro quo' when we quote a very similar saying of Cicero (Brutus, § 71): 'Nec dubitari debet quin fuerint ante Homerum poetae'.

That there must have been epic poets before Homer who composed lays in hexameter metre is self-evident, unless we suppose that the inventor of the metre brought it himself to Homeric perfection. Who these poets were is for ever a secret; yet if we think what genius the creation and elaboration of the hexameter pre-supposes, we must feel that among them was one perhaps greater than Homer, for I consider the invention of the Hexameter to have been the greatest achievement of the Human Spirit, between the evolution of language and the introduction of writing, among the Greeks: it rendered possible both Iliad and Odyssey; it assisted the memory, and thus ensured their preservation; until writing was, as I may say, discovered by the Greeks, this was the form of every composition meant to survive; and not until writing came to supersede it, and to perform more effectively the office it had performed, did the hexameter fall into neglect, just as calligraphy fell into neglect upon the discovery of printing.

The inventor is said to have been Olen, a name coined no doubt to satisfy those who wanted information on the point, and who were quite contented when they were dogmatically told something definite.

Of pre-Homeric poetry there seem to have been three great streams, when the Greeks were originally coming into Greece, after leaving the other Indo-Germans, viz., the Thracian, Phrygian, and Cretan. To try to be more definite than this is idle. Orpheus, a pre-Homeric poet of whom we hear a great deal, is purely mythical—a poethero, an ideal bard; Ribhu is the Sanscrit name. As for Musaeus ('servant of the Muses'), and Eumolpus ('the good chaunter'), their names are transparent; Thamyris, too, seems to be but a pre-historic Fata-morgana of the later 'Blind Maeonides' of tradition. Chrysothemis, Philammon, Linus, Pamphos, Hyagnis, Bakis, and Olympus, the pupil of satyr Marsyas flayed by Apollo, these of Pausanias' mentioning, and the host of pre-Homeric poets whose names were given by Demetrius Phalereus (Schol., γ. 267,* and

* All through I cite the Iliad by Greek capitals; the Odyssey by small letters.

Suidas, v. Θάμυρις), may be consigned to the same limbo as 'Old John Naps of Greece'.*

For pre-Homeric poetry the Homeric poems themselves, and whatever light we can derive from Indian literature, furnish the oldest authority and best evidence that we can have : it is vain to seek information, as the Germans do, in the fictions of late writers who were as ignorant of the facts of the case as we are. Judging, therefore, merely from the Homeric poems, epic lays seem not only to have existed before them, but actually to have become somewhat artificial, mechanical, and dead. To show their artificial and mechanical nature, I need only call attention to the fixed and stock epithets, some of them indeed as old as the Vedas, δοτῆρες ἐάων, datāras rasūnām; certain formulæ like ὧδε δέ τις εἴπεσκε; and ever-recurring numerations. How often do we hear of something continuing nine days, and being completed in the tenth? how often of something thrice attempted, and thrice failing? For seven years is Aegisthus king (γ. 304); for seven years is Odysseus with Kalypso (η. 259); for seven years is the beggar in Egypt (ξ. 285). To show its partial numbness and deadness, I need only refer to the epithets Τριτογένεια, 'Αργειφόντης, and Φιλομμειδής, which the epic poets seem to use without understanding their meaning.

* *Taming of the Shrew*, Act I. Sc. ii. 95 :—

'Why, sir, you know no house nor no such maid,
Nor no such men as you have reckon'd up,
As Stephen Sly and Old John Naps of Greece,
And Peter Turph and Henry Pimpernell,
And twenty more such names and men as these
Which never were nor no man ever saw'.

We cannot, however, establish with certainty the existence of any definite cycle of legends, any 'Sagenkreis', anterior to Homer, because the passages which seem to suggest
such a cycle occur only in the Odyssey, which will be shown
hereafter to be later than the Iliad : I refer to such passages
as μ. 69, *sqq.*, where the tale of the Argo is spoken of as
being known to all (πᾶσι μέλουσα), or to θ. 500 where Demodocus is represented beginning as it were at a certain
chapter in the legend of the Trojan War (ἔνθεν ἑλών). The
only reference in the Iliad to such pre-Homeric epic lays
is in I. 189, the κλέα ἀνδρῶν that Achilles sings, and we
cannot do better than give to such lays this name in per-
petuity.

Poetry pervaded all Greek life; but at the different periods of the development of Greek civilization different kinds
were perfected—'some grew to honour, some to shame'—
heroic, didactic, dithyrambic, satiric, gnomic, tragic, comic,
bucolic, epigrammatic—all waxed and waned, all had their
day. Destiny, looking upon the different sorts of poetry
amongst the people, discerns some little sign of differentia-
tion—some characteristic for natural selection in one kind
more than in another—and forthwith marks out this kind
for future development and renown. So from the many
kinds of pre-Homeric poetry which were popular amongst
the masses, and of which we find mention in the Iliad—the
Threnos, the Hymn, the Paean (A. 473, X. 391), the Linus,
the Hymenaeus, the dancing songs whether warlike or festal,
and the κλέα ἀνδρῶν—the last had the mark of distinction,
and were therefore chosen for cultivation and renown, were

the favourites of fate, and outstripped their fellows in the race for fame.

Indeed some of the songs of the people never rose to fame at all, nor did any poet of great genius deign to lift them out of their obscurity and marry them to his immortal verse, as for instance the cradle-songs, βαυκαλήματα and ναυναρίσματα; the beggar-songs, χελιδονισμοί and κορωνίσματα; the working-songs, whether πτιστικά and κελεύσματα, or the ἱμαῖον μέλος, and ἐπιμύλιοι; fables, χαρώνεια; drinking-songs, παροίνια; the *aubade*, διεγερτικόν; and the riddle, γρῖφος.

That Homer was in doubt whether the development of the γρῖφος or of the epos was his true vocation in life seems as certain as any other *soi-disant* fact about him given by late writers: it was commonly stated that he died of grief and vexation at not being able to solve a riddle.

I take it for granted, then, that the hexameter was in full swing before Homer; that *epic* lays were already composed in that metre; that already their style and diction had become definitely fixed, formal and technical, and in some few instances even archaic; then came the Mighty One,—Homer,—and by the torrent of his genius marked the channel in which epic poetry should ever after flow; the Mighty One who laboured, and into whose labours, as we shall show, lesser men entered without the slightest effort, as the Cæsars succeeded the great Julius, or the emperors Charlemagne.

It will be the object of most of the following chapters to show how the Iliad and Odyssey are the united product of

the genius of Homer and of his successors. I believe that
Homer's great merit—the merit which makes him 'a name
for ever'—was his seeing that the hexameter, the epic, the
tale of the Trojan War, the heroes Achilles and Odysseus,
were the elements out of which the poetry of the future was
to be made. From amongst the vague and formless legends
of his day he chose those of the Trojan War for immortality,
and fixed them in rigidly-defined form by his genius: his
successors might add to it, but could not alter its shape and
the main features which he had given it. For fully two
centuries after his death that crystallized mass of poetry
kept slowly augmenting like an Alpine glacier. We can
imagine the divine spirit of the poet looking down with
majestic pride from the heaven of his immortality upon
the gradual advance of his work— .

> 'The Glacier's cold and restless mass
> Moves onward day by day ;
> But I am he who bids it pass,
> Or with its ice delay.'

II.

I⊤ is not unusual for English books to speak of Wolf's
'Prolegomena ad Homerum' as though the views therein
contained were till then unknown and uncreate, and as
though in the year 1795 they sprang suddenly into the world
armed for battle, and terrible as Athene from the head of
Zeus. Such a view is unwarrantable. Many of the ideas
which the book contains had been put before the modern
world a long time previously. Jacob Perizonius, in his 'Ani-
madversiones Historicae' (1684), had stated that the Homeric poems were not originally committed to writing;
Bentley, in 1713, mixing truth and falsehood in a strange
haphazard way, had said 'Homer *wrote* (!) a sequel of songs
and rhapsodies to be sung by himself for small earnings and
good cheer at festivals and other days of merriment: the
Iliad he made for the men; the Odyssey for the other sex.
These loose songs were not collected together in the form of
an epic poem till 500 years later'. That the poems did not
impress Bentley's mind with the idea of their original unity
of design is plain from his words, which are otherwise of
little worth, being quite unsupported by proof, and assum-
ing as incontrovertible that Homer *wrote*. Similar guessing,

with the additional drawback of being at once dogmatic and systematized, characterizes the book of François Hedelin, Abbé d'Aubignac, which, from a comparison of the Homeric lays with the French *chansons*, represented the Iliad and Odyssey as the merest patchwork : the absence of proofs for his assertions, and the obvious ignorance of the writer, were fatal to his theory. A perusal of the book nearly cured Wolf of scepticism, for indeed the Abbé goes too far : not content with demolishing Homer, he proceeds to disparage all Greek literature, from which, he says, he never learned anything worth speaking of : a statement, as Wolf slyly remarks, true, and moreover the only thing true in his whole book.

On Giambattista Vico, however, the book seems to have made a more favorable impression, for in his ' Principi di Scienza nuova' (Nap. 1730), he maintains that Homer was no historical personage, but a mere Ideal, and that his name means ' joiner of lays,' a view which meets with corroboration from recent etymologies of the name.*

Another forerunner of Wolf was Thomas Blackwell, Professor of Greek in Aberdeen, whose book, ' An Enquiry into the Life and Writings of Homer, London, 1735', is unfortunately chiefly epideictic, and of little critical value. The author shows that Homer was merely the topmost blossom of all the rich efflorescence of Ionian life; that he was the child of his time as much as Shakspere was; and that he

---

* G. Curtius, however, maintains that it must have a passive sense, ' fitted together '; so that it would not be the name of a poet, but of his perfectly-finished work.

looks on life with the same clear eyes, the same simple and natural feeling. Soon after came an 'Essay on the Original Genius of Homer, London, 1769 ', by Robert Wood, a Minister of Foreign Affairs, and friend of the Earl Granville of that day. In the year 1742 he had travelled in the East, visiting Egypt, Palmyra, and Troy ; and on his return to England, as a foretaste of that banquet which the detailed account of his travels should furnish, he got some few copies of this Essay printed and circulated *privately* among his friends (for being a person of quality he objected to his books being sold in the common shops). The Essay is important, not only on account of the acuteness and daring which characterize it, but also as an attempt, the first in modern times, to identify the scene of the Iliad with the actual Troad as existing in the year of grace 1742. It is an old story by this time how successful later discoverers, going on Wood's lines, have been, and the achievements of Dr. Schliemann in especial have made him known throughout the world.

In 1783 Wolf was appointed Professor in Halle, and soon after edited the Odyssey and Iliad, with prefaces in which we see a faint glimmer of the views he afterwards publicly set forth. To mature these views he collected for ten years all the material that could throw any light upon the Homeric poems; but it was not till the publication of the Scholia of the Venetian MS. by Villoison that he had proper apparatus to work with. Half a century previously Antonio Bongiovanni had given to the learned world a short account of a Venetian MS., sister to the one which it was

Villoison's glory to edit in 1788.   It is a year for ever me-
morable, and marks an epoch in classical scholarship.

Jean Baptiste Gasparde d'Ansse de Villoison was still a
young man when, in 1781, he discovered the manuscript
which has made his name immortal, but he was already
known as a scholar through editing the Lexicon of Apollonius, which he had unearthed in the Library of Saint
Germain des Prés.   The Venetian MS., or, as it is called,
Codex Venetus Marcianus A, is of the tenth century, and
besides the text contains the Scholia, which are principally
the criticisms of Aristarchus as reproduced by Aristonicus,
Didymus, Herodian, and Nicanor, but very often they are
verbal quotations from Aristarchus himself.   The publication of these Scholia threw such a flood of light upon the
Homeric poems that all previous knowledge of their history
seemed mere darkness.   In these Scholia, and in Villoison's 'Anecdota Graeca', which are two quarto volumes of
gleanings from hitherto unpublished material in the Library
of Saint Mark, Wolf found much food for meditation till
1795.   In that year he could keep silence no longer: the
scepticism which he had subdued and kept under for nearly
twenty years at last bursts forth: 'Jacta est alea', he cries,
'ad quam certe non imparatus accessi'.

Wolf's 'Prolegomena' forms an excellent propaedeutic
to the Homeric question: it is a celebrated book, but one
little read outside Germany, and the quotations that one
occasionally finds made from it are made at second-hand.
The fame it gained for its author upon its first appearance is

almost incredible ; and yet, strange to say, a second edition of it was not printed till 1859. The book is octavo, and the full title is 'Prolegomena ad Homerum, sive de operum Homericorum prisca et genuina forma variisque mutationibus et probabili ratione emendandi, scripsit Frid. Aug. Wolfius. Halle: 1795 '. The following chapter will be mainly an abstract of its contents, with some necessary criticisms.

III.

The book opens by distinguishing between the *recognitio* and *recensio* of texts; the former being a kind of *à priori* guessing at the right reading; the latter being based upon a careful examination and collation of MSS. As far as Homer is concerned, all the MSS. at first accessible to Wolf were so late as to be but of little use: they are not at all as old as some which we have of Herodotus, Plato, or Isocrates; and yet the text of these authors is far from perfect. Bad, however, as are our MSS., far worse were those worked on by the Alexandrian critics, to whose untiring labours we owe our text in its present state.* As for ever getting at the original form of the poems, Wolf deems it sheer folly to think of such a thing: and we may rest well content if we make our present copies as good as those which were used by Plutarch, Longinus, and Proclus.

Wolf decries former editors for not giving Scholia, &c.,

---

* The few fragmentary papyri of the first century which we possess contain no readings better than the Vulgate. They are often disfigured by barbarous mistakes made by slaves whom the booksellers employed to multiply copies of the text for the market, and who seem not to have understood Greek. Some more papyri, found last year at Fayoum, are at present being examined by scholars at Munich, and may in time yield some profitable results.

and for having never read even Eustathius, quoting Barnes' boast, 'Eustathii intima scrinia se compilasse', and convicting him of a deliberate falsehood. To Ernesti, however, he gives high praise: 'Tantum aberat ille a perversâ opinione eorum qui hodieque hunc textum, qualis paullatim forte fortunâ factus est, genuinam ac prope μουσόπνευστον habere videntur; istorum exemplo Buxtorfianorum, qui eandem rem olim praedicabant de Hebraico codice suo, quum ab eo omnem ingenii et tantum non rationis humanae usum arcerent, ea quoque tanquam θεόπνευστα reveriti quae nunc a doctis vitiosissima putantur.'

Villoison's Homer furnished invaluable information, but it failed to satisfy the extravagant hopes which had been raised about it amongst scholars who had for a long time previously been hearing the names of Zenodotus, Aristarchus, Crates, Alexion, and of all the other Alexandrian critics, and who expected the publication of their commentaries and διορθώ-σεις. Of these Villoison's book contains only the 'shreds and patches' which Time has left, and which show what a vast amount of commentary formerly existed on the poems, and no doubt was still extant in the fifth and sixth centuries of our era. Wolf eulogises the Venetian Scholia, comparing them to the Jewish Masora, and vaunting their superiority, and then proceeds in no very modest strain to recount his own labours in preparing an edition of Homer previous to Villoison's publication. He had read, he tells us, the ponderous commentary of Eustathius several times, and made careful extracts from it; had collected all the Scholia then extant; had perused every lexicographer, grammarian, or

c

ancient author, in whom any quotations from Homer could
be found, and above all, had studied the poems of his Alexandrian imitators.   He had elaborated all this material,
when suddenly, by the publication of the Venetian Scholia,
his labours were for ever superseded, and to his no small
astonishment he found that Eustathius, till then the infallible authority on all matters Homeric, had been nearly as
badly off as himself; for that prolix divine had not so good a
text as the one in the Library of Saint Mark, and dropped
into utter disgrace as a commentator when compared with
the newly-published scholiasts, 'non tantam, quanta vulgo
fruitur, laudem meruit; plurimam debet jacturae doctiorum
scholiorum.'   Yet these scholiasts themselves often indulge
in dreary ineptitudes; but as they were men speaking
Greek, which had not yet become a dead language, they
not unfrequently explain difficulties with an ease unknown
to later scholars, and by reading them one makes acquaintance with the sort of studies which were in vogue amongst
the teachers of Cicero, Horace, and Virgil: 'non ambitiose
hoc dici plures loci Ciceronis, Senecae et aliorum, docent,
atque omnis ratio grammaticae et liberalis institutionis apud
Romanos.'

The goal that Wolf set before him was to reconstitute
the text of Homer, so that one of the ancient critics, Longinus for instance, would have been satisfied with it.   He
then proceeds to a history of the text, which he divides into
six periods—(1) the first reaching from the origin of the
poems to the time of Pisistratus, who is said to have collected and formed them into two complete poems; (2) from

Pisistratus to Zenodotus, who first inaugurated the criticism afterwards cultivated with such success by the Alexandrians; (3) from Zenodotus to Apion ('propter artem interpretandi poetae, ut Seneca scribit, totâ Graeciâ circumlatum'); (4) from Apion to Longinus, and his pupil Porphyry, both of whom emended and explained the poems; (5) from Porphyry to the Athenian Demetrius Chalcondylas, who brought out the first printed edition; (6) from Demetrius Chalcondylas to the end of the eighteenth century.

Some may wonder that works like the Iliad and Odyssey, in which one meets so few gross mistakes, should demand the great labour which Wolf imposed upon himself. It must be remembered, however, that the critic is more exacting than the ordinary reader, and often has his suspicions roused by the very smoothness of a passage and the apparent absence of faults, and he often forces us to accept some unattractive reading whose long descent is duly attested in preference to some *parvenu* no matter how charming: 'saepe enim severiore judicio, quod a veterrimarum auctoritatum collatione ducendum est, plane efficitur ea omnes numeros veritatis habere, in quibus maxime offensae sint; alia autem incertae aut nullius fidei esse, quae perquam probabili et festivo sensu niteant'.

There are readings which are in all the MSS., and which must be rejected, as λύσαιτε (A. 20); Πιερίῃ (B. 766); ἐπόψιον (Γ. 42). Some of these are very ancient, and have excellent authority; but Wolf, who cares little for great names if they are nothing more than names, wishes it were possible to know in what state each critic received the text from his predecessors, and what changes he introduced into it, 'ridetur *cor Zenodoti et jecur Cratetis;* an Aristarcho ea ubique acies mentis et judicii fuit, ut ab eo dissentire sit nefas?'

Verses, too, are found in all the MSS. which are certainly interpolations, as for instance N. 731, which even in the Venetian Codex is not obelized, and yet has no more authority than those verses which are sometimes quoted as Homer's by ancient authors, but which will not fit anywhere into our present text. Among the ancients, as among ourselves, the text met with much superstitious reverence. Lucian would not hear of a single traditional line being set aside; but, on this principle, one would blindly accept whatever text might be accidentally extant in one's day, and would cherish every *lapsus calami* as a special beauty-mark, *e. g.* ἰχῶρ (E. 416) for ἰχῶ; ὁμίλῳ (I. 545) for ὁμίλου.

The Greeks themselves had not any standard text of Homer: from the quotations which both Hippocrates and Aristotle make, we see that their texts must have differed considerably from ours, and Wolf proves, by instancing many variants, that the text called 'the edition of the casket', possessed by Alexander the Great, has not survived in ours. Indeed as the poems were composed without the aid of writing, and for a long time preserved by memory only, it is more than likely that the very first copies which were written must have differed considerably from one another, and that these differences quickly gave birth to others. An interesting analogue is presented by the MSS. of Dante which vary considerably within twenty years of his death, and thus render the fixing of his text well-nigh hopeless. How difficult then, nay, how impossible it must be, to restore the Iliad and Odyssey to their original form, especially if they are the work not of one but of several bards.

It is desirable, therefore, that we should find out at what period the Greeks first made use of writing. And when examining the Iliad and Odyssey, we must above all things eschew notions about the evolution of epic poetry which we may have derived from the Aeneid or Paradise Lost. In Homer we find fresh and vigorous genius, and little of that elaborate art which characterizes the latter poems. The erudition attributed to Homer by commentators is quite chimerical; yet many who would perhaps readily grant that Homer was unlettered are quite shocked to hear that he was illiterate, although this fact only serves to heighten our estimate of his genius. We can scarcely conceive how he could do without writing, just as we wonder at the old navigators doing without the compass, or Cæsar and Alexander fighting battles and storming cities without gunpowder. We must not, however, by laying too much stress on vague words and expressions, go too far, and conclude, says Wolf, that Homer could not count save on his fingers (πεμπάζομαι); nor, on the contrary, from the word εὐνομίη conclude that there were then written codes of law; nor must we take γράφειν and σῆμα as denoting the actual writing of alphabetic signs.

Of the origin of their alphabet the Greeks themselves knew nothing; late authors naïvely quote prose and verse of a period anterior to Cadmus, 'Mirum est, inquit Plinius,

quo procedat Graeca credulitas! nullum tam impudens men-
dacium est, quod teste careat.' The form of the Greek
letters points to their Phœnician origin; but granting that
the Greeks had an alphabet, and had even carved a few
inscriptions, yet this would not prove writing to have been
in general use. At that early time writing had not become
the indispensable necessity of life it is nowadays, and
poetry could well do without it. Papyrus was probably not
obtained in large quantities till the seventh century, when
Egypt was opened to the Greeks (Herodot. v. 56): before
that, writing, thinks Wolf, was confined to stone, wood,
and metal. 'Sed folia Sibyllis et amantibus relinquimus
etsi illius moris vestigium quoddam videri possit in ἐκφυλ-
λοφορίᾳ et in petalismo Syracusano'. The Greeks did not
use linen like the Romans, and though the preparation of
skins for MSS. may, as Herodotus says, have preceded the
use of papyrus, yet even when the means of writing were
abundantly provided, it took many years before the Greek
alphabet was perfected. At Athens it was only in 403 B. C.
that the alphabet of twenty-four letters was adopted. The
Ionians, no doubt, were the first to adopt the Phœnician
characters and to use writing; though Kirchhoff in his recent 'Studien' is opposed to this view.

In 664 B. C. we are told that, for the first time in Greece,
written laws were formulated for the Locri Epizephyrii by
Zaleucus. In the time of Solon public inscriptions at
Athens were βουστροφηδόν, that is, going from right to left,
and then from left to right. Writing need not have become
common until prose began, for prose cannot exist without

it; and though the poets Archilochus, Alcman, &c., must have written their poems, still it would not be common until the time of Pherecydes of Syros and Hecataeus, of Miletus, who range between 550 B.C., and 500.

Though the Homeric poems imply that the heroes knew nothing of writing, it has been doubted whether Homer may not himself have been acquainted with the art. Josephus says he was not, and probably expresses the ordinary Greek belief, ὅλως δὲ παρὰ τοῖς Ἕλλησιν οὐδὲν ὁμολογούμενον εὑρίσκεται γράμμα τῆς Ὁμήρου ποιήσεως πρεσβύτερον. . . . . καί φασιν οὐδὲ τοῦτον ἐν γράμμασιν τὴν αὑτοῦ ποίησιν καταλιπεῖν, ἀλλὰ διαμνημονευομένην ἐκ τῶν ᾀσμάτων ὕστερον συντεθῆναι, καὶ διὰ τοῦτο πολλὰς ἐν αὐτῇ σχεῖν τὰς διαφωνίας.

The two passages in the Iliad supposed to speak of writing know nothing of an alphabet: in H. 175 the κλῆροι are only arbitrary symbols scratched on wood or pebbles, which the herald carries round to the chiefs, that he who threw one into the helmet may recognise it: accordingly ἐπιγράφειν in v. 187 means to scrape or scratch. The other passage, Z. 168, 169,

πέμπε δέ μιν Λυκίηνδε, πόρεν δ' ὅγε σήματα λυγρὰ,
γράψας ἐν πίνακι πτυκτῷ θυμοφθόρα πολλά

presents no difficulty; all the old scholiasts are agreed upon the point: γράφειν is equivalent to χαράσσειν or ξεῖν, σήματα to εἴδωλά τινα, and πίνακα to σανίδα or ξυλάριον.

In the poems, then, there is absolutely nothing which would lead us to infer the existence of writing, and the history of their transmission seems to establish the very con-

trary. We may well accept the words of Rousseau : ' Si
l'Iliade eût été écrite, elle eût été bien moins chantée, les
rhapsodes eussent été moins recherchés et se seraient moins
multipliés'. In Homer's time there was no necessity for a
poem to be *written :* if it was a poem at all, it would pass on
from generation to generation, ' vivu' per ora virum.' It is
only in the present day that poems have to trust for immortality to beautiful typography and a binding in 'congenial
calf'; it is only modern poets who deliberately set themselves to the task of writing 'for posterity.' The Homeric
bards composed for the immediate applause of their hearers,
as we see from the cases of Phemius and Demodocus, and
at a later period from what the rhapsodist Ion says in Plato
of his recitations. All sorts of poems, even those of Xenophanes (Diog. Laert. ix. 18), used to be recited by such
rhapsodists. The most famous school of them was at Chios ;
it was a family of Homerids (the most celebrated being
Cynaethus, Ol. 69), who sung Homer's poems, and who
themselves also composed : ' atque ex hoc factum esse puto,
ut tam multa carmina illorum temporum, oblitteratis rhap-
sodorum, a quibus confecta essent, nominibus, quum ab aliis
et aliis subinde repeti solerent, tandem falsis auctoribus
assignata et ad extremum ἀδέσποτα circumferrentur '.

In Homer's time the calling of bard was quite special,
and followed by men wholly devoted to it : these bards, and
afterwards the rhapsodists, recited purely from memory ;
and even in the time of Socrates,* when a fashionable craze
for collecting MSS. of Homer, similar to that in modern

* Xen. Mem. iv. 2, 10.

times for collecting Elzevirs, took possession of the biblio-
phils of Athens, the recitations of the rhapsodists were
made without the aid of book or written copy. Of course
their memories when carefully cultivated soon became mar-
vellously retentive, and the poems were no doubt handed
down in the schools of the rhapsodists with as much jealous
care as that which guarded religious learning amongst
the Hebrews. The words technically appropriated to
poetry and poets all point to oral instruction : διδάσκειν
δράματα, docere ; μανθάνειν, discere partes ; διδάσκαλοι, ὑπο-
διδάσκαλοι, ἀντιδιδάσκαλοι, &c.

Once these schools of rhapsodists were firmly established,
the Homeric poems were quite as safe in their keeping,
although unwritten, as they would have been in libraries
and MSS., so elaborate and careful was the training to
which neophytes were subjected. The Alexandrian critics,
who had no more idea of the disintegrating criticism of
nineteenth century Germans than they had of gunpowder
or dynamite, attributed most of the variants to these rhapsodists ; and no doubt the rhapsodists did occasionally make
mistakes in single words, or perhaps now and then one
of them 'greatly daring' deliberately changed the position
of a verse ; and often, no doubt, some rhapsodist of high
poetic power would interpolate verses of his own into
the poems it was his profession to recite. That they had
poetic genius is plain from the Hymn to Apollo, which
is confessedly later than Iliad or Odyssey. It is well
known that both poems of Homer were recited only in
parts at a time—parts, too, arranged in different orders,

and each generally with a special name. These names
are given at the beginning of the rhapsodies by Aelian and
Eustathius, and by many other writers, who often quote
Homeric passages under these titles. The parts were of
very uncertain length, nor did they, as we may infer from
Eustathius, coincide with the division into books made by
Aristarchus : the Ἀλκίνου ἀπόλογος, for instance, embraced
four or five books of the Odyssey, an amount which could
not be got through with ease at one recital. Others, however, are shorter, as the Διομήδους ἀριστεία (E and part
of Z), Θεομαχία (Υ and Φ), Δολώνεια (K), &c. Their
titles, however, and length were not definitely fixed, but
varied according to the exigencies of recitation, or the
caprice of the reciter.

Under such conditions then as we have pointed out it
is quite impossible to imagine bards composing poems of as
great length as the Iliad and Odyssey in their present state.
Not even Homer, exclaims Wolf, could have done it, 'de-
cem linguis, ferrea voce, aeneis lateribus'; no, he would
surely have required pen, ink, and paper for it. But
granted that he had them, and had written his poem, would
he not have been in the same plight as Robinson Crusoe
when he had built his boat, unable to launch it into the
world of publicity ? For though some men of exceptional
acquirements may have used writing at that early time, yet
we cannot postulate a reading public; and without written
copies and a reading public how could even a Greek
audience, in an age when scenic acting was unknown, sit
out an epic of 15,000 lines, and grasp its beauty as a whole !

The Odyssey is, in the main, dominated by one idea—
the Return of Odysseus; but in the Iliad we cannot be
quite sure what is the chief subject of the poem. If one
were to take the opening lines in their strict sense, the
poem should end with the eighteenth Book; but if all the
Books are to be brought under one great idea, then the
majority of them will be in celebration of the *ira memor*
of Achilles, and all of them of his glory. Wolf suggests
that the opening line may have originally begun—

ΚΥΔΟΣ ἄειδε θεὰ . . . .

The connexion between the Books is so slight, and the
inconsistencies which they contain so numerous and so vital,
that Wolf sees in the Iliad no more than a mere juxtaposition of independent rhapsodies. Would it not be strange,
he asks, that from amongst the many stories of the war
just one only—the Iliad—should remain to us 'perfect and
entire, wanting nothing'? and would it not be still more
strange that we should hear nothing of other stories 'done
into verse', too? It would be strange, indeed : and the explanation is, that our Iliad consists of just these very stories
collected together, and made to fit into each other as well as
they can. Were four different poets, says Wolf, to treat of
the war, their collected poems could not differ from one another more than parts of the Iliad do from other parts. The
subject of the Ἰλιάς in its present state is certainly not the
wrath of Achilles, but infinitely more ; and that the wrath
did not dominate the whole poem seems to have been the
feeling of those superstitious ancients who wondered why

Homer *began* such a splendid work with the ill-omened word μῆνις.

In the Odyssey, on the other hand, we have a whole put together by some bard in an age when subordination of details to the main subject had begun to be better understood. We can well imagine that the sojourn of Telemachus with Nestor and Menelaus, of Odysseus in Ogygia, and the tale of his wanderings which he tells to the Phæacians, were composed and sung apart by themselves, without any intention that each should be an integral part of a great future poem, a poem which when put together would be more than the mere aggregate and sum of its components, having had breathed into it the breath of life,—plot and organization. It is quite erroneous to think that what is indispensable to any such work of literature in the maturity of a nation, viz., duly-articulated plot, was understood so early in the development of the Greeks. That the Homeric poems were originally without it seems plain, from the fact that their imitators, the 'cyclic' poets, are all destitute of plot; for Aristotle naïvely remarks that Homer was the only one of the epic poets who knew how to invent and develop a single action : ' Quam sero Graeci in poesi didicerint totum ponere, permulta docent '. In didactic poetry we must come down to the age of Xenophanes and Parmenides to find works well composed, with a fundamental idea and a well-sustained plan. There is hardly any plot at all in Hesiod. It is mere sophistry to declare that the ships' catalogue is an integral part of the Iliad : had it been wanting, no one would ever have discovered that the poem, to be complete, stood in need of it.

Wolf has found many breaks in the continuity of the poems: for example, at Σ. 356–368, where the disturbing element, a quarrel between Zeus and Hera, is shown by the Scholia to be an interpolation. There are many similar examples in the Odyssey; but most absurd of all is the case of Pylaemenes, who though slain by Menelaus in the fifth book of the Iliad, yet weeps among the mourners at the death of his son Harpalion in the thirteenth. A good instance in the Odyssey is at δ. 620, where we are hurried away, sooner than one would wish or expect, from the pleasant discourse of Menelaus, not to return again till the fifteenth book. Now after δ. 620 four verses follow which are very harsh, owing to the strangeness and ambiguity of their language. Eustathius explains δαιτυμόνες, not in accordance with the usage of Homer as *guests*, but as *hosts*, τοὺς τὴν δαῖτα ἐτοιμάζοντας. He also explains ἀλόχους in a not less unusual sense, *maid-servants*, as they were the concubines of the suitors, and he refers the whole passage to the hall of Odysseus, not to that of Menelaus. Barnes took ἀλόχους to mean wives of the sons and friends of Menelaus. Madame Dacier thinks it refers to Sparta, probably being misled by the θείου βασιλῆος; but μῆλα ἄγειν recalls the suitors to our memory, αἰεὶ μῆλ᾿ ἀδινὰ σφάζοντες, and μνηστῆρες in v. 625, appears to go very well with the servants preparing the banquet: but, be this as it may, the sudden shifting of the scene from Sparta to Ithaca is clumsily managed, and the voice that we hear singing is not the voice of Homer.

I wonder no emendator has as yet obliterated these troublesome verses, and by marking the change of scene as simply as at ρ. 166, won for himself a name amongst the critics. Certainly had this been done, or had v. 625 been made the beginning of a new book, I imagine no one would ever have discovered that the passage had been tampered with.

The putting together of the Homeric poems, like the proverbial building of Rome, was not the work of a single day, nor of a single man, nor even of a single age. The Alexandrian critics set aside the end of the Odyssey from ψ. 297, and the last book of the Iliad, as later additions.

Perhaps the best way to throw light on the origin of the poems is to detail their subsequent history. From the tradition that Lycurgus introduced the poems into Peloponnesus from Ionia we may obtain a small precipitate of fact, viz., that before his time few rhapsodies were known to the Spartans, but that he increased their number, and that thereafter Homer was held by them in high esteem. From the days of Lycurgus to those of Solon the rhapsodists sung the poems according to their own caprice; at Athens, however, Solon ordained that they should be sung at the Panathenæa, ἐξ ὑποβολῆς,* that is, in the natural order of the events they celebrated; elsewhere the rhapsodists were masters of the situation, and adopted whatever order they chose, reciting the Ὁπλοποιία before the Λιταί,

---

* Tradition states a further order of Solon's, namely, that they were to be recited ἐξ ὑπολήψεως. This is explained by Bernhardy as implying fixed divisions, or lays in the poems, which were to be sung entire.

and sometimes even before the Λοιμός. Solon thus did much for the unification of the poems at their recitation, and the work so well begun by him was completed by Pisistratus: the lays chanted in every order, or rather disorder (confusa, διεσπαρμένα, διῃρημένα, σποράδην ᾀδόμενα) by the rhapsodists, were collected, say the ancients, and arranged in their proper order by him, and for this they give him high praise. If Pisistratus did no more than this, he deserves no more fame than a printer who rearranges the disordered sheets sent to press by a careless author, 'omnino tantum in hoc negotio relinquunt homini, qui ex eo ipso maximam famam eruditionis consecutus est, quantum hodie interdum negligentiores scriptores relinquunt curae typographorum.' Wolf thinks that Pisistratus did not *rearrange* them at all, but rather arranged them for the first time, duly organizing and articulating them. The Doloneia, according to the Alexandrian critics, was originally a separate poem, and it was made an integral part of the Iliad by Pisistratus, who placed it where it now stands. There is an absurd story that the *raison d'être* of Pisistratus' edition was to supply copies of the poems for the Athenians, whose own had been destroyed by fire, and that Pisistratus established a commission to collect material from all quarters of Greece, and to publish an authorized text. Now this sounds anachronistic enough, but it is too much to be told by Eustathius that Zenodotus and Aristarchus took part in it along with Onomacritus ! Wolf cannot help being severe: 'nos, qui scire nobis videmur quid inter fabulam et historiam intersit, illic historiam sub fabula agnosci-

mus, simili eruendam modo quo versati sunt viri docti in
Judaïco commento de LXX. interpretibus'.

Whatever the work of Pisistratus may have been, it left
much that might still be done by others, and which never
was done, not even by the Alexandrians themselves, as we
see from verses quoted by Plato* and others which are not
to be found in our Homer.   It is impossible to form a definite idea of the text as settled by Pisistratus; Hipparchus
followed the example set by his father, and then other
editors took up the task, διασκευασταί as they are called,
which in Aristarchus' use of the word is almost equivalent
to interpolator.

* Rep. II. 379.   See Bergk. G. L. 1, 887.

IV.

THE second period of the history of the Homeric poems, viz., from Pisistratus to Zenodotus, is scarcely less obscure than the first. Until the age of Pericles, Homer was known throughout Greece almost solely from the recitations of the rhapsodists, and not from reading. Cynaethus of Chios, the most famous of the rhapsodists, and reputed author of the Hymn to Apollo, was contemporary with Pindar. During this period the philosophers attack Homer on moral grounds, while others defend him, reading into the poems all kinds of allegorical meanings, which would transform the poet into a sage philosopher and grave theologian. Later on, many of the sects, especially the Stoics, showed the greatest zeal in discovering these ὑπόνοιαι. Aristarchus, however, opposed this, and everywhere adhered to the literal meaning; yet this did not deter the philosophers from finding weighty ἀπόρρητα and doctrines of their own all through the poems, and it has continued to be a favourite pursuit even to the present day. The Sophists, on the other hand, only used the poems as a source whence to draw difficult problems, which required the subtlest ingenuity to solve. These προβλήματα, or ἀπορίαι and their λύσεις, in which

D

afterwards the learned *alumni* of Alexandria occupied themselves so much, were very fashionable in the schools of the
philosophers and Sophists; nor must we seek elsewhere the
origin of critical study which those very ἀπορίαι in many
instances rendered indispensable.   Two emendations of the
kind remain, which were made by Hippias of Elis;* the
place for the first of which, were it not for Aristotle's passing
notice (*Poet.*25), would never have been discovered, so altered
is our text.   It is B. 15, where at that time, instead of
the words Τρώεσσι δὲ κήδε' ἐφῆπται, was read pretty nearly
as at Φ. 297, διδόμεν δέ οἱ εὖχος ἀρέσθαι.   It was thought im-
pious to represent Zeus as promising what was not to happen
(Wolf compares 1 Kings, ch. 22); therefore Hippias, with
sophistical subtlety, altered the word δίδομεν to διδόμεν, the
infinitive for the imperative, so that by the change of an
accent the blame might fall not on Zeus but on the Dream.
The other passage is ψ. 328, to which he gave its present
form.†   Where, if Hippias was the first to expunge οὐ, and
if his contemporaries handed down such readings as θηλυτε-
ράων in φ. 454 for the τηλεδαπάων of Aristarchus, we see,
without going further into the matter, what faults disgraced
the copies of that day.

     In the time of Pericles copies of Homer were used in the
schools for boys, though the instruction was chiefly given
orally.   Afterwards it became usual to collect texts of
Homer, as we read Euthydemus did,‡ and this may have

---

* Bergk., G. L. G. p. 891.
† Σκύλλην θ', ἥν οὐ πώποτ' ἀκήριοι ἄνδρες ἄλυξαν.
‡ Xen. M. S. ιv. 2. 1.

naturally suggested their collation, which was not, however, carried to any great extent. We know of eight famous διορθώσεις previous to that of Zenodotus: two by individual scholars, Antimachus and Aristotle; the remaining six the town editions, of which some few variants are preserved to us. But let us here, once for all, do away with the notion that the critics of that day were like those of the present time: they did their best, no doubt, to restore to Homer his original and genuine form, but their attempts were very vague and rash, and aimed chiefly at making the bard everywhere consistent, and removing any passages which they considered deficient in merit, and occasionally adding beauty where there was little before. And just as a man of taste and talent, but unskilled in criticism, would deal with some old poetic relic of our language, which he might find in a fragmentary state and with many variants inserted in the margin, even so, Wolf thinks, those early editors treated the poems; so far were they from that sternness which takes care lest anything be introduced which was not written by the author of the book. In fine, all early emendations proceeded upon the *aesthetic*, not upon the *critical* judgment.* The editions called αἱ ἀρχαῖαι in the Scholia are also, no doubt, earlier than Zenodotus.

Villoison has shown that Antimachus the editor was no other than Antimachus the poet. Of the διόρθωσις of Aristotle, ἡ ἐκ νάρθηκος ἔκδοσις, we know but little, except that Alexander the Great carried it with him during his conquer-

---

* How infantile were the first essays in criticism is plain from the procedure of Aristophanes in his *Frogs*.

ing career, and professed as much admiration for Homer's poetry as Napoleon Buonaparte is said to have had for Macpherson's. Editions are mentioned of an unknown Euripides, and an unknown Nessus of Chios. The poet Philetas of Cos, the master of Zenodotus, is also said to have corrected the text. Later than Zenodotus we find three poet-editors : Aratus for the Odyssey, Rhianus for the Iliad, and Apollonius Rhodius for general textual criticism. Alexandria becomes the birth-place of grammatical studies, and under the Ptolemies grammarians and commentators spring up with startling rapidity.

Most of the authors, whose variants and critical remarks are quoted in the Scholia or in Eustathius, are grammarians who treated special Homeric questions, and were not editors or even commentators in the strict sense at all. They were either ἐνστατικοί (that is, proposers of subtle difficulties in the poems), or λυτικοί (those who solved them), and their writings had ceased to exist long before the Scholiasts made the compilations which we now possess ; indeed, even the recensions and expositions of the best critics, *i. e.* Zenodotus, Aristophanes, Aristarchus, and Crates, were not then extant : in fact, from the time of Augustus on, scholars contented themselves with making abstracts of the works of the great critics, copying scholia, and compiling lexicons. Of these, one by Apollonius, though in a fragmentary state, is extant, and has been edited by Villoison.

It is difficult to get a clear idea of what was done by Zenodotus of Ephesus, whom Suidas calls the first corrector, διορθωτής, of the text. The scholiasts attribute to him all sorts of ineptitudes: even a tiro would be ashamed of the absurd readings attributed to him; and so numerous are the verses 'athetized' that he leaves Homer but a shadow of his former self ('nonnullis visus est Homerum prope ex Homero tollere'); often removing the very finest passages, 'contaminating', curtailing, enlarging, as he thinks fit, and treating the Iliad as though he were the author and composer of it himself—'omnem sibi in Iliada velut in propium opus arrogat potestatem'; so violent and capricious was criticism at its commencement. Yet Wolf has a fellow-feeling for Zenodotus, and quotes Ausonius in his honour—

'Maconio qualem cultum quaesivit Homero
Censor Aristarchus normaque Zenodoti'.

To Zenodotus is attributed the correction of φή for ὡς, B. 144, and many changes of syntax, as well as the substitution of more modern forms for old-fashioned or obsolete ones; also the correction of many mistakes which had arisen from the imperfection of ancient writing, the non-separation of words, or from the rapidity with which copies were multiplied for sale.

After Zenodotus comes his pupil Aristophanes of Byzantium, in the reign of Ptolemy Philopator (φιλόμηρος, Wolf styles him) and Epiphanes. Although his attention was chiefly devoted to the tragic poets and to his namesake's comedies, yet whatever he did for Homer was sound and excellent: some of his readings are quite as good as those of our common text, and his corrections not unfrequently win the approval of Aristarchus. This is no small praise,

for Aristarchus was regarded by the ancients as the king of
critics; indeed his name has become proverbial for severity;
yet of the 800 books which he wrote on literary questions
almost nothing remains, although, thanks to the Venetian
Scholia, his recension of Homer is tolerably well known to
us.   The commentaries of Didymus and Aristonicus were
abstracts, and often word-for-word transcriptions of Aristarchus' commentary on the Iliad.

Wolf treats Aristarchus rather unfairly; but there is
a good deal of truth in his estimate of the great Alexandrian.   He shows that Aristarchus was not a critic in the
same sense as Bentley or Valckenaer: from Horace's words,
' Fiet Aristarchus', he concludes that he was more an inter-
preter and judge of poetry than a textual critic, and maintains that he dealt with the Homeric poems as Varius and
Tucca would have dealt with the unfinished poem of Virgil,
had they not been prevented by the request of Augustus and
of their dying friend.   To a Greek or a Roman, a critic
meant a connoisseur in literature, a man like Maecius Tarpa.
The aim of Aristarchus' criticism was not to restore the
poems to their original condition, but to give them the ele-
gance demanded by prevailing taste and fashion, so that
the greatest of poets might not seem awkward amongst the
brilliant Alexandrian savants: ' forma genuina illis fuit ea,
quae poetam maxime decere videbatur.   In quo nemo non
videt omnia denique ad Alexandrinorum ingenium et arbi-
trium redire'.

Ammonius says there was but one edition by Aristarchus: the bad readings which are attributed to him are not

really his, but are merely the old ones allowed to stand unaltered : as he did not introduce into the text the readings of
which he himself approved, they remained only in notes
and scholia.   To Aristarchus belongs the glory of having
first fixed the rules of Homeric grammar ; it was natural,
therefore, that where a slight correction would bring the text
into accordance with his rules, he should make that correction; but when this was impracticable, he declared the passage spurious, as K. 397–399, for instance, on account of μετὰ
σφίσιν, *inter vos*.   Apollonius Rhodius, however, had taken
no offence at this meaning of the pronoun, and had even
used it as a first person plural, II. 1277.*   Perhaps, therefore, Aristarchus carried his grammatical pedantry too far.
We have seen how justly he rejected allegorical explanations of the poems, and limited himself to common sense :
yet even in this he goes too far, and often lays himself open
to the charge of ψυχρολογία.   In E. 860, and Ξ. 148, where
Ares and Poseidon shout as loud as ἐννεάχιλοι ἢ δεκάχιλοι,
he introduces the correction ἐννεάχειλοι ἢ δεκάχειλοι !   This
can only be paralleled by his conjecture in Pindar, *Pyth.*
III. 76, where, thinking the stride of Apollo was too long, he
read for βάματι ἐν πρώτῳ, βάματι ἐν τριτάτῳ !   In his use of
the obelus Aristarchus seems not to have marked lines which
we should consider spurious, but those which he thought
unworthy of Homer, and which Homer, had he been trained
in the schools of Alexandria, would himself have con-
demned : ‘obelum ab Aristarcho non tam iis versibus esse

* Both Apollonius and Aratus use their pronouns with great license.

praepositum, quos crederet Homeri non esse, quam his omnibus, qui ei viderentur digni reprehensione minusque digni
loco suo vel absolutissima arte principis poetarum.'   Yet
though Aristarchus may have carried his self-importance
too far, he was in the main right when he felt that the
critic who would emend these poems whose early history
was so strange—orphans, as it were, of noble birth—must
above all things free them from aught misbecoming their
divine origin : 'non quid cecinerit Homerus, sed quid canere
debuerit, spectare debuit emendaturus'.

'Hence,' says Wolf, 'it is plain that we have not Homer's
poems in their original freshness and vigour as they were
known to his contemporaries, but that we receive them,
wasted as by a long illness, continued from the time of Solon
to that of the Alexandrians, during which arrangers, inter-
polators, and correctors, subject the poems to whatever course
of treatment they think fit.'   Scholars had long suspected
this, but the publication of the Venetian Scholia placed it
beyond all doubt.

Crates of Mallos is the last critic of whom Wolf treats.
He belongs to this period, and founded at Pergamum a
school similar to that of Alexandria, and almost as famous.
He did his best to read all the science of his day into
the poems, and make Homer out as great a polymath as
himself.

Wolf never completed the ' Prolegomena', which were
published in their present fragmentary state; but, incom-
plete though they are, they give us a fair outline of the

external history of the text,* and of the amount of knowledge or ignorance possessed by the ancients with regard to the origin and proper form of the poems. As to their authorship or origin, in many respects the Greeks knew even less than we: Aristarchus himself appears to have been ignorant of the existence of the digamma ; therefore, putting the ancients aside, let us turn with the moderns to the poems themselves, and try what we can learn from their nature and contents. Perhaps we shall not be altogether unsuccessful in our attempt to unweave that glorious ' double rainbow' which spans the mist and darkness surrounding the cradle of European civilization.†

* This is now supplemented by Lehrs and Ludwich very considerably, in separating the Scholia as to origin and tradition.

† In his recently-published 'Aristarch's Homerische Textkritik nach den Fragmenten des Didymos dargestellt und beurtheilt,' Ludwich maintains (p. 27) that the great Alexandrian's criticism was only *tentative ;* he establishes (p. 16) against Ammonius, as Lehrs has done also, that there were two editions by Aristarchus, a point on which Wolf hesitated.

V

THE Homeric poems are the oldest works of European literature, and were the earliest achievement of the Greek race, for which, as for all cultivated nations since, they established the high-water mark of intellectual excellence, and now for nearly three thousand years have remained unapproached and unapproachable in their freshness and beauty above all other works of literature and art. They have become, as it were, a part of Nature to us and to other cultivated Indo-Germanic peoples. To the transient generations of men they seem everlasting as the hills themselves. They are older than the city called Eternal; and in another three thousand years, when that city may be nothing but a name, they will still be as fresh and lovely as a summer dawn.

The influence that the Homeric poems exercised on the subsequent literature of Greece can scarcely be overrated. Greek epic poetry is but an echo, and later on, a conscious imitation of them. Aeschylus, the founder of Greek tragedy, calls his poems but 'crumbs from the Homeric banquet'. Amid Sophocles' merits it is not the least that his treatment of character is 'Homeric'. History first accepts the myths and traditions of Homer as true, moulds its style after them, and soon interprets seriously the germs of fact which it believes they contain. Philosophy, too, as soon as she begins to ponder the problem of Humanity, sees in the Homeric poems the great 'fact' to be dealt with, and either tries to expel the poems from their place in education, or else, by importing into them her own views, to claim Homer as an ally and support. Phidias, the greatest of Greek sculptors, confessedly borrowed from Homer the conception of his Zeus, which was set up in Olympia, the centre and focus of Hellas, and which was acknowledged by all as a satisfactory embodiment of the Hellenes' idea of the Most High. To Athens, that other focus of Hellas, Homer was all in all: and to imagine Greek life without the Iliad and Odyssey is as impossible as to imagine it without sun-shine or air.

In Europe educators have wisely used the Homeric poems to sweeten the often bitter draught of schoolboy learning: and many—looking back on years of life deso-lated by school routine in remote towns, where the light of culture flickered and went out—remember how their hearts leaped at the sudden sunlight that burst on them when they first read Homer, and how his caressing verse made divine amends for their long journey through the gloomy desert of 'useful' knowledge. Everybody knows what an awakening in Elysium it was to Keats when he first read Chapman's English rendering of the poems; and it is an old story now how great a boon Voss conferred on the German nation by his translation of Homer into the vulgar tongue: anyone who looks into the literature of the time will see what a deep sensation it produced, and how Homer's poems became in art and poetry the canon of Truth and Nature. Goethe's words have become a familiar aphorism: 'Homer stellt die Existenz dar, wir gewöhnlich den Effect: er schildert das Fürchterliche, wir fürchterlich, er das Angenehme, wir angenehm'. Lessing, in his famed 'Laocoon', seems not to know whether Homer is more true to Nature, or Nature to Homer.* The French and Italian have their translations by Madame Dacier and Monti, the Slav and even the Irish Kelt have theirs by Schukoffsky and MacHale.† The Greeks gave the greatest honour to Homer's memory, and indeed deified him, nor has their high estimate of his genius been set aside by succeeding ages.

But all the calm light that rested on the godlike head of the deified Homer has been within the last century darkened and overcast; and amidst a 'mighty pother' of storm and thunder he has been caught away from our eyes like a second Romulus. He is gone, and in vain we seek him sorrowing.

The Iliad and Odyssey, commonly called the poems of Homer, are not the work of one poet; but each is a collection of separate lays by different bards. Of the two the

---

* Cf. Pope, *Essay on Criticism*, 1. 134:

    'And when to examine every part he (*i. e.* Virgil) came,
    Nature and Homer were, he found, the same'.

  † Schukoffsky's version is of the *Odyssey;* Archbishop MacHale's is of the first six books of the *Iliad.*

Iliad is the elder collection. On a festal evening, in some rich man's home, the lay was sung to the accompaniment of the Kithara. Probably it was of moderate length, and treated only of a single exploit glorifying the ancestry of the entertainer. Lays which dealt with the same subject—the siege of Troy for instance—tended to fuse together, having more natural affinity for one another than for those which treated of some alien subject. As this war surpassed all others in interest, the 'tale of Troy divine' was most often demanded by audiences, and so the separate lays of separate bards dealing therewith were brought closely together until they formed wholes, one of which by the natural law of survival proved itself the fittest. While other collections perished by neglect, the 'fittest' throve and augmented, and finally, being brought to Athens, it was fixed in writing by Pisistratus. The poems are the poetic growth of a long period of time, conditioned by natural laws like language itself, and, like it, in nowise the work of a single individual.

This was the obvious conclusion to be drawn from Wolf's 'Prolegomena ad Homerum'. It caused the most widespread commotion in Germany, not merely among scholars, but among the general public, who had been all bewitched by the charm of the Homeric poems a few years previously in Voss's translation. Fichte and Humboldt adopted Wolf's views, and Goethe eulogized the great critic in verse:—

'Erst die Gesundheit des Mannes, der, endlich von Namen Homeros
    Kühn uns befreiend, uns auch ruft in die völlere Bahn!
Denn wer wagte mit Göttern den Kampf, und wer mit dem Einen?
    Doch Homeride zu sein, auch nur als letzter, ist schön'.

These names suffice to show how Wolf's theory influenced
the best minds of Germany on the question : but quite apart
from Homer, Wolf's work is of the highest importance in
the science of history and criticism, owing to the conscien-
tiousness of his method. For almost twenty years he had
in silence pondered and proved the thoughts which he un-
folded in his 'Prolegomena'; for twenty years he had untir-
ingly investigated the traditions of antiquity, the poems
themselves, and all that cultivated men of any age or country had written about them; and after his twenty years of
study he resolved, though with inward repugnance, to yield
to the inexorable force of reason, and abandon errors which
had become most dear to him. Fr. Schlegel, a man whom
no one will suspect of taking delight in the overthrow of
time-honoured beliefs, bestows the highest praise on Wolf's
work :—'Through the spirit of disinterested love of wisdom, science, and truth that it breathes—through its con-
centration, and the skilful concatenation of such a long
chain of evidence—it is a model of research'.

Many scholars have since followed the path pointed
out by Wolf, minutely examining the connexion between
the poems and their dialectic and metrical form; carefully
reviewing all notices of Homer or Homeric poetry in ancient authors; and studying closely the growth of Greek
culture in connexion with the literary development of other
nations; for all these *momenta* must meet with their due
and proper consideration if we are to arrive at a trustworthy result. Lachmann (who applied Wolf's principles
to old German poetry) confined himself strictly to the struc-

turo and connexion of the Iliad, contributing much of the
very highest value in that department. So numerous and
so excellent are the writings of others on the subject,
especially of Nitzsch, Bäumlein, Nägelsbach, Düntzer, Friedländer, and Jacob, that they have interested not scholars
merely, but the general public of Germany in the 'Homeric
Problem'. And amongst other good results it is not the
least that they have freed the subject from the limitations
of pretended historical facts. The answer to the question
of original unity, or subsequent union of originally independent lays, can only be sought in the poems themselves.

In the poems themselves. Theoretically this sounds very
well, but in practice it often means leaving the decision to
subjective inclination and individual feeling; yet the fact
that convictions are divided ought not to make us give up
hope that we may obtain a fair solution by careful study;
and poems of the extent of the Iliad and Odyssey, by minute comparison of their separate parts, afford a standard
which very considerably limits the uncertainty of subjective
views. Let us first examine the Iliad.

The events and actions which the Iliad presents to us
have a tolerably close connexion with each other. The host
of the Achaeans are already in the tenth year of their effort
to take Troy by way of vengeance for the crime of Paris; but
Achilles, the bravest of the Greeks, deeply mortified at an
insult put upon him by Agamemnon, the leader of the army,
resolves to avenge the wrong done him by withdrawing from
the combat. Thetis, the goddess-mother of Achilles, by her
prayers obtains from Zeus the promise that the Greeks shall

suffer defeat until Agamemnon repent his injustice and offer
satisfaction. Then follows the fulfilment of the promise. At
first the daring of the Greek chieftains stems the tide of
Trojan valour, but soon the Greeks fall into such distress
that Agamemnon sends an embassy of the noblest men in
the army to pray for reconciliation with Achilles, and
offer full satisfaction. But Achilles' thirst for vengeance is
still unslaked. The distress of the Greeks must intensify,
the Trojans must press into the camp, and the burning of
the ships must threaten them with complete destruction,
before he can bring himself to give up his rancour and
throw off his inaction. It is the next day which brings
matters to the crisis. The bravest Greeks retire wounded
from the field, Hector breaks through the gate and rampart
of the camp, even the mighty Ajax cannot stop him, and
soon a ship is set on fire. Hereupon Patroclus, the trusty
companion of Achilles, begs him to help the Greeks in their
hour of need, or at least to allow himself and the Myrmidons
to take part in the fight. Achilles gives permission. The
timely succour brought by Patroclus turns the fortune of the
day, and lured on by his success, contrary to the express
command of Achilles that he should do no more than defend
the camp, he presses boldly on the flying Trojans. But soon
he falls, and with difficulty is his dead body, already stripped
of its armour, rescued from the enemy. On learning the
heart-rending tidings, Achilles comes to the rampart, and
merely by his battle-shout awes the Trojans and drives
them back. Next morning Agamemnon gives full satisfaction for his insult, and Achilles discards his rancour,

burning with desire to avenge his beloved friend. This vengeance he wreaks in the renewal of the fight, and slays, after many heroes of lesser note, Hector, the hope and pillar of Troy. The burial of Patroclus, the funeral games in his honour, the giving back of Hector's body to the aged Priam and the death-lament over it, close the epic.

This brief sketch will suffice to recall the main features of the poem. One cannot possibly review it without immediately perceiving the clear connexion of the whole, and the grouping of details about a common centre. But admiration of the Homeric poems has advanced a step further than this, and has made the discovery that the whole Iliad is dominated by a single thought, a leading idea, a *motif*, running all through it, and in the following way is the doctrine formulated: 'To Achilles' righteous and just resentment the Most High Ruler of the world grants satisfaction; but human passion drives into excess and malignity resentment which in itself was just. Achilles sins in rejecting the proffered atonement, and through the death of his dearest friend pays the penalty for his excessive wrath'.

Who would deny that the course of events in the Iliad is peculiarly suited to the expression of this great moral idea? Who is ignorant of the fact, that the right measure of excess and defect—the Mean—is that notion which through a natural tact the Greeks of every age considered the Ideal of the Good and Noble? Yet it is much to be doubted whether in the Iliad, as we have it now, and as the old Greeks had it (be it a single conception or a union of sepa-

rate elements), we can find the presentation of that idea
dominating the whole, or can even fairly read it into the
poem. In fact, we are justified in giving the statement
an unhesitating denial. It is NOT for righteousness' sake
that Zeus grants full vengeance to the wrathful Achilles;
he owes a debt of gratitude to Thetis for former kindnesses,
by means of which she moves him to grant her request.
The rejection of the proffered atonement by Achilles is NOT
the point on which the subsequent action turns : no notice
is taken of it afterwards, where there is every need of its
being mentioned, and Zeus, without the slightest indication
of displeasure at Achilles for being so implacable, remains
true to his promise to obtain satisfaction for him through
the ever-increasing distress of the Greeks. When Patroclus falls, neither God nor man regards it as a punishment for the excessive wrath of Achilles; he is slain by the
direct action of a god friendly to the Trojans, and because
he transgresses Achilles' express command in pressing on the
retiring enemy. The *motif* which we were to find running
through the poem is on all vital occasions not only wanting,
but there is another, essentially different, occupying its
place. One must, as it were, stand far away from the
Iliad, and take a very distant view of it indeed to
arrive at the conclusion that any single thought domi-
nates the whole.

As soon as we leave the merest general outline, and approach the details of its execution, weighty considerations
force us to give up all thought of a continuous whole.
Difference of style and manner one cannot hope to make

generally understood; and as to the grounds for doubt which depend upon the contents of the poem, so great is their number and complexity, that it is quite impossible to convey an adequate idea of them without entering into a minute and lengthy examination; yet here we may give a slight foretaste to show their general nature, and the basis they afford for theory.

Such discrepancies as that of the same hero being killed on different days and by different adversaries may be passed over as trifles; they only occur in the case of unimportant names, and incongruities of the kind in a long poem might readily be set down to forgetfulness in the poet even on the presupposition of single authorship. But there is something further which deeply affects the main action itself.

There are three days of battle, the detailed account of which occupies the greater part of the Iliad: the first is tolerably favourable for the Greeks though deprived of Achilles, and reaches from the second almost to the end of the seventh book; the second—which tells of the distress of the Greeks, Patroclus's fight and death, and ends with the appearance of Achilles on the scene of battle—embraces from the eleventh to the eighteenth; and finally the third—in which is recounted Achilles' vengeful slaughter of the Trojans, and the slaying of Hector—occupies the twentieth, twenty-first, and twenty-second books. On closer acquaintance we meet the greatest difficulties. Zeus promises in the first book to bring about the defeat of the Greeks to satisfy the wrathful Achilles: yet so far is this

from taking place, that at the end of the first day's fighting the Greeks have decidedly the best of it. Again, on
the second day, the account of the commencement of the
battle begins briskly : after eighty verses we hear that
as long as the sun was mounting the heaven the luck was
equal; but after that, *i. e.* after noon, the decisive change
began ; yet further on, when we have through five books
followed the many vicissitudes of the fight, and have learnt
events which must have occupied a considerable time, viz.—
the battle round the rampart of the Greeks, the storming of
its gate after obstinate resistance, Poseidon's help given to
the Achaeans, the cozening of Zeus by Hera, his sleep, and
the assistance he lends to the Trojans on awaking, their
rallying, the fight round Ajax's ship, Patroclus's prayer to
Achilles for permission to succour the Greeks, the arraying
of Patroclus and the Myrmidons, and a large portion of the
combat in which they engage—after all this, though 4000
verses previously we were expressly told it was noon, we
learn that it is still noon, or nearly noon, for the sun
is in the mid-heaven. Arbitrarily to excise some passages
between the two notices of noon, as later enlargements of
the originally compact relation, avails but little, for the
whole development of the fight—which is to bring about
the appearance of Patroclus—and a considerable portion of
the battle shared in by him, fall into a period which has
no existence, viz., between two points of time which are
expressly stated to be identical.

The appearing of Patroclus on another occasion is just
as strange. At the beginning of the unfavourable turn of

events in the eleventh book he is sent by Achilles in hot haste to inquire who is the wounded man that Nestor is bearing from the battle.   Patroclus is in such a hurry to fulfil his impatient lord's command, that he refuses Nestor's courteous invitation to seat himself in his tent.   Soon, however, this haste is all forgotten ; and during the storming of the rampart by Hector, during the many reverses of fortune which occupy four long books, Patroclus remains in the tent of the Greek chief placidly conversing; nay, stranger still, when he finally, in the sixteenth book, returns to Achilles he brings no answer to the commission laid upon him, nor is a word said about his having been sent out at all.

Similar want of consistency we find all through the poem, no matter how vivid and intuitively intelligible the separate episodes may be : even scenes which are most closely united often will not fit in with the whole state of the fight, or the manner of it, or the place where it is carried on.   We have mentioned how Agamemnon sends an embassy of the noblest men in the army to Achilles to offer reparation so complete that we wonder it is not accepted, yet shortly after Achilles speaks as if the embassy had never been sent at all (Π. 71) :

> (Τρῶες) τάχα κεν φεύγοντες ἐναύλους
> πλήσειαν νεκύων, εἴ μοι κρείων Ἀγαμέμνων
> ἤπια εἰδείη.

Of the part which Poseidon takes in the battle on one occasion we have two separate and irreconcilable accounts (N. 345–360, and N. 10–39).   In the later passage he is represented 'stealing secretly forth from the grey salt sea'

(v. 352), and 'avoiding to give open aid' (v. 356) to the
Argives; yet in the earlier passage, where his glorious coming from Samothrace with chariot and horses is described,
there is not a thought of secrecy or concealment. Again in
Λ. we find a prophecy of Zeus about the immediate future
which is irreconcilable with what follows. Zeus (vv. 191–
194) promises that when Agamemnon is wounded and retires
from the combat he will 'give Hector strength to slay till
he come to the well-timbered ships, till the sun goeth down
and sacred darkness draweth on'. Soon after Agamemnon
is wounded and leaves the fight; but Hector, instead of
pressing on victoriously with god-given strength, and hew-
ing his way towards the ships, is himself wounded by Diomede (vv. 355, 356):

> στῆ δὲ γνὺξ ἐριπὼν καὶ ἐρείσατο χειρὶ παχείῃ
> γαίης· ἀμφὶ δὲ ὄσσε κελαινὴ νὺξ ἐκάλυψεν·

and as soon as he gets breath again he leaps into his chariot
and drives away! So, too, in Θ. we come upon a jarring
discord: Zeus prophesies that Achilles will rouse himself
(vv. 475, 476):

> ἤματι τῷ, ὅτ' ἂν οἱ μὲν ἐπὶ πρυμνῇσι μάχωνται
> στείνει ἐν αἰνοτάτῳ, περὶ Πατρόκλοιο πεσόντος.

Now ἤματι τῷ is never used to signify the immediate future,
yet it is on the evening of the very next day that Achilles
appears at the trench, and the fight over Patroclus's dead
body was in the open field and *not* at the ships. So patent
were these inconsistencies that Aristarchus struck out the
lines as later interpolations. But perhaps even more re-

markable are the irreconcilable narratives describing the
death of Patroclus, which are in immediate juxtaposition.
In Π. 793–815 we read how Apollo stripped him of his
armour; yet in P. 125–187, and still more expressly in
v. 205, it is stated that Hector did so.

Here are inconsistencies which cannot be set aside. We
may be captivated by the life-like vividness and power of
the separate parts and of individual episodes, but the effort
to hold fast the thread of the narrative ends in utter failure.
We cannot maintain our equilibrium, but, as though in a
mighty ocean-current, are swept away out of our steady
course. Yet in an age where there was no other way to
make acquaintance with a poem but by hearing it recited,
surely it must have been necessary that above all things the
plot should be simple, easily comprehended, and clear.

Quite different is the impression left by the account of
the battle of the first day (reaching from the second to the
seventh book), which, though it be inconsistent with what we
are led to expect from A., yet is in itself, if we make some
inconsiderable exceptions, clear and intelligible. Who that
has ever read the Iliad can forget the striking picture of
Helen amongst the Trojan grey-beards as they sit viewing
the Greeks from the wall of Troy; the delicately-finished
sketch of Pandarus, the beauty of which Lessing has ap-
preciated so well; the heroic deeds of Diomede, the chival-
rous scene where he meets with Glaucus; and, finally, the
parting of Hector and Andromache, which, though often
imitated, has never been surpassed in its touching beauty
and truth? But though each separate portion is so fine that

it is hard to give the preference to any one of them,
yet their union with one another cannot be accepted
without hesitation. There are too many events crowded
together for us to consider them as taking place succes-
sively on one day; and the connexion of scene with scene
is anything but clear.

These books begin with the arming of the Greek heroes,
which is splendidly pourtrayed: the muster of the host and
the names of the chieftains occupy nearly 400 lines; all
points to the beginning of a great general engagement;
and there follows—a truce, and the single combat of Paris
with Menelaus. A solemn agreement, ratified with sacrifices
and oaths, that if Menelaus be victor Helen and the treasures shall be restored, is wantonly broken; and yet later,
on that very same day, Hector is represented as proposing a
second single combat without covenanting for any prize of
victory, and almost without a thought of the previous combat. The Greeks, too, without a word of reproach for the
former perfidy of the Trojans, accept the challenge; and
still more strange, though the former combat resulted in
their favour, though in the general action they had been
superior, yet their bravest chieftains have not courage for
the fight, and need Nestor's reproaches to rouse them from
their dismay. Among these cowards is Diomede, who on
this very day had courage enough to fight with Ares and
to vanquish him. But even before this we find Diomede's
prowess has all evaporated most mysteriously, for scarcely
has he driven Aphrodite and Ares from the field, when
upon meeting Glaucus he inquires with most punctilious

piety whether he be a god or no, 'since in a combat with the gods no man should engage'.

It will not be necessary to enumerate here any more contradictions of this kind, though the abundance of them invites one to do so; for in the two parts of the Iliad under review, that is, in almost half of the entire poem, the host of considerations that present themselves would take up too much space, and we can only attempt by some obvious instances to point out their kind and their signification. Whoever would wish to find full confirmation of the importance of these contradictions will not seek it in the writings of those who have so convincingly established the dissonances, but will rather turn to the best essays of the opposite school, which vainly tries to prop up the unity of the poem. The artful interpretations and sophistical subtleties which are resorted to by the conservatives are the best justification our disbelief can have. When a poem like the Iliad—at one time through a few hundred lines, at another time through nearly a thousand verses—has characters and situation strongly marked, and expressed even in the most trifling details with the greatest clearness; and yet in the verses immediately following foregoes all that this preceding situation implied, and abandons the 'feeling' of the former passage; and when this sort of discord pervades the poem—occurring not so much in the separate episodes, as in their uniting together to form a greater totality—we are naturally led to the conclusion that those single narrations are the original elements, and that their union was an afterthought.

Though the narrative of Diomedes' meeting with Glaucus is in its kind as excellent as that of his *Aristeia*, yet it
can neither have been composed nor intended as a continuation of that narrative.   Hector's proposal of single combat,
the fear of the Greek chiefs to fight with him, Nestor's reproaches and admonitions, are all excellently told; but as
incidents of the same day, on which the Achaeans are cheated
of the prize of a previous single combat, and of a day on
which they are completely victorious, they are simply incongruous.   Facts of this kind speak so loudly that one cannot
be deaf to them, and their consideration has brought about
an unanimity on certain points between the opposing parties.
No one really familiar with the question at issue any longer
thinks that an individual poet, by name Homer, created
the whole Iliad in its present shape and extent.   That the
authors of the Iliad in its present state had older separate
lays to work on—by the expansion, development, and
piecing-together of which they formed a collective poem—
that the incongruities, or as they are more mildly termed
discrepancies, which present themselves arise from this patch-
ing, is acknowledged even by the intelligent upholders of the
unity of conception.   Extreme conservatives think it sufficient to remark how difficult it is to point out expressly
the older and independent elements, and maintain that the
value of the Iliad rests not on the beauty of its separate
episodes, but on its grandeur as a whole.   The first objection is quite beside the mark : the point at issue is, whether
the poem did or did not spring from such elements—and
upon this considerable unanimity is now felt.   The propor-

tion which the subsequent additions bear to the original germ will be set in a clearer light by further examination and discussion.   The question, whether we are to consider the separate episodes or their grouping together as of higher value, may well be left unanswered.   We may remark, however, that the composition of comprehensive and delicately-articulated epic poems—compared with that of simple lays, dealing each with a separate adventure—is a marked advance in epic literature.   The greatness of Homer lies in making this advance beyond the older poets, and originating an extensive and duly-organized poem, which was subsequently still more extended and skillfully articulated by later bards, sometimes with more, sometimes with less, success.   The origination of the Iliad, therefore, in contradistinction to its subsequent elaboration and augmentation, is a fact of the highest significance in the evolution of the Greek Epos.

What we have just said makes for the superiority of the poem, in its character of an articulated whole, to other lays of its own time, rather than to its own separate elements; for, with all its greatness, we must never forget that in the Iliad the inconsistencies are so obvious and so vital that, when once pointed out, they cannot be glossed over; and though for centuries thousands of readers, bewitched by the entrancing beauty of the poetry, heeded them not, it was not owing to any deficiency in power of observation, but rather because the separate portions fascinate so irresistibly that one does not regard their mutual connexion and interdependence, being transported with enchantment,

like the boatman who forgets the reefs as he listens to the
song of the Lorelei :

> 'Den Schiffer im kleinen Schiffe
> Ergreift es mit wildem Weh ;
> Er schaut nicht die Felsenriffe
> Er schaut nur hinauf in die Höh'.

What Goethe and what Lessing admired in the Iliad was
not its totality, but the exceeding beauty of separate parts ;
and I think we do not lose, but rather gain, when we feel
that these are complete in themselves, and cease to regard
the Iliad as the work of one man—a miracle, or a 'lusus
naturae'.

Hitherto our attention has been directed to the Iliad
only : now we shall briefly discuss the Odyssey. The plea
for the unity of design in the Odyssey is not based upon the
well-considered limits of its subject-matter, and the grouping of its many details about a common centre, but rather
on the skilful and complicated plaiting of the whole. The
despite Odysseus suffers at the hands of fate during his
return, and afterwards from the suitors, all serves to one
end, to show the character of the hero ; his endurance and
circumspect prudence are superior to perils by sea and perils
by land : neither the love of pleasure, nor the magic of goddesses' beauty, nor the naïve sweetness of the maiden who
befriends him in his distress, can avail to ease his yearning
for his home, or overmaster his love for his wife, who is
equally true to him, 'pure, lovely, and without reproach'.

The story of which this is the leading *motif* is not arranged according to the order of events ; the commencement

of the poem places us already at the end of the wanderings
of Odysseus, which are narrated not by the poet in his own
person, but with much greater effect by Odysseus himself
when a guest amongst the Phaeacians, and quite assured of
his safe return.   Three strands of narrative—the proceedings
in Odysseus's house, the journey of Telemachus to his father's
companions in arms, and Odysseus's wanderings—at first run
parallel to one another, but by degrees are gradually plaited
together into a single thread; and Odysseus and Telemachus, returning almost simultaneously to Ithaca, master and
slay the enemies in their house.   That this skilful arrangement is the result of mature design, and that this complexity
of plot is an advance, in the art of composition, upon the
consecutive arrangement of the Iliad will readily be con-
ceded, but will not give us much help towards deciding
whether the Odyssey in its present form was *originally*
single in its design, or is an excellent piecing-together of
older poems not originally designed to coalesce, or is an expansion and development of a germ originally much simpler.
But against the first of these there are the following irre-
futable arguments:—First, with regard to the plot as just
pointed out, it is only by taking a very general and abstract
view indeed that we can regard it as an indication of unity
of design.   The third and fourth books contain really nothing which has the remotest bearing on Odysseus; they
deal with the return of the heroes from Troy (expressly
exclusive of Odysseus).   The character of the hero, which is
so well sketched in the first half of the poem, suffers fatal
degradation in the second half; and though it would be too

much to declare it a parody or caricature of the preceding
representation, yet the contrast is so very marked that we
cannot see how one and the same poet could have composed
both. How, for instance, could the poet who represented
Odysseus braving the horrors of the Cyclops' cave, and in-
flicting such vengeance on the slayer of his companions, all
unaided by the gods, represent him enduring so unmanfully,
nay protracting and almost courting, such despiteful usage
at the hands of the ' wanton dissolute boys' who seem never
to have engaged in any war save that of words—he the
πτολίπορθος, and assisted at every turn by Athene herself?
In fact his endurance in this part of the poem is more
worthy of the 'captator Ulixes' of Horace's Satire (II. 5)
than of the wave-worn warrior of the previous books.*

We said that the Odyssey. was more complicated than
the Iliad : so loose, however, is the connexion between the
two separate lines of action, that the narrative of Telemachus's expedition is perfectly otiose, and the expedition itself
quite futile. But apart from this, the sutures are very
plain where this narrative is joined on to the other. At
the commencement of the fifth book, to get us back from
the Telemachy to the Odyssey proper, an assembly of gods
is held whose deliberations are out of harmony with what
we read of in the first book, and are related in verses which
are a cento from other parts of the poem.† On the other

* The dreary repetition of the insults heaped on Odysseus finds a parallel
in the dreary battle-scenes which are tiresomely repeated in the sixteenth and
seventeenth books of the Iliad.

† The Odyssey opens with the promise of Odysseus's return given by Zeus to
Athene, to effect the accomplishment of which the goddess proposes the sending

hand, when we are to pass from the account of Odysseus's arrival in Ithaca to that of Telemachus, in the fifteenth book, Athene is put into requisition; but unfortunately she leaves Odysseus, with whom she has been much busied, a long time *after dawn*, and yet arrives that very day *before dawn* in Lacedaemon; the points of time are expressly marked as they require to be, and this precludes the possibility of the passages being composed by the same poet.

Another important argument against unity of design is, that the groundwork of the narrative, which must surely be clear in the mind of an individual poet, is by no means clear, but varies. Now these variations cannot be explained as 'freie Dichtungen' which, though violating strict logical consistency, are often deliberately introduced by a poet into his work for the sake of adding some special charm or beauty, thus justifying their existence; for the variations to which we refer add no special charm or beauty, but are rather blemishes and disturbing elements. For example; the god whose wrath is visited on Odysseus is at one time Helios, at another Poseidon: there are also diffe-

---

of Hermes to Kalypso, *while she herself goes to Ithaca. Athene indeed goes to Ithaca*, but Hermes is not sent, though his mission is much more needed. Afterwards, when the interpolator has done with the less important episode, he lays the blame of the delay, which is really his own, on Zeus, to whom he represents Athene as coming with complaints, reminding him of his promise, and getting Hermes sent. But there is another inconsistency: Telemachus intends that his journey shall be of brief duration, and that his absence from home shall remain a secret (β. 374). In strict accordance with this intention he refuses Menelaus' invitation to stay longer at his Court, and for very excellent reasons (δ. 594). And yet after all he remains more than twenty days in Sparta, viz., all the time occupied by the return of Odysseus from Ogygia to Scheria, by his stay at Scheria, and his voyage thence to Ithaca.

rent accounts of the number of the suitors, of their abodes, and of the length of time they have been carousing in Odysseus's house, of their bringing marriage gifts or not, of the outward form and appearance of the hero himself, of the age of Telemachus, of the attempt of the suitors on his life, of the name of a most important personage (Eurykleia, Eurynome) within Odysseus's house. Here are inconsistencies, exhibited most convincingly by Jacob and Fäsi, which cannot be set aside.

A third argument of the greatest possible weight, but not very capable of demonstrative proof, is derived from the difference of style and poetic merit of different parts, which will be perhaps best felt by comparing the wretched confusion of the twentieth book with the crystalline clearness of the sixth.

Sometimes it is very hard to say which of two similar passages in the Odyssey is to be considered the original, and which the copy; for a scene often makes its appearance in a slightly-altered form: indeed the whole poem is haunted by these 'doubles', a characteristic which differentiates the Odyssey from the Iliad. In addition to those instances of variation and repetition mentioned above, we may call attention to the two solitary goddesses Kirke and Kalypso, who on account of their many resemblances are constantly in after ages confounded, as we see from Pausanias' account of the figures on the Chest of Kypselos (Lib. v. xix. 7): Εἰσὶν οὖν ἐν σπηλαίῳ γυνὴ καθεύδουσα σὺν ἀνδρὶ ἐπὶ κλίνῃ, καὶ σφᾶς 'Οδυσσέα εἶναι καὶ Κίρκην ἐδοξάζομεν ἀριθμῷ τε τῶν θεραπαινῶν, αἳ εἰσι πρὸ τοῦ σπηλαίου καὶ τοῖς ποιουμένοις ὑπ' αὐτῶν. Now it was Kalypso that lived in a grotto, not Kirke, although the rest of the scene evidently is from the Kirke-episode (κ. 348–360). In the same way we have two wonder-working speeders of Odysseus o'er the sea, Aeolus and Alcinoos;* the similar prophecies of Kirke and Teiresias; the ill-timed slumbers of Odysseus which are twice fraught with disaster. In the second half of the poem stools and baser missiles are flung thrice at the hero,† when once would have sufficed. He is recognised by dogs on four different occasions;‡ on four different occasions, to audiences not entirely different, he gives deceptive accounts of himself, which, though similar, do not agree in the chief points.§ Penelope, too, is always ready to fall asleep no matter what hour it is;‖ Odysseus' constant begging and eating is carried on to such an extent as to draw down the ridicule of the ancients (see Athenaeus, x. 412 b); to say nothing of the signs from heaven which the gods never tire of repeating.¶

Lachmann dissected the Iliad; Kirchhoff has dissected the Odyssey with as much conscientious care as acuteness. His theory is that the Odyssey is a systematic re-editing, by a poet or poets of moderate abilities, of an original germ incorporated with kindred lays, and further enlarged

---

* It is worth while remarking that first we are told the Phaeacian ships go without sails or rowing, and yet afterwards they are rowed.

† ρ. 360–491; σ. 346–428; υ. 284–344.

‡ ξ. 29; π. 4, 162; ρ. 291.

§ ν. 257–286; ξ. 199–359; ρ. 419–444; τ. 172–248.

‖ δ. 793; π. 450; σ. 188; υ. 54; φ. 357; ψ. 5.

¶ ο. 160–165, 525–528; ρ. 160, 541; τ. 535; υ. 103, 345; φ. 411–413; χ. 240.

F

by freely-invented additions; that the original germ itself,
viz., the return and adventures of Odysseus, is not a
simple lay like those which go to form the Iliad, but
belongs to a period when the art of poetry had greatly
developed, and that the amplifications, such as we have
pointed out, and later additions, belong to a period when
the creative power of epic poetry was nearly effete, and
mere prolixity was supplanting force. If we may be allowed a Euhemeristic interpretation of the story that the
Iliad was the production of Homer's youth, and the Odyssey
of his decay, we would say that the Iliad is the child of
youthful epic poetry, and the Odyssey the offspring of its
age.

It is the fashion amongst some scholars to compare the
evolution of Greek epic poetry with that of the sagas and
legends of other nations, from China to Peru, on a principle no other than that of 'obscurum per obscurius'; and
to refer the reader, who, it is taken for granted, is omniscient
or nearly so, if not to the 'epics' of Polynesians, Aztecs,
Eskimo, and Tartars, at least to the Indian Mahâbhârata,
the Scandinavian Edda, the Finnish Kalevala, the Nibe-
lungen-Lied, and the Chansons de Geste : far be it from
us, however, to essay such an eagle-flight,

'Di meliora piis, errorem et hostibus illum';

therefore let us proceed in the following chapters to a more
minute examination of the internal evidence of the Homeric
poems themselves.

VI

THE Homeric poems were produced and orally preserved by bards of whom we find idealized pictures in the Odyssey. These bards live at the courts of princes, and their themes are similar to that of the Iliad and Odyssey : the quarrel of Odysseus and Achilles (θ. 72), the taking of Troy by the wooden horse (θ. 499), the tale of Ares and Aphrodite (θ. 226), and the return of the Greeks from Troy (α. 325). They alone sing, and never do any of their hearers attempt to meddle with what is the exclusive profession of the bards. Once and once only do we read of anyone not a bard by profession singing such lays, and that person is no less than Achilles, the goddess-born, to whom the poet does not grudge a share in his skill and art (I. 186). Lachmann and Grote, therefore, are doubtless wrong in talking of the epic lays as though they were mere 'Volkspoesie', as in the poems themselves the people are represented as quite mute, and it is not from their traditions that the poet gets his themes, but by direct inspiration of the muse (θ. 63). In fine, from internal evidence it is plain that epic poetry on the Tale of Troy had become emphatically 'Kunstpoesie', practised and jealously guarded by a special caste of professional singers.

F 2

The bard is represented as singing lays which are most in fashion (θ. 74); the newest poems are expected of him, and he does not sing merely the lays of others, but is himself a composer, welcomed and invited to kings' courts (ρ. 382), living for his art and by his art alone. We must further notice that he is not represented as singing for the whole people, but only for a select audience of chiefs and nobles.

We have broken away from tradition : what are we to set in its place ? By what hypothesis shall we explain the present state of our Iliad and Odyssey ? Wolf never aimed at being constructive ; Lachmann's ' Liedertheorie ', though brilliant, starts from the $\pi\rho\tilde{\omega}\tau\omicron\nu$ $\psi\epsilon\tilde{\upsilon}\delta\omicron\varsigma$ of ' Volkspoesie ', which we see the Homeric poems were not. Nitzsch, starting with a floating capital of popular lays, maintains that the poems are not a mere juxtaposition of them, but a whole, which Homer has animated and vivified by the introduction of a great moral idea ; and though interpolations are common, yet that their number is not very great. Grote's theory is a somewhat modified form of Lachmann's, for he talks about other lays (B.-H., I.-K.) already pre-existent in the Trojan 'Sagenkreis' or $'I\lambda\iota\acute{\alpha}\varsigma$, as he names it, which grouped themselves about the Achilleis or Wrath of Achilles, a poem dominated by one idea, and forming the nucleus of our present Iliad.

Yet all these scholars are right in agreeing that the poems in their present state are not the work of one poet, but contain many subsequent additions. That these additions are really subsequent and not even cotemporary,

much less older than the original germ as the believers
in 'Volkspoesie' and in the 'Sagenkreis' suppose, may
be proved once for all by a decisive example. That
the Doloneia (K.) was not originally an integral part of
the Iliad but that it was subsequently added, and that it
presupposes the 'Wrath of Achilles' is shown by the fact
that in it the Trojans are represented as bivouacking in
the open field in front of the Achaean camp : this fixes the
point of time during which its action is laid as no other than
that when Achilles in his wrath has withdrawn from the contest, since (I., 352), Achilles says—

> ὄφρα δ' ἐγὼ μετ' Ἀχαιοῖσιν πολέμιζον
> οὐκ ἐθέλεσκε μάχην ἀπὸ τείχεος ὀρνύμεν Ἕκτωρ
> ἀλλ' ὅσον ἐς Σκαιάς τε πύλας καὶ φηγὸν ἵκανε,

so that it must have been composed strictly with reference
to the absence of Achilles during his Wrath.

It must not be supposed that the 'Epic Cycle' was
put together from materials furnished by the imaginary
'Sagenkreis' of Grote and others. That the Epic Cycle
is wholly the poetical 'creation' of later bards, and was
composed strictly with reference to the Homeric poems, is
plain from the fact that the Cypria end where the Iliad
begins, and that the Aethiopis begins where the Iliad leaves
off. The Nostoi and the Telegonia stand in similar relationship to the Odyssey. Welcker,* from the scanty evidence at his disposal, has done his best to establish that the
poets of the 'cycle' show many traces of imitation of the

---

* Ep. Cycl. II. 13 and 285 ; also Kirchhoff, Od., p. 331, seqq.

Homeric poems : for instance—in the Aethiopis of Arctinus, Memnon, son of the Dawn, comes to the help of the Trojans, and having slain Antilochus, the dearest friend of Achilles, is himself slain just as is Hector in the Iliad. Similarly in the Nostoi of Hagias of Troezen, the story of Menelaus' wanderings is probably copied from the fourth book of the Odyssey, where that hero himself tells his adventures to young Telemachus. Wherever the stories in the cyclic poems differ from those in Homer, we are no doubt right in attributing the variations not to differing current traditions, but to the invention of some later bard who felt an individual preference for alterations and improvements of his own.

That such variation was wholly due to the bard's own poetic genius, an instance taken from the Iliad will show. All through the poem Achilles has a boding of imminent death ; but this, vaguely represented at one time (Φ. 112),

όππότε τις καὶ ἐμεῖο ᾿Αρει ἐκ θυμὸν ἔληται,
ἢ ὅγε δουρὶ βαλὼν ἢ ἀπὸ νευρῆφιν οἰστῷ,

is at another more definite (Φ. 277),

ἤ μ᾿ ἔφατο Τρώων ὑπὸ τείχεϊ θωρηκτάων
λαιψηροῖς ὀλέεσθαι ᾿Απόλλωνος βελέεσσιν,

till at last (X. 359) the dying Hector speaks with prophetic clearness :

ἤματι τῷ ὅτε κέν σε Πάρις καὶ Φοῖβος ᾿Απόλλων
ἐσθλὸν ἐόντ᾿ ὀλέσωσιν ἐνὶ Σκαιῇσι πύλῃσι.

The poet introduces such variations merely to meet the exigencies of the moment for poetical effect.

It may be well to give some further instances, to show how there was really no definite tradition on a given point, and how passages were composed quite irrespective of one another. According to A. (100 and 431) Chryseis comes from Chryse and is brought back thither, yet Achilles tells his mother that it was at Thebe, the city of Eetion, that she was taken captive (A. 366). From verse 392 it would seem that Briseis was captured on the same occasion, and yet in T. 60 we read that she comes from Lyrnessus (cf. v. 296), and in the Catalogue (B. 690) both towns are united together.* In Z. 395 we find an expansion of the story of the taking of Thebe, and learn how Andromache was the daughter of Eetion, and how her father was slain at the storming of the city.

Similarly in the Odyssey we find no fixed and unalterable tradition, but see how the bards could alter it as they chose. Twice are we told the story of the death of Agamemnon (γ. 246, δ. 511). On the first occasion Nestor relates how Aegisthus beguiles Klytaemnestra, and, assisted by her, murders Agamemnon. On the second occasion Menelaus hears from Proteus of the return of Agamemnon and of his death. Now, though this latter account is the more circumstantial, Klytaemnestra is not mentioned as having taken any part in the murder, whereas her crime is the main theme of Nestor's narrative.

Nestor's narrative, therefore, is an enlargement of the passage in the fourth book, as the story of his own experience is in like manner an enlargement of the account

* Strabo, XIII. 584, § 7; 611, § 61, and Venetian Scholia on A. 366.

which Menelaus gives: nay, more than this, it is an interpolation as well, because we see from γ. 193 that the poet had no intention of relating the death of Agamemnon at all, since Nestor there takes it for granted that the story is known to everybody—a supposition apparently confirmed by Telemachus's answer (v. 203). Accordingly the sudden eagerness of Telemachus, some fifty lines afterwards (v. 248), to hear about it is very ill-timed, and had the original poet told the story in full in the fourth book, the interpolator would probably have let Telemachus wait patiently till then; but knowing that the story would eventually be told incompletely, he could not refrain from here telling it, as he thought it ought to be told. In the Nekyia (λ. 405) both passages are combined, and the death of Cassandra added.

These are fair instances of the way in which the Homeric poems, and the stories contained in them, gradually developed in the hands of imaginative bards.

When those who first essayed Homeric criticism found various improvisations of the poet in one book and not in another—improvisations merely suited to the occasion and of no further import—they were often much puzzled, and sometimes exalted such difficulties to the rank of 'indications of separate authorship.' In Z. 431 Andromache, with that charming naïveté which characterises her, tells a little wifely fib, about an imaginary escalade, that she may thereby detain her husband in safety in the city. The ancients (Strabo XIII. 598) were greatly distressed that Homer had given no account of this escalade in the

previous books, and after the most mature consideration
it was decided that the passage describing it must be lost!
Similarly, when Agamemnon (H. 113) wishes to detain
'auburn-haired' Menelaus from single-combat with Hector,
he tells him that even Achilles is afraid to meet the brave
Trojan—a statement which has caused great perplexity
among the critics, who can find nowhere any corroboration of Agamemnon's words. But perhaps the most ab-
surd instance of $\psi\nu\chi\rho\delta\tau\eta\varsigma$ is finding difficulty in the skin
of wine, by the help of which Odysseus takes vengeance
on the Cyclops (ι. 195 and 163). We are told that Maron,
priest of Apollo in Ismarus, whose life he had spared,
had given it to him; and yet in the account of the
adventures among the Kikones it is never mentioned!

Such poetical inventions ('freie Dichtungen') are extremely frequent, and have no other object than to lend
some adornment to that which might seem prosaic without them. Thus, in Z. 289, when costly garments, 'the
work of Sidonian women,' are mentioned, in order to give
them a more worthy history and higher importance, the
poet invents a voyage of Paris to Sidon, which is never
afterwards mentioned when it has once served its turn.
Similar to this is the descent assigned to an unimportant
hero when Homer is introducing him to the reader: for
instance, Othryoneus (N. 362), and Asteropaeus (Φ. 139).

Sometimes in these 'freie Dichtungen' the later poets
go a little too far, and thus convict themselves in the very
act of interpolating and amplifying: for instance, in the

account of the adventures in the Cyclops' cave, we do not
hear of Antiphos at all; and yet, before Odysseus, who was
the only one who could bring news of what had happened
there, gets back to Ithaca, we find (β. 17) old Aegyptios
in the Ithacan assembly relating to his hearers how his son
Antiphos was the last to be eaten by the Cyclops! Odysseus
himself, too, though asleep at the time when his companions
conspired to open the wind-bags, yet afterwards can tell all
they said, and who was the prime mover in the traitorous
act; he also relates the proceedings of the Olympic Council,
though he was on earth at the time and could have known
nothing about it; but perhaps the most curious instance
of 'freie Dichtung' rising superior to Logic, is to be
found in the case of Amphimedon, who, though killed in
χ. 284 before he had discovered that the insulted beggar was Odysseus, yet is aware of the fact in Hades, and
is aware also of the fact that it was Odysseus who had
removed the arms out of the suitors' way with the aid of
Telemachus; though how he could have learned all this
is hard to see.   Kirchhoff ventures upon a jocular explanation, supposing that Hermes, while conducting the
shade of Amphimedon down to Hades, may have explained the situation to him to beguile the tedium of the
journey!

These instances, which some may think trivial, have been
soberly advanced by many scholars as indications of separate
authorship, and curiously enough they occur in passages
which will be shown hereafter on independent grounds to

be of later date, and by a different bard. To show how
different in kind are the logical inconsistencies which are
likely to occur in *a work by a single mind* let us take
some instances from Dante.

The Spirits in Purgatory are represented as shadowy
forms through which the sun can shine; the shadows have
no shadow, and Dante is amazed to see that he alone
throws a shadow on the ground,

> I' vidi
> Solo dinanzi a me la terra oscura (*Purg.*, III. 20).

So bodiless are these phantom forms, that in the third circle
of Hell Dante passes over a mass of sinners lying on the
ground, and his foot passes through them as though they
were not there at all. Yet after he has shown so clearly
how unsubstantial they are, he represents them as feeling
heat, cold, and other sensations : indeed one instance is
almost ludicrous, where Dante himself causes an unsubstantial shadow to shriek with pain by pulling that
shadow's unsubstantial hair :—

> 'Io avea già i capelli in mano avvolti,
> E tratti glien avea più d' una ciocca,
> Latrando lui con gli occhi in giù raccolti ;
> Quando un altro gridò : Che hai tu, Bocca ?
> Non ti basta sonar con le mascelle,
> Se tu non latri ?' qual diavol ti tocca ?—(*Infer.*, xxxii. 103.)

Again when Virgil meets his fellow-countryman, the trou-
badour Sordello, they embrace passionately :

> 'O Mantovano, i' son Sordello
> Della tua terra.   E l'un l'altro abbracciava'.—(*Purg.*, vi. 74.)

Yet when Statius would fain embrace his feet, Virgil tells
him it is impossible:

> 'Frate,
> Non far, chè tu se' ombra, e ombra vedi; '

to which Statius answers that his great love for Virgil made
him for the moment forget that he was a shadow:

> ' Or puoi la quantitate
> Comprender dell' amor ch' a te mi scalda,
> Quando dismento nostra vanitate,
> Trattando l' ombre come cosa salda '—(*Purg.*, xxi. 131–136.)

Similarly Dante tries thrice to embrace his friend Casella,
but cannot; his arms pass through the shadow and return
to his own breast (Purg. ii. 76–91); yet in the 'Inferno'
we read how he is lifted and carried by Virgil (xxiii. 50).*

Let us now examine some passages in the Odyssey which
seem to be unconscious reminiscences of the Iliad, and therefore make for the supposition that the Iliad was already in
existence at the time of their composition.

On two different occasions in the Iliad (T. 334, Ω. 488) is
Achilles filled with sorrow for his lonely father Peleus, especially when the sight of aged Priam brings the sad lot of
desolate Peleus so vividly before his mind. Of this we have
an echo in the Odyssey (λ. 494), where we see the same lov-
ing solicitude felt by him even in the abode of the dead.

Again, when Helen, the most lovely woman of the world,
is charming her boy-guest Telemachus with a tale of Troy,
she thrills him with a story of how his father ventured into
Ilion and slew many Trojans, which is 'the counterfeit

* 'Dante Alighieri, sein Leben und seine Werke, von Hartwig Floto, Stutt-
gart, 1858.'

presentment' of the Doloneia. When Menelaus mentions Odysseus's victory in the arena at Lesbos (δ. 341), we feel that the poet has before his mind a similar victory over Ajax in the Iliad (Ψ. 700).

But still more important evidence that the Odyssey presupposes the Iliad, is the fact that the poets of the Odyssey, with the fixed desire to invent 'some new thing', when recounting any former achievement of Odysseus, studiously try to avoid re-handling any deed of prowess already treated in the Iliad, and tell us things which the singers of the Iliad knew nothing of; in δ. 269 Odysseus' self-possession inside the wooden horse is praised; in ε. 308 he calls to remembrance the fight round Achilles' dead body; in θ. 219 he says that he is second only to Philoctetes in shooting with the bow; in θ. 75 and 499 we hear of the quarrel of Odysseus and Achilles; and it is by no means the result of chance that Patroclus, who is so all-important in the Iliad, speaks not a word when he appears in the Nekyia (λ. 468).

Other evidence that the Iliad is prior to the Odyssey may be derived from the fact that the words of the two greatest heroes of the former poem are parodied in the later. Everyone knows the words of Hector when he bids his wife cease from useless anxiety about his life, and then, 'taking his last embrace', adds that war is for men alone, and most of all for him (Z. 490–493):

> ἀλλ' εἰς οἶκον ἰοῦσα τὰ σ' αὐτῆς ἔργα κόμιζε,
> ἱστόν τ' ἠλακάτην τε, καὶ ἀμφιπόλοισι κέλευε
> ἔργον ἐποίχεσθαι· πόλεμος δ' ἄνδρεσσι μελήσει
> πᾶσιν, ἐμοὶ δὲ μάλιστα, τοὶ Ἰλίῳ ἐγγεγάασιν.

Everybody knows these noble verses, but everybody perhaps
does not know the ignoble parody of them put into the
mouth of Telemachus in the Odyssey (a. 355–364), where
he is represented as a precocious youngster ordering his
mother to go about her business, and adding that *talking*
is for men alone, and most of all for him !

ἀλλ' εἰς οἶκον ἰοῦσα τὰ σ' αὐτῆς ἔργα κόμιζε,
ἱστόν τ' ἠλακάτην τε, καὶ ἀμφιπόλοισι κέλευε
ἔργον ἐποίχεσθαι· μῦθος δ' ἄνδρεσσι μελήσει
πᾶσι, μάλιστα δ' ἐμοί· τοῦ γὰρ κράτος ἔστ' ἐνὶ οἴκῳ.

This parody is at least comic; but the parody of the
words which Achilles speaks on the occasion of the Embassy
(I. 312, 313) is irredeemable :

ἐχθρὸς γάρ μοι κεῖνος ὁμῶς Ἀΐδαο πύλῃσιν,
ὅς χ' ἕτερον μὲν κεύθῃ ἐνὶ φρεσίν, ἄλλο δὲ εἴπῃ.

The moral majesty of these lines stamps them deeply in the
memory.   But the irreverence of some buffoon has put them
into the mouth of Odysseus when transformed into a beggar;
Eumaeus has warned him not to tell any of the hackneyed
falsehoods that beggars usually tell, to which Odysseus re-
plies that there are beggars and beggars, but that he is a
very superior sort of beggar, winding up by a parody of
Achilles' words such as we might expect from the mouth of
Thersites (ξ. 156, 157) :

ἐχθρὸς γάρ μοι κεῖνος ὁμῶς Ἀΐδαο πύλῃσιν
γίγνεται, ὅς πενίῃ εἴκων ἀπατήλια βάζει,

'The beggar who a beggar's tale will tell
To me is Hateful as the Gates of Hell'.

That Odysseus in his disguise should thus lig
apply the words of righteous resentment, which he .
spoken on the occasion of the Embassy, is as incredible a
that the poet of the Presbeia could thus carelessly traduce
his own work.

The desire to say or sing 'some new thing,' which we
have noticed in the poets of the Odyssey, seems to be the
final cause of the Telemachy; for the poet who invented
the Nostoi which it contains, and which were decidedly
'new' compositions ('neue Erfindungen'), had no other
way of introducing them into the Odyssey than by this
skilful device of getting them told to Telemachus.   So
Telemachus is made to undertake the journey to Sparta
to hear these *nostoi*, and not, as the poor boy thinks, to
hear tidings of his father: he goes ostensibly in obedience
to divine promptings, but really at the bidding of the
poet.

Owing to this desire of 'some new thing,' we find in the
Iliad also later additions of the same kind, which, apart
from their immediate value as forming an integral part of
the whole, have a separate interest in themselves: for instance, the story of Bellerophon (Z. 152), of Meleager (I. 524),
of the assembling in Aulis, and the prodigy of the sparrow
(B. 304).   Now, from the manner in which these passages
are 'inlaid,' and their own intrinsic slightness, it seems
clear that they were never independent lays existing apart
from the rest of the poem, but rather that they were specially composed for the positions they now occupy.   So
far, therefore, is the Iliad from being a selection and

Everybod~ion of separate lays self-existent, and forming an
does ~sive floating mass of poetry ('Die Sage vom trojani-
rschen Kriege'), that as there is no evidence for the existence of such a 'Sagenkreis' before the Iliad, the 'Sagen'
can only have come into existence subsequently, as augmentations of the Homeric poems.

No hypothesis hitherto advanced as to the origin of
the poems has met with general acceptance. But from the
many which have been advanced, and from the careful
special studies made by scholars, we may glean something
of value. We have seen that the Iliad and Odyssey of
the present day have undergone various changes, and are
no longer in their original state. We have seen many
diversities between different parts, and how sometimes a
conception, vague at first, gradually increases in precision
and definiteness, as for instance the manner of Achilles'
death.*   On occasions like these we may well suppose that
one passage, accepting the other as an unalterably existing fact, merely imitates, enlarges, and improves upon it,
and is of course subsequent to it in date of composition.
Now this is an exact characterization of the relations which
exist between the greater part of the Odyssey and the Iliad.
As extensions of the story in the Iliad we find in the Odyssey the slaying of Antilochus by Memnon (δ. 187, λ. 468,
522), the taking of Troy by the wooden horse (δ. 269,
θ. 492, λ. 523), Odysseus's entry in disguise into Ilion
(δ. 240), and in the strife of Odysseus and Achilles (θ. 77)
we have an unmistakable reference to the Iliad:

* See p. 70.

ἄναξ δ' ανδρῶν Ἀγαμέμνων
χαῖρε νόῳ, ὅτ' ἄριστοι Ἀχαιῶν δηριώωντο.
ὣς γάρ οἱ χρείων μυθήσατο Φοῖβος Ἀπόλλων
Πυθοῖ ἐν ἠγαθέῃ, ὅτ' ὑπέρβη λάϊνον οὐδὸν
χρησόμενος· τότε γάρ ῥα κυλίνδετο πήματος ἀρχὴ
Τρωσί τε καὶ Δαναοῖσι Διὸς μεγάλου διὰ βουλάς.

Here is the βουλὴ Διὸς of the Iliad reiterated. But another mark shows that it is later than the Iliad, namely, that Agamemnon consults the oracle at Pytho: the Iliad knows nothing of oracles, and the issue of the war is foretold in Aulis by Kalchas.

Many indications too may be found in the Odyssey of a higher and therefore later state of culture and civilization than what we find in the Iliad. In the latter there are only the familar trees, pine, oak, beech, ash, poplar, alder, and willow, but in the Odyssey we have the recently acclimatized fig (ι. 183), cypress (ε. 64), cedar (ε. 64), and palm (ζ. 163). The olive also, which is frequent in the Odyssey, is only once mentioned in the Iliad, and there too as a rarity, in the simile at P. 53 :

οἷον δὲ τ ρ έ φ ε ι ἔρνος ἀνὴρ ἐριθηλὲς ἐλαίης
χώρῳ ἐν οἰοπόλῳ, ὅθ' ἅλις ἀναβέβρυχεν ὕδωρ,
καλόν, τηλεθάον.

Indeed there are many references in later literature to the acclimatization of the olive in Greece, which was said to have been introduced by Athena, and planted at Colonus, or on the Acropolis at Athens.* More too is known about the world: Egypt, which is little known in the Iliad

---

* Soph. O. C. 701, sq. ; Hdt. 5, 82.

F.J. 381), is much more familiar to the Odyssey, and twice is the island of Pharos named (δ. 351, 227).

The religious ideas of the two poems also differ. The ancients noticed that the messenger of the Gods in the Iliad was Iris, but in the Odyssey Hermes. Only in the late-added Ω does Hermes go on a mission. That Iris was known to the Odyssey, in her capacity of messenger, is clear from the play on the name in σ. 6 :

> *Ἶρον δὲ νέοι κίκλησκον ἅπαντες
> οὕνεκ᾽ ἀπαγγέλλεσκε κιὼν ὅτε πού τις ἀνώγοι.*

The idea of a life after death is more developed in the later poem, and we find mention of Elysium. In the questioning of Teiresias, and the strange rites recounted, we seem to have a reference to oracles of the dead which were wholly unknown to the Iliad. The interest which the gods take in the doings of men is more of a moral nature in the Odyssey than in the Iliad, as we see from ρ. 484, where it is said the gods wander unseen amongst men, watching their deeds of piety or sin,

> *ἀνθρώπων ὕβριν τε καὶ εὐνομίην ἐφορῶντες.*

The Mythology is also different. In the Iliad, Helen (Z. 345) says she wishes the storm-wind had carried her away :

> *ὥς μ᾽ ὄφελ᾽ ἤματι τῷ ὅτε με πρῶτον τέκε μήτηρ
> οἴχεσθαι προφέρουσα κακὴ ἀνέμοιο θύελλα
> εἰς ὄρος ἢ ἐς κῦμα πολυφλοίσβοιο θαλάσσης.*

Here we have the storm-wind merely as one of the elemental forces of nature. The poet of the Odyssey is not satisfied with such vagueness; he becomes more definite, and imagines a Ἅρπυια dwelling at the estuary of the Okeanos: in υ. 63, *seqq.* we have the intermediate link:

ἢ ἔπειτα μ᾽ ἀναρπάξασα θύελλα
οἴχοιτο προφέρουσα κατ᾽ ἠερόεντα κέλευθα
ἐν προχοῆς δὲ βάλοι ἀψορρόου Ὠκεανοῖο.

But most remarkable is it that in the Iliad (Ξ. 225) Olympus is a mountain on the borders of Thessaly and Macedonia, whereas in the Odyssey (ζ. 42, *seqq.*) it is an ideal heaven.

In the language of the poems, too, we find much to mark the different stages of their development. It will be sufficient to give one decisive instance. In the Iliad we meet the expression πόλις ἄκρη, or ἀκροτάτη, again and again (Z. 257), but never the compound ἀκρόπολις, which is the only form used in the Odyssey (θ. 494, 504). That the compound was evolved out of the former expression cannot be doubted. Other differences in the language of the poems may be noticed: different epithets are employed for the same object, and the same epithet is employed in different senses; εὔκυκλος, for instance, applied to the 'shield' in the Iliad, and meaning 'round,' in the Odyssey to the 'chariot,' and meaning 'well-wheeled.' In the Iliad ἐξοπίσω is used only of *place;* in the Odyssey only of *time:* in the Odyssey certain inflectional forms as ἔριν and φιλίων occur, which are wholly unknown to the Iliad, ἔριδα and φίλτερος being the forms which it uses.

In outward shape and expression also the Odyssey shows how much it is indebted to the Iliad. At the slaying of the suitors, in the twenty-second book, many verses are taken bodily from the older poem, as

δούπησεν δὲ πεσών, ἀράβησε δὲ τεύχε' ἐπ' αὐτῳ, and
ὤιμησεν δὲ ἀλείς, ὥστ' ἀιετὸς ὑψιπετήεις.

The reader has seen that the apparent unity which is supposed to pervade the poems in their present form is indeed little more than an *apparent* unity, that in many places the poems show unmistakable signs of having been retouched by other hands. This is easiest to detect in those cases where one passage copies another, for instance, in Π. 419 *sqq.*, where the poet, trying to express the conflict in nature of Benevolence and iron Necessity, represents Zeus, contrary to Fate's decree, wishing to save Sarpedon from death at the hands of Patroclus, but yielding to the opposition of Hera, who dissuades him from such unlawful desires. This passage closely resembles X. 166, where, before the death of Hector, Zeus wishes to save him, but is successfully opposed by Athene. That the latter is the original and the other a copy may be inferred from the fact that Hector's death is necessary to the poem, but Sarpedon's death is not.

In the case of single verses or groups of verses we find that an earlier passage is frequently used to help out a later one, and often that verses splendidly suited to their original position are in a later passage singularly out of place. In Π. 214, when Achilles arms the Myrmidons, the serried battalion is made up of men closely packed like stones in a wall:

ὣς ἄραρον κόρυθες τε καὶ ἀσπίδες ὀμφαλόεσσαι·
ἀσπὶς ἄρ' ἀσπίδ' ἔρειδε, κόρυς κόρυν, ἀνέρα δ' ἀνήρ·

ψαῦον δ' ἱππόκομοι κόρυθες λαμπροῖσι φάλοισι
νευόντων· ὡς πυκνοὶ ἐφέστασαν ἀλλήλοισιν.

Here, as in all poetry worthy of the name, we find means fitly adapted to the end in view; for after this marshalling of the host, a long decisive battle follows: but in N. 131, where the same verses occur, there is nothing to justify their presence; they are not used of the deliberate marshalling of a host for battle, but of a *sudden rallying* of the Greeks by Poseidon during the heat of conflict.

But there are worse instances: instances of a stiffness of language and a numbness of imagination, which brand the passage in which they occur as a late composition. In Ψ. 39 we read

αὐτίκα κηρύκεσσι λιγυφθόγγοισι κέλευσαν
ἀμφὶ πυρὶ στῆσαι τρίποδα μέγαν.

Why λιγύφθογγοι? Because the poet of the passage, being of a sluggish imagination, chose to take the epithet which he found ready-made in B. 50, and so well suited to that passage:

ἀυτὰρ ὃ κηρύκεσσι λιγυφθόγγοισι κέλευσε
κηρύσσειν ἀγορήνδε κάρη κομόωντας Ἀχαιούς.

Of course it will be objected against this argument that λιγύφθογγοι is a stock epithet, but the very fact that an epithet has become a stock one is a sure symptom that early spontaneity has gone, and the creeping paralysis of composition has set in.

We have seen (*a*) that the Odyssey is later than the Iliad, (*b*) that in both poems some parts are easily discernible as later than others; and now it remains (c) to attempt the separation of the later from the earlier portions. The subject of the Iliad is the quarrel of Achilles and Agamemnon, the withdrawal of Achilles from the war, the consequent defeat of the Achaeans, and the burning of the ships; then follow the fight and death of Patroclus, the reconciliation of Achilles with Agamemnon, and the vengeance wreaked on Hector. The distinguishing feature of the Odyssey is, that in the detailed account of the return of Odysseus the narrative of his previous adventures is inlaid in the form of a tale told by the hero himself.

VII

THE wrath of Achilles is the *motif* in the Iliad which should by its dominant persistence characterize the original parts of the poem. Therefore, since the wrath of Achilles is utterly absorbed into his passion to avenge Patroclus, the books which follow after the death of Hector do not belong to the original design. There is no reason, of course, why the poet should not have enlarged and continued his poem if he chose, but that it was probably another who did so may be gathered from the fact that Menelaus' speech (Ψ. 570) borrows much from the other parts of the Iliad, as Bekker has shown in his notes. The Greek too, in some places, seems faulty, as at v. 679, δεδουπότος Οἰδιπόδαο for ἀποθανόντος: a use apparently derived from the expression δούπησεν δὲ πεσών, regardless of the special meaning in that phrase. In Ω. 283, *seqq.*, we may notice that the prayer of Priam is an imitation of Π. 220, *seqq.*, where Achilles in a very moving passage sends forth the Myrmidons, and prays for them to Zeus, standing in the middle of the court, beaker in hand. Mr. Gladstone has noted that this is the only occasion in the Iliad where one man prays for others. In the imitation, not only are the words stolen, but the *mise en scène* is stolen as well. That a different poet introduced the imitation seems more likely than that the poet of the fine passage in Ἰl. afterwards mechanically repeated himself in Ω.

Lachmann has pointed out the passage which probably suggested the subsequent addition of the λύτρα to the already finished 'Wrath of Achilles': it is X. 410, *seqq.* When Hector falls by Achilles' hand, and is about to be dragged away by him, Priam, who sees it all from the battlements, is about to rush forth in the violence of his grief, and implore Achilles in the name of his father Peleus to use the body mercifully.

In Ψ. 664, Epeios, the future builder of the wooden horse, makes his appearance first, and the poet who feels that he is introducing amongst the familiar heroes of the earlier books an alien who will be looked upon coldly, makes him apologise for his intrusion in explaining why he has never been heard of before (Ψ. 670) : and so naïvely discloses the fact that he is a late-comer, not only into the action of the poem, but into the poem itself.

We must notice that these concluding books here under discussion do not stand in loose juxtaposition with the preceding ones. The poet, whoever he may have been, who composed them, dexterously transforms events in the preceding books into a kind of preparation for this poem of his: the taking, for instance, of twelve Trojans in Φ. 26, *seqq.*, as requital for the death of Patroclus, is made to serve as introduction and preparative to Ψ. At the ἆθλα, although the poet adroitly introduces Diomedes (v. 291, *seqq.*), with the horses which he had taken from Aeneas in a preceding book (E. 319, *seqq.*), yet, strange to say, he never mentions those of Rhesus, which Diomedes captured in K. (465-503) ; a fact which seems to show that this book (Ψ.) was composed before the Doloneia.

We shall now proceed to the ninth and tenth books, in which we have the embassy to Achilles and the Doloneia preceded by a setting of sentinels. Grote (II. 179), as we stated previously, has shown that the embassy is not part of the original design ; and Schömann (Opusc. III. 17) has singled out Phoenix for his attacks. The allegory of ἄτη and the λιταί is quite unique of its kind, and not in accordance with the manner of the other books. The Doloneia, which even the ancients regarded as no integral part of the poem, has been shown by Nitzsch (Sag., p. 225) to be a later addition ; and we may notice the epithets τλήμων and πολύτλας given to Odysseus (vv. 497-248), which correspond with his character in the Odyssey ; πτολίπορθος, too (v. 363), seems to point to the important part he took in the capture of Troy, and is an epithet specially reserved for him in the Odyssey. It is to be observed that these books, like those at the conclusion of the poem, are not mere loose additions, but that the poet who added them took great care about their setting, linking them skilfully with what precedes and with what follows (Σ. 448, *seq.* ; T. 140, *seq.* ; 172, *seqq.* ; 192, *seqq.*). Another point which may be mentioned as characteristic of these amplifications is, that they are introduced by some new *motif* different from the main *motif*, and useless to the action of the poem as a whole ; the main-

spring does not set them going : the new departure is merely
to introduce the interpolated poem, and when that end is
served the new *motif* is allowed to drop, so that the main
action of the poem is not harmed, but is in no way advanced
by the interpolation.   Thus the Embassy fails in its purpose
and comes to nothing, and the Doloneia leads to no important result—in fact they were never meant to do so—their
final cause is simply to introduce later and very excellent
poetry, and if that poetry be good, then in the mind of
the author their existence is justified.

Kayser has shown that the eighth book is little more
than a cento from other parts of the poem.   We may draw
attention to the scales of fate (v. 69, *seqq.*), which are taken
from the magnificent passage in the twenty-second book.
The object of this eighth book is simply to procure for
the Presbeia a suitable position.

We next turn to the second book, which contains the
arming and marshalling of the Achaeans occasioned by the
deceptive Dream sent by Zeus to Agamemnon.   These events,
though they partially satisfy the expectations roused in the
first book, yet upon closer examination are full of difficulty.
German scholars* have shown that the two narratives united
in this book differ from one another, and are to some extent contradictory, viz., the Arming of the Greeks, and the
Proving of them by Agamemnon—the πεῖρα, as it is called,
which is first suggested in a council of the elder chiefs
(v. 73).

The πεῖρα bids fair to frustrate the arming of the host

* Lachmann, p. 8-13; Köchly, Opusc., i. 1-48, 69, *seqq.*: Bergk, p. 554.

until it is itself cancelled and set aside—a fact which shows
us clearly that the arming is the main object, and therefore the older poem, and that the πεῖρα is an 'inlaid' addition originally unknown to the passage : the intention of the
poet in adding it was to pourtray for us the disposition of
the Greek army, tired of the long war, and yearning to
return home. For this reason he has laid his scene expressly
in the tenth year of the siege. The fact that the war has
dragged on its weary length for ten years constitutes the
temptation of the Greeks, and also constitutes their deliver-
ance out of that temptation, since it is precisely because the
tenth year of the war has come that they may now hope for
speedy victory. The poet, however, does not take as much
trouble as we have done to explain how the πεῖρα is to be
connected with the rest of the poem ; he is by no means ex-
plicit ('die Motivirung ist sehr mangelhaft') ; but he makes
us amends by the graphic pictures he has given us of the
breaking up of the assembly, and of Thersites, upon whose
vileness the overflowing imagination of the poet has conferred an undeserved immortality, as did the amber in Mar-
tial's epigram* upon the reptile it surrounded.

The πεῖρα is later than the Arming ; and quite in accordance with this fact is the important part which Odysseus
plays in it ; he is called πτολίπορθος (v. 278) by an anachronism such as we have pointed out above, and which betrays
an acquaintance with the Odyssey, as does v. 260, where he
says with pride *that he is the father of Telemachus* (who
must, in accordance with Homeric chronology, have been at

* IV., 59.

this time about eleven years old), a fact referred to nowhere else in the Iliad except in the ἐπιπώλησις, which
Köchly shows to have borrowed much from the passage
before us.

That a poet anxious to sing the Wrath of Achilles should
immediately digress into a dry catalogue of ships (484, *seqq.*)
is such a patent absurdity that no one will contend for the
κατάλογος being part of the original poem.   Probably it was
the very latest addition made, as will be shown hereafter.   It
had a special interest in itself as a description and geogra-
phical division of Greece, but the absurdity of giving it in
the tenth year of the siege is obvious, though in an account
of the commencement of the war it would be very appropriate, and might be made as splendid as the mustering of
the clans in Virgil's *Æneid* (VII.).   As poetry, its worth is
insignificant.   It is nothing but a dry and prosaic rendering of a subject poetically handled in the 'Teichoskopia'
and in the 'Epipolesis'.   Köchly sees in v. 362,

κρῖν᾽ ἄνδρας κατὰ φῦλα κατὰ φρήτρας Ἀγάμεμνον,

the verse which occasioned the catalogue.

To proceed now to Books III.-VII.: Düntzer* and Grote
have shown that originally these did not belong to the
poem.   It has been stated that the will of Zeus to
avenge Achilles' insult by the defeat of the Greeks is the
leading *motif* of the poem.   In Book III. this is quite forgotten; even the deceptive Dream is forgotten; for otherwise Agamemnon, filled as he is with confidence that he

---

* Homer, u. d. Epische Cyclus, p. 58. *seqq.*

will immediately take Troy, would never give his consent
to the single combat. Indeed at the beginning of Book IV.
Zeus himself seems to have forgotten his promise to Thetis,
and appears to take no special interest in either side, and
the battle is decided in favour of the Greeks.

Books III.–VII. therefore may be detached from the rest
of the Iliad; yet even they do not form a totality—a
complete whole : Grote has pointed out that for the latter
part of these scenes, viz., the building of the wall, there is
no sufficient reason, since the Achaeans, after their successes,
need not concern themselves so much about their safety.
The only reason the poet has for building the wall is to
to have it ready to be stormed afterwards, since, from a
military point of view, the first year of the war (Thucyd.
I., ii.) was the proper time for its erection. Connected with
this is the truce which renders its building possible, and
probably also the single combat of Hector and Ajax,
which serves as introduction to the truce. Apart from these
scenes, and forming a group in themselves, stand the
earlier scenes (Books III.–VI.) : viz. the introduction to the
battle (Γ. 1 to Δ. 421), Hector's going into the town, and
the Aristeia of Diomedes (Δ. 422–H. 16). But even these
are not all of the same age or by the same poet. Köchly
has shown that the Teichoskopia is an interpolation in the
combat of Menelaus and Paris, since it interrupts the action,
and contains circumstances which are inconsistent and at
variance with it : for instance, in Γ. 145, *seqq.*, Helen is
represented sitting amongst the Trojan elders, to whom

she is pointing out the Greek heroes, whereas in v. 384, when Aphrodite goes to bring her to Paris, she is seated amongst the women in the tower.

Even the ancients had been perplexed by this Teicho-skopy: they could not believe that Homer would commit such a blunder as to represent Priam in the tenth year of the war asking for the *first* time who the besiegers of the city were. The combat of Menelaus and Paris, which contains this late-added episode, has been proved by Kam-mer (O. p. 21, *seqq.*) to be itself a late addition, since it is ignored in the Aristeia of Diomedes in passages where mention of it would have been unavoidable, were not the Aristeia a composition of earlier date : for in-stance, on Hector's going into the town no one asks how this all-decisive combat went; on Hector's meeting Paris (Z. 325, *seqq.*) and reproaching him for his remissness, he says not a word of the combat, though it would have been the richest subject for reproof. It follows therefore that of Books III.–VII., the Aristeia remains as the oldest part, but even this is not one complete whole; it falls into two portions, viz., the two battle scenes (Δ. 422–Z. 72), and the going of Hector into Ilion, his parting from Andromache, and his return to the battle-field with Paris (Z. 72–H. 16).

The ostensible cause ('motivirung') of Hector's going into the town is to order a prayer to be offered to Athene that she may check the valiant Diomedes (Z. 96); but it is to be remarked that in the battle scene immediately

preceding it is Polypoetes and Agamemnon, and *not* Diomedes, who have been dealing death to the Trojans. Haupt,
Geist, and Köchly, have discussed the matter with great
acuteness: we may be content with remarking that this
has the characteristic of all interpolations, a new *motif*
different from the main one, which is dropped and comes
to nothing when it has served its turn. Here the *motif* for
Hector's going into the town is to offer prayer to Athene,
which leads to nothing. Now had the same poet been the
author of this book and of the Aristeia, how could he have
refrained from emphasizing the tragic contest between the
Trojan's 'prayer of faith' to Athene and the active help
she is all the while giving to their foes the Greeks (E. 736,
seqq.) Everyone will remember the verses in 'In Memo-
riam' where Tennyson has treated of such irony:

> 'O mother, praying God will save
> Thy sailor,—while thy head is bow'd,
> His heavy-shotted hammock-shroud
> Drops in his vast and wandering grave.'

Indeed if the same poet had composed both episodes, he
could not have avoided accentuating the contrast by some
such comment as Shakspere's in 'King Lear':

> 'As flies to wanton boys, are we to the gods,
> They kill us for their sport'.

There can be no doubt therefore that here we have the
work of different bards; and furthermore, that the Aristeia
must be the later of the two, since otherwise the tragic contest
would be strongly accentuated, which is totally disregarded
by the passages as they stand at present. Some ancient

reader, feeling the contrast and trying to clear Athene of duplicity in receiving the Trojans' gifts and giving them the consent which silence proverbially implies, while really rejecting their petition, inserted line Z. 311, which represents the statue of Athene refusing with a nod. His insertion, however, did not escape detection, as we see from the Venetian Scholia on the line. The Ἕκτορος καὶ Ἀνδρομάχης ὁμιλία, therefore, is earlier than the Aristeia of Diomedes, which was composed as an afterthought to justify the earnest prayers of the Trojans against Diomedes.

Naber* has shown that the parting of Hector from Andromache, sad as it is with boding and presentiment, seems intended to prepare us for his immediate death, which is not however related till the twenty-second Book. Yet it is strange that Andromache, when she sees her husband dragged away by the enemy, never thinks of their last parting. Naber explains this by supposing that the sixth Book was composed later than the twenty-second. This supposition is borne out by many instances of imitation, and also by the fact that in the sixth Book many points have gained a precision and definiteness, and the legend has undergone a development which in its earlier stage (X.) it did not possess. In the older Book the name of Hector's wife is not mentioned (v. 437); but in the more recent one, not only does the poet give her a name, but tells us of her previous history, and even goes so far as to give a derivation for the name of Hector's son.

Naber maintains that the Ἕκτορος καὶ Ἀνδρομάχης

* 'Quaestiones Homericae,' p. 156.

ὁμιλία, when originally composed, cannot have been so far removed from Hector's death as it is now: a theory true, and in agreement with what we have just shown, viz., that H.-K. were originally absent from the poem. Let us, however, adduce further evidence. It is this: the Aristeia cannot have ended where it now ends, viz., at the beginning of H., for there it is violently broken by the interpolated Books (VII.-X.), and its termination and proper conclusion is not found till Λ. 369, *seqq.;* the break is where Hector, after going into Ilion and bidding the matrons offer up prayers against Diomede, returns to the battle-field accompanied by Paris, who is splendidly described (Z. 506, *seqq.*), and whom the poet evidently intends to perform great feats of war; but no sooner has the poet got him fairly on the field of battle than the impertinent interpolator comes and proclaims a truce (during which he pits Ajax against Hector in single combat); and not until Λ. 369 will this interpolator withdraw, and allow Paris to wound Diomede and drive him from the field. This is the end and termination proper of the Aristeia of Diomedes; this is its satisfactory conclusion; and we see how it was for this the poet was preparing us when he put into Hector's mouth the praise of his brother's prowess as they left Ilion together (Z. 520-523).

H

VIII.

LET us hasten on to what may be called the second half of the Iliad, Λ.–Χ. These Books have no unity or proper connexion with one another;* and we can point out the later portions with considerable certainty. The Reconciliation of Agamemnon and Achilles is unmistakably of later date than the Presbeia, and is moreover quite superfluous, since Achilles' resolve to avenge Patroclus is quite unconditional, and is sufficient to bring him into the field without any reconciliation at all. The Hoplopoïa is also later, since it presupposes the Presbeia (Σ. 448, τὸν δὲ λίσσοντο γέροντες Ἀργείων), and imitates it. The Meeting of Achilles with Aeneas and Asteropaeus (Υ. 176, *seqq.*, Φ. 148) is an imitation of the meeting of Glaucus and Diomede (Ζ. 119, *seqq.*), which occurs in a Book we have shown also to be late. The withdrawal of Aeneas from the battle by Poseidon in Υ. is imitated from his withdrawal by Apollo in E., which has been shown to be very late; and that the Death of Sarpedon in Π. is copied from that of Hector has been already stated.

We will now proceed to the Errand ('Botengang') of Patroclus. In the course of the eleventh Book, Agamemnon, Diomedes, Odysseus, Machaon, and Eurypylus are succes-

* G. Hermann, opusc. v. 59, *seqq.*

sively wounded (v. 595). Achilles sees Machaon being
borne out of the fight by Nestor, but, not recognizing him,
sends Patroclus (v. 610) to find out who the wounded man
is. Away goes Patroclus, and for very haste will not sit in
Nestor's tent, though courteously invited to do so; yet after
all he delays there while Nestor dilates upon the doings of
his youth, nor leaves until the old hero, moved by the increasing distress of the Greeks, charges him to use every
endeavour to rouse Achilles to the war, but in case he cannot
succeed in this, then to get Achilles to give him his own
armour and send him into the fray, that the Trojans, mistak-
ing him perhaps for Achilles, may abandon the fight (v. 795,
seqq.). Fired by this advice, Patroclus hastens from the tent,
but meets the wounded Eurypylus limping from the battle.
The disabled hero begs him to bind his wound and help him
to his tent. Patroclus does so, declaring all the while that he
is hurrying to Achilles (*not* to fulfil his errand, and bring news
that Nestor's wounded friend is Machaon, but) to rouse him
to do battle (v. 838, *seqq.*). Yet after all he lingers there in
Eurypylus' tent, while the rising tide of war surges round the
rampart of the Achaeans; while even the god Poseidon has
to come to the assistance of the hard-pressed Greeks; while
Zeus is lulled to sleep by Hera; while Hector is wounded,
and the Trojans put to flight; and not till Zeus wakes from
his slumber; not till Hector returns and renews the success
of the Trojans; *i.e.* not until the fifteenth Book (390–404), do
we hear of Patroclus again; and then he tells his host Eurypylus that he can tarry no longer, since he is hastening to
urge Achilles to the war, using the *very words* which Nestor

H 2

used (402, *seqq.*). At the opening of the sixteenth Book we find Patroclus, having failed to rouse Achilles, obtaining leave to don the hero's armour, and entering the conflict; then follows his death, the loss of the armour, the Hoplopoïia, and the slaying of Hector.

In this Errand of Patroclus we find the characteristic mark of an interpolation, viz., the introduction of a counterfeit or mock motive ('schein-motiv'); for the sending of Patroclus to inquire after Machaon is nothing else, since upon his return the object of his mission is forgotten, and he does not even tell Achilles that it was 'only' Machaon: the 'schein-motiv' is quietly allowed to drop when it has served its turn in bringing Patroclus to Nestor that he may get from him the idea of donning Achilles' armour (the 'Waffentausch'), which is but a new 'schein-motiv' to introduce the Hoplopoïia.

And now for this other 'schein-motiv', viz., the donning of Achilles' armour by Patroclus, that the Trojans may mistake him for Achilles. This is merely a device of the later poet (or interpolator if you will) to lose the arms in order that he may have an opportunity of bringing in his splendid Hoplopoïia. Now, that in the original poem Patroclus went forth in his own armour, and that this masquerading in Achilles' armour was subsequently 'inlaid', is plain from the fact that when Patroclus does go forth none of the Trojans for an instant mistake him for Achilles. From the matter-of-fact way in which his appearance on the field is related (Il. 278),

Τρῶες δ᾽ ὡς εἴδοντο Μενοιτίου ἄλκιμον υἱόν,

it is plain that the original poet had not the faintest conception that Patroclus was wearing Achilles' armour, and would
no doubt have been indignant at the later poet presuming
thus to enter Achilles' tent, and to thrust his services as
armourer so officiously upon Patroclus.

But when the later poet has at last got Patroclus into
the field, arrayed from head to foot in such flawless armour,
he is at his wits' end how to get him killed: so Apollo has
miraculously to strip all the armour off again, and thus
expose Patroclus defenceless to the weapons of the Trojans.

Patroclus is killed, and shortly after we read with astonishment that Hector strips off his armour (P. 125),

Ἕκτωρ μὲν Πάτροκλον ἐπεὶ κλυτὰ τεύχε᾽ ἀπηύρα.

What! did the interpolator actually make Patroclus wear
Achilles' armour over his own?

But even when the interpolator has at last successfully
managed to have all the armour lost, he cannot make up his
mind what its subsequent history is to be. In P. 129, *seqq.*,
Hector brings the armour to his chariot, and gives it to his
attendants to carry into the town; but afterwards he follows the chariot, overtakes it, and dons the armour: later on
(X. 323) there is no mention, though we might well expect
it, of his having done so; and from P. 231 we may infer that
he did nothing of the kind,* for there he promises, to anyone
who will bring him the dead body of Patroclus, half the armour—a promise which seems to show that the poet of the
passage regarded the body as not yet despoiled.

* Bergk., Gk. Lit., p. 620.

We see, then, that the 'Waffentausch' is a later addition, and therefore all the episodes which depend on it are later also. The object of the 'Waffentausch' is to pave the way for the Hoplopoïia, and in order to get this a niche in the Homeric Temple of Fame, its poet is resolved that 'all causes shall give way', as we shall now see.

When Menelaus sends Antilochus (P. 691, *seqq.*) to announce the death of Patroclus to Achilles, and to summon him to rescue the body of his friend, the interpolator will not let Antilochus deliver his message in full, but only allows him to announce Patroclus' death; for the interpolator has pressing business of his own on hand, viz., to bring Thetis up out of the green-sea depths at the exceeding bitter cry of her son, that she may procure for him the Hephaestus-wrought armour; he will not therefore allow Achilles to attempt the obvious and immediate duty of rescuing his friend's body until it has been definitely settled that there is to be a Hoplopoïia, and then we find Hera sending Iris to bid Achilles show himself to the combatants, and by the terror of his voice put the Trojans to flight (Σ. 148, *seqq.*).

The obvious conclusion to be drawn is, that in the original poem Achilles was informed of his friend's death by the messenger from Heaven, and at once, as was natural, went forth and rescued the body. The sending of Antilochus to summon Achilles to rescue the body is a 'schein-motiv', which is quietly dropped when its real object is achieved, viz., to get Thetis to come up out of the sea, and thus lead on to the Hoplopoïia.

On independent grounds, principally those of diction, Kirchhoff has pointed out that the conversation of Thetis and her son is a late addition, and is an expanded imitation of the similar passage in A. (v. 357, *seqq.*) ; and Bergk adds that the list of Nereids, though very interesting to the etymologist, is not of very high poetic merit, and has all the completeness of a later addition.*

To sum up, then : the ' Change of Armour' is a later addition, having its commencement in Nestor's advice in B., and finding its conclusion in the Hoplopoïia of the eighteenth Book. We may take, as a further piece of evidence, the fact that at the beginning of Π., when Patroclus has obtained permission to don Achilles' armour, the poet proceeds through verse 101,

ὣς οἱ μὲν τοιαῦτα πρὸς ἀλλήλους ἀγόρευον,

back to the field of battle, and tells how Hector hurls a torch into one of the ships, and how Achilles, seeing the flames, cries out to Patroclus (v. 126) :

ὄρσεο διογενὲς Πατρόκλεις ἱπποκέλευθε . . .
δύσεο τεύχεα θᾶσσον, ἐγὼ δέ κε λαὸν ἀγείρω.

That this passage is inconsistent with the other is plain, and that the latter is γνήσιος and the former νόθος can be doubted by none. Moreover, in the lines which follow (130-145), describing the donning of the armour, no attempt is made to show that it is Achilles' armour which Patroclus puts on, if we except the bare assertion that it is so, in lines 140-144, which Zenodotus omitted.

* Gr. Lit., p. 627.

The amplification of the poem by this 'Waffentausch' is typical of all its amplifications. They were not cotemporary with the original poem, still less were they prior to it in date. They do not actually harm the main action of the poem; they merely lengthen and protract it unduly. The author of them always casts about till he finds a plausible pretext for introducing them, and tries closely to unite and make them one with what precedes and follows. They are thus conditioned to a considerable extent by the already existing poem; and hence arise unavoidable inconsistencies and contradictions.

Even after the deduction of all the scenes connected with the 'Change of Armour', the residuum is not self-consistent, nor the work of one poet. The twelfth Book opens with the mention of the final destruction of the wall around the ships by Poseidon, Apollo, and Zeus. The Trojans storm it, having first, in accordance with the advice of Polydamas, dismounted from their chariots, and formed into five companies; but Kayser* has pointed out that all this is inconsistent with what immediately precedes. For in Λ., when we took leave of the Greeks, so far were they from being driven back into their strongholds, that they were decidedly victorious.

The connexion of N. with M. is just as bad. Lachmann showed long ago that the one cannot be considered a continuation of the other, since N. knows nothing of the five-fold attack organized by the Trojans in M. Bergk is, no doubt, right in saying that in the original poem there was not only no Teichomachy, but no wall around

* Hom. Abh., p. 56.

the ships; for otherwise the catastrophe would not be the fight *around the ships*, but rather the fight at the rampart which defended them. The rampart is as useless to the poem as it was to the Greeks; and Bergk all but expresses regret that Poseidon, Zeus, and Apollo, when obliterating it from Troy, did not obliterate it from the Iliad as well.

Kayser,* who believes the rampart to have been an historical reality, thinks that in the time of the poet who composed the passage all traces of the actual wall had disappeared by the action of natural forces. That the action of Natural Forces should afterwards be transfigured into Divine Agency is nothing unusual; and we will point out further on how the later poets, with more and more freedom, introduced the gods as actors into these scenes of bygone history without any feeling on their own part, or on that of their audience, that there was anything absurd in their so doing : though no doubt both the poets themselves and their audiences would have felt the absurdity of introducing the gods into contemporary history. We may remark that the poet of this passage, whoever he may have been, seems to have had some local knowledge of the topography of the place from his enumeration of the streams in M. 19, *seqq.*

The beginning of the thirteenth Book is marked by the active part which the gods begin to take in the actual fight, and which they continue to take till the twenty-second Book. Not to trouble the reader with the circumstantial proofs whereby it has been shown that the scenes where the gods are introduced are later additions, we will carry him by an easy

* Hom. Abh., p. 56.

à priori road to the point at which German scholars have arrived by the painful *à posteriori* method. The closer we are to any historical event the more truthfully and practically is it related, and even though poetically treated is not garbled with mythology: only after a considerable lapse of time does the marvellous creep in when the poet and his audience are far from the facts. Using this axiomatic principle as our criterion, we may distinguish the earlier portions from the later additions; and we will find that the results tally with the results arrived at on independent grounds.

In the oldest part of the Iliad, viz., A., we see how sublime is the poet's conception of the part which the Heavenly Powers take in the war (v. 5)—

$$\Delta\iota\grave{o}s\ \delta'\ \grave{\epsilon}\tau\epsilon\lambda\epsilon\acute{\iota}\epsilon\tau o\ \beta o\upsilon\lambda\acute{\eta}—$$

the old bard feels that the gods are high above man; that in some mysterious and awful way they

'Shape his ends, rough hew them how he will'.

It is only later that their action is particularized, and I may say vulgarized: in a late passage of the Odyssey the gods are represented as in Hesiod wandering unseen amongst men (*ρ*. 487), observing their good or evil deeds—

$$\grave{a}\nu\theta\rho\acute{\omega}\pi\omega\nu\ \ddot{\upsilon}\beta\rho\iota\nu\ \tau\epsilon\ \kappa a\grave{\iota}\ \epsilon\grave{\upsilon}\nu o\mu\acute{\iota}\eta\nu\ \grave{\epsilon}\phi o\rho\hat{\omega}\nu\tau\epsilon s.$$

In the Aristeia of Diomedes, too, which has also been shown to be late, the poet does his best to inform his hearers of the very latest discoveries in theological science; he lets them know that the gods are wrapt in mist, and therefore invisible to ordinary men (E. 127, 186, 356); that their blood is not blood at all, but that it should be called by its proper scientific name ἰχώρ (339). Athene's equipment is accurately detailed (736, *seqq.*); the poet gives us a glimpse of Heaven and Olympus (749, *seqq.*); he explains the rapidity of the gods' motion (770); and finally here, and here only, do we find mention of the cap of Hades (775).

Let us now take an instance of how the same theme is treated by an earlier and by a later poet. In the combat between Hector and Achilles, when the moment for deciding between them comes, Zeus is represented as weighing the destinies of both: Hector's scale sinks, and he is doomed to death (X. 212, *seqq.*). It is a conception unrivalled for simplicity and grandeur; it is the conception of Homer. But in immediate juxtaposition is another, and I believe a later, treatment of the subject by some poet who could not bear that the closing scene should be so brief and decisive. When Zeus (v. 167, *seqq.*) sees Achilles pursuing Hector, he is moved by compassion for the Trojan hero, and asks the gods is there no way by which he may be rescued. Athene offers violent opposition, Zeus yields, and sends her down to earth to do as seemeth her fit. She lends her assistance to Achilles, but what need of assistance when Fate has already decided that Hector is to die (v. 179, πάλαι πεπρωμένον αἴσῃ); what need of Zeus idly questioning the gods when he knows the scales of Fate proclaim victor and vanquished? The loving-kindness of Zeus, overruled by higher law, is pathetic in the extreme, but does not prove the passage to be early. Nay, there is one half line the incongruity of which is most

startling.   It is where Apollo, who has come as we are to
suppose to help Hector, leaves him (v. 213):

ᾤχετο δ' εἰς ᾽Αίδαο, λίπεν δέ ἑ Φοῖβος ᾽Απόλλων.

What ! ᾤχετο δ' εἰς ᾽Αίδαο of a person still alive ; of a person
whose fighting occupies the next fifty lines (- 300) ; and of a
person whose actual death is finally described in the following words :

᾽Ως ἄρα μιν εἰπόντα τέλος θανάτοιο κάλυψεν·
ψυχὴ δ' ἐκ ῥεθέων πταμένη ᾽Αϊδός δε βεβήκει,
ὅν πότμον γοόωσα λιποῦσ' ἀδροτῆτα καὶ ἤβην.

We may then regard the direct share which the gods
take in the conflict in Books N.-X. as a late addition. In
Z. the gods take neither side ; and this Book, as we have
stated previously, was probably the oldest of the later additions.   I may remark that, if we regard such immediate
interference of the divinities as absent from the original
poem, the inconsistency between the end of the first and the
beginning of the second Book is at once removed.

Amongst the many late additions which we have pointed
out in the Books Λ.-X., we may draw attention to N. 361-
672 (which we will name the Aristeia of Idomeneus) as
being one of the earliest.   Ajax and Hector are absent from
it ; and it bears the mark of all additions, viz., that it does
not materially affect the progress of the plot.   That Ajax
and Hector were originally the chief figures in every battle-
scene may be inferred from the fact that the poets feel bound
to account for their absence in battle-scenes where they do

not appear (Λ. 163, 497, 542; N. 674). Though this passage seems to be a later addition, yet Idomeneus appears to
have been an actor in the original poem. But not so the
Thracian Rhesus (K. 435), of whom we have no previous
mention, and who, as the poet naïvely tells us, is a late-
comer to Troy; so, too, Epeios, in the twenty-third Book, as
we have seen; so, too, Asteropaeus, who, though he appears
once or twice (M. 102; P. 217, 351), yet has for chief rôle to
be killed in an encounter with Achilles (Φ. 139, *seqq.*), which
is but a copy of the meeting of Diomedes and Glaucus.

The Lycian heroes, Glaucus and Sarpedon, are also late-
comers. Sarpedon appears in the Teichomachy, which has
been shown to be a late composition (M. 290–429), and then
is not heard of again for a long time. In Π. 419–683 we
find the account of his death by Patroclus, imitated from the
slaying of Hector by Achilles. Zeus wishes to save him;
Hera forbids it, but suggests that his body may be carried
to Lycia and there receive burial (τύμβῳ τε στήλῃ τε, Π. 457).
There are some internal inconsistencies, too, as if the poet
did not quite grasp the situation which he wished to develop:
for just previously Zeus is represented as sitting on Ida, and
Hera on Olympus, while in this passage they are represented
as sitting together; and soon after Zeus gives command to
Apollo to carry out the plans they have resolved on (v. 666),
though Apollo is far away upon the plain. Zenodotus was
of opinion that the whole dialogue between Zeus and Hera
should be left out. The simile in Π. 482, *seqq.*, is taken
word for word from N. 389, *seqq.*

The Lycian heroes are treated with great sympathy and

honour by their poet, and are even placed above Hector, whom both Glaucus and Sarpedon rebuke and scornfully remind of his duties (E. 471, M. 310, P. 140). This high position which the Lycians occupy in the poem is to be attributed to the Muses having already become mercenary, ἀργυρωθεῖσαι πρόσωπα, at the time when these Lycian additions to the poem were made. The poet who sung their praises was a dependent at the courts of some of their descendants— those of Glaucus, for instance, who resided in some of the Ionian towns (Herodot. I. 147). These princes, not contented with being glorified by the renown of their ancestor Glaucus, actually force the bard to go further, and glorify Glaucus himself by the renown of *his* ancestor Bellerophon, whom the bard represents as of the purest Greek blood, coming 'from Ephyre and central Argos'; for such genealogies must have been peculiarly grateful to the vanity of these residents in Asia Minor. It may be remarked that when the late-comer Glaucus enters the battle and the poem simultaneously, the poet makes Diomedes, who is a figure in the old poem, ask who he is, adding naïvely that he never saw him before. In the Ἀλήιον πεδίον we probably have a local reference which may give us a clue to find where the poet of the passage dwelt.

We may see, too, how influences of a similar kind brought Aeneas into the poem. In the Troad there were probably descendants of the hero (Υ. 307):

νῦν δὲ δὴ Αἰνείαο βίη Τρώεσσιν ἀνάξει
καὶ παίδων παῖδες, τοί κεν μετόπισθε γένωνται.

Strabo (XIII. 607, *seqq.*) says they ruled in Skepsis; to flatter them the poet lavished praises on their ancestor Aeneas, representing him as the son of Aphrodite, and such a favourite of the gods that they twice rescue him from death.

Polydamas, also, is a late-comer, and has 'the badge of all his tribe'—futility; he does not affect the main action at all; his frequently-offered advice is never taken;[*] and we should notice that in Σ. 249, *seqq.*, we are told for the first time who he is, which seems to indicate that this is his first appearance in the poem.

On the Greek side, Diomedes was the first new arrival; then Nestor, who appears only in passages already proved to be late: he, too, has 'the badge of all his tribe'—taking no part in the battles,[†] and giving advice not followed. His attempt to stop the strife between Achilles and Agamemnon (A.) fails in its object, and indeed is a disturbing element in the development of the situation, since the reply of Achilles, suggested by Nestor's interference, is inappropriate and gratuitously insolent (vv. 297–303). In all probability Nestor was originally absent from the scene, and v. 244 was followed immediately by v. 304, an arrangement which would be far more effective, and I may add more dignified, than the present arrangement of the scene.

Nestor, like the Lycian heroes, owes his place in the poem to his descendants. Those of the Lycians were princes in Miletus,[‡] and no doubt made it their study to win the favour of a poet who could confer upon the founder of their

---

[*] Bergk., Gr. Lit., pp. 609, 628.
[†] Kayser, Hom. Abh. p. 54, *seqq.*; Lachmann, p. 59; Bergk. p. 614.
[‡] Herodotus, i. 147; Strabo, xiv. 633; Pausanias, vii. 2.

house such deathless fame. Furthermore, to the poet himself the praise of Nestor must have been a theme peculiarly
welcome, affording as it did opportunities for picturesque
narrative of youthful exploits, and for inculcating all sorts
of valuable lessons in practical·wisdom. With Nestor, naturally enough, his sons Antilochus and Thrasymedes came
into the poem.

Next comes Odysseus : he, too, generally appears in later
passages in the πεῖρα, the ἐπιπώλησις, the Presbeia of the
ninth Book, the Doloneia, &c. Very often a passage where
he is mentioned 'shows the cloven-foot' by such anachronisms as the epithets, τλήμων, πολύτλας, πολυμήχανος, &c.,
which especially suit his character as pourtrayed in the
Odyssey, and are therefore, probably, considerably later
than the original poem.

So, too, Menestheus with the Athenians occurs in later
passages ; and Phoenix, whom we will leave to Bergk's
tender mercies (Gr. Lit., p. 596).

We see, then, that the Iliad had in its early and original
state far fewer heroes to take part in the action, which was
therefore marked by a simplicity which contrasts strongly
with the vast crowd of 'lords, ladies, captains, soldiers,
heralds, messengers, gentlemen, and attendants', which at
present throng it ; and perhaps we have an indication of
this simplicity where Agamemnon, threatening that he will
indemnify himself for the loss of Chryseis (A. 138), says :

$$\text{ἐγὼ δέ κεν αὐτὸς ἕλωμαι}$$
$$\text{ἢ τεὸν ἢ Ἀιαντος ἰὼν γέρας ἢ Ὀδυσῆος ;}$$

and six lines further on (v. 144):

εἷς δέ τις ἀρχὸς ἀνὴρ βουληφόρος ἔστω
ἢ Αἴας ἢ Ἰδομενεὺς ἢ δῖος Ὀδυσσεὺς
ἠὲ σὺ Πηλείδη.

Does the poet here mean to name for us, at the very outset, the *dramatis personae* of his poem? Does Homer use but four or five characters for his poems, as the early painters used but four or five colours for their pictures?

Kammer, in his Homeric Studies, has acutely remarked that throughout Y.-X. Achilles fights *on foot*, with which the harnessing of the chariot-horses described at the end of the nineteenth Book is inconsistent, and is therefore probably a later addition. Kammer's observation seems to hit the mark, for Achilles' chief glory is his swiftness of foot; he is called ποδάρκης or πόδας ὠκὺς, and he justifies his right to these titles by his speed on the final day of combat.

His chariot is not brought into the poem again till X. 395, where Hector is bound to it, and dragged away. Of course, if the chariot itself is a later addition, the dragging of Hector is also later, which we might infer from another consideration, viz., that it serves to introduce Ω., the Ἑκτορος λύτρα, which is confessedly late.

Kammer's shrewd remark will apply to other heroes also beside Achilles; Ajax and Hector, Hector and Patroclus, fight at the critical moment on foot; the fight at the ships is on foot; Patroclus is on foot when he is slain, and his companions are on foot when they protect his dead body, which is finally borne from the field on their shoulders; and the

I

Telamonian Ajax with his great shield is always a fighter on foot.

In all these battles, though chariots are sometimes mentioned, yet we nowhere find any clear conception of their use in the fight. We hear of them now and then, but soon after we must picture to ourselves the fight going on without them. Every careful reader of Λ.-P. will see that this is so. In Π. 358 Hector is fighting on foot, when suddenly we read (v. 367):

$$\text{Ἕκτορα δ' ἵπποι}$$
$$\text{ἔκφερον ὠκύποδες σὺν τεύχεσι.}$$

Where had these horses been all the while?

In the arming of Patroclus, amongst the verses which describe the yoking of the chariot there occurs the representation of the Harpies (Π. 150, *seqq.*), which show that the passage is late upon comparison with Z. 345, and because it shows connexion with the Odyssey. In M. 50, *seqq.*, we find a clear conception of the employment of the chariots in strict relation to the conditions of the fight. Here the combatants dismount from them before the rampart. This passage, however, occurs in the Teichomachy, which we have shown to be an aftergrowth.

Only in the fifth Book, which we have proved to be one of the 'epigoni', do we find real fighting in chariots, especially that of Diomede and Aeneas.

Accordingly, since the parts of the poem in which the fighting is on foot contain the battles which are of chief importance, and are most decisive, they must be regarded as

the earlier; from which it follows that the chariots and cha-
riot-fights are on the whole later additions. We might infer
this from independent historical considerations, since horse-
breeding is a luxury which was late in coming amongst the
Greeks: and not till Ol. 25 (680 B.C.) did a team run at
Olympia.* That it was from the Asiatics that the Greeks
learned the delight of having splendid horses may be inferred from the legend of Pelops, who is represented as
coming from Phrygia, and by the victorious swiftness of his
chariot winning a bride in Pisa. Excavations at Mycenae
have brought to light war-chariots depicted on vases: but
had such chariots been used before Troy there would be,
no doubt, some mention in the poems of their transport
across the Aegean. In all probability the old Aeolic poem
of the original Homer knew nothing of chariots; and not
until the poem had made its home amongst the Ionian
towns, with their wealth and splendour, were chariots introduced. And thus the later poet endowed the heroes of the
past with all the magnificence of his own age and civilization, careless of anachronism, careless of inconsistency, careless even of the customs of his race; for we know of no
instance where chariots were actually used *in war* by the
Greeks unless in the revolt of the Cyprians against Darius
(Herodot. v. 113).

Beside the passages which we have discussed as after-
growths, there are many others of less extent which certainly appear to be of still later origin. In the Patrocleia
we referred to the death of Sarpedon (Il. 419–697); but still

* Eusebius, Chronic. i. p. 195, Schöne.

I 2

earlier in the book come his two companions, sons of Amiso-
darus, the Chimaera-keeper (Π. 327), who presuppose Sarpedon, and carry us back to the narrative of Glaucus (Z. 119,
seqq.).   We have referred to the part which Apollo takes in
confounding and disarming Patroclus as not belonging to
the original poem, and therefore the wounding of Patroclus
by Euphorbus, which follows the disarming, and the slaying
of Euphorbus by Menelaos (P. 3–118), appears to be a later
addition.

The simplicity of the action in the sixteenth Book is
disturbed by similar foreign elements.   Hector practically
disappears from the field for a while—at least he does nothing
noteworthy.   In v. 362 we are told vaguely that he stemmed
the onset of the Greeks and protected the Trojans; then suddenly, in v. 367, we hear of him hurrying away in his chariot
and offering no opposition, though Patroclus all but scales
the walls of Troy.   In the scenes, too, after Patroclus' death
there are many futilities.   The battle rages round the hero's
dead body, but the narrative is so overloaded with detail
that the main point is quite lost sight of.   Although, for
instance, we read (P. 319) that the Trojans are almost
driven back into Ilion, and the reader might naturally think
there was now a favourable opportunity for rescuing the
body, yet the Greeks engaged in the fight do not seem to
have thought so.   In lines 426–542 Automedon, Patroclus'
charioteer, comes back into the mêlée, and monopolizes the
attention of Hector and Aeneas.   Now, if ever, is the time
for the rescue ; but no, the Greeks seem to have forgotten
what they are fighting for.   There is no *advance* in the

action; we have merely a juxtaposition of loosely-connected lays, whose increase or diminution is a matter of no concern; the golden rule to be observed in interpolating them being, to allow the Greeks to obtain only as much success as is consistent with victory ultimately declaring itself for the Trojans—a result necessitated by the already-existing poem. In one passage, indeed, the poet, whoever he was, seems to have been tempted to allow the Greeks to break this golden rule, and to carry all before them: in v. 321 he says :

'Αργεῖοι δέ κε κῦδος ἕλον καὶ ὑπὲρ Διὸς αἶσαν,

where Διὸς αἶσα is the predetermined issue of the fight.

Υ.–Χ. show many signs of re-handling in the fights of the gods, the struggle of Achilles with Scamander, and his meeting with Aeneas. When these are removed there remains a natural succession of single contests, such as we might expect to engage Achilles as he presses on to meet Hector. And let us here remind the reader of the relationship which exists between the twenty-second Book and the fifth and sixth. Hector's parting from his wife seems intended to prepare us for his approaching death, which, as we have said, seems originally to have followed it more closely. Andromache's lament in the twenty-second Book makes no reference to the last parting from her husband; whence we conclude that the Lament existed before the Parting; and there are many little points in which they agree curiously: for instance, we find the πόλις ἄκρη mentioned in X. 172 (ἐν πόλι ἀκροτάτῃ), and v. 383 (πόλιν ἄκρην), just as in Ζ. (88, 257, 297, 317); whereas in the other books the name usually employed is Πέργαμος ἄκρη (Υ. 52, Ε. 460), or Πέργαμος (Ω. 700).

We may observe, in passing, the great beauty of the twenty-second Book, and of the older parts of the twenty-first (v. 99, *seqq.*); a beauty only equalled in the sixth. The conversation of Hector with Helen or Andromache, and that of Glaucus with Diomedes, is marked by an originality and loveliness, of which there is a plentiful lack in those scenes descriptive of 'excursions and alarums' which follow, and which we believe were interpolated wholesale between the 'Parting' and the 'Death of Hector'.

Yet although a very chaos of additions of all sorts seem to have gathered about the original poem, none of them could have existed as an independent entity, separate from the rest of the poem, and having sufficient interest in itself. All presuppose what precedes and follows—all are accommodated to the position they occupy. If any of them were now to be removed from its position, it would no doubt be missed; since as there was usually some point in the original poem which suggested the later addition, so that later addition usually coloured all others which were afterwards added. All are developments of a given situation; and as they had to conform themselves to its unalterable exigencies, the prevention of slight inconsistencies was unavoidable: thus Γ.-Η., though they lack the leading 'motiv' of the poem (*i. e.* the will of Zeus obtaining satisfaction for Achilles by the defeat of the Greeks), yet are all acquainted with the immediate situation, viz., the absence of Achilles, whose wrath is often referred to (Δ. 512, Ε. 788, Ζ. 99, Η. 228).

No matter what additions, therefore, the later poets made, they had above all things to take the greatest care not to snap the chain of sequence in the old poem, lengthen that chain as they might. So when they introduce a 'motiv' which, if not cancelled, would eventually interfere with the original one, they cancel it quietly when they have made as much use of it as they want. After the covenant, which serves to introduce the single combat of Alexander and Menelaus, follows the breaking and cancelling of it. The πεῖρα of Agamemnon, too, ends in nothing. The gods who are introduced into the fight effect nothing decisive; they only counterbalance each other: the original course of the poem is merely delayed for some time by such additional scenes, and when they are over, the old point of departure is resumed, to which the interpolator faithfully carries us back. Sometimes, however, he fails to realize the position, and completely grasp the situation: for instance, he makes Achilles say in the Presbeia (I. 346) that Agamemnon, with the other princes, may ward off fire from the ships (v. 602); though how Achilles, being no prophet, and having never read the Iliad, could have known they were about to be burned is hard to see.

The reader has seen how the additions to the poem were not simultaneous but successive; and that the later poets were acquainted, not only with the original germ, but with the subsequent accretions as well; and as each poet received a complete whole from his predecessors, so he handed it on to his successors enlarged, but still a complete whole. Of these enlargements the one most easily made was the length-

ening of the poem by the last books: there was nothing here
to be done except to take care that the joining should be skilful and undetected by the critical nail. More difficult was the
'inlaying' of a passage, which was generally managed by a
'schein-motiv'; the clearest instance being Achilles' command to Patroclus to bring word who is the wounded man
he sees passing, a 'motiv' dropped as soon as the poet has
got Patroclus into conversation with Nestor. So, too, the
'schein-motiv' of Hector's going into the town is to command the offering up of prayers to Athene; but that the
'real-motiv' is to give us those charming domestic pictures
which occur in Z. must be obvious to all.

In the first half of the Iliad most of the additions are
quite 'new' scenes inlaid: in the second half they are usually
mere 'developments' of the already existing material, often
specially suited to the requirements of the audiences.

It is interesting to follow the growth of the later passages. We remarked elsewhere that the ἐπιπώλησις is later
than the Aristeia of Diomede: we find in it Agamemnon
chiding Diomede (Δ. 372, seqq.), just as Athene had chided
him in the earlier passage (E. 800), and telling him how
much braver his father Tydeus was. He then goes on to
relate the incident which the goddess had related to Diomede, but does so more explicitly, adding new matter to
the tale (v. 391, seqq.) :

> οἳ δὲ χολωσάμενοι Καδμεῖοι κέντορες ἵππων
> ἂψ ἄρ' ἀνερχομένῳ πυκινὸν λόχον εἶσαν ἄγοντες
> κούρους πεντήκοντα· δύω δ' ἡγήτορες ἦσαν
> Μαίων Αἱμονίδης ἐπιείκελος ἀθανάτοισιν

υἱός τ' Αὐτοφόνοιο μενεπτόλεμος Πολυφόντης·
Τυδεὺς μὲν καὶ τοῖσιν ἀείκεα πότμον ἐφῆκεν·
πάντας ἔπεφν', ἕνα δ' οἶον ἵει οἰκόνδε νέεσθαι·
Μαίον' ἄρα προέηκε θεῶν τεράεσσι πιθήσας.
τοῖος ἔην Τυδεὺς Αἰτώλιος.

Now this, a new addition to the history of Tydeus, is merely a copy of the account of Bellerophon's brave doings related in (Z. 187, *seqq.*) :

τῷ δ' ἄρ' ἀνερχομένῳ πυκινὸν δόλον ἄλλον ὕφαινεν
κρίνας ἐκ Λυκίης εὐρείης φῶτας ἀρίστους
εἷσε λόχον· τοὶ δ' οὔτι πάλιν οἰκόνδε ἀρίστους
εἷσε λόχον· τοὶ δ' οὔτι πάλιν οἰκόνδε νέοντο·
πάντας γὰρ κατέπεφνεν ἀμύμων Βελλεροφόντης.

For in the history of Tydeus (A. 398) the words θεῶν τεράεσσι πιθήσας are inappropriate. Surely no omens of heaven are needed for sending a vanquished man home to relate the story of a defeat, whereas it is quite different in the original passage (Z. 183) :

καὶ τὴν μὲν κατέπεφνε θεῶν τεράεσσι πιθήσας,

where nothing but obedience to the signs of heaven could have nerved the hero against the dread Chimaera.

So grew the Tydeus tale; and let it be noticed that here (Δ.) first are his adventures brought into connexion with the 'Seven against Thebes'. To this is added that Sthenelus, defending himself and his lord Diomedes against the reproaches of Agamemnon, maintains that they are better than their fathers (Δ. 406) :

ἡμεῖς καὶ Θήβας ἕδος εἵλομεν ἑπταπύλοιο,

whereas Tydeus perished in the attempt.

This answer is only new in its application, for the words are taken from Diomede's conversation with Glaucus (Z. 222, κρqq.), and of course this is the earliest mention of the war of the Epigoni.

Let us now review our results. The first addition to the original poem, as far as we can make out, was the ῞Εκτορος καὶ ᾽Ανδρομάχης ὁμιλία, ostensibly occasioned by the success of Diomedes, and serving as introduction for the death of the Trojan hero: in this was then inlaid the meeting of Glaucus and Diomedes. Such is the content of the sixth Book, whose proper conclusion, as we have shown, is the wounding of Diomedes in the eleventh Book, but which is now separated from its proper context by all kinds of interpolations. Next was added the detailed Aristeia of Diomedes (E.), and the battles of the gods; and here first were chariots brought upon the field. The single combat of Menelaus and Alexander was used as introduction to these scenes, and in it was inlaid the Teichoskopy. The second Book was enlarged by the πεῖρα, to which then the ἐπιπώλησις was added. In the second half of the Iliad parts of the thirteenth Book (Idomeneus) perhaps belong to the old poem: at all events the germ of the book seems to have been known to the poet of the Teichomachy, which was an aftergrowth. Owing to the duration and length of the battle came a break—the single combat of Ajax and Hector—which, as we have said, follows the earlier one too closely. The poet-interpolator who stops the battle here has, of course, to set it going again, and he effects this by the Aristeia of Agamemnon. The Teichomachy necessitates the building of the wall, which in its turn necessitates the truce.   Later still was added the Presbeia (with the eighth Book); to which was added the Doloneia, which appears to be later than the ἐπιπώλησις.   The Presbeia was then copied in the Reconciliation of Agamemnon and Achilles in the nineteenth Book, as is plain from the fact that Agamemnon's disparagement of Ἄτη (T. 84, seqq.) makes use of the Allegory in I. 505, seqq., and can scarcely be said to improve upon it.

The second half of the Iliad underwent considerable alterations, owing to a later poet arming Patroclus in Achilles' armour, that the loss of it may lead on to the Hoplopoïïa, and introducing this change of armour by means of the errand of Patroclus, which in its present form appears to be later than the Presbeia (for as Kayser has pointed out, Λ. 786, seqq., is taken from I. 254, seqq.).   Other important changes were made by the introduction of gods into the combat of men: their action extends from N. to X.; and amongst them the Διὸς ἀπάτη deserves especial mention.   The death of Patroclus is much influenced by this innovation, and is copied in the ‘Death of Sarpedon’, whose fight with Tlepolemos in the fifth Book is later still.

In the tumultuous fighting of the last two days of battle we find much imitation of the fifth Book: part of the twentieth, viz., the meeting of Hector and Achilles, is an imitation of the combat of Menelaus and Alexander, since Υ. 443, seqq., is taken from Γ. 380, seqq.   Γ., on the contrary, is later than the ‘Armour-Change’, since Γ. 333 is taken from Π. 134.

Finally, the burial of Patroclus and the ransom of

Hector were added at the close, after some insignificant preparations in the preceding Books. One of the very latest additions seems to have been the Ships' Catalogue in the second Book.

This will suffice to give in outline the results of the foregoing discussion, and the reader will observe that it by no means professes to solve all difficulties, and to be as unimpugnable truth as a Euclidean theorem; but that it is a rational hypothesis of the gradual evolution of the poem, and a fair attempt to determine the respective antiquity of its episodes, and to mark the several ages of these members of the Homeric family.

We have hitherto been dealing with the 'Epigoni'; let us now turn to the parts which remain, and which consequently formed the original poem: they are A. (except the end), the conclusion of O., the beginning of Π., and portions of the later Books till the twenty-second, with perhaps part of the thirteenth. These told of the quarrel of Achilles and Agamemnon; of the dream sent by Zeus, and the marching out of the Achaeans; of their defeat by Hector; of the fire hurled into the ships; of the sending forth of Patroclus with the Myrmidons; of his death, and the difficult recovery of his body by his friends; of Achilles' return to the battle; and the slaying of Hector.

Such was the argument of the poem. The actors, besides Achilles and Agamemnon, were Odysseus, Ajax, Hector, and Patroclus, with perhaps Idomeneus. The narrative was much shorter and more rapid than at present. The opening of the first Book is brief and compact, contrasting strongly with the parts which we consider to be of later date. We have not in it the luxuriant richness of detail, the similes and numerous epithets, which are lavishly used in passages less important to the progress of the poem. How simple, for example, is the description of Apollo's use of the bow here (A. 49), and what wealth of detail the poet has squandered at Δ. 105, *seqq.*

The account of the burning of the ships is characterized by the same vigorous and curt style (Π. 119, *seqq.*) :

γνῶ δ' Αἴας κατὰ θυμὸν ἀμύμονα ῥίγησέν τε
ἔργα θεῶν, ὅ ῥα πάγχυ μάχης ἐπὶ μήδεα κεῖρε
Ζεὺς ὑψιβρεμέτης, Τρώεσσι δὲ βούλετο νίκην.
χάζετο δ' ἐκ βελέων· τοὶ δ' ἔμβαλον ἀκάματον πῦρ
νηΐ θοῇ, τῆς δ' αἶψα κατ' ἀσβέστη κέχυτο φλόξ.
ὣς τὴν μὲν πρυμνὴν πῦρ ἄμφεπεν· αὐτὰρ Ἀχιλλεὺς
μηρὼ πληξάμενος Πατροκλῆα προσέειπεν·
ὄρσεο διογενὲς Πατρόκλεις ἱπποκέλευθε·
λεύσσω δὴ παρὰ νηυσὶ πυρὸς δηΐοιο ἰωὴν·
μὴ δὴ νῆας ἕλωσι καὶ οὐκέτι φυκτὰ πέλονται.
δύσεο τεύχεα θᾶσσον, ἐγὼ δὲ λαὸν ἀγείρω.

Let anyone compare the descriptions of the fight on less momentous occasions and the difference will be quite clear : in Λ. 544, *seqq.*, when Ajax is retreating, a long detailed simile accompanies the fact; but at the burning of the ships, when the Greeks are sustaining the mightiest and most momentous of defeats, we read merely χάζετο δ' ἐκ βελέων. How many names we find in other parts of the poem, but here we know not who it is that hurls the fire into the ships, for here it is the action and progress of the poem that is of chief importance, and not the persons. Beyond shadow of

doubt, in the old poem there were very few of those mono-
tonous and valueless detailed descriptions of battle-scenes
which are so massed together in the present poem. The
poetic worth of the Iliad does not depend upon its scenes of
carnage, but rather on those passages in which we are far
removed from the field of battle, and in which the poet in
his incomparable way depicts human life and thought.

That the germ of our present Iliad was a vigorous and
brief poem, to which new compositions were gradually added
and carefully united, is a theory not very unlike that of
Lachmann : the additions are, so to speak, separate poems
hung upon one thread; but our theory differs from his
' Lieder-theorie', in believing that these poems probably
never had any separate existence, but that they were expressly composed to amplify an already-existing whole. At
every stage of its evolution the Iliad was a complete poem.
Every bard who rehandled it—either by expanding something which it already contained, or by filling up what he
considered its deficiencies, or by inserting some entirely new
poem of his own creation—always did so with a clear understanding that he must not interfere too much with its
features as a whole. It is quite impossible to believe that
any collector, or mere διορθωτής, gathered up the portions
and put them together.

As the contents of the poem were thus enriched by manifold augmentations, its form also became richer, the representation more perfect, and the poet's use of language more
masterful. The older portions are simple; the later luxu-
riantly ornate. From the earlier poets the later ones learned

much, and not unfrequently surpassed them; yet, on the other hand, it often happens that in not using what they have learned in its original sense, but in giving it some new application, they put the jewels of epic poetry to sorry misuse.

IX

WE have seen how the Wrath of Achilles was expanded into an Iliad. Let us now see how this tale of Troy was itself augmented and brought to a conclusion by a later poem—the Odyssey. In it the return of the heroes from Ilion could be narrated very appropriately, since Menelaus returns to his home, and Orestes avenges his father, in the eighth year after the fall of Troy (δ. 82, γ. 305, *seqq.*); and Odysseus, who is the last of all to get back, returns in the tenth.

From the Odyssey we get an idea of a time when the taste for epic poetry has become general, and the tale of Troy is known everywhere; not only the Ithacans and Phaeacians, but even Aeolus, wishes to hear (κ. 15):

>"Ιλιον 'Αργείων τε νέας καὶ νόστον 'Αχαιῶν·

the siege of Troy forms part of the Sirens' song (μ. 189, *seqq.*) :

>ἴδμεν γάρ τοι πάνθ', ὅσ' ἐνὶ Τροίῃ εὐρείῃ
>'Αργεῖοι Τρῶές τε θεῶν ἰότητι μόγησαν·

and Odysseus, sitting as a stranger before Penelope, says (τ. 108) that her fame reaches the heaven.

That epic poetry is more widely spread, and that the poet has become more self-conscious, is evidence of the very

strongest kind that a long period of time and a wide gulf
lie between the Odyssey and the Iliad. But still more important is the advance which it shows in art by the skilful
arrangement of its plot, by which events, widely diverse in
time, and happening in places far removed from each other,
are yet all related within very confined limits. The poet
has with great skill divided his material, and introducing us
into the very midst of the hero's wanderings, has chosen the
moment of calm afforded by his stay amongst the Phaeacians as the point of departure for relating the rest of the
hero's adventures, adroitly making the hero himself narrate
them. The *Nostoi* of the other heroes have been proved to
be later compositions than the Nostos of Odysseus himself ;
therefore it must not be supposed that the whole Odyssey is
the work of one poet. Nitzsch, Grote, Düntzer, and Kammer,
although contending for the unity of the poem, do not
maintain that it is the work of a single mind. Köchly has
separated it into several independent lays ; Kirchhoff has
done his best to show that it is made up of poems from
many sources ; and Kayser has shown that the component
parts belong to different periods.

No one in Germany any longer believes in the complete
unity of the Odyssey : the last books, as in the case of the
Iliad, are a late continuation, as even Mr. Gladstone has
brought himself to acknowledge, and they relate what happened after Penelope recognized her husband. In the Scholia
on ψ. 297, and in Eustathius, we find it remarked that Aristophanes and Aristarchus closed the genuine Odyssey at
v. 296, and declared the remainder spurious. In more mo-

K

dern times Spohn* has gone carefully into the matter, and
proved conclusively that it is a later addition : it tells how
Odysseus relates his adventures to Penelope ; how next morn-
ing he goes with Telemachus to the country to visit his father
Laertes; how the suitors conducted by Hermes go down to
Hades; how the vengeance of their relatives is averted by
Athene; and in fact how all 'ends happily'. Spohn, and
since his day Liesegang, have pointed out how these books
contain many verses taken from other passages, and sometimes ill-suited to the place where they are forced to do duty.
The descent of the suitors into Hades occasions a second
Nekyia, which is beyond a doubt meant to complete that in
the eleventh Book, introducing, as it does, conceptions quite
new and unknown to the former narrative, viz., the Λευκὰς
πέτρη, the πύλαι Ἡελίου, and the δῆμος ὀνείρων. Here, too,
for the first time, we find Hermes as guide of the dead ; and
we should also remark that in the account of the burial of
Achilles (ω. 60) the Muses have for the first time attained
to the definite number of after times—nine.

We have said elsewhere that the Telemachy did not belong to the poem in its original state : it is but poorly united
with the return of Odysseus, and does not in any way help
to bring it about, since Odysseus does not meet his son until
they have both returned to Ithaca. In the assembly of the
gods, at the opening of the poem, it is resolved that Hermes
shall be sent to Kalypso to effect the return of Odysseus, and
that Athene shall go to Ithaca to arouse his son. The latter
takes place, and its consequences are followed out to their

* 'Commentatio de extrema Odysseae'. Leipzig, 1816.

end; but the former and more important part is neglected till the fifth Book, when the gods effect it, without however seeming to know anything of their former resolutions in a.[*] Here we see how little the poet understood the management of two plots which should be evolved simultaneously: he allows one to develop, the other to stand still. To the poet of the Telemachy, the Telemachy is an end in itself; he cares not that it should contribute any material assistance to the Odyssey proper; and Kirchhoff is right in saying that its final cause is the desire to relate the Nostoi of the other heroes, especially of Agamemnon and Menelaus. Now these Nostoi are compositions of later date than the Nostos of Odysseus, that is, than the original germ of our Odyssey; therefore, à fortiori, the Telemachy must be of later date than the Odyssey proper: and accordingly, just as we might expect, we find it borrowing (β. 93, seqq.) verses almost word for word from the older poem (τ. 138, seqq.).

Many have thought that the Telemachy existed once as a separate poem, quite independent of the Odyssey; but Telemachus's journey is too devoid of result to be the subject-matter of a separate poem, or to form anything but a mere episode; and we should observe that its dependence on the Odyssey is not confined to the first Book, but extends to the later Books as well. It stands in close relationship with the slaying of the suitors as recompense for their insolence in the house of Odysseus and in the assembly of the people, and is composed strictly in reference to their subsequent punishment, as are the wishes and prophecies in γ and δ.

* Hennings, p. 151, seqq.

The issue is unmistakably foretold by the portent and its explanation in the assembly (β. 141–176, and 235, *seqq.*, 281, *seqq.*). The spokesmen amongst the Suitors, too, are the same as in the later books : we must conclude, therefore, that the Telemachy was never self-existent, but was composed deliberately for the position it now occupies.

It serves also to bring father and son together when they do arrive in Ithaca : for on arriving from Sparta, Telemachus goes first to the swine-herd Eumaeus, and there meets his father, agrees on the policy to be adopted against the suitors, and all through the remaining books acts in collusion with him. It was an old source of wonder why Odysseus stayed so long and so aimlessly with Eumaeus, but the explanation is simple. It is not the hate of the gods or the cruelty of fate which keeps him still absent from his home, but the poet of the Telemachy, who pens him in the swine-herd's steading till Telemachus thinks fit to return from Sparta. So, too (π. 130), the poet sends Eumaeus ostensibly to announce to Penelope the safe return of Telemachus, but really that father and son may speak together in private and arrange their plans.

This mutual understanding between father and son appears continually in the later books : therefore, if the Telemachy is an aftergrowth, *à fortiori* must these be so. We find confirmation of this view in the arguments advanced by others on independent grounds, and drawn from the number of similar scenes which are repeated in these books : twice do the suitors plot the death of Telemachus, and twice fail to effect it (π. 361, *seqq.*; v. 241, *seqq.*); thrice is Odysseus the mark of missiles (ρ. 462, σ. 394, ν. 299); thrice does he quarrel with the insolent maids (σ. 311, τ. 60, ν. 6).

All through these later books the insolence of the suitors is the too dominant note which the poet makes as harsh and jarring as he can: he seems to think that the sympathies of his audience are on the side of these young gentlemen, and that everyone will be filled with indignation at the merciless vengeance of Odysseus, unless he can show that their conduct went beyond even those limits permitted to such distinguished *jeunesse*. The poet does not go quite as far as Schiller in his 'Wilhelm Tell', and actually add a special scene in formal defence of Odysseus against the charge of murder; but yet, fearing that in spite of the pre-ceding insults and indignities so tediously detailed there may be some still unsatisfied, he cannot help, as it were in his final 'charge' to such persons (χ. 285, *seqq.*), calling their attention to the insult of Ktesippos (ν. 284, *seqq.*), and the attempt upon the life of Telemachus (χ. 53).

The second half of the Odyssey has been so carefully examined by German criticism, that we can now offer a rational theory of its development.

When Odysseus lands at Ithaca, Athene comes to him, and, to make him unrecognizable, transforms him into an old and ragged beggar (ν. 397, *seqq.*). This transformation is temporarily cancelled that he may be recognized by Tele-machus (π. 155, 454), but immediately afterwards she trans-forms him again, and in this disguise he endures all the insults heaped upon him in his house; but we must observe that at the end of the action, when Odysseus is recognized by

Penelope, the transformation is not cancelled. From this
Kirchhoff has with great acuteness inferred that in this
Recognition-scene the original poet did not represent Odysseus as a beggar at all, but as the hero-errant, so worn by
time and marred by calamity that even his wife, whose every
thought is of him and him alone, knows him not. Kirchhoff, with admirable poetic taste, declares this to be the older
and original *motif* of this 'Continuation' (Fortsetzung) of the
Nostos proper. The recognition of her husband by Penelope
is the great scene to which the rest of the poem should lead
up, and it is its fitting conclusion. Penelope is the heroine
of Greek Epos, the faithful wife and mother, suffering many
sorrows, but still so lovely in her sorrow—an ideal for the
Pagan world that contrasts not unfavourably with the Ma-
donnas of Christendom. If Kirchhoff is right, as I believe
he is, we have a very simple criterion by which to separate
earlier passages from later; all those in which Odysseus acts
as a disguised beggar having no part nor lot in the old
Odyssey.

This conclusion agrees admirably with what was previously stated, viz., that the second half of the Odyssey and
the late Telemachy are closely bound together. The following instances will show this connexion :—When Athene is
transforming Odysseus she tells him that his son is still in
Sparta (*v.* 412, *seqq.*). Eumaeus tells of the plot laid against
Telemachus' life as he returns (ξ. 174) ; then comes the recognition by Telemachus; the mutual understanding between
father and son ; the subsequent indignities, and the slaughter
of the suitors. In all these scenes we have the Kirchhoffian

double mark of late composition—dependence on the Telemachy and the beggar-motif.

In the original germ of the Odyssey—the Nostos proper
—Odysseus is still in the prime of life, a hero of princely
beauty and bearing; and as such he leaves the land of the
Phaeacians. But in the later 'Continuation' (Fortsetzung) a
new *motif* was introduced, viz., the change wrought in his
appearance by years of wandering and suffering. Then
came a still later bard; who, feeling that the 'Continuation'
was inconsistent with the Nostos, attempted to reconcile
them by the introduction of the 'transformation by Athene.'
His attempt did not quite succeed, however, as the reader
will have noticed, since in the 'Recognition' scene, already
existent and unalterable, it was impossible to introduce
the requisite cancelling of the transformation which had
actually been effected for an interval upon a previous
occasion.

We have drawn attention elsewhere to the numerous
repetitions in these later books, and we may point out a
certain feebleness of graphic power which is quite peculiar
to them. In the Eumaeus scenes there is a weak talk-
ativeness which is quite out of accord with the older parts
of the poem, and, in the effort to present us a picture of a
faithful servant, the poet goes too far, making Eumaeus at
the very first sight of Odysseus (ξ. 29, *seqq*.), and, while
in the act of protecting him from the dogs, lament the
absence of his master and the troubles with the suitors.
In the Eumaeus scenes Kayser has drawn attention to the
misuse of many traditional expressions, and the useless

addition of many unmeaning formulae borrowed from other
passages: for instance, v. 420:

> οὐδὲ συβώτης
> λήθετ' ἄρ' ἀθανάτων· φρεσὶ γὰρ κέχρητ' ἀγαθῇσι·

and v. 432:

> ἂν δὲ συβώτης
> ἵστατο δαιτρεύσων· περὶ γὰρ φρεσὶν αἴσιμα ᾔδη.

The τόξου θέσις, by which is to be decided who shall wed
Penelope, is certainly a later addition or interpolation: there
is no sufficient reason for its existence, since there is nothing
in the poem to compel Penelope to such a step; and sudden
and startling though her resolution be, it is not followed by
the effect which we should expect. No one expresses astonishment; no one expresses joy; all seem to regard it as a
matter of course. Afterwards, the fight with the suitors is
quite inconceivable in its improbability: we must regard
them as perfectly inert, for though some proposals of defence
are made, not a finger is raised by them; and the poet who
has not genius enough to pourtray the victorious combat of
one man with so many, and yet knows that the given
result (ἀέθλια καὶ φόνου ἀρχὴν) must be attained, tries to
get through with his task as fast as he can. Niese has
drawn attention to the badness of the Greek in the lines
(φ. 2, 3):

> τόξον μνηστήρεσσι θέμεν πολιόν τε σίδηρον
> ἐν μεγάροις Ὀδυσῆος ἀέθλια καὶ φόνου ἀρχήν.

Surely bow and arrows are not ἀέθλια, a word usually
meaning 'prizes of contest'; surely, too, πολιόν τε σίδηρον
would never suggest to the mind twelve axes.

But worse than this is its burlesquing of the Iliad. In φ. 246, we read how Eurymachus, not being able to string the bow, 'in his great heart groaned mightily.'

ἀλλά μιν οὐδ᾽ ὣς
ἐντανύσαι δύνατο· μέγα δ᾽ ἔστενε κυδάλιμον κῆρ.

How inappropriate, nay, how sacrilegiously, these words are used will be plain by comparing the passage from which it is taken in the Iliad, K. 11, *seqq.*, where Agamemnon is lying sleepless in his bed :

ἤτοι ὅτ᾽ ἐς πεδίον τὸ Τρωικὸν ἀθρήσειε
θαύμαζεν πυρὰ πολλὰ, τὰ καίετο Ἰλιόθι πρό,
αὐλῶν συρίγγων τ᾽ ἐνοπὴν ὅμαδόν τ᾽ ἀνθρώπων.
αὐτὰρ ὅτ᾽ ἐς νῆας τε ἴδοι καὶ λαὸν Ἀχαιῶν,
πολλὰς ἐκ κεφαλῆς προθελύμνους ἕλκετο χαίτας
ὑψόθ᾽ ἐόντι Διὶ, μέγα δ᾽ ἔστενε κυδάλιμον κῆρ.

How beautiful here—how incongruous and misplaced there !

We may regard Books ν–χ as forming a group, from which many individual scenes may be cut out without interfering with the march of the action. The proceedings in Odysseus' house, which begin in the seventeenth Book, are capable of an indefinite amount of expansion, and the poets recur again and again to the lawlessness of the young nobles, and degrade Odysseus to a very beggar in his words and acts, as well as in his dress. In reading the boxing-match with Iros, we seem to be far, far removed from the greatness of the heroic age, and can trace in such scenes the beginning of the later comic epos. But amidst these scenes of degradation there is a scene 'among them, but

not of them,' which shines forth all the more brightly
by contrast with those about it: it is the 'Conversation'
of Penelope with her foreign guest in the nineteenth Book.

The introduction to this conversation in ρ. 508, *seqq.*,
is obviously a later addition. In it Penelope, who wishes
to hear some news of her husband from the stranger, tells
Eumaeus to bid him approach, whereon Eumaeus relates
all he knows about him, and is then dismissed; the interview being postponed till evening. Now Eumaeus relates
not only all he knows, but also much more which he does
not know, for Odysseus (ξ. 199, *seqq.*) had told him a very
different story; but what he says agrees with the tale
afterwards told to Penelope by Odysseus, and therefore,
as we must conclude, is borrowed from it: moreover, we
should observe, that when the interview does take place
Penelope is represented as knowing nothing about the
stranger's history, although she had been already informed
of it by Eumaeus. Plainly then the ' induction ' to the
' Conversation ' is a later composition than the conversation
itself.

Niese has pointed out how none of the preceding scenes
will serve as induction, and Kammer has successfully abo-
lished the claims of the scene which immediately follows,
describing the washing of Odysseus' feet by Eurycleia, to
rank with it as of equal antiquity, so that the episode of
the conversation stands quite alone.

Its subject-matter is remarkable (τ. 100–316). Penelope
asks the stranger his name, but he prays her not to seek
to know it, for to utter it causes him the greatest pain.

Hereupon Penelope relates how sorely she is distressed, how countless suitors seek her hand, how she has sought to keep them afar by the guile of the web, but that now she knows not what to do—her parents urge her to marriage, and her son grows impatient. The stranger then declares his name, and tells, moreover, how in Crete he lodged Odysseus on his way to Troy. Penelope bursts into tears, and her guest tries to console her, telling her how he has heard from the Thesprotians that her husband is at hand.

Now here it must be remarked that for the first time we have a clear statement of the difficulties in which Penelope is placed (ν. 130, *seqq.*). Of the web by which she beguiled the suitors, and which is inseparably associated with her name, not a word is said elsewhere in the second half of the Odyssey.* Whether it be Athene, or Eumaeus, or Telemachus who is relating to Odysseus the doings in his house, Penelope's web is never mentioned. The later poets who made Telemachus the chief figure in Odysseus' house, and added all those dreary scenes of objective degradation, could not realize the subjective state of Penelope, so vividly put before us here by the old poet—could not catch the delicate perfume of this 'flower that bloomed i' the shade,' nor pourtray her love, so potent in its constancy; they had no eye but for the obvious brutalities of the suitors, and repeatedly call our attention with very anxious concern to the waste occasioned by them in Odysseus' house. Nowhere else is Penelope's sorrow and perplexity

---

* Except ω. 126, *seqq.*; in the Telemachy we have it, β. 93, *seqq.*, in verses taken from τ.

so clearly represented; and a further note of difference between this scene and the later ones all round it is the growing impatience of Telemachus, who is not so represented elsewhere.

A further proof that this passage is older than those which surround it, is that from the tale here told by the pretended stranger those many tales which occur in the second half of the Odyssey are taken: ν. 256, *seqq.*; ρ. 419, *seqq.*; τ. 75, *seqq.*, are taken from ξ. 199, *seqq.*, the tale told by Odysseus to Eumaeus, and this is itself taken from τ. 303, *seqq.*, our present passage.

In ξ. 158, *seqq.*, the stranger, to confirm his statement that Odysseus will soon return, although sitting in Eumaeus' hut, swears somewhat inappropriately by the hospitable board and hearth of Odysseus, to which he has (not yet!) come:

> ἴστω νῦν Ζεὺς πρῶτα θεῶν, ξενίη τε τράπεζα,
> ἱστίη τ᾽ Ὀδυσῆος ἀμύμονος, ἣν ἀφικάνω·
> ἦ μὴν, κ. τ. λ.

On the contrary, how appropriate is the expression in its original place (τ. 303, *seqq.*), when the stranger is sitting at the hearth and in the house of Odysseus:

> ἴστω νῦν Ζεὺς πρῶτα θεῶν ὕπατος καὶ ἄριστος,
> ἱστίη τ᾽ Ὀδυσῆος ἀμύμονος, ἣν ἀφικάνω·
> ἦ μὴν, κ. τ. λ.,

and let the reader notice how θεῶν in passing from the original into the copy has been damaged.

Now the tale in the fourteenth Book is an integral

part of the action extending from ν. to χ., and dominated
by the beggar-motif, and is, as we see, copied from the
'Conversation' of Penelope and Odysseus; therefore it
follows that the 'Conversation' is older than these books—
a conclusion further strengthened by the fact that in this
interview Odysseus is not represented as a beggar, but only
as a stranger. Seeing, then, that this episode is older than
its surroundings, it necessarily follows that it must originally have held some position other than that which it now
holds, and that the march of the action must have been
different from what it is at present.

Kammer remarked that this episode was inconsistent
with what follows. Eurycleia is the only one who will wash
Odysseus' feet, and she speaks of the scornfulness of the
maids, so that it is plain Odysseus is again transformed
into a beggar.

There is, however, one other passage where the original
motif of the 'Continuation' is plainly perceptible, viz.,
the 'Recognition' scene. Like the 'Conversation,' it is
older than the passages all round it; the scenes which
precede it, describing the slaying of the suitors, are dominated by the beggar-motif, and are, therefore, of later
composition; and if we strike them out, we can see how
natural is the reserve and doubt of the gentle lady who
is so numbed by sorrow, that even the coming of her hero-
husband cannot at once vivify her poor heart with joy:
whereas, if those scenes are allowed to remain, surely her
scepticism must appear obstinate, and the secret, known
only to Odysseus and herself, must appear childish after

he has given such triumphant proof of his identity as the slaughter of the insolent suitors.

What then remains but to connect the ' Conversation' with the ' Recognition,' thus pre-supposing an original poem very different from the present one: in it the slaying of the suitors has no place, and is not needed ; for what so natural as that ' the foolish suitors to a wedded lady' should withdraw upon the safe return of her husband. If we picture to ourselves the poem without the Telemachy, and the suitor-scenes connected therewith, *i. e.* the majority of Books ν.–χ., then there being no *insolence* of suitors, there will be no need of punishment for them, and the conclusion of the Odyssey will be no less satisfactory than at present. The poem will consist of two parts—the old Nostos, in which Odysseus is yet in his prime, and the somewhat later ' continuation,' in which he is represented as much worn by years of suffering.

This poem then, being such as we have pictured it, underwent considerable enlargement, two new *motifs* being added. At one time the insolence of the suitors is presented to us in all its forms necessitating their death at the hands of Odysseus, and so completely does it throw the older ' continuation' into the shade as to reduce it to the rank of occasional episodes : at another time we have the noble old *motif*, namely, that the ' wise world-wandering stranger, guest of many a king in many a land,' was so altered by time and calamity that on his return home he was unrecognizable. We have this afterwards rendered more plausible and probable, but at the same time degraded and spoiled, by his transformation into a beggar, whom suitors and servants despitefully use, while in this disguise he learns his true friends and faithful servants.

How greatly the old *motif* was injured may be seen by the way in which Penelope's grief for her husband's unknown fate is set aside, and the wasteful excess in Odysseus' house is dwelt upon as the sole cause of sorrow. Penelope is thrust more and more into the background by the later bards, while Telemachus is brought forward. She is the heroine of the old poem—she is the cause of the whole complication and the mighty concourse of suitors; yet, in the greater part of the poem in its present state, it is plain that the later poets did not rightly know what to do with her; they make her frequently appear before the suitors in an objectless and aimless manner, when one would expect her to be sitting retired in her chamber.

X

It is accepted now by German scholars that amongst the adventures which Odysseus relates to the Phaeacians, the Nekyia of the eleventh Book is of late date, for as Köchly remarks, the poet would not have caused Odysseus to journey to Teiresias for information when he intended to give him much better and more complete information afterwards through Circe.

It is a late addition, and, moreover, is later than the Telemachy; for in the account which it contains of Agamemnon's death (λ. 405, *seqq.*) its poet puts into requisition the two passages which are separate in the Telemachy, and to the fuller of the two, which represents Klytaemnestra as taking part in the murder, is added the figure of Kassandra: moreover, κ. 539, *sq.*, is taken from δ. 389, *sq.*; and a very strong proof that Odysseus cannot have been with Teiresias in the old poem is, that when the hero is parting from the Phaeacians he expresses a wish that he may find his wife and his friends at home well (ν. 42, *sq.*):

> ἀμύμονα δ᾽ οἴκοι ἄκοιτιν
> νοστήσας εὕροιμι σὺν ἀρτεμέεσσι φίλοισι.

Now it is quite impossible that Odysseus should speak

thus had he heard the words of Teiresias; and we should remark, too, that in his wish he does not refer to his son Telemachus, which seems a proof that in the old poem Telemachus did not play the important part which he does afterwards. Kammer notices that Kalypso, when foretelling to Odysseus the troubles that await him, speaks only of those which befall him during his return, apparently knowing nothing of the suitors; and as no such knowledge can be assumed on the part of Odysseus, we hence derive another element of proof that the suitor-scenes were unknown to the old poem.

Köchly sees an important criterion of the relative age of the several parts of the poem in their difference of style. Vigour and masterly conciseness mark the older parts, as, for example, the adventures among the Kikones and the Loto-phagi, with Aeolus and the Laestrygonians ; which with the voyage of Odysseus past the Sirens, past Scylla and Charybdis, as well as the slaying of the oxen of the Sun, he declares to be the nucleus of the original poem. A little later, perhaps, is the Kyklopeia, a masterpiece of art : in it the narrative proceeds more leisurely, and in the dialogue the contrast between the speakers is strongly marked : the adventures with Kirke seem to be still later ; and it is to be noted that Odysseus' companions, who in the older parts of the poem were mere lay figures, have here developed, and take a marked share in the action —to one of whom, who takes the chief part in opposing Odysseus, the poet gives a name, Eurylochus ; though in the adventures with Aeolus such definiteness of detail had

L

not yet been attained by the legend, and the companions
had not yet been provided with a spokesman.   In κ. 34
we read only

οἱ δ᾽ ἕταροι ἐπέεσσι πρὸς ἀλλήλους ἀγόρευον,

and in v. 37,

ὧδε δέ τις εἴπεσκεν ἰδὼν ἐς πλήσιον ἄλλον.

This expansiveness and detail is a mark of lateness, and the
ancients very justly, but for a different reason, regarded
the augmentation of the adventures at Thrinakia, by the
introduction of Lampetie, as later than the rest of the
episode. Lampetie is represented by the interpolator as
announcing to the Sun the destruction of his cattle. What
need of a messenger, ask the ancient critics, when the Sun
sees everything, and when the older poet expressly reminds
us of the fact in the verses—

δεινοῦ γὰρ θεοῦ αἴδε βόες καὶ ἴφια μῆλα
'Ηελίου, ὃς πάντ' ἐφορᾷ καὶ παντ' ἐπακούει.

This difference of style will be found one of the best
criteria for distinguishing the various stages of poetic development to which the several parts of the Odyssey belong.
To what stage it will assign the Telemachy and the suitor-
scenes is patent to all.

XI

At the beginning of the Odyssey we are told that, alone amongst all the gods, Poseidon is wrathful with Odysseus, because he blinded his son, the Kyklops (*a.* 20, 68). But it is strange that, in the account of the wanderings of Odysseus, which follow the Kyklopeia, we nowhere meet with a single indication that the Kyklops' prayer was answered. Poseidon does nothing whatever to avenge him, or to satisfy his own anger; and the final storm which destroys Odysseus' ships and drowns his crew is brought about by Zeus and Helios.

Düntzer was the first to suggest that the prayer of the Kyklops was later than the rest of the episode, and Kammer finds confirmation of this hypothesis in the fact, that after the Kyklops states his descent from Poseidon, Odysseus scornfully makes reply in verses which read like a later imitation of his previous mockery. We may also notice that the poet, who in *ι.* 106, *seqq.*, gave such an excellent description of the land of the Kyklops and its inhuman inhabitants, can scarcely have conceived of them as the sons of gods: indeed Polyphemus himself declares he recks not of the gods at all (v. 273, *seqq.*) Whence we may infer, that as in v. 412 Poseidon is for the first time mentioned as his

father, the genealogy was thence transferred to *a*, and
the wrath of Poseidon made a *motif* of the poem.

In the later poem, as Poseidon is the oppressor of
Odysseus, so Athene is his protector: she effects his return,
counsels and guards his son, smoothes the way for him
amongst the Phaeacians, and in Ithaca stands by him continually. Now, in the older poem, the 'Wanderings' of
Odysseus, it is quite the contrary, as Kayser has justly
remarked, and on no occasion does she assist him. The later
poet seems to have been painfully conscious of this inconsistency; so in ζ. 325 he makes Odysseus complain that till
then Athene had never heeded his prayers; and the poet
goes on to explain this neglect as arising out of her regard
for Poseidon; and later on (ν. 341, *seqq.*) he represents
Athene excusing herself to Odysseus on the same plea.
Therefore, if Poseidon be a later addition to the poem, *à
fortiori* must Athene be so; and this is quite in harmony
with the results obtained by other methods. In the parts
which we declared to belong to the old poem she takes no
share; it is in the Telemachy and the second half of the
Odyssey that she is so busy.

In the Iliad we pointed out how the direct interference
of the gods in battle marked a later period of Epic art; so
too in the Odyssey their interference occurs in the more
recent passages.

We have now got two criteria of lateness for the first
half of the Odyssey—the introduction of gods and amplitude
of details. In the ἀπόλογος we have no gods and marvellous
conciseness: in the passages which, as it were, envelop and

surround the ἀπόλογος, we find the gods introduced, and
more expansion and detail; that is, the return from Ogygia,
and the sojourn amongst the Phaeacians (ε–θ).

This inference is, in the case of the fifth Book, *i. e.* the
voyage from Ogygia to the Phaeacians, curiously confirmed
by some peculiarities of its verses. When Kalypso, in
accordance with Hermes' bidding, tells Odysseus that he
is free to depart whither he will, and must now build a
raft, he thinks she has some evil design, and demands an
oath from her in the following words (v. 177, *seqq.*) :

> οὐδ' ἄν ἐγὼν ἀέκητι σέθεν σχεδίης ἐπιβαίην,
> εἰ μή μοι τλαίης γε, θεά, μέγαν ὅρκον ὀμόσσαι
> μή τί μοι αὐτῷ πῆμα κακὸν βουλευσέμεν ἄλλο.

Now how unreasonable this is. Odysseus, as he frequently
tells us, has experienced nothing but good at the hands of
Kalypso—she received him when a helpless outcast, has
treated him kindly, and is exceedingly anxious to marry
him; yet, in spite of all, he feels this exaggerated mis-
trust; and what is the meaning of making her swear she
will do him no further (ἄλλο) harm?

The explanation is that the verses are taken bodily from
κ. 342–344, where Kirke has transformed Odysseus' companions into beasts, and has attempted to transform him
too. He has threatened her with the sword, and now she
is urgent that he shall lie with her. Odysseus answers :

> οὐδ' ἄν ἔγωγ' ἐθέλοιμι τεῆς ἐπιβήμεναι εὐνῆς,
> εἰ μή μοι τλαίης γε, θεά, μέγαν ὅρκον ὀμόσσαι
> μή τί μοι αὐτῷ πῆμα κακὸν βουλευσέμεν ἄλλο.

From comparison of the two passages, it is clear that the

poet of ε has borrowed from κ, and therefore that the adventures with Kirke must be older than the Return from Ogygia, and, consequently, older than the Assembly of Gods in the beginning of the poem, at which that return is resolved on.

Closely connected with the return from Ogygia is the arrival of Odysseus at the land of the Phaeacians, and his sojourn amongst them. Here we find that amplitude of detail which is the mark of later passages, and here we find also that other mark, interference of gods, the wrath of Poseidon, and the help of Athene. The books which deal with the Phaeacians, especially the seventh and eighth, have experienced many augmentations. The description of the garden of Alkinoos (η. 103-131) was long ago proved by Friedländer* to be very late. In the eighth book, too, re-handling is apparent where Odysseus is twice moved to tears by the song of Demodokus, and twice does Alkinoos notice it and bid the singer cease, as we are told in the very same words (θ. 62. seqq.; 469, seqq.). It is only on the second occasion that the incident furthers the action of the poem, and Alkinoos asks Odysseus' name. Of the two similar scenes the first is the older, for it develops naturally from what precedes; in the second, Odysseus himself requests the bard to sing, and then is violently affected by emotion. Probably v. 92 is to be joined with v. 532, and all that now intervenes, i. e. the games and the tale of Ares and Aphrodite, were originally absent. Even the ancients found cause of offence in this tale (266-369), though it

* Philol. VI. 669, seqq.

was not without defenders amongst them.* They noticed
that in the Iliad Aphrodite is not the spouse of Hephaestus,
and they thought that this passage was not the work of
Homer but of Demodokus—a criticism not very wide of
the mark, for the passage treats of the Gods in a manner
different from the rest of the poem, and, though not the
work of Demodokus, is certainly the work of some poet
other than the Homer of the Iliad.

We have seen that Kalypso, the Assembly of Gods, and
the Return from Ogygia, were later compositions: indeed
the reason of Kalypso's existence, as one might gather from
her name, seems to be merely to keep Odysseus seven
years concealed from all men, so that his wanderings may
occupy as many years as did the siege of Troy, and that he
may be the last of the heroes to return home, thus rendering it possible to include the narrative of their return in his.

Now were the Kalypso episode originally absent, it
follows as a matter of course that the hero would come
to the land of the Phaeacians, not from Ogygia but from
Thrinakia, after his shipwreck and the death of his companions, for their impiety in slaying the oxen of the Sun.
In the second half of the Odyssey we find evidence for this,
which is all the more convincing from its being unde-
signed. We have shown elsewhere that the 'Conversation'
of Odysseus and Penelope in the nineteenth book is one
of the oldest portions of the second half of the Odyssey.
In this interview the supposed stranger tells what he knows
of Odysseus (v. 272, *seqq.*) :

* Schol. Aristoph. Pax. 778 ; Schol. Od. θ. 266 ; Schol. Il. Σ. 382.

ἀτὰρ ἐρίηρας ἑταίρους
ὤλεσε καὶ νῆα γλαφυρὴν ἐνὶ οἴνοπι πόντῳ,
Θρινακίης ἀπὸ νήσου ἰών· ὀδύσαντο γὰρ αὐτῷ
Ζεύς τε καὶ Ἥλιος· τοῦ γὰρ βόας ἔκταν ἑταῖροι.
οἳ μὲν πάντες ὄλοντο πολυκλύστῳ ἐνὶ πόντῳ·
τὸν δ᾽ ἄρ᾽ ἐπὶ τρόπιος νεὸς ἔκβαλε κῦμ᾽ ἐπὶ χέρσου,
Φαιήκων ἐς γαῖαν, οἳ ἀγχίθεοι γεγάασιν,
οἳ δή μιν περὶ κῆρι θεον ὡς τιμήσαντο
καὶ οἱ πολλὰ δόσαν, πέμπειν τε μιν ἤθελον αὐτοὶ
οἴκαδ᾽ ἀπήμαντον· καί κεν πάλαι ἐνθάδ᾽ Ὀδυσσεὺς
ἦην, κ. τ. λ.

Here the stranger is not romancing, but is giving the theme
of the earlier part of the poem, with this single exception,
that in our present Odyssey the hero, when he leaves
Thrinakia, does not come at once to the Phaeacians, but
to Kalypso.

The Odyssey in the old form which we postulate must
have had a different commencement from that which it
now has, the Telemachy and the voyage from Ogygia
being absent.   How the poem was introduced can be
made out pretty plainly from the opening verses, which
even the later poets allowed to remain unaltered as Induction to the whole :

Ἄνδρα μοι ἔννεπε, μοῦσα, πολύτροπον, ὅς μάλα πολλὰ
πλάγχθη ἐπεὶ Τροίης ἱερον πτολίεθρον ἔπερσε,
πολλῶν δ᾽ ἀνθρώπων ἴδεν ἄστεα καὶ νόον ἔγνω,
πολλὰ δ᾽ ὅ γ᾽ ἐν πόντῳ πάθεν ἄλγεα ὅν κατὰ θυμὸν,
ἀρνύμενος ἥν τε ψυχὴν καὶ νόστον ἑταίρων.
ἀλλ᾽ οὐδ᾽ ὧς ἑτάρους ἐρρύσατο, ἱέμενός περ·
αὐτοὶ γὰρ σφετέρῃσιν ἀτασθαλίῃσιν ὄλοντο,
νήπιαι, οἳ κατὰ βοῦς Ὑπερίονος Ἠελίοιο
ἤσθιον· ἀυτὰρ ὅ τοῖσιν ἀφείλετο νόστιμον ἦμαρ.

Kirchhoff, Köchly and some others, wondering why the

destruction of the companions should be mentioned here, supposed that the lines were interpolated; but they are not so, they are extremely opposite; for ἀλλ' οὐδ' ὥς refers closely to νόστον ἐταίρων, and the verses seem to be an almost certain proof that here began the Odyssey proper, with Odysseus' arrival amongst the Phaeacians; and one can almost continue the passage with the verses from τ.

> τὸν δ' ἄρ' ἐπὶ τρόπιος νεὸς ἔκβαλε κῦμ' ἐπὶ χέρσου
> Φαιήκων ἐς γαῖαν οἳ ἀγχίθεοι γεγάασι.

After the Procœmium came the narrative of his landing and of his sojourn with the Phaeacians, more concisely, however, than at present: then came the ἀπόλογος, the story of his return to Ithaca, and of his restoration to his wife.

XII

LET us now review the results of our investigations. The old Odyssey begins with the coming of the hero to the land of the Phaeacians: he tells his name and his adventures with the Kikones, Lotophagi, Aeolus and the Laestrygones, at Thrinakia, and perhaps too with the Kyklops. Later on was added the narrative of how he was brought to Ithaca by the Phaeacians; how he comes as a woe-worn stranger into his wife's presence, and the 'Recognition-scene' finally ends the poem. The style of this old Odyssey is most strongly marked in the ἀπόλογος: conciseness and simplicity are its main features: the poet brings us from one scene of wonder to another with the simple words, constantly repeated,

$$\text{ἔνθεν δὲ προτέρω πλέομεν ἀκαχήμενοι ἦτορ}$$

(ι. 62, 105, 565; κ. 77, 132).

The next addition to this poem was perhaps the Kyklopeia: then came Kirke, and at the same time the Sirens, with Skylla and Charybdis. A still more important creation was Kalypso, who, by detaining the hero seven years at Ogygia, and thus increasing his term of sorrow to ten years, gives Telemachus time to grow up, and thus renders it possible for later bards to compose a Telemachy. Soon after Kalypso's entrance into the poem came the introduction of the other gods, especially of Athene and Poseidon : then came the Olympian assembly, and this afforded occasion for the journey of Telemachus, which in turn afforded occasion for the introduction of the nostoi of the other heroes. With the Telemachy came the suitors and their lawless revelry in Odysseus' house, and then, as a necessary consequence, their slaughter by the hero.

After the Telemachy was composed, the ἀπόλογος was augmented by the Nekyia, and then, after numerous slight alterations and additions, the poem was concluded by the meeting with Laertes, the descent of the suitors to Hades, and the averted vengeance of their kinsmen.

We have previously shown how the Odyssey borrowed much from the Iliad : it will be well to give here a few instances where later additions to the Iliad seem to have borrowed from the Odyssey. Epeios, who appears in none of the battle-scenes of the Iliad, has been introduced at the funeral-games of Patroclus, from the Odyssey, where he is celebrated as the builder of the wooden horse (θ. 493, and λ. 523) : hence we conclude that Ψ is later than θ. The κατάλογος, too, seems to have been influenced by the Odyssey, since it mentions the bow-man Philoctetes (B. 718, seqq.), with whom we first become acquainted in the Odyssey. Besides these passages, Kayser has shown that in the eleventh book the preparation of Nestor's meal (Λ. 628, seqq.) is imitated from the Kirke episode (κ. 233, seqq.), but traces of such influence are rare.

Hermes, as messenger of the gods, seems to have found his way into the Odyssey from the twenty-fourth book of the Iliad; at all events, in the older Kirke-episodes he is in no sense a messenger. That Iris, the usual messenger of the gods in the Iliad, is known also to the Odyssey in that capacity, is plain from the nick-name Iros (σ. 5, *seqq.*) given to the beggar Arnaeus because of his running on errands.

We have tried to show how the Iliad and Odyssey gradually developed, how to the old scenes and persons new ones were added, as Diomede and Nestor to the Greeks, and the Lycians to the Trojans in the Iliad. Similarly in the Odyssey were added Philoctetes, Memnon, and Eurypylus. The names of some of these later additions are so transparent that one can see at a glance how entirely they are creatures of the poet's own imagination, called after the *rôle* that is assigned them, and not traditional personages of some legend possessing more or less reality: for example, Dolon, Thersites, Astyanax, Neoptolemus, Kalypso, Telemachus, and Nausikaa.*

The stormers of Ilion were originally only the Achaeans, of whom Achilles' followers, the Myrmidons, were especially conspicuous. But with the new heroes new tribes come into the poem, and we read of Boeotians, Athenians, Lokrians, Epeians, Phthians, and Ionians, who are counterbalanced on the Trojan side, not merely by the Lykians, but by a host of barbarians—Kilikians, Mysians, Mäonians,

---

* Welcker, Ep. Cycl. II., p. 11, *seqq.*

Paphlagonians, Paeonians, and Thracians. We have a poetical review of them in the Teichoskopia and the Epipolesis, and at a later period a detailed account is given in the κατάλογος of all Hellenic tribes as having shared in the Trojan war.

Originally the Iliad was merely a lay, with Achilles for hero, and his wrath for subject. Perhaps joined with it was a 'Rape of Helen' (Z. 212); for in the first book the background of the poem is very vague and obscure: only as we proceed do the shadows light up; and in books which were shown to be late are we told the origin and commencement of the Expedition; in the πεῖρα we first read of the assembling of the host at Aulis, and learn the duration of the war. Afterwards the later poets introduced many heroes and tribes to enrich and augment the work; and though at times careful to show by the oft-repeated formula, οἷοι νῦν βροτοί εἰσι, how distant was the age they were depicting, yet they did not scruple to introduce what even an uncritical audience must have recognized as anachronisms, viz., chariots and mercenaries, for mercenaries the ἐπίκουροι seem to have been. In P. 220, seqq., Hector reminds them that they are now wanted to do that work for which they have received previous food and support: in Σ. 288, seqq., we hear of actual pay being given them from the treasures of Ilion.

In the κατάλογος, which has been shown to be later than the Odyssey, we find not only that the number of the heroes has increased, but that all are localized with a knowledge of Greece proper which is as extensive as it is precise;

and the legend of the war is itself augmented by the mention here for the first time of the fate of Protesilaus, and a
fuller account of Philoctetes than is given in the Odyssey
(B. 698, 718).

As the poems gradually developed the gods were introduced, and to the imaginative bards theology proved as plastic
a material to work in as history. Accordingly, in Σ. 382 we
find that Charis is wife of Hephaestus, while in the Odyssey
his wife is Aphrodite : in Φ. 196 we find Okeanos is merely
the source of all streams and waters ; in Ξ. 201 we find he
has already developed into the origin of the gods themselves
(θεῶν γένεσις). So, too, personal beings are evolved out of
pure abstractions ; as, for instance, the Fates (Ω. 49) out of
μοῖρα, the Harpies out of θύελλα, and last of all come the
Λιταὶ and Ἄτη (I, 502, T. 91).

The Homeric poems are a laboratory wherein the tale of
Troy is brought to perfection, and other tales inaugurated and
partially developed ; as, for instance, the war against Thebes ;
but how far the composer of such passages was working upon
material already in existence is hard to say, since the poet is
of course the child of his age, and naturally adopts whatever
is 'in the air' at the time : we may, however, be confident
that by means of the Homeric poems, and by their means
only, did subsequent generations learn aught of the Trojan
War. No doubt many a court poet introduced genealogies
of heroes, to flatter the pride of his noble patrons who
claimed descent from them. The earliest is, perhaps, that
of Glaucus, in the story of Bellerophon ; then we have
that of the Trojan princes (Υ. 213, *seqq.*) ; of Agamemnon

(B. 100, *seqq.*), of Diomedes (Ξ. 144, *seqq.*), and of Achilles (Φ. 187). Even the mention of the heroines in the Nekyia may be assigned to the same influence. The Hesiodic catalogue of heroines is a copy and amplification of the Homeric one, with little further merit than that it is more comprehensive.

We cannot say for certain where the Homeric poems first came into existence; but it is not improbable that the Wrath of Achilles is Aeolic: Killa and Tenedos (both Aeolic) are mentioned in the oldest part of the Iliad (Α. 38), and this origin would account for the many Aeolisms in the poem. This would accord very well with the most trustworthy tradition as to Homer's birthplace, namely, that it was Smyrna, which was originally Aeolic and afterwards became Ionic. There can be no doubt that the poem attained its present dimensions by the additions of Ionian bards, who would naturally Ionize the older Aeolic portions; but who often, if they had no Ionic equivalent, whether metrical or other, for some Aeolic word, would allow that word to stand unaltered, and who often, in the poems which they composed for the amplification of the legend, would affect Aeolisms, partly to lend an air of archaism to their work, and thus disguise the lateness of its production, and partly to adorn it with what had come to be regarded as the proper diction of epic poetry.

Amongst the Greeks on the coast of Asia Minor the poems first throve, and as these Greeks never lost the consciousness that they were settlers from the other side of the Archipelago, they took especial interest in the accounts of the home and descent of the heroes, so that the poem had a constant ten-

dency to become more and more universal in character, and
to lay aside the local limitations which may have marked its
origin.

We should remark that the poems seem to belong to
a period in which the migrations of the Hellenic families had
long ceased. In the κατάλογος we find Greece portioned out
just as in later times: and though the Dorians are not
mentioned as occupying Peloponnesus, we must not draw
any hasty conclusions from this fact, for even in historic
times they are seldom referred to by this name. And since
in Central Greece the tribes are mentioned as occupying the
same relative positions as they did afterwards, we may well
conclude that the Dorians were already settled in Peloponnesus when the Catalogue was composed.

We find the Boeotians (the Kadmeians are always spoken
of as belonging to an age preceding the Trojan War), Lokrians,
Phokians (P. 307), Aetolians (N. 217, seqq.), and even the
Athenians, in their well-known abodes. In the Presbeia,
wealthy Orchomenus and Pytho are mentioned (I. 381, 404 ;
λ. 459). Of the Peloponnesus the poet's knowledge seems
even more exact. Argos is always mentioned as the leading
state, and at the beginning of history we know that the
Dorian Argos *was* the leading state in Peloponnesus, and
did not decline till the eighth century. From Z. 157, seqq., it
would seem that Corinth (Ephyre) belonged to her, since
Bellerophon is there represented as a subject of the Argive
Proetus. Occasionally mention is made of Mykenæ and of
Sparta : of Mykenae twice as the kingdom of Agamemnon,
and on both occasions in late passages (Λ. 46 ; H. 160). We

know that Sparta rose to eminence subsequently, and therefore, as we might expect, we hear more about her in the late
Telemachy.   Messene is mentioned but once (φ. 15), not
unnaturally, lying as it does beyond Argos and Sparta, and
only obtaining renown by its overthrow.

The frequent mention of Herakles may, perhaps, be due
to Doric influences and to families who claimed descent from
him: his landing on Cos (Ξ. 250 ; O. 26) may contain an
allusion to some Doric colony founded there, and we have a
direct reference (τ. 177, Δωριέες τε τριχάϊκες) to Dorians
occupying Crete, and that too in a passage believed, with
good reason, to be one of the earliest.

We do not find any collective name for the Greeks in the
Homeric poems.   In the Iliad, and in a borrowed passage
in the Odyssey (λ. 496), Hellas generally means no more
than a part of Thessaly.   It seems to have a wider signification
in the formula ἀν' Ελλάδα καὶ μέσον Ἄργος ; but by the time
the κατάλογος was composed the distinction between Greek
and barbarian had already advanced so far that we find
the words πανέλληνες (B. 530), and βαρβαρόφωνος (ν. 867)
employed.   It is not merely Greece, however, that is known
to the poets of the Iliad ; for we find mention of the Cili-
cians and of Cyprus, of Phoenicians and Sidonians, even
of Egyptian Thebes (I. 381), and of the Aethiopians.   The
poets of the Odyssey show further acquaintance with the
world : the Phoenicians are frequently mentioned ; the
island Pharos (δ. 354) is specially named ; many a descent
on Egypt is made by pirates from Crete, which brings to
our minds Minos, θαλασσοκράτωρ ; the Libyans occur in

M

δ. 85; and, finally, the Sicels (ν. 383), and the land, Sicania (ω. 307).

In these later passages we find a knowledge of the western world which is quite foreign to the other parts of the poems, in which the west is an utterly unknown region; in the oldest part of the Odyssey—the Wanderings of Odysseus —the journey into the Unknown Realms of Fancy begins when the hero fails to double Malea and the storm drives him past Cythera (ι. 80, *seqq.*).   The Aegean Sea, on the contrary, and its coasts, are very well known to both poems; also the nearest neighbours of the Asiatic Greeks, the Phrygians, Carians, Leleges, Maronians, and Mysians: the Paphlagonians are mentioned too, and (B. 847) some of their towns on the coast of the Black Sea.   Sidon is always mentioned as the capital and seaport of Phoenicia; Tyre is not referred to even once—from which we may conclude that the latter town had not yet risen to eminence—a fact which, were more but known of Phoenician history, would give us valuable assistance towards fixing the date of the poems.   In the Presbeia (I. 381) we have mention of Egyptian Thebes, which was most famous under the rule of the first two Kings of the twenty-second dynasty (934–898, B.C.), of whose military splendour there is, perhaps, a reminiscence in this passage.

Kirchhoff has wasted much ingenuity in trying to fix dates for the poems, but his theories have broken down.   We cannot attain to any real certainty.   The mention of Sicels and of Sicania need not force us to assign a very late date to the passages where they occur, since, of course, the planting of colonies there in B. C. 734 naturally compels us to pre-suppose very long previous intercourse and acquaintance with that land and its people.

We say then that the Iliad and Odyssey were fully finished before the first Olympiad; but how long they were in process of formation none can tell : gradually they and the legend they contained increased, ever gain-ing fresh increments from the poetic genius of kindred minds to whose keeping they were entrusted, and whose mighty heirloom they were.

XIII.

FAR more startling, however, than any inconsistencies or contradictions in the context of the poems is the fact that their language is a mixture of dialects—a fact which out-weighs even the marked difference in the vocabulary of the Iliad and Odyssey.*

This moment has been brilliantly weighed by Fick in his attempt to restore the Odyssey to its original dialect, and his daring theory is as follows :—

The word-forms which we meet in Homer, he asserts, are of two kinds, good Greek and barbarisms, the former actually used at some period and somewhere in Hellas, the latter arising from misunderstandings and subsequent edit-ing. These forms had no real existence outside of the Ho-meric poems, or the epics which the Alexandrians composed, and of course must be set aside in any attempt to restore the Homeric poems to their original state.

---

* Prof. Munro gives the following words as peculiar to the Iliad :

ἄποινα, γέφυρα, κασσίτερος, λοιγός, νόθος, φηγός, λαιψηρός, ζάθεος, ἐκη-βόλος, ἕκατος, χραισμέω, χωρέω, μαρμαίρω, παμφαίνω, εἶθαρ, τύνη.

To the Odyssey :

ἤλεκτρον, γείτων, βασίλεια, ἑστίη, πτωχός, πτωχεύω, χρήματα, δέσποινα, ἐλπίς, ἐλπωρή, ἐσθής, ἁγνός, θεουδής.

Pisistratus' edition of the text, in which Fick believes, would have employed the old Attic way of writing, using E and O for ε, η, ει, and o, ω, ου, and not doubling the consonants. After the archonship of Euclides, such a text would need to be all re-written (not without many mistakes) into the characters of the Ionic alphabet. Accordingly, E being mistaken for ει, instead of η, gave θείομεν for θήομεν. Nauck has worked this vein with rich results, as in restoring in Ω. 789, ἤγρετο, 'collected himself', for ἤγρετο, 'awaked,' ΕΓΡΕΤΟ. Further, Onomacritus and his colleagues would often be in doubt owing either to defective or contradictory traditions as to how an open syllable should be written, and apparently cut the Gordian knot by giving the contracted Attic form as in η. 145, θαύμαζον δ᾽ ὁρῶντες, for ὁρίοντες or ὁράοντες, leaving it to the reader to restore whichever form he would. Afterwards, when the poems were re-written from the old Attic into the Ionic characters, shortly after 400 B.C., so little was known of the Homeric dialect that the opposition between metre and form was surmounted by simple repetition of the vowel; for instance, ἰχθυάαι out of ἰχθυᾶι, φόως from φῶς, &c., and so a swarm of unreal forms was called into existence which are easily got rid of when one understands their origin.

Attic forms when they occur must have got into the text very late indeed: ὧν, for instance, which is the common Greek form, must in every case be read for οὖν, which was peculiarly Attic.

Even when we have set aside the non-Greek forms and this Attic intruder, we have not a single dialect remaining, but a strange mixture of Ionic and an A-dialect, which is none other than old Aeolic. This mixture is plain in the use of ᾱ and η forms side by side, as νύμφη beside θεά and νυμφάων. That such mixture is not original cannot be doubted; the point at issue is whether the older parts of the poems were originally Aeolic or Ionic.

The ancients decided for the latter, not unnaturally, owing to the name and fame of the epic school of poetry at Chios. Now Fick, accepting Kirchhoff's division of our present Odyssey into—(1) the old Return from Troy, with the (2) vengeance of Odysseus; (3) the Telemachy, and (4) a later Return, with the conclusion, maintains that Kynaithos of Chios, the author of the Hymn to Apollo, first bound those together, and that, as he was an Ionian, he used that dialect chiefly, which would therefore characterize the passages used for soldering, interpolating, and continuing; but that the real and original germ of Homeric poetry is in the Aeolic dialect; and that at Aeolic Smyrna there was a community of bards who used this dialect in their poems, and who, when Smyrna became Ionic, about 700 B.C., emigrated to Chios, where they themselves and their poem were Ionized. This Ionized Aeolic then became the dialect of our text, and of later epic poetry.

The proof of the Aeolic origin of the poems lies in the language; the digamma forbids us to regard them as Ionic, and forces us to accept the other alternative. For instance, the vocalized digamma in such Homeric forms as ἀυίρνον, ἀυίαχοι, ἀγαυός, &c., correspond exactly with the Aeolisms ἀυάτα, αὔηρ, ἄυελλα; and even the absence of digamma in some forms, as ὑρέω, finds a parallel in Aeolic ὄρημι (Sapp. 2, 11).

Amongst the Ionian cotemporaries of Homer (850 B.C.) the digamma had already gone out of use, at least there is no trace of it in the oldest Ionic poets or inscriptions. Aeolic, too, is the accent, as may be seen in μητίετα, ἐυρύοπα, ἄμμες, ἀκαχήμενος, ἄλλυδις, &c. Aeolic, too, is the *psilosis* in ἄλτο, ἄμαξα, ἀμβροτεῶ, ἀβροτάζω, ἀμόθεν, ἄμυδις, ἦμαρ, ὤριστος, &c.

Psilosis must of course be introduced in the poems in every case where the Ionic dialect had it, as ἀπικέσθαι, κατῆσθαι, ἄρματα, and when this is done so few rough breathings remain, that we may substitute for them the Aeolic psilosis.

After examination of the remaining Aeolisms of Homer we arrive at this law, to which there is scarcely an exception, ʻthat Aeolisms are only to be found where the Ionic dialect had no metrical equivalent for themʼ, or where there was no word exactly corresponding to them in meaning. This throws a flood of light upon the subject of mixed dialects, and shows that this mosaic of forms did not arise, like that in Spenser's *Fairy Queen*, from a deliberate design to use an artificial dialect, but by a translating of the old Aeolic poems, word for word, into Ionic, in which, when there was not at hand a ready equivalent for any given word, that word was left unaltered, in its Aeolic form, amidst the surrounding Ionic.

For instance, the Aeolic forms of the feminine a-declension, νύμφᾱ, νύμφας, νύμφαι, were transformed into the Ionic equivalents νύμφη, νύμφης, νύμφηι, but the gen. pl. νυμφάων was allowed to stand because the Ionic gen. pl. νυμφέων was not metrically an equivalent: similarly θεά was allowed to stand, because there was no corresponding Ionic form θεή (the correct form being ἡ θεός).

Aeolic, too, is the metrical treatment of words, thus contrasting sharply with the Ionic. The sharpening (verschärfung) of vowels on which the ictus falls is very common in Homer, both at the beginning and in the middle of words, both before vowels and consonants, and in the latter case is excellently shown by the doubling of the consonant, as in ἔλλαβε. That this was a favourite peculiarity of Aeolic poetry is well known from fragments of Alcaeus and Sappho. Theocritus, too, in his Aeolic idylls, 28, 29, 30, adopts this as a vital peculiarity of the dialect: it must not be confounded with the Ionic lengthening of a vowel on which the ictus falls, the Ionic ἠγερέθονται, ἠγαθέη, ἠνορέη, being represented in Aeolic by αὐερέθονται, ἀγγαθέα, ἀννορία: ε in Ionic becomes through the ictus ει (a spurious diphthong); so we find in Homer forms like εἰλήλουθα alongside of others like ἔλλαβε; similarly ο becomes ου, as in οὔνομα, Οὔλυμπος.

Other metrical considerations, too, seem to make for an Aeolic rather than an Ionic origin: an initial vowel in Homer can in thesis follow another vowel, but among the old Ionian poets this is not the case throughout. Homer allows it in the dactylic ending of the first, in the main caesura of the third, and in the caesura of the fourth (hephthemimeris and so-called bucolic caesura), positions in which it does not occur amongst the Ionians.

Even tradition harmonizes with the supposition that the poems were originally Aeolic, since of the many birthplaces of Homer Smyrna is always named first. Now Smyrna was founded by Aeolians, and did not become Ionic till it was conquered by the Colophonians,* which may well have caused the Homeridae to emigrate from Smyrna to Chios, where the poem was Ionized, dropping the digamma, and replacing Aeolic by Ionic words.

In an Italian copy of the manuscript, περὶ ᾿Αριστάρχου σημείων we find the words τὴν δὲ ποίησιν (῾Ομήρου) ἀναγιν-ώσκεσθαι ἀξιοῖ Ζώπυρος ὁ Μάγνης Αἰολίδι διαλέκτωι· τὸ δ' αὐτὸ καὶ Δικαίαρχος. If this was Dichaearchus of Messina, the celebrated pupil of Aristotle, and the author of the book περὶ ᾿Αλκαίου, his opinion that the poems were originally Aeolic is of the very highest importance.

A former generation of scholars being convinced that the Homeric poems originated amongst the Ionians, found no difficulty in discovering all sorts of natural capacity in the Ionians for epic poetry ; but Fick maintains that to the un-biassed observer the truth seems quite the contrary. Ionic poetry from Kallinos to Hipponax shows a coarse realism, which is quite at variance with the spirit of Homeric poetry with its dream of a grander and a nobler past. But the keynote of Homer is that of Aeolic poetry ; both spring from deep feeling, of which the old Ionians knew nothing. The 'Lament' (Ψ and Ω) is half lyrical, and is the link between the old order of poetry and the new.

By far the most satisfactory argument that the poems

* Mimnerm 9; Herodot. 1. 149; Paus. vii. 5. 1.

were originally Aeolic is that they lend themselves so easily
to retranslation into that dialect, whereby we obtain a homo-
geneous poem freed from the chaos of forms which fill our
present text. Only ballad-singers or learned students like
Apollonius Rhodius, or our own Edmund Spenser, could use
such a composite medium—an artificiality which would be
wholly repugnant to poetry of such natural freshness and
vigour, though the later Ionian poets no doubt found little
difficulty in adopting such a style, as the occasional Aeolisms
which yet remained in the poem had grown familiar to their
ears.

We must not call such a composite medium a 'language
of art' (Kunst-dialect), for on such principles Fick remarks:
the heroes of Fritz Reuter's story ('Ut mine Stromtid'),
Uncle Braesig, carpenter Schulz, and sexton Suhr, would be
talking the language of art without knowing it, and a sen-
tence like ' ich segge dir, dat du mi das bliewen lässest ',
would be a masterpiece.

But to return after our digression. If the poems were
originally composed in Aeolic, and subsequently translated
into Ionic, it follows that when, in turning our present text
back into Aeolic, we come upon Ionic forms which resist all
our efforts to render them, we may rest assured that the
passages in which they occur are later additions by an
Ionian.

Kirchhoff has, with considerable appearance of truth,
divided the Odyssey into four epics—(1) the old Nostos of
Odysseus; (2) the later continuation, which Kaiser calls the
τίσις Ὀδυσσέως; (3) a more recent return of Odysseus; and

(4) the Telemachy. Now, Fick's researches aim at showing that these four epics were composed in Aeolic, but that their fusion together, that is, the Odyssey as we have it at present, is the work of an Ionian of the seventh century, and that he was no other than the Homerid Kynaithos of Chios, who first published his compilation in Smyrna, 660 B.C.

Fick points out how great a help to the memory, at a time when the poems were not fixed in writing, must have been the symmetrical articulation of the old Nostos of Odysseus as given by Kirchhoff: it consists of ten portions of 250 verses each, and contains five lays; (a, β, γ, δ, κ) the narrative of the poet in his own person, and (ϵ, ζ, η, θ, ι) the tale told by Odysseus, these two totalities containing within them the smaller totalities (a, β) before Scheria; (γ, δ) in Scheria; (ϵ, ζ) the Kyklopeia; and (η, θ) the Nekyia. To remember the Odyssey in its present arrangement, with its many changes of action and of scene, would almost necessitate the presupposition of a written copy.

The τίσις 'Οδυσσέως, or the vengeance of Odysseus on the suitors (ν. 185; ψ. 296), was originally composed as a continuation of the Nostos. The older form of the τίσις is enlarged by a later poet, who introduces new elements, and sometimes merely repeats the old ones. The transformation of Odysseus, for instance, is new; but the loyal herd, Philoitios, is copied from the good swineherd, Eumaeos, and the insolent Melantho from the disloyal Melanthios.

The later return of Odysseus, he supposes, was originally related in the third person, and was afterwards woven in with the ἀπόλογος by the editor. The subject is principally the folly and sin of Odysseus' companions, and the vengeance which the sun-god wreaks upon them.

The Telemachy is sometimes entitled ἡ ὀιωνοί, and is full of signs and prophesyings of the return of Odysseus. We have a φήμη (β. 35); the omen of birds of Halitherses (β. 146, sq.); the revelation of Athene (γ. 371); the prophecy of Proteus (δ. 351, sq.); Helen as θυμόμαντις (ο. 163, sq.); and lastly, Theoklymenos' and Telemachus' direct prophecies in ο. 224, sq.

XIV

I MUST not leave the subject without treating of what has been done, or rather left undone, in Homeric criticism by the English classical school.

In 1808 Payne Knight, who had been considerably influenced by the 'Prolegomena', brought out an eccentric work, 'the Iliad restored to its original form', that is to say, with the digamma replaced, and certain arbitrary changes of spelling, &c., introduced. This bibliographical wonder was published in the grand style; there were only fifty copies printed, so that in a few years they were rareties in the market, and fetched large prices, till in 1820 a second edition in quarto was published. Although it contains many absurdities, the work is of importance as a practical attempt to rise superior to the Wolfian dogma, that we cannot, in reconstituting Homer, get back beyond the text as arranged by the Alexandrians; for Knight will not bow to mere authority, but professes himself a follower of common sense: 'saepe fit ut ludibria vulgi philosophorum deliciae sint: et Plato, Zeno, Berkeley, Hume, etc., serio tractaverint quae quivis e trivio homunculus jure risisset. Hujusmodi homunculum me esse fateor: neque exquisitiore aliquo ingenii

acumine sed communi hominis cujusvis sensu in re criticâ
uti.' He then proceeds to establish the separate authorship
of Iliad and Odyssey, but believes staunchly in the unity
of each poem.

The influence of Payne Knight, however, was more than
counterbalanced by the elaborate refutation and scholarly
erudition of Colonel Mure, who carries his conservatism so
far that he is not only behind Wolf, but actually behind
the Alexandrians. He will not admit, for an instant, that
the Iliad and Odyssey are by different authors, and so jealous is he of the rights of the divine bard, that he will
scarcely grant that (ψ. 296–ω), though rejected by Aristarchus, is an interpolation.

Mure studied the Germans who preceded him, but only
did so when his mind was already made up on the question,
and when the application of the axiom ' that a work by an
individual author may contain many inconsistencies ', was
capable of becoming almost indefinitely elastic in his hands.
His strongest argument for single authorship, namely, that
many different bards would not all have selected the tenth
year of the war for their theme, shows how deliberately he
blinds himself to the fact pointed out by many Germans,
that many passages in the poem cannot possibly have been
intended to belong to that year—for instance, the catalogue,
the view of the army from the Trojan walls by Helen and
Priam, and the duel between Paris and Menelaus. He
seems also quite untouched by the argument directed by
Wolf against the single authorship of the Iliad, viz. that
in a poem which should describe the defeat of the Greeks

we read of scarcely anything but their successes, the number
of slain Trojans largely preponderating over the number of
slain Greeks.   On general resemblance between the books
he lays too much stress, while inconsistencies and contradictions are too easily condoned as unavoidable in such a long
work, composed when writing was unknown, and intended
for an uncritical audience.   In Mure the English conservative view of the poems has found its clearest expositor, and to
the opponents of that view a hearing has been accorded, but
not much more.   In his criticism Englishmen have readily
acquiesced, pleased, as they are, with its broad method, and
wearied by the minuteness and frequent puerilities of the
opposing school, and accepting as self-evident his proposition
that 'general resemblance is a stronger argument for single
authorship than proportional discrepancy'.   Mure maintains
that it is the natural difference of subject-matter which occasions the difference between Iliad and Odyssey, and he easily
exposes the absurdity of deducing proof from such facts as
that a Lesche and columns are mentioned in the Odyssey,
but not in the account of the camp before Troy.   Good arguments, however, do not suffice him, and he has recourse
to sophistry.   It is an *ignoratio elenchi*, to use the illustration
of a painter exhibiting his work in public, for every passing
dilettante to draw his brush through the part which he may
consider *defective :* the critics do not give their opinion on
what is defective, but on what they consider to be the work
of *different* hands, the later work being often better than the
earlier.

To argue, as he does, for the genuineness of the Doloneia,

that it is not *unworthy* of Homer in matter or style, is quite
beside the mark ; yet it is no unusual defence of any passage
against which objection is taken.   On other occasions we can
hardly regard him as serious, as when he shrewdly explains
away the old objection of the Chorizontes, that Hephaestus'
wife is Aphrodite in the Odyssey, but Charis in the Iliad.
Are we really to believe that after Aphrodite's infidelity
with Arês, Hephaestus divorced her, and married again,
and that Homer in his poems intended to convey to us this
fact, a matter of which the later Greeks were ignorant ?

But now Colonel Mure has been succeeded by Mr. Gladstone, who is nothing, if not of a party.   He has practically
adopted his predecessor's position with an impatience of con-
tradiction, however, that is all his own.   He adheres to one
Homer, author of both Iliad and Odyssey, and he employs
the greatest ingenuity in tracing through the various books
many slight resemblances which he forces to do duty as
evidence of single authorship.   Indeed, whatever Mr. Gladstone has advanced of importance on the question proper is
but a detailed exposition of what Mure had broadly stated,
accompanied by much sentimental admiration and devotion
to an imagined Homer.   Mure had at least accorded the
Germans, up to his day, a hearing, but Mr. Gladstone's ears
are as the adder's.   From his three-volume work, ' Homer,
and the Homeric Age', published in 1858, it is plain that
he not only has neglected the Germans, but has not even
gone through Wolf, of whose book he mentions little more
than its date of publication.   Indeed it would scarcely be
worth while noticing Mr. Gladstone's work on the question

proper, were it not that by the publication of his Juventus
Mundi, eleven years afterwards, he called the attention of
the world to the fact that during that long interval he had
consistently avoided acquainting himself with what had been
said of a subject on which it pleased him to be dogmatic.
Yet even this neglect might have been pardoned in one so
busy with public affairs, did he not subsequently by the publication in 1878, of a primer meant for the widest diffusion,
maintain the views of thirty years ago as obstinately as
ever, and with such utter disregard of the opposing school
that no reader would ever suspect that a view contrary to
his own prevailed so widely on the Continent.

But apart from German criticism, which he so shunned,
it is strange that, though his great fellow-countryman Grote,
whose judgment on the Homeric question is so sound and
impartial, had long been trying to teach the English world
sense, yet Mr. Gladstone is quite untouched by his influence.
Indeed Grote seems to have foreseen Mr. Gladstone's case
with prophetic clearness when he says, 'No man can pro-
duce arguments sufficiently cogent to contend against opposing preconception'. Grote's attempt to resolve the Iliad is
a very sensible one. Although a unity pervades the Iliad,
although 'it is no mere congeries but an organism', yet he
sees that it 'presents the appearance of a house built upon a
plan comparatively narrow, and subsequently enlarged by
successive additions'; and his division of an Achilleis (A, Θ,
Λ–X) from an Ilias (B–H, K), afterwards augmented by
books Ψ and Ω, is substantially correct, and has found a
supporter in Prof. Geddes. The Odyssey he accepts as a

N

totality ; but this may be pardoned him, since in his day it had not been subjected to the rigid examination which it has since undergone at the hands of Kirchhoff.

With the exception of Prof. Geddes, Mr. Mahaffy, and some few others, the great body of English scholars is apt to decline expressing any opinion at all upon the question, or else they follow Mr. Gladstone's lead, no doubt owing to the great fame he has won in other fields, so that his views require especial attention.

Mr. Gladstone's first book, ' Homer and the Homeric Age ', treats the matter as a parergon, one of the objects of the work being to prove the providential government of the world, from which it is surely a far cry to the Homeric question. The author maintains that, for discussing the subject, knowledge of the text is the one thing needful; but surely such knowledge would keep him from such an incorrect statement as that which he makes in his ' Primer ', published thirty years after—' *Almost the only* real discrepancy of the text is the case of Palaemenes, leader of the Paphlagones, who is slain by Menelaus in the fifth book, but weeps among the mourners at the death of his son Harpalion in the thirteenth ' (p. 25). His hackneyed argument that the types of character and the facts all through the poem are much the same is of but little importance. Surely if one wrote a poem on the same subject at the present time one would not dare to depart very glaringly from the traditional types in the story.

Later we find Mr. Gladstone tripping in his logic. After he has used the word Homer, as meaning the author of both

Iliad and Odyssey together, or at least of either of them
separately, he says it is absurd to believe in a multitude of
Homers. But even on the supposition that there were two
Homers, they could scarcely be said to constitute a multitude ; and on the other hand if a multitude of bards con-
tributed to frame the poems, they would not be all *Homers*
in the sense which Mr. Gladstone attaches to the word. Yet
so pleased is he with this logical fallacy, that he calls it an
'overwhelming' proof of the unity of authorship ; and then
goes on to say that the 'ordinary' reader will of himself
perceive the unity of the poems, 'and as he continues to believe therein the belief will grow stronger': but such belief
is a very different thing from proof.

And here let us give a definite instance of Mr. Gladstone's beliefs preconceived and out of relation with fact.
He asserts of Thetis (p. 76) that she 'has not lost the arch-
ness of coquetry'; and when she grasps Zeus' chin (after
the earnest manner of a suppliant), Mr. Gladstone tells us
that 'she having already embraced him by the knees with
one arm, and *touched him under the chin* with her right hand,
POUTINGLY *insists* that he shall say aye or nay'. Such a
scene is not of Homer's imagination surely, but of Mr.
Gladstone's.

Or again, to take another instance of Mr. Gladstone's
à priori theorizing. We have seen that he is intuitively
certain one poet was author of the poems; he is also intuitively certain that this author deliberately accommodated
sound to sense. 'Homer varies incessantly the velocity of
his movement and the weight of his tread, in due proportion

to the subject he is exhibiting. . . . When he has to describe
the rapid motion of the flying chariots, or when he tells of
the light velocity of the mares that had Boreas for their
sire, the rapid, that is to say, the short syllables of each
verse are increased to eight or even ten. . . . When, on the
other hand, he has to describe hard, heavy blows, or the
massive constituents of an abundant banquet on the tables,
and on two similar occasions, he goes so far as to exclude
short syllables altogether, by what are termed spondaic
lines'.   Now in the Iliad one line is dactylic in every 4·91,
and in the Odyssey one in 5·23 ; and of these dactylic lines
the majority in nowise express ' velocity of movement '. For
instance, A. 30, ἡμετέρῳ ἐνὶ οἴκῳ ἐν ῎Αργεϊ τηλόθι πάτρης.
The nature of the hexameter is such that the dactyls, as a
matter of course, preponderate over the spondees.   Of spondaic lines Mr. Gladstone, in both Iliad and Odyssey combined, only instances four ; but a fifth would have shown
him how untenable was his theory, viz. B. 813, τὴν ἤ τοι
ἄνδρες Βατίειαν κικλήσκουσι, where the poet has used as many
spondees as possible, but where there is obviously no mimicry
of the sense intended.   But perhaps the best refutation of
the theory is, that when the funeral of Patroclus is described,
on which occasion, if ever, spondaic lines are wanted, there
are actually two sequences of five dactylic lines.   In fact
there are thousands of dactylic lines in Homer which are
not mimetic.   The occasional correspondence, therefore, of
sound and sense in other dactylic lines cannot be said to be
intentional—in fact the very contrary may almost with certainty be inferred from the fact that in the lines Ψ. 362–533,

devoted to the chariot race, where, if anywhere, 'velocity of movement' is continually recurring, *the proportion of dactylic lines is not only less than the proportion of such lines in the Iliad separately, or the Odyssey separately, but is actually less than the proportion of such lines in the rest of the same book.*

In his etymological disquisitions, too, we find this same tendency to theorize *à priori.* He says (p. 102): 'It seems that the Pelasgian tongue supplied both peninsulas (Greece and Italy) with most of the words relating to the primary experience, and to the elementary wants and productions of life; but not with those of a more arduous range, such as war, art, poetry, and song. . . . Speaking generally (p. 96), the words of Latin and Greek which most closely correspond are words relating to the commonest objects of perception, and the primary wants of life, and forms of labour'. Under which head the following are given by way 'not of exhaustion, but of example':

κοινή, *cena.*	μηρός, *femur.*
σῖτος, *cibus.*	βραδύς, *tardus.*
ἀτρύγετος, *triticum.*	ῥέζω, *rex.*[*]

Of course in 1858 it was natural to follow Niebuhr, Bishop Marsh, and Döderlein; but in 1869 to have no more recent authority than a book published in 1838 is inexcusably behind-hand.

Grote's theory, which we have seen had so little effect in England, though spoken of with respect in Germany, and indeed forming an epoch in Homeric criticism, has been

---

[*] 'Hom. Stud.' p. 300.

accepted in the main by Prof. Geddes, who believes that our
Iliad is made up of an Achilleis and an Ilias combined, and
that the author of this Ilias is also the author of the Odyssey; but like Grote he admits too easily the unity of the
Odyssey, yet without being able to plead Grote's excuse; for
Prof. Geddes' criticism is quite irrespective of the Germans,
and might have been penned before the Odyssean researches
of Kirchhoff and Kayser, so little is it affected by them; yet
this may perhaps be condoned on the plea of originality and
independence.

Prof. Jebb's intended work on Greek literature is unfortunately still unpublished; but from what he has said in
his 'Primer of Greek Literature', it would seem that he is
merely inclined to follow Bergk's lead, and place Homer between 940–850 B.C.   He is a decided Chorizontist, and is of
opinion that Homer was born at Smyrna, and the poems
were originally composed in Ionic.

Mr. Paley has pursued a course of his own, which is as
eccentric as it is original.   He took the precaution to veil his
theories, on their first publication, by the thin disguise of a
Latin dress—'Homeri quae nunc extant an reliquis cycli
carminibus antiquiora jure habita sint'.   The view he sets
forth is, that our Iliad and Odyssey did not exist till the end
of the fourth century, B.C.—in fact, till the time of Plato,
who is the first author whose quotations tally with our present text; and that then our 'Homer' was vamped together
by a certain Antimachus of Colophon, from old, and, till then,
obscure legends of the Cyclic poems.

To support this view Mr. Paley draws arguments (1) from

the infrequency of references to our Iliad and Odyssey in
the early lyric and tragic poets, though by them Homer is
often spoken of; (2) from the absence of scenes taken from
the Iliad and Odyssey upon the vases of this period, although
other epic subjects are constantly depicted.   Mr. Paley also
(3) sees confirmation of his theory in many more modern
Attic forms and false archaisms which occur in the language
of the poems; furthermore (4) he believes that until Periclean times writing and writing materials were not common
in Greece, and therefore that the composition of the Iliad
and Odyssey was till then impossible.

Now, that the poets and potters do not handle themes
treated of in the Iliad may be explained, as Mr. Paley admits, on two hypotheses, viz. that they ignored them, or that
they deliberately avoided them.   Mr. Paley chooses the
former alternative, and it suits his theory to do so; but in
all probability the latter is the true explanation.   What
poet would be foolhardy enough to rival Homer, and re-
handle some scene treated with such consummate art by the
first of poets?   What dramatist would venture to present
upon the stage the parting of Hector and Andromache?
what actor to act it? what artist to depict it?   Is not
this avoidance of the subjects treated by Homer the very
highest homage?   Would not the Greeks, to whom the
Homeric poems were what the Bible is to us, have been
likely to resent any alterations made by a playwright in
legends which had acquired a sacred character, and were
looked upon with the deepest reverence?   Would not the
potters have been more likely to depict upon the vases, in

preference to Homeric scenes which would make large demands on their imagination, scenes from popular tragedies giving the *pose plastique* which they had presented to their eyes from day to day? And, though not making direct reference to Homer, surely Sophocles, to say nothing of Herodotus, is filled with his spirit. Yet how this can be accounted for on Mr. Paley's theory is hard to see.

Mr. Paley sets the use of writing far too late; the inscription at Abu Simbel of Greek soldiers in the service of Psammetichus, which we must assign at the very latest to B.C. 600, more probably to 650, shows that writing even then was not uncommon, at least among the aristocrats. But apart from this, the odes of Pindar and the plays of Aeschylus, which of course needed writing for their composition, are anterior to the date which Mr. Paley assigns to writing. Moreover, Plato, who is Mr. Paley's sheet-anchor, inasmuch as he is the first author whose quotations from Homer agree with our text, though brought forward as a witness on Mr. Paley's side, unfortunately testifies against him, for he expressly says (Rep. x. pp. 595, c. 598, D., 607, A.) that Homer was the father and originator of tragedy, *i.e.* that our Homer (for Plato's Homer, as Mr. Paley admits, is our Homer) preceded the *tragici*, that is Thespis and all the rest. Herodotus, too, speaks of Homer as the author of the *Iliad* (II. 116), *i.e.* as our Homer, and places him 400 years before his own time. Here then is the opinion of two literary Greeks of great eminence, and in these we may well acquiesce in preference to the hypothesis that, in an age sensitively alive to all things intellectual, two such splendid bodies of poetry as the Iliad and Odyssey should come into existence without making a stir, and, stamped with the name of Homer, should pass current alongside of the inferior material which we must suppose to have borne that name till then. It is in his choice of a new Homer, however, that Mr. Paley is perhaps most unhappy ; for Antimachus, so far from being the *author* of the poems, was only the *editor* of a recension of them, and his acknowledged works, the 'Thebais' and 'Lyde', were overloaded with learning and pedantry.* The period at which Antimachus composed the poems, Mr. Paley says, was after the Tragic poets, and before Plato, which is much as if one should say, after Shakspere, and before Bacon.

On the paucity of references to our Iliad and Odyssey in the writers before Plato Mr. Paley's theory is chiefly based ; but from what remains of those writers, if we but interpret the facts aright, we shall find that a conclusion diametrically opposed to that of Mr. Paley must be drawn. For instance, from Pindar, Nem. 7. 20, ἐγὼ δὲ πλέον' ἔλπομαι λόγον Ὀδυσσέος ἢ πάθεν διὰ τὸν ἁδυεπῆ γένεσθαι Ὅμηρον, Mr. Paley quite arbitrarily dogmatizes that this does not refer to our Odyssey, because other poems, too, dealt with the story of Odysseus—'Nam plurima de Odysseo noverunt tragici de quibus silet Homerus'—and that these other poems were called Homeric by Pindar, and actually were so, our 'Homer' not having yet come into existence ! That the usual acceptation of the passage is the right one is manifest from the fact, that it is only our Iliad and Odyssey that

* Prof. Mahaffy's 'Hist. of Gr. Lit.' I. 146, 192.

represent Odysseus' character favourably; and that he is traduced and represented as a trickster by almost every other poem, and this treatment of his character began with the cyclic poets.

When Euripides in the Cyclops introduces Silenus and his rout, Mr. Paley thinks this is evidence that he is following some legend different from our Odyssey; but surely we must allow Euripides credit for sufficient originality to vary the Homeric story, especially in a Satyric drama, where Silenus and his followers are indispensable. In the same way, too, in Aeschylus' Ransom of Hector, we must explain the existence of the band of Phrygians which accompanies Priam to redeem Hector's body: they do not come from our Homer, nor from the work of any other old poet, but direct from Aeschylus' imagination, to form the chorus necessary to his play. Mr. Paley might as well assert that Sophocles must be following some legend different from that of Aeschylus and Euripides, because he varies the story of Philoctetes, whose island Aeschylus and Euripides represent as inhabited, while Sophocles represents it as deserted. In Homer the reference is indecisive, the words used being merely Λήμνῳ ἐν ἠγαθέῃ.

But a more glaring, and indeed ludicrous inability to understand the significance of facts, is where Mr. Paley maintains that because Aristophanes in the *Wasps* (v. 180, *seqq.*) represents old Philocleon, when trying to escape from durance and return to the Courts, as essaying flight beneath an ass, and exclaiming that he is Outis, there must therefore have been in existence some other legend which represented Odysseus escaping beneath such an animal. On another occasion, however, Mr. Paley has even surpassed himself in bald literalness of interpretation—' Ex ejusmodi rhapsodiis, ut opinor, non ex Odysseâ nostrâ, Aeschylus Clytaemnestram, ἀμφίσβαιναν ἤ Σκύλλαν τινα, οἰκοῦσαν ἐν πέτραισι ναυτίλων βλάβην, nominavit' (Agam. 1204).

If we should grant that the argument drawn from the silence of the poets proved anything, it would prove too much; for though Mr. Paley admits that the raw materials from which our Homer was subsequently manufactured were previously in existence, yet the obvious avoidance of re-handling these materials would furnish as valid an argument against their existence in the raw as in the manufactured state.

With regard to the language of the poems, Mr. Paley, with his usual contempt for the sound guidance of German etymologists, has chosen his own path, and has been misled by an *ignis fatuus*. Surely nothing can be more impossible than that the poems were composed in the new Attic dialect, and besprinkled with old epic phrases to give them an archaic look. Surely if this were the case, the contrast between them and the genuine old epics then extant would have been too marked for Plato or the Alexandrians to accept them. The occurrence of Atticisms can prove no more than that the poems underwent a certain modernizing which was perhaps inevitable. But this modernizing was only one of external form, for the spirit of the poems is quite uninfluenced by the spirit of republican Athens, which would be impossible had they been composed at the epoch Mr. Paley suggests.

We have said that English scholars are usually apt to
decline expressing any opinion at all on the question; and
the most remarkable instance of this is the Provost of Oriel.
He, if any man, may well be thought to have such intimate
knowledge of the poems as would render him competent to
pronounce an opinion, yet he shrinks from doing so, hesitat-
ing and vacillating in the most painful manner; and though
he has read the Germans, and uses the facts which men with
decided views have accumulated, yet he will not assent to
the conclusions which are obviously to be deduced therefrom.
One sees this all through his 'Homeric Grammar'.* Facts
there stated show what the Germans admitted long ago,
viz. that as the diction of I, K, Ψ and Ω, differs from that
of all the rest, these four books had not the same author
as the others. Adopting the language of the Germans, he
constantly speaks of 'false archaisms'; but such language is
unmeaning in Mr. Munro's mouth until he first decide at
what time Homer lived. Yet so much does he dread an
Aeolic Homer, that he will commit himself to no inferences
whatever.

But it is not merely in his Homeric Grammar that Mr.
Munro so studiously avoids giving any opinion, but even
in his latest work,† which publicly professes to deal with
the question, his judgment is in suspense. Even on the
ninth book he cannot decide, and keeps shifting his position in the most unsatisfactory manner; and the most one
can get from him is that, like Sir Roger de Coverley, he

---

* 'A Grammar of the Homeric Dialect'.   Oxford: 1882.
† 'Homer's Iliad', I.-XII.   Oxford: 1884.

thinks 'there is a good deal to be said on both sides of the
question '. On the Doloneia he is more definite, not so
much on account of any reasonable arguments advanced by
the moderns, as because of the authority of the Greek commentators ; and yet he sighs to think that this authority is
not confirmed by the *oldest* scholia. To strengthen authority
he gives a statement of the reasons which have been given for
the lateness of the book—(1) that it comes in awkwardly ;
(2) is cumbrous, and lacks proportion ; (3) that Rhesus and
his Thracians are mentioned nowhere else ; (4) that the diction contains late formations ; (5) with instances of a post-
Homeric use of the article ; (6) pseudo-archaisms ; (7) ἅπαξ
εἰρημένα, words common to the Odyssey, but not to the rest
of the Iliad ; and that (8) the style and tone are dissimilar
to the rest of the Iliad. Now if these reasons, separately
or collectively, are potent to support the tradition of the
ancients concerning the lateness of this book, why are they
not valid in the case of other books, or other passages?
Why will Mr. Munro not be content to accept tradition on
its own merits without trying to strengthen it by arguments, whose validity in other cases he is so shy of ad-
mitting ?

In his prefatory remarks on the ninth book we read : 'this
is not the place for a full discussion of the question whether
it be part of the original Iliad or not '; which seems to mean
no more than that Mr. Munro has not yet made up his mind
on the matter ; nevertheless he essays to oppose Grote, whose
arguments (he asserts) do no more than show that the ninth
book, if it is an addition, is a skilful and effective one ;

as if those who maintain that a passage is late maintain also that it is bad.   But Mr. Munro almost in the same breath retracts the plea of genuineness for which he is contending, distrustfully adding, ' other arguments have been found in (1) peculiarities of language, and in (2) allusions indicating a more advanced state of knowledge than is found elsewhere in the Iliad ; (3) discrepancies with other books, and (4) the strange allegorical passage beginning at verse 502, *sqq.*'   And then he diplomatically takes his leave with the remark that after all, as the style of the book is unequal, ' it may be doubted whether the sustained rhetoric of the speeches is quite Homeric'.   I can well understand the perplexed reader exclaiming in the words of Terence, ' Fecisti probe ; incertior sum multo quam dudum '.

Of Fick's daring theory, for some criticism of which all may fairly have looked with hope to Mr. Munro, he has not ventured to say a word.   In his Grammar he had put it off— ' It is impossible to discuss a theory such as this in the brief space which can be given to it here '.   In his more recent book, however, he has become such an obscurantist that Fick's name is not even mentioned, and all notice of what has been said on the question is dismissed in fourteen octavo pages, which give a bare skeleton of what was done between Wolf's and Grote's time.   Here Mr. Munro ' sets up his everlasting rest ' at a point where Friedländer left the matter in 1853, with his tract, ' Die homerische Kritik von Wolf bis Grote '.

APPENDIX.

I.

THE RELATION BETWEEN THE MYCENAEAN AND HOMERIC AGE.

FROM the antiquities which remain at Mycenae it is certain that a civilization extremely high existed in Greece long anterior to the Homeric age, probably about 1000 B.C. The external culture of this age was decidedly Eastern in its characteristics, and in the Homeric poems some faint traces or echoes of these yet remain. After this period of material splendour had passed away, there was a relapse amongst the Greeks as to external culture into what one might almost term barbarism, though intellectually there was great advance. The uncleanliness of the Homeric house is quite remarkable, as well as the extreme simplicity of the food, which is usually but meat and bread. Nowhere are fowl and vegetables mentioned, and fish, the delicacy of after times, is regarded as a miserable means of support.* The fortifications of abodes in the Epos are no longer of hewn stone, as in the Mycenaean period, but of wood and earth.

At Mycenae the mode of burial was essentially different from that in the Homeric poems, and, without doubt, earlier. In Homer the body is burnt on a pyre; the bones, when collected, are placed in a metal urn, buried in the earth, and covered with a mound. At Mycenae the graves are cut out of the rock, and contain skeletons; they hold ashes, too, but these are of burnt

* μ. 329–331, δ. 368, 369.

offerings, similar to those of Achilles at the burial of Patroclus
(Ψ. 166–169), or the victims in the Odyssey, slain beside a cenotaph
in honour of the dead (a. 291, β. 222). On one skeleton flesh and
muscle is to be seen, which indicates that some method of embalming was used. Wax was employed by the Persians for the purpose of preserving the body, and honey by the Babylonians—a
process not unknown to the Greeks—the Spartan king Agesipolis,
who died of fever in Chalcidice in B.C. 380, being brought home to
Sparta covered in honey (Xen. Hell. v. 3, 19). That the process
of embalming had not been quite forgotten in Homer's time may
be inferred from his use of the word ταρχύειν, and other echoes are
also to be found ; the body of Hector, for instance, lies in state for
nine days ; that of Achilles for seventeen. Thetis keeps Patroclus'
body fresh with nectar and ambrosia poured through the nostrils
(Τ. 38, 39)—a process which is too realistic to be mere fiction ; and
the dead bodies on pyres (ψ. 170, ω. 24, 68) are surrounded with
vessels of honey, which seems a reminiscence of the older custom.

In Mycenae the faces were covered with masks of gold, as in
Egypt and the East ; the walls were covered with plates of metal,
and the dresses were ornamented with gold leaf sewed on, of which
custom we find an echo in Θ. 43, and Ν. 26, where Zeus and Poseidon clothe themselves in gold : the golden breastplates, too,
reminding one of that of the high priest of the Jews, seem remembered in the Aegis on Pallas' breast. There are to be found at
Mycenae also seals and carved stones, neither of which are to be
found in Homer, for Odysseus has no other means of securing his
chest of treasure (θ. 443–448) than a curious knot. Rings are not
amongst the ornaments made by Hephaestus, nor amongst the
suitors' gifts to Penelope, but they are numerous at Mycenae ; and
on the whole the Mycenaean age was externally more brilliant
than the Homeric, not owing to any self-developed art or manufacture, but to the importation of these works of art and luxury by
the Phoenicians ; for to the higher civilization of the East the early
Greeks at first willingly surrendered themselves, but from the
Homeric age onwards they asserted their own individuality. In
Mycenae the walls are of hewn stone, with carvings on them ; in
Homer there are no stone fortresses, but only ditches, mounds, and

palisades; gravestones, indeed, are mentioned, but not as sculp-
tured. In some respects, however, the Homeric age is more advanced than the Mycenaean; for instance, the fibula is not to be
found in Mycenae, and the arrow-points are sometimes made of
stone.

The great difference between the Mycenaean and Homeric age
is to be accounted for by the Dorian invasion of Peloponnesus; the
vanquished withdraw to Ionia, and have there to establish a foot-
ing for themselves. In the Epos, Mycenae is still called πολύ-
χρυσος, but after the Dorians had thoroughly occupied the country,
gold became so rare, that when the Spartans in the first half of the
sixth century wanted gold to make a statue of Apollo, they had to
send to Sardis for it (Herod. I. 69). Amongst the exiled Ionians,
too, culture naturally ebbed; the bodies of their friends they
burned, and, owing to the insecurity of their abode, for ease of
transport stowed the ashes in urns. They further had to think of
the necessary and useful, rather than of the ornamental, so that
we find among them no beautiful stone fortresses like those at
Mycenae, but simply military works, such as are mentioned in the
Epos. We know that the wall round the ships was of wood and
earth, and from the fact that Poseidon fears (H. 445) it will eclipse
the fame of the wall of Troy which he and Apollo built, it appears
that that wall, too, was of earth and wood.

The classical representation of the scenes from the poems is
quite misleading, although familiar to most of us, the heroes being
represented as naked, the women in the garb of Periclean times,
and in the background pillared temples. At Alexandria there was
no such study as archaeology, and in the poems themselves there is
naturally no deliberate description of those everyday surroundings
with which all were familiar, so that the Greeks easily slipped into
the error of picturing to themselves the Homeric age as being like
that in which they themselves lived. How absurd is such an anachronism may be seen from the fact that the Thracians are highly
civilized in the Epos, and not, as we read of them afterwards, barbarians and drunkards. They are armed like Achaeans, but more
splendidly, and not as in Herod. VII. 75. They were *en rapport* with
Eastern civilization through the instrumentality of the Phoenicians,

O

who were the great means of communion between the peoples of
that age, and from whom were heard stories of the short summer
nights of the north, and of the Pygmies of Africa. It was Phoenician imports and works of art that first stimulated the imagination of the Greeks. In E. 462, the poet represents Ares, when
inspiring the wavering Trojans with courage, as appearing in the
form of the Thracian Acamas, which would in the classic period
of the fifth or fourth century have excited laughter. The bivouac
of the Thracian Rhesus is very orderly, his chariot and armour
beautiful; the goblet which Priam gives with the other valuables
as ransom for Hector is a splendid present from the Thracians.
Afterwards the Thracians relapsed into barbarism; but at the
period of which we speak the Greeks were inferior to them in external culture; indeed, the Locrians (N. 712–721) have not iron
helms, shields, or ash spears, but only bows; and in ρ. 384 we
read how the practisers of useful arts are summoned from abroad;
and it is a Lydian or Karian woman who is mentioned as staining
ivory, from which we may conclude that works of art and luxury
were chiefly imported.

The graves at Mycenae are to be regarded as prior in date to
the Dorian conquest, which took place in the tenth century. This
then marks the superior limit, at a considerable time after which
we may fix Homer's date; the inferior limit is marked by the pictures on the vases found near the Dipylon in Athens, which closely
represent Homeric manners; the men in their usual daily dress are
girded with swords: greaves are worn; bodies lie in state, covered
from head to foot with a pall; there are funeral games, with tri-
pods for prizes. These vases must be later than Homer, because
already the making of them had become a trade, and similar ones
are found widely in Asia Minor, and in the neighbouring islands,
whereas in Homer nothing of trade or the industrial spirit is known
at all. Furthermore, the Dipylon vases represent the ships with
rams or rostra, while the Homeric ship is ἀμφιέλισσα, i.e. 'curved'
symmetrically at both ends.

We must further be on our guard against confusing the Homeric costume and that of the classical period, even though the
same words be used for both. The women's garb in Homer is

tight-fitting to the bust, τανύπεπλος, an epithet which is to be
explained not as ἑλκεσίπεπλος, but as 'stretching' the robe—as τα-
νυπτέρυξ, 'with wide-stretching pinions', τανύφλοιος, 'with smooth-
stretched bark'. The girdle was worn loosely over the hips, and
tied low in front (βαθύζωνος), which explains the epithet βαθύκολ-
πος, the κόλπος being that part of the garment which reached from
throat to girdle; this opened down the front, as we see from the
ἑανός (Ξ. 180) which Hera puts on fastened with ἐνεταί, while of
course the later Dorian and Ionian χιτών was fastened on the
shoulder by a περόνη or πόρπη. Similar also was the mode of
wearing the peplos which Antinous gave to Penelope (σ. 292), and
which was furnished with twelve περόναι : this explains the phrase
κόλπον ἀνιεμένη, 'throwing open her bosom', reminding one of
ἀνιέναι πύλας; whereas, if the garb were fastened on the shoulder,
we would expect some compound of κατά. It is by means of this
opening that the nurse of Eumaeus contrives to secret the stolen
goblet, since from the figures on the vases we see the opening at
the neck and for the arms is too small to allow anything to pass by
these apertures, and the central division is marked very distinctly.
From the girdle down the robe fell straight and foldless. Wool was
probably the chief material used in its manufacture; but that linen
robes, probably from Egypt and Phoenicia, were also common
seems clear, from the use of such epithets as σιγαλόεις, λιπαρός
(Χ. 406), &c. That this divided robe was essentially Oriental and
non-Hellenic is certain from the figures on monuments in Egypt
and elsewhere.

Pre-hellenic, too, and thoroughly Oriental is the use of many-
coloured garments. In classical times white was in vogue, because
it allowed the eye to rest on the bodily form without the distractions
of colour and pattern; but in Homer we constantly meet the epithets, ποικίλος, παμποικίλος, and read of garments embroidered with
δαίδαλα πολλά (Ξ. 178). Andromache's web has θρόνα ποικίλα,
and there are figured scenes in that of Helen (Γ. 125–128). In
classical times there was nothing of the sort, since the folds in
which garments were worn would have interfered with the scene
pourtrayed, while the Homeric garb, fitting the body tightly,
showed off the design. Not till the Greeks in Alexander's time

began to orientalize, did these early dresses and the breast-division
come into fashion again.   Both Aristophanes and Plato mention
coloured and figured cloaks as excessive luxuries (Plut. 530 ; De
Rep. 8, p. 557, c.).

Pre-hellenic, too, was the woman's head-dress :

> τῆλε δ᾽ ἀπὸ κρατὸς βάλε δέσματα σιγαλόεντα,
> ἄμπυκα, κεκρύφαλον τ᾽ ἠδὲ πλεκτὴν ἀναδέσμην
> κρήδεμνόν θ᾽, ὅ ῥά οἱ δῶκε χρυσέη Ἀφροδίτη.

From Etruscan monuments we see that the πλεκτὴ ἀναδέσμη is a
ribbon wound up round the κεκρύφαλος, which is a kind of vertical
stiff chignon fastened to the head by a band, ἄμπυξ, while the
κρήδεμνον is a mantle-hood thrown over all.   The κεκρύφαλος cannot be taken as a net thrown over the hair; it is essentially Oriental, and of course this is the only place where either it or the
πλεκτὴ ἀναδέσμη is mentioned.   It is worth while noticing that
in Ξ. 170-185, where Hera's toilet is described, no such chignon
is mentioned, but the mantle (κρήδεμνον) is placed directly upon
the head, which seems to show that the two passages before us are
of different dates.

We must not picture to ourselves the hair of the heroes, although worn long, as free and flowing—a mode of wearing it which
first appears in the sculptures of the time of Myron and Phidias,
and in the red figured vases.   The hair, though long, was probably
bound together in a mass, and conventionally arranged : indeed we
have almost certain confirmation of this supposition from Λ. 385,
τοξότα, λωβητήρ, κέρᾳ ἀγλαὲ, παρθενοπῖπα, where κέρᾳ ἀγλαὲ cannot mean bow-man, for κέρας is never used in the singular for a
bow, nor is ἀγλαὸς 'bright', used for ἀγαλλόμενος, 'exulting in ':
and besides, κέρᾳ ἀγλαὲ would be a weak repetition of τοξότα, although such an interpretation wins the approval of Aristarchus :
κέρας must mean, as the old scholiast explains it, and as antiquities
prove, a horn-like arrangement of the hair ;* besides, the word is
thus used by Archilochus, as we see from the scholion on ω. 81,

---

* Cf. Juv. xiv. 165, madido torquentem cornua cirro, and also Servius ad.
Aen. xii. 89, cornua autem sunt proprie concinni.

οἱ νεώτεροι κέρας τὴν συμπλοκὴν τῶν τριχῶν ὁμοίαν κέρατι· τὸν κεροπλάστην ἄειδε Γλαῦκον, Ἀρχίλοχος.

Euphorbus (P. 52) wears his hair artificially arranged, πλοχμοί θ᾽ οἳ χρυσῷ τε καὶ ἀργύρῳ ἐσφήκωντο, and in many graves are found gold spirals which were used for binding the hair in the manner of ringlets. So we read of Amphimachus, leader of the Karians (B. 872):

ὃς καὶ χρυσὸν ἔχων πόλεμόνδ᾽ ἴεν, ἠΰτε κούρη.

The conventional arrangement of the hair was resumed in later times, but was abandoned in the classical period. Thucydides (I. 6, 2) mentions that the Ionians and Athenians, as late as the fifth century B.C., wore the κρώβυλος fastened with τέττιγες. Nor must we picture to ourselves the women with a shower of hair, but with carefully plaited tresses, as we see from (Ξ. 175):

ἰδὲ χαίτας
πεξαμένη, χερσὶ πλοκάμους ἔπλεξε φαεινούς,
καλοὺς ἀμβροσίους ἐκ κράατος ἀθανάτοιο.

The masks found at Mycenae show that the beard was worn conventionally in a wedge-shaped form, and this gains some confirmation from the fact that the razor is mentioned, though in a late book of the Iliad.* Probably the upper lip was shaved, as in Egypt, and to this Archilochus refers (frag. 60):

οὐ φιλέω μέγαν στρατηγὸν οὐδὲ διαπεπλιγμένον
οὐδὲ βοστρύχοισι γαῦρον οὐδ᾽ ὑπεξυρημένον.

From Plutarch (Cleom. 9) we learn that at Sparta, the most conservative of states, this custom long prevailed. We should remark, too, as an important note of difference between the Homeric and the classical age, how seldom is mentioned the bath, that luxury of after-times. Pre-hellenic, too, is the delight in strong perfumes (Ξ. 171–174), which seem not merely to have been used for the person, but even to scent rooms (θαλάμῳ εὐώδεϊ κηώεντι) and garments (εἵματα θυώδεα).

* ἐπὶ ξυροῦ ἵσταται ἀκμῆς, K. 173.

The error of believing in a single Homer is not more incorrect than this one of picturing the men and women of the poem in classical costume, after the manner of Flaxman. For example, the scene of Helen amidst the elders on the Trojan wall, as presented to the imagination of the poet, was perhaps something of the following kind :—Priam and the elders, clothed in tight-fitting chitons, many of them wearing carefully-arranged linen garbs, reaching to the very feet, with straight and foldless mantles of red or purple drawn round the back and shoulders, some with rich patterns, the king's, perchance, with a battle-scene upon it ; their faces, with shaven upper lip and formal wedge-shaped beards, set as in a framework of hair, bound in gold spirals, and hanging down on each side. Helen wearing a richly embroidered peplos, strongly perfumed, and showing by its close fit the contour of the lovely form beneath. Glittering on her breast are the golden fibulae which fasten the divided bosom of her dress ; round her throat a necklace of gold and amber; her hair elaborately plaited, the head probably overtopped by the stiff κεκρύφαλος, round which is twisted the ἀναδέσμη, on her brow the golden ἄμπυξ, and over all, as a foil to the richly-coloured picture it sets off, the hood (κρήδεμνον, καλύπτρα) of white linen. It is a scene of conventional form and various colour essentially Eastern, and lacking the dignified freedom and just proportion of the true Hellas.

It is a curious fact that, though tools of iron are often mentioned in the Epos, weapons are usually spoken of as made of bronze. If we except the suspected verse (Δ. 123) which ascribes to the arrow of Pandarus an iron point, the club of the Arcadian Areïthoos (H. 141–144) is the only iron weapon mentioned in the Iliad ; while in the later Odyssey (π. 294, and τ. 13) the line

$$\text{αὐτὸς γὰρ ἐφέλκεται ἄνδρα σίδηρος,}$$

shows that when these verses were composed the weapons must have been more commonly made of iron, although the later poets who expanded the Epos, still using the conventional style, represented the combats as carried on with bronze weapons, only occasionally thus letting slip something which showed how times had changed.

As regards the use of the war-chariot we find the same conventional treatment common in the poems, seemingly a faint echo of Mycenaean times; for that chariots were in use in Mycenae is plain from the pictures on the pottery.   In the Homeric poems chariots are frequently mentioned, but no clear account is given of their use in the actual combat.   To judge from the figures on the seals found at Mycenae, the corselet and greaves of metal which were afterwards so common in the Homeric age were then unknown, and were only adopted by the Greeks after the Dorian invasion—a fact which shows how hard a fight the immigrants into Ionia had to establish themselves.   That this later equipment was thoroughly satisfactory, and that the steady bronze-clad hoplite made a powerful impression on the Eastern imagination, is clear from a story told by Herodotus (II. 152), how, when Psammetichus had taken flight into the marshes, an oracle declared that he would be able to avenge himself if bronze men should rise out of the sea.   The prophecy was fulfilled when heavy-armed Ionians and Karians landed at Sais, and entering his service, vanquished his foes.   The μίτρη and the oval shield, however, which are so usual in Homer, almost immediately dropped out of use.

A reader of the Homeric poems must ever bear in mind how many Eastern influences affected the Greeks of that age—influences which afterwards lost their power on Greek life; in fact, if a modern were magically transported into the megaron of an Ionic prince, and even were a Homeric bard singing there, yet from the conventional style of art, and the manifold variety of colour which would everywhere meet his eyes, he would feel as though he were sitting in Nineveh at the court of Sanherib, or at Tyre in the palace of King Hiram, and not in a company of Greeks.

But in spite of Orientalism in external matters, intellectually, in conception, feeling, and thought, we already find in the Epos all that individualizes the Greek race of after-times.   Perhaps most remarkable is the dislike of everything objectless and purposeless which is apparent all through the Epos, and which was so distinctive of the later Greek.   Thoroughly Hellenic is the glowing enthusiasm for physical beauty.   In the poetry of no other people is there anyone who approaches Helen in the elemental power which

her beauty exercises. Nor does this aesthetical appreciation con-
fine itself to youthful forms, but extends even to the old. When
Achilles looks upon the beautiful face of aged Priam he is moved
by the same feeling of admiration as that which inspired the Athenians when they ordained that the most beautiful old men should
be θαλλοφόροι at the Panathenaea. Even in the cult of the nude,
which was afterwards so highly developed, the Epos shows that
the first step has been already taken. When Hector is slain by
Achilles, and stripped of his armour, and the Greeks coming about
him marvel at the beauty of the naked body (X. 369), they already
display the same aesthetic sensibility which, many centuries afterwards, the Athenian soldiers displayed at Plataea, in presence of
the slain Persian general, Masistios (Herod. ix. 25). In X. 71–76,
Priam says it matters not if a youth lie slain and naked, for he is
lovely to look upon, but an old man lying thus is a sorry sight. A
contemporary of Sophocles would scarcely have spoken otherwise,
yet in the Homeric age this feeling is quite abstract, and has no
direct influence on manners. It is still regarded as disgraceful for
a man to be naked amongst men (B. 262). In the boxing and the
wrestling match the loins are girded (Ψ. 683, 700); and not until
the 15th Olympiad does the Lacedaemonian Acanthus dare to run
naked.*

Thoroughly Hellenic, too, are the forms of the gods, as pourtrayed in the poems. There occur, indeed, many hideous conceptions, but these did not admit of modification by the poet, partly
perhaps because they were fixed through Oriental influence, and
partly because they had already struck root in the minds of the
common people. We need only instance hundred-handed Briareus,
the giants Otus and Ephialtes (λ. 305–311), nine fathoms long, and
nine ells broad, and Scylla, with her twelve feet, six necks, six
heads, &c.

The early poetry of no other nation shows such genius for the
plastic arts as the Homeric. The poet of the shield of Achilles
shows his ability to conceive a pictorial whole, perfect in itself, and
inspired by one idea, and he groups his pictures on principles un-
surpassed even at the best period of the arts. It took more than a

---

* Thucyd. i. 6, 4; Pausan. v. 8, 3; Dionys. Hal. vii. 72.

century before the Greeks could represent such a pictorial whole, except to the imagination. It took still longer for the heroes, so sharply individualized in the Epos, to find expression in marble or bronze. Not until Phidias was the Homeric Zeus revealed to the eyes of men.

II.

VILLOISON'S PROLEGOMENA.

VILLOISON had been sent on a literary commission to Venice in 1781, by King Louis XVI. While there he collected the unedited scholia on the Iliad, and arranged them for publication. The MS. which contained them was in the library of St. Mark, No. 454. It is in folio, and of the tenth century, that is, two hundred years prior to Eustathius. The calligraphy is most careful, and displays ancient characteristics and ancient orthography to be found nowhere else. The text of the Iliad presents us with the hypodiastole, the hyphen, and inter-aspiration. The hypodiastole ($\dot{\eta}$ $\dot{\upsilon}\pi o\text{-}$ $\delta\iota a\sigma\tau o\lambda\dot{\eta}$) resembles our comma, and has been preserved by some editors to distinguish $\ddot{o}$, $\tau\epsilon$ ($\ddot{o}$ $\tau\epsilon$) from $\ddot{o}\tau\epsilon$; $\ddot{o}$, $\tau\iota$ ($\ddot{o}$ $\tau\iota$) from $\ddot{o}\tau\iota$; $\tau\acute{o}$ $\tau\epsilon$ ($\tau\acute{o}$ $\tau\epsilon$) from $\tau\acute{o}\tau\epsilon$, &c. Porphyry says it was used to separate words that one might confuse when closely written, as $\ddot{\epsilon}\sigma\tau\iota\nu$, $o\ddot{\upsilon}s$ and $\ddot{\epsilon}\sigma\tau\iota$ $\nu o\hat{\upsilon}s$, which were usually written without division ($\epsilon\sigma\tau\iota\nu o\upsilon s$). The hyphen ($\dot{\eta}$ $\dot{\upsilon}\phi\acute{\epsilon}\nu$), a little curve placed beneath the line, marked the union of the factors of a compound word, as $\dot{o}\nu\epsilon\iota\rho o\pi\acute{o}\lambda os$, $\kappa o\rho\upsilon\theta a\acute{\iota}o\lambda os$, or showed that one idea was intended to be conveyed by two words written separately, as $\pi\acute{\upsilon}\kappa a$ $\pi o\iota\eta\tau o\hat{\iota}o$, $\pi\upsilon\lambda\acute{a}\rho\tau ao$ $\kappa\rho a\tau\epsilon\rho o\hat{\iota}o$. In case of tmesis, where a preposition is separated from its verb, the preposition bears no accent. With regard to inter-aspiration, there were several usages; but the principal one was to mark the etymology of compound words when the second

component was from a word beginning with a vowel or ρ. Thus
Aristarchus wrote ἐξέσίην in Ω. 235, to show that the word came
from ἐξ and ἵημι. The manuscript gives at A. 8, ξυνέηκε, and
the scholion on the passage is δασύνεται τὸ ξυνέηκε. Before the
invention of Ξ, and the long vowel Η, the symbol for which had
originally been used to mark the aspirate, forms like ΚΣΥΝΗΕΕΚΕ,
or ΚΣΟΝΗΕΕΚΕ, were common, since the old Greeks wrote o for
υ, as well as for ω and ου. Sometimes the inter-aspiration served
to distinguish two words which were exactly alike in form, as
Εὐρύαλος, the proper name, and εὐρύάλος the adjective. In writing εὐρύάλος, the adjective, the inter-aspiration showed that the
idea of the sea was in the word. In writing the proper name,
Εὐρύαλος, there was no need to draw attention to the connotation
of the word, what it denoted being the main point. In an inscription on the Farnese column we find ΕΝΗΟΔΙΑ for ἐνοδία, from
which it is clear that the inter-aspiration was usual in early writing, and not a mere conventionality of the Alexandrians. This is
also proved by the fact that the word ταῶς was written ταῶς by
them. The word is not of course a compound; ταῶς stands for
ΤΑΗΩΣ, Aeolian ταϝῶς, Latin pavo. The old aspiration Η of the
Ionians and Athenians was sometimes an equivalent of the Aeolic
digamma, or of the β, which the Pamphylians, according to Hera-
clides, were accustomed to place between the vowels.

Much in the same way the old grammarians, as Porphyry tells
us, used always to put upon the letter ρ, even when single and in
the middle of a word, either the smooth or rough breathing; when it
was joined with a tenuis they gave it the smooth breathing: when
joined with an aspirate, the rough; as, for instance, Ἀτρεύς,
κάπρος, but χρόνος θρόνος. Examples of this use are frequent in
the Marcian Codex, which gives not only the old readings, but also
the old orthography of the Alexandrians.

A remark of Porphyry in his book, περὶ προσῳδίας, is worth
quoting:—ἰστέον ὅτι ἐπὶ συμφώνου τίθεται ἑνὸς μόνου, τοῦ ρ, ἡ
δασεῖα καὶ ἡ ψιλή· ἐπὶ τοῦ ῥώμη, καὶ ῥέω, τίθεται ἡ δασεῖα· ἐπὶ δὲ
τοῦ ῥάρος, ὃ σημαίνει βρέφος κατὰ τοὺς Αἰολεῖς, ψιλή . . . καὶ διὰ
τί, ῥάρος ψιλοῦται ὅτι ἡ Αιολὶς γλῶττα τὸ ψιλοῦν τὰ στοιχεῖα
φιλεῖ.

An interesting example of the strictness of the ancient grammarians' orthography is to be found in Θ. 206, where εὐρύοπα Ζῆν' ends the line, and αὐτοῦ begins the next. Of course Ζῆν' is for Ζῆνα, the final letter of which is elided by synapheia with the αὐτοῦ following. It is wrong, therefore, to write Ζῆν by apocope, as some do. The Alexandrians all maintain that it is a case of elision—nay more, Aristarchus says the ν does not belong to the verse it appears to terminate, but rather to the beginning of the next, and that the true orthography is Ζῆ-ν', αὐτοῦ, as the Venetian MS. writes it. Compare the scholion on Ω. 331 : οὕτως τὴν συναλοιφὴν διεῖλεν Ἀρίσταρχος, Ζῆ-ν', ἐν ἀρχῇ τοῦ στίχου τὸ ν θείς. Eustathius, too, gives the old rule, εἰ μέσον δύο φωνηέντων εὑρέθη σύμφωνον ἐν ἁπλότητι, ἢ συνθέσει, ἤ καὶ συναλοιφῇ, τῷ δευτέρῳ, τουτέστι τῷ ἐπαγομένῳ φωνήεντι, ἀκολουθεῖ.

The old grammarians who busied themselves with the emendation of manuscripts used not only to correct the mistakes of copyists, but used to place above doubtful vowels the symbols which we employ to mark longs and shorts. It is a remarkable fact that this usage does not occur even once in the Venetian MS. The grammarians, too, if we are to believe Porphyry, used to place grave accents on every syllable which had not the acute nor the circumflex. But the uselessness of this habit caused it to be abandoned, since of course every syllable which has not the τόνος proper has the grave accent. Besides, it was only in books meant for learners that even the accents which we use were employed ; in all other instances the accent was only affixed in cases of ambiguity or difficulty, or on account of the peculiar and unusual prosody of the dialect which the author used. Not until the seventh century of our era did it become usual to mark the accent of every word.

Villoison dwells at great length upon the cunning craftsmanship of Aristophanes of Byzantium in devising symbols for marking accents, breathings, quantity, divisions of a word, union of two words with one another, and punctuation of sentences and paragraphs.

The Venetian MS. gives all these details of orthography, but it does more, for it gives before a countless number of lines the critical signs which the Alexandrians used, the ὀβελὸς, ὀβελὸς σὺν

ἀστερίσκῳ, ἀστερίσκος καθ᾽ ἑαυτὸν, διπλῆ καθαρὰ, διπλῆ περιεστιγμένη, ἀντίσιγμα ἄστικτον, ἀντισιγμα περιεστιγμένον, κορωνίς, &c.,
to mark lines spurious, obscure, corrupt, or remarkable, false readings of Crates, emendations of Aristarchus or Zenodotus, peculiar
orthography, &c. These signs, which never before were published,
Villoison gave in his edition with full explanations taken from the
till then unedited pages of the MS. 483.

These marks not only show us the verdict passed upon certain
verses by Aristarchus, but also inform us what later critics thought
about such a verdict. Everybody remembers how Lucian (Ver.
Hist. II. 20) asks the shade of Homer what verses are spurious,
and what are genuine, and how that good old soul claims all as
his, and scoffs at the critics, Zenodotus and Aristarchus, for their
ψυχρολογία and want of poetic feeling. Callistratus composed a
book against the extremes to which the critics went (their τολμή-
ματα or παρατολμήματα, as he called them), and another against
athetizing, πρὸς τὰς ἀθετήσεις. Fragments of this book and of
those of Didymus Chalcenterus, περὶ τῆς Ἀρισταρχείου διορθώσεως,
have been preserved in the Venetian scholia, in which are also
quotations from the works of Ammonius of Alexandria, Tryphon,
Ptolemaeus Ascalonites, Dionysius Thrax, and Parmeniscus, either
defending or impugning the opinions of Aristarchus. Demetrius
Ixion, too, is quoted at Z. 437, ἐν τῷ πρὸς τοὺς ἀθετουμένους.

Amongst the many marks in the Venetian MS., one is peculiar,
made by dropping wax upon the parchment. Villoison had seen
the same mark in MSS. at Amorgos, Patmos, and on Mount Athos,
and he acquiesces in the explanation given by Ernesti in his Index
Latinitatis Ciceronis under *Cerula*, viz. that the ancients use it
to mark passages which they wished to examine further, or with
which they found some fault.

In the inner margin of the MS. are carefully given the various
readings (often much better than the common ones) of very old
copies, and of those public 'city' editions, of which we hear in
connexion with Massilia, Chios, Cyprus, Crete, Sinope, and Argos.
Villoison in a note draws a comparison between the fate of the Homeric poems and of the Koran. Both were originally unwritten.
The Homeric poems were divided into books by Aristarchus, just

as Plato's Laws were by Philippus Opuntius, and so the Koran
was divided by later Imams.   About the true readings there are
the same disputes in either case.   Various states—Cyprus, Chios,
Crete, Sinope, Argos, Massilia—took care that public editions of
Homer should be preserved, and so Mecca, Medina, Cusa, &c., did
the same for Mohammed, and these single copies, just as the Vulgate ἡ κοινή, busy the acuteness of the most learned interpreters.

The MS. gives variants from the editions of Zenodotus, of
Callistratus, of the poet Rhianus, a contemporary of Ptolemy
Euergetes, of Sosigenes, of Philemon of Crete (who is not to be
confounded with the grammarian Philemon, who was born in
Attica : perhaps, however, we should read instead of Κρητικόν,
κριτικόν, a title which may have been given him to distinguish
him from his namesake the comic poet), from those of Aristophanes
of Byzantium, of Antimachus the epic poet, and of Apollonius
Rhodius, whose book 'against Zenodotus' is quoted by the scholiast on N. 657, and from it most of the readings given as his are
perhaps taken.

Constantly, too, we find editions referred to as αἱ πολιτικαὶ
ἐκδόσεις, by which we are to understand editions publicly preserved, or made by certain States, as those mentioned above.   Opposed to these are the αἱ κατ' ἄνδρα, which private individuals got
made for themselves, just as Cassander, according to Athenaeus,
had a revision of Iliad and Odyssey made for his own use.   It is
possible, however, that these editions were so named when the
editor who was responsible for them was known, for the town-
editions are anonymous.   Both private and town-editions were
more accurately written and revised than those which were for
sale on the book-stalls (τῶν εἰς πρᾶσιν γραφομένων βιβλίων), and
which, as Strabo tells us (XIII. p. 419), were made by ignorant
copyists, and subjected to no correction.   These are the copies
called the Vulgate, αἱ δὲ κοιναί (Il. Ω. 214, 314).   They are also
called δημοτικαί and δημώδεις, unless, indeed, these are to be regarded as the πολιτικαί.   Our common text is filled with the readings of the κοιναί; hence Villoison concludes that our common text
is not even that of Aristarchus.

Everywhere we come across the name of this great critic, and his

queenly edition, ἡ Ἀριστάρχου, ἡ Ἀριστάρχειος, ἡ κατὰ Ἀρίσταρχον
ἔκδοσις or διόρθωσις or ἀνάγνωσις. Sometimes two editions by him
are mentioned, and different readings are thus quoted from them,
ἐν τῇ ἑτέρᾳ τῶν Ἀριστάρχου οὐκ ἐφέρετο καθάπαξ· ἐν τῇ ἑτέρᾳ . . .
Thus on K. 159, ὄρσεο· διχῶς ὁ Ἀρίσταρχος· ἔγρεο, καὶ ὄρσεο.
The same scholia again on K. 397–399 mention that Ammonius
Alexandrinus, who succeeded to the school of Aristarchus shortly
before the time of Augustus Cæsar (ὃς καὶ διεδέξατο τὴν σχολὴν
Ἀριστάρχου), first marked these three verses with dots, and then
finally struck them out. So, too, in many other Greek mss., the
copyists first dotted words which they thought should be cancelled,
ἵνα μὴ τὸ βιβλίον ἀκαλλές τε ὁρῶτο, καί τινα τρόπον ἀμυχὲς,
ξεσμάτων ἐπιφερομένων, and this usage is seen also in the case of
the dotted obel, which was placed before lines, the condemnation
of which was open to some doubt. Ammonius wrote a book entitled, περὶ τοῦ μὴ γεγονέναι πλείους ἐκδόσεις τῆς Ἀριστάρχίου
διορθώσεως, which is cited in a note of Didymus. To reconcile
this with what we have said, we must suppose that Aristarchus
allowed one set of readings to stand in his text, while he gave
those which he approved in his commentaries, and that after his
death these were made into what was known as his second edition.
We find mention of another book of Ammonius launched against
the περὶ Ὁμήρου of Athenocles.

The collector of our scholia, whoever he was, seems to have
belonged to the school of Aristarchus, as when speaking of it he
frequently uses the expression, οἱ ἡμέτεροι. However, he gives
expression to his own ideas also, and often refers to his own books,
ἐν ἑτέροις ἡμῖν εἴρηται. He even goes so far as to correct Aristarchus in certain details of accentuation, &c. He seems to belong to
a rather early period, while the Aeolic and Ionic dialects were yet
flourishing, as we may gather from what he says (O. 536), παρὰ
δὲ Αἰολεῦσι κύμβη καλεῖται; (O. 545), ἔτι παρ᾽ Ἴωσι; (B. 117),
ἕως νῦν παρ᾽ Ἴωσιν: he may, however, be here merely quoting
some old note of a period long prior to that in which he himself
lived.

A single instance will suffice to show the pains which the scholiast of this Venetian ms. took in collecting from every available

source whatever of value there might be relating to Homeric poetry. In Γ. 406, no one had suspected there was anything wrong; the Pseudo-Didymus, Eustathius, Clarke, Ernesti, all had passed it over. The common reading is Ἧσο παρ' αὐτὸν ἰοῦσα, θεῶν δ' ἀπόειπε κελεύθους: of course the proper reading is θεῶν δ' ἀπόεικε κελεύθου. Our scholiast quotes from Didymus: Ἀρίσταρχος ἀπόεικε διὰ τοῦ κ ἀντὶ τοῦ ἀπόειπε, καὶ χωρὶς τοῦ σ κελεύθου· θαυμάσειε δ' ἄν τις, ἡ ἑτέρα διὰ τοῦ π, πόθεν παρέδυ. οὔτε γὰρ ἐν ταῖς Ἀρισταρχείοις, οὔτε ἐν ἑτέρῳ τῶν γοῦν μετρίων ἐμφερομένων πέφυκεν· καὶ οὐ μόνον ἐν ταῖς ἐκδόσεσιν, ἀλλὰ καὶ ἐν τοῖς συγγράμμασιν ἀπαξάπαντες οὕτως ἐκτίθενται.

Crates of Mallos (sometimes called the Homeric, sometimes the critic), contemporary of Ptolemy Philometor, and the introducer of grammatical studies into Rome, wrote a commentary on Homer in nine books. He is occasionally referred to in the scholia, and his book appears to have been called Ὁμηρικά. Chrysippus the Stoic, Aristophanes of Byzantium, Parmenion, Clearchus, and Apollodorus, are also quoted, as well as certain γλωσσογράφοι, amongst whom, at A. 99, are Apollonius the sophist, and his master, Apion. Quotations are made from Apollonius Dyscolus, Apollonius of Tyana, Apollonius, son of Theon, son of Molon, son of Cheris, Diodorus of Tarsus, Dionysius of Thrace, and amongst many others of the same name, Dionysius of Alexandria, whom Didymus calls ὁ ἀπ' Ἀριστάρχου. Then come a host of Ptolemies, of whom we will but mention him of Ascalon, author of a book on the school of Crates, and on the variants of the Odyssey. Zoilus, too, obtains dishonourable mention. At E. 4, we read, Ζωΐλος ὁ Ἐφέσιος κατηγορεῖ τοῦ τόπου τούτου, καὶ μέμφεται τῷ ποιητῇ. This Zoilus was born at Ephesus, but was by descent of Amphipolis. At A. 129, we read, Ζωΐλος ὁ Ἀμφιπολίτης καὶ Χρύσιππος ὁ στωϊκὸς σολοικίζειν οἴονται τὸν ποιητήν. So, too, Porphyry on K. 274: Ζωΐλος, ὁ κληθεὶς Ὁμηρομάστιξ, γένει μὲν ἦν Ἀμφιπολίτης ... ὃς ἔγραφε τὰ καθ' Ὁμήρου, γυμνασίας ἕνεκα, εἰωθότων καὶ τῶν ῥητόρων ἐν τοῖς ποιηταῖς γυμνάζεσθαι· οὗτος ἄλλα τε πολλὰ Ὁμήρου κατηγορεῖ, κ.τ.λ. Then come the names of fifty others who wrote books on Homer.

But more important than this multitude of authorities is the

fact that the scholiast has preserved a considerable part of the book
of Didymus Chalcenterus on the revision of Aristarchus, of Herodian's book on the accents and breathings of the Iliad, of Nicanor's
on the punctuation of the poems, and the symbols of Aristonicus
with his commentary. These latter, the Ἀριστονίκου σημεῖα μετὰ
ὑπομνηματίου, are really the symbols used by Aristarchus, and their
signification. At the end of each book of the Iliad the scholiast
conscientiously repeats the titles of the four works from which
he drew most of his observations:

> παράκειται τὰ Ἀριστονίκου σημεῖα καὶ τὰ Διδύμου
> περὶ τῆς Ἀρισταρχείου διορθώσεως, τινὰ δὲ καὶ
> ἐκ τῆς Ἰλιακῆς προσῳδίας Ἡρωδιανοῦ
> καὶ ἐκ τοῦ Νικάνορος περὶ τῆς Ὁμηρικῆς στιγμῆς.

Herodian, the son of Apollonius Dyscolus, and the heir to his
learning, established himself in Rome, and was a great favourite
of Marcus Aurelius. Nicanor, contemporary with Hadrian, was
surnamed Στιγματίας and νέος Ὅμηρος, on account of the nature of
his works. Countless poets and prose writers are mentioned in the
scholia, and invariably whenever a variant is given, the authority on
whom it depends is named also.

Wolf is usually regarded as the originator in modern times of
the Homeric question; but we may observe that the germ of his
theory was clearly stated by Villoison, in 1788, in the following
paragraph—'Hisce scholiis, nunquam antea vulgatis, maxima Homericis versibus lux affunditur; loca obscura illustrantur; veterum
ritus, mores, mythologia, geographia, explicantur; germana et sin-
cera lectio constituitur; variae variorum codicum et editionum lec-
tiones atque criticorum emendationes perpenduntur. Homericum
enim contextum, qui memoriter a rhapsodis recitabatur quique
omnium ore decantabatur, jam pridem corruptum fuisse constat;
cum fieri non potuerit, quin multa necessario demerent, adderent,
immutarent diversi diversarum Graeciae regionum rhapsodi. Homerum scripto consignavisse sua poemata negat Josephus, in limine
prioris libri contra Apionem; et huic opinioni favere videtur Dionysii
Thracis scholiastes ineditus, narrans Homeri carmina, quae in sola

hominum mente ac memoria conservabantur, nec exarata erant, periisse tempore Pisistrati, et hunc ideo praemium iis proposuisse, qui Homericos versus ipsi afferrent ; et proinde multos, pecuniae avidos, Pisistrato suos versus pro Homericis venditasse '.

Homer, like all great writers, had to suffer at the hands of editors, correctors, and interpreters. Thus Aratus, himself a poet and author of a critical edition, on asking Timon, as Diogenes Laertius tells us (I. 9, 600), how one might arrive at the genuine and true poems of Homer, was told, ' By avoiding the emended texts, and getting an old copy by good luck ' (εἰ τοῖς ἀρχαίοις ἀντι-γράφοις ἐντυγχάνοι, καὶ μὴ τοῖς ἤδη διωρθωμένοις). Leo Allatius indulges in a similar paradox, ' Si petas quaenam antiquarum editionum accuratior, melior, ἀσφαλεστέρα, ac magis genuina fuerit, dico, antiquitatis judicio, emendatiorem fuisse Aristarchicam ; meo, nullam ; sed illam omnium optimam existimo, quae a nullo fuerit correcta'; for your corrector often passes on from the writings to the writer himself, and dictates to him what he should have written, and often so alters an author's works, that were the author himself to come to life he would repudiate with loathing those writings which once were all his joy.

Villoison says that Cynaethus of Chios, whom he supposes to have first put the poems in their proper order, injured them considerably, and hence the necessity of the diorthoses. And Eustathius (Iliad, p. 16) says, τοῦ ἀπαγγέλλειν τὴν Ὁμήρου ποίησιν σκεδασθεῖσαν ἀρχὴν ἐποιήσατο Κύναιθος ὁ Χῖος· ἐλυμήναντο δὲ, φασὶν, ἐν αὐτῇ πάμπολλα οἱ περὶ τὸν Κύναιθον, καὶ πολλὰ τῶν ἐπῶν αὐτοὶ ποιήσαντες, παρενέβαλον· διὸ καὶ διωρθώθησαν αἱ Ὁμηρικαὶ βίβλοι.

Cicero thinks (de Oratore, III. 33) that it was Pisistratus who gathered the limbs of torn Homer : ' In illa autem librorum dispositione et separatione, quae non ab Homero ipso sed ab Aristarcho facta est, admittenda, non consentiunt veteres, nec eam semper sequuntur'. Whence the necessity of criticism. Villoison reminds us of the legend of the burial of the MSS. of Aristotle, and their faulty restoration by Apellicon of Teos. What utter folly then it is to think that the poems in their present state are as they issued from the mouth of the divine singer ! ' Eant nunc, et veterum auctorum

P

in omnibus locis veram et germanam lectionem πατροπαράδοτον, et
proinde sacrosanctam, accepisse, et ipsammet Homeri, Aristotelis,
Hippocratis, etc., ubique manum tenere se, sibi persuadeant ho-
munciones in arte critica, in historia litteraria, et in antiquitatis
studio prorsus hospites et peregrini'!

So, too, Origen in his commentary on St. Matthew complains of
the carelessness of the copyists, and of the sacrilegious daring of
some correctors, by whose alterations the MSS. of the New Testament are filled with disagreement : πολλὴ γέγονεν ἡ τῶν ἀντιγράφων
διαφορὰ, εἴτε ἀπὸ ῥᾳθυμίας τινῶν γραφέων εἴτε ἀπὸ τινῶν μοχθηρᾶς
τῆς διορθώσεως εἴτε καὶ ἀπὸ τόλμης τῶν τὰ ἑαυτοῖς δοκοῦντα ἐν τῇ
διορθώσει προστιθέντων καὶ ἀφαιρούντων. So Plato's laws have
been interpolated by Philippus Opuntius ; the works of Hippocrates by his son Thessalus, who collected and arranged them ;
and Villoison details the many corrections which Galen had to
make in the text rectifying the alterations of Thessalus, and the
subsequent editors, Capito and Dioscorides.

A good instance of the rash emendations which were sometimes
introduced into Homer is at A. 453. Phoenix is telling of the
advice his mother gave him (παλλακίδι προμιγῆναι, ἵν' ἐχθήρειε
γέροντα) to avenge her of her husband's insults. He says, τῇ
πιθόμην καὶ ἔρεξα· πατὴρ δ' ἐμὸς αὐτίκ' ὀϊσθεὶς πολλὰ κατηρᾶτο.
Now as Phoenix was always represented as a model of virtue,
Aristodemus of Nisa reconciled this passage with the common
legend by reading τῇ οὐ πιθόμην, οὐδ' ἔρεξα, not considering for
an instant how, under such circumstances, the ὀϊσθεὶς which follows is to be explained, nor heeding the scansion of the line.

Similarly in the same episode vv. 458–461 were rejected by
Aristarchus, and we only recover them from Plutarch :

> τὸν μὲν ἐγὼ βούλευσα κατακτάμεν ὀξέϊ χαλκῷ·
> ἀλλά τις ἀθανάτων παῦσεν χόλον, ὅς ῥ' ἐνὶ θυμῷ
> δήμου θῆκε φάτιν καὶ ὀνείδεα πόλλ' ἀνθρώπων,
> ὡς μὴ πατροφόνος μετ' Ἀχαιοῖσιν καλεοίμην.

Plutarch says the verses are very apposite, showing Achilles
the terrible extremities to which anger may lead. He says that

Aristarchus rejected them through fear (ὁ μὲν οὖν 'Αρίσταρχος ἐξεῖλε ταῦτα τὰ ἔπη φοβηθείς), apparently that some one might accuse Homer of giving Achilles a guardian unsuited to his duties. We see from this that Aristarchus' taste was not always infallible. Here he was not content with obelizing the verses, but ousted them altogether, διὰ τὸ ἀπρεπές no doubt, as in so many other cases. We may infer from the fact that these verses are not in any of the мss. that our text is that of Aristarchus.

Very far-fetched, too, is the explanation of A. 6, διαστήτην ἐρίσαντε, which the grammarians read διὰ στήτην ἐρίσαντε, quarreling on account of a woman, as we learn from the scholiast Diomedes. Porphyry well remarks in the preface of his 'Ομηρικὰ ζητήματα (where he confesses that the meaning of many words is unknown, and that there are difficulties which many pass over and of which they are not aware, deceived by the apparent clearness of the poems which we study when mere boys, and which we think we understand when perhaps we are altogether in error): ἐν τοῖς 'Ομήρου ποιήμασιν ἀγνοεῖται πολλὰ τῶν κατὰ φράσιν . . . ἡμεῖς ἐκ τῆς παιδικῆς κατηχήσεως περινοοῦμεν μᾶλλον, ἐν τοῖς πλείστοις, ἢ νοοῦμεν, fort souvent nous tournons autour du sens d'Homère, sans pouvoir le saisir. On Ψ. 422, where Callimachus confounds ἁματροχιάς with ἁρματροχιάς, Porphyry advises us to deal leniently with those who make mistakes, seeing that Callimachus, excellent grammarian, careful critic, famous poet, and passionate imitator of Homer though he was, yet mistook the meaning of words. From the Venetian scholia we see that Archilochus, Simonides, and Antimachus, made similar mistakes. Surely the errors of these men, who were so much nearer to Homer than we are, and whose native language was Greek, should give us pause in Homeric criticism. It was the delight of these scholars to raise all sorts of difficulties for solution; ἐνστατικοί was the name they gained for themselves, ὥσπερ ἔνστασιν πρός τινα ποιούμενοι. It is supposed that Apollonius Dyscolus got his name (δύσκολος, the Pozer) from the cruxes he devised, ὅτι ἐν ταῖς γυμνασίαις δυσλύτους ἀπορίας ἔλεγεν. Zenodotus wrote a book called λύσεις 'Ομηρικῶν ζητημάτων, and we have part of another by Porphyry. Those who furnished solutions of these puzzles were called λυτικοί. The Venetian мs. ' Qui *Homerus variorum totius antiquitatis criticorum* vocari potest', contains many of these ἀπορήματα, ἀπορίαι, προβλήματα or ζητήματα, as they are called, with the λύσεις as well.

The library of St. Mark has another ms. of the Iliad, No. 453, containing some scholia. It is of the eleventh century. Antonio Bongianni had made extracts of the scholia on A, and published them as early as 1740. Villoison gives those on all the books, omitting merely some absurd Byzantine etymologies. No. 453 agrees in many points with No. 454, and with the Leyden and Moscow mss., and supplies many deficiencies and lacunae of the others.

Bergler had transcribed the scholia from the Hamburg copy of the Codex Lipsiensis in the Pauline library, having begun the task in 1717, and ended it three years afterwards, but he never published them. Villoison is filled with sorrow at the fate of *poor Bergler* (infelix ille Berglerus), whose life was in so many respects like his own. He had, at the invitation of Prince Maurocordato, gone into Wallachia, but the fall of his patron forced him to fly from Bucharest, and he died in extreme wretchedness in Constantinople. The transcript, which went as far as P. 38, passed into the hands of Burchard Menken, and then into Bentley's. A copy of the transcript was found amongst the books of Christopher Wolf which had come into the possession of the Hamburg library. Villoison got a loan of this through his friend the Duke of Weimar, and extracted all the notes which were not already in his collection. That the scholia are very late is plain, because on M. 225, ὁ Θεσσαλονίκης, *i.e.* Eustathius is quoted. Villoison marks the Hamburg extracts with L, those from the Venetian ms. 454, with A, and those from 453, with B. Some notes from Porphyry, hitherto unpublished, and copied by Vernazza from Vatican mss., complete the collection. They had been presented to Villoison, as he takes care to tell us, by Count Zuliani, the Venetian Ambassador at Rome.

Villoison omitted to mark the accents, not because other scholars had set him the example, but to diminish the number of typographical errors; for while the book was being printed at Venice he was travelling in Germany, France, Greece, and Turkey. However, John Antony Colet, who was a scholar as well as a printer, took great pains with the book, preparing the new type necessary to mark the critical signs, and transcribing from No. 454 the text of the Iliad which precedes the scholia. The omission of the accents is a source of much perplexity, since the notes of Herodian, dealing as they do principally with accentuation, are in their present state mere enigmas.

The remainder of the Prolegomena is a most garrulous account of Villoison's travels in Greece and Asia Minor during the printing of his book. It was no luxurious tour in his day, but a journey fraught with many dangers, from which he returned barely in time to write the preface we have been translating. Its style is unique ; it is a chaos of proper names, titles of books, figures of every kind, quotations in different languages, peculiar symbols, abbreviations, italics, Greek in uncial letters, parentheses, notes, digressions, and appendices. He sows with the whole sack ; pell-mell he scatters about his ideas on the Iliad, and on many other things quite unconnected with it. The Latin is excellent, but the sense of order and proportion is wanting. Villoison felt this himself, and puts forward as his best apology to the reader the fact that it could not be otherwise. How, he asks, could he write elegantly, when homeless and in a foreign land, having barely escaped a grave in the waters of the Aegean ; with life imperilled on land or sea, in country or in city, by burning houses, brigands, plague, and pirates, worn out by his travels and their unavoidable fatigues ?

III.

THE CRITICAL SIGNS.

τὰ παρατιθέμενα τοῖς Ὁμηρικοῖς στίχοις σημεῖα ἀναγκαῖον γνῶναι τοὺς ἐντυγχάνοντας.

διπλῆ ἀπερίστικτος (>—).   This is also called the διπλῆ καθαρὰ, and is used to mark a word which the poet uses but once, as ΚΡΗΓΥΟΝ in A. 106.   >— Μάντι κακῶν, οὐ πώποτέ μοι τὸ κρήγυον εἶπες· ἄπαξ γὰρ εἴρηται ; to mark an expression peculiar to Homer ; to confute the chorizontes ; for reference to notes, mythological, historical, grammatical, or literary ; to notes relating to Attic syntax ; to mark words with several meanings ; ἡ διπλῆ καθαρὰ ἢ ἀπερίστικτος παράκειται πρὸς τὴν ἄπαξ εἰρημένην λέξιν καὶ πρὸς τὴν τοῦ ποιητοῦ συνήθειαν, καὶ πρὸς τους λέγοντας μὴ εἶναι τοῦ αὐτοῦ ποιητοῦ Ἰλιάδα καὶ Ὀδύσσειαν, καὶ πρὸς τὰς τῶν παλαιῶν ἱστορίας καὶ σχηματισμοὺς, καὶ ἑτέρας ποικίλας χρείας, καὶ τὰ ἐναντία μαχόμενα τῶν νοημάτων.

ἡ δὲ περιεστιγμένη διπλῆ (>÷) is used to mark false readings of Zenodotus, Crates, and Aristarchus ; πρὸς τὰς Ζηνοδότου καὶ Κράτητος γραφὰς, καὶ αὐτοῦ Ἀριστάρχου.

ὁ δὲ ὀβελός (–) is used to mark the condemnation, or athetizing of verses as interpolated ; πρὸς τὰ νόθα καὶ ἀθετούμενα.

ὁ δὲ μετὰ ὀβελοῦ ἀστερίσκος (-※) is used to mark an interpolated verse wrongly borrowed from some other passage in the poems ; ἔνθα εἰσὶ μὲν τὰ ἔπη τοῦ ποιητοῦ, οὐ καλῶς δὲ κεῖνται, ἀλλ᾽ ἐν ἄλλῳ.

ὁ δὲ καθ᾽ αὑτὸν ἀστερίσκος (※) is used to mark verses which occur in two or more passages, but legitimately according

to the opinion of the critics. Of course such formulae as τὸν δ'
ἀπαμειβόμενος . . . are not marked: ἔνθα καλῶς εἴρηνται τὰ ἔπη ἐν
αὐτῷ τῷ τόπῳ ἔνθα κεῖνται.

τὸ δὲ καθ' αὑτὸ ἀντίσιγμα (ͻ) is used to mark an inverted
construction, or an anacoluthon ; πρὸς τοὺς ἐνηλλαγμένους τόπους
καὶ μὴ συνᾴδοντας ; as at B. 188, where the scholium is διὰ τὴν
τάξιν τῶν ἑξῆς, τὸ ἀντίσιγμα. So at v. 192, τὸ ἀντίσιγμα, ὅτι ὑπὸ
τούτων ἔδει τετάχθαι τοὺς ἑξῆς παρεστιγμένους τρεῖς στίχους· (203–
205) εἰσὶ γὰρ πρὸς βασιλεῖς ἁρμόζοντες, οὐ πρὸς δημότας· Οὐ μὲν
γάρ πως πάντες . . .

τὸ δὲ περιεστιγμένον ἀντίσιγμα (ͻ̣) is used to mark tauto-
logy ; ὅταν ταυτολογῇ καὶ τὴν αὐτὴν διάνοιαν δεύτερον λέγῃ ; as
at Θ. 535–540, where Pluygers' note is 'Antisigma apponebat
Aristarchus, quod in libris, quos ante oculos haberet, conjunctae
extarent quae eorumdem locorum in antiquis libris traditiones
essent diversae.'

ἡ δὲ κορωνίς (ꜜ) seems to have been used to mark the ending of a scene, or a transition from one to another. In the early
MSS. of the Iliad it was used to mark the end of each rhapsody,
that is to say, each division of the poem which had a separate
name, and was the subject of a recitation : ἰστέον ὅτι αἱ ῥαψῳδίαι
Ὁμήρου, παρὰ τῶν παλαιῶν, κατὰ συνάφειαν ᾔνωντο κορωνίδι μονῇ
διαστελλόμεναι, ἄλλῳ δὲ οὐδένι· τῆς δὲ κορωνίδος τοῦτό ἐστι τὸ
σημεῖον (ꜜ), λέγεται δὲ ἀπὸ μεταφορᾶς τῆς ἐν τοῖς πλοίοις ἀνα-
κεκαμμένης κορωνίδος.

Κεραύνιον (Τ) seems to have been used to obelize several
verses together. Aristarchus used to place the obel before each
verse, but later critics seem to have employed the ceraunion for
the sake of brevity. It consists of one obel, written horizontally
in the usual manner, and another vertically, of whatever length
may be required to cover all the spurious verses. It was not often
used (ἐστὶ μὲν τῶν σπανίως παρατιθεμένων).

We meet another sign in the Venetian mss., viz. Ϲ. This is a symbol used by the Byzantine grammarians to draw attention to any remarkable passage. It occurs at B. 203–205.

There is yet another sign ($\div$) which is affixed where Aristarchus was in doubt whether the passage was spurious or not; it may be called the demi-obel (Lehrs. v. 1, 9).

The κερέα α τοῦ α / is unexplained.

And so is the ω askew πλάγιον ⳍ.

INDEX.

Q

THE END.

DUBLIN : PRINTED AT THE UNIVERSITY PRESS.

DUBLIN UNIVERSITY PRESS SERIES.

THE PROVOST and SENIOR FELLOWS of Trinity College have undertaken the publication of a Series of Works, chiefly Educational, to be entitled the DUBLIN UNIVERSITY PRESS SERIES.

The following volumes of the Series are now ready, viz. :—

Six Lectures on Physical Geography. By the REV. S. HAUGHTON, M.D., Dubl., D.C.L., Oxon., F.R.S., *Fellow of Trinity College, and Professor of Geology in the University of Dublin.* 15s.

An Introduction to the Systematic Zoology and Morphology of Vertebrate Animals. By ALEXANDER MACALISTER, M.D., Dubl., *Professor of Comparative Anatomy in the University of Dublin.* 10s. 6d.

The Codex Rescriptus Dublinensis of St. Matthew's Gospel (Z). First Published by Dr. Barrett in 1801. A New Edition, Revised and Augmented. Also, Fragments of the Book of Isaiah, in the LXX. Version, from an Ancient Palimpsest, now first Published. Together with a newly discovered Fragment of the Codex Palatinus. By T. K. ABBOTT, B.D., *Fellow of Trinity College, and Professor of Biblical Greek in the University of Dublin.* With two Plates of Facsimiles. 21s.

The Parabola, Ellipse, and Hyperbola, treated Geometrically. By ROBERT WILLIAM GRIFFIN, A.M., LL.D., *Ex-Scholar, Trinity College, Dublin.* 6s.

An Introduction to Logic. By WILLIAM HENRY STANLEY MONCK, M.A., *Professor of Moral Philosophy in the University of Dublin.* 5s.

Essays in Political and Moral Philosophy. By T. E. CLIFFE LESLIE, Hon. LL.D., Dubl., *of Lincoln's Inn, Barrister-at-Law, late Examiner in Political Economy in the University of London, Professor of Jurisprudence and Political Economy in the Queen's University.*

The Correspondence of Cicero : a revised Text, with Notes and Prolegomena.—Vol. I., The Letters to the end of Cicero's Exile. By ROBERT Y. TYRRELL, M.A., *Fellow of Trinity College, and Regius Professor of Greek in the University of Dublin.* Second Edition. 12s.

Faust, from the German of Goethe. By THOMAS E. WEBB, LL.D., Q.C., *Regius Professor of Laws, and Public Orator in the University of Dublin.* 12s. 6d.

The Veil of Isis; a series of Essays on Idealism. By THOMAS E. WEBB, LL.D., Q.C., *Regius Professor of Laws, and Public Orator; sometime Fellow of Trinity College and Professor of Moral Philosophy in the University of Dublin.* 10s. 6d.

The Correspondence of Robert Southey with Caroline Bowles : to which are added — Correspondence with Shelley, and Southey's Dreams. Edited, with an Introduction, by EDWARD DOWDEN, LL.D., *Professor of English Literature in the University of Dublin.* 14s.

The Mathematical and other Tracts of the late James M'Cullagh, F.T.C.D., *Professor of Natural Philosophy in the University of Dublin.* Now first collected, and edited by REV. J. H. JELLETT, B.D., and REV. SAMUEL HAUGHTON, M.D., *Fellows of Trinity College, Dublin.* 15s.

[Over.

A Sequel to the First Six Books of the Elements of Euclid, containing an Easy Introduction to Modern Geometry. With numerous Examples. By JOHN CASEY, LL.D., F.R.S., *Vice-President, Royal Irish Academy; Member of the London Mathematical Society; and Professor of the Higher Mathematics and Mathematical Physics in the Catholic University of Ireland.* Third Edition, enlarged. 3s. 6d.

Theory of Equations : with an Introduction to the Theory of Binary Algebraic Forms. By WILLIAM SNOW BURNSIDE, M. A., *Erasmus Smith's Professor of Mathematics in the University of Dublin ;* and ARTHUR WILLIAM PANTON, M.A., *Fellow and Tutor, Trinity College, Dublin.*

The Parmenides of Plato : with Introduction, Analysis, and Notes. By THOMAS MAGUIRE, LL.D., D. LIT., *Fellow and Tutor, Trinity College, Dublin.* 7s. 6d.

The Medical Language of St. Luke : a Proof from Internal Evidence that "The Gospel according to St. Luke" and "The Acts of the Apostles" were written by the same Person, and that the writer was a Medical Man. By the REV. WILLIAM KIRK HOBART, LL.D., *Ex-Scholar, Trinity College, Dublin.* 16s.

Life of Sir Wm. Rowan Hamilton, Knt., LL.D., D.C.L., M.R.I.A., *Andrews Professor of Astronomy in the University of Dublin, and Royal Astronomer of Ireland, &c. &c.:* including Selections from his Poems, Correspondence, and Miscellaneous Writings. By ROBERT PERCEVAL GRAVES, M. A., *Sub-Dean of the Chapel Royal, Dublin, and formerly Curate in charge of Windermere.* Vol. I. (1882) ; Vol. II. (1885) ; each 15s.

Dublin Translations : Translations into Greek and Latin Verse, by Members of Trinity College, Dublin. Edited by ROBERT YELVERTON TYRRELL, M.A. Dublin, D. Lit. Q. Univ., *Fellow of Trinity College, and Regius Professor of Greek in the University of Dublin.* 12s. 6d.

The Acharnians of Aristophanes. Translated into English Verse by ROBERT YELVERTON TYRRELL, M.A. Dublin, D. Lit. Q. Univ., *Fellow of Trinity College, Dublin, and Regius Professor of Greek.* 2s. 6d.

Evangelia Antehieronymiana ex Codice vetusto Dublinensi. Ed. T. K. ABBOTT, B.D. 2 Vols. 20s.

The Eumenides of Æschylus : a Critical Edition, with Metrical English Translation. By JOHN F. DAVIES, M.A., Univ. Dubl., : D. Lit., Q.U.I. ; F.R.U.I. ; *Professor of Latin in the Queen's College, Galway.* Demy 8vo. 7s.

The Homeric Question. By GEORGE WILKINS, B.A., *Ex-Scholar, Trinity College, Dublin.* Demy 8vo.

A Treatise on the Analytical Geometry of the Point, Line, Circle, and the Conic Sections, containing an account of its most recent extensions. By JOHN CASEY, LL.D., F.R.S., F.R.U.I., *Member of the Council of the Royal Irish Academy, and of the Mathematical Societies of London and France; and Professor of the Higher Mathematics and Mathematical Physics in the Catholic University of Ireland.* Crown 8vo, cloth. 6s.

In the Press:—

The Æneid of Virgil, translated into English blank verse. By REV. CANON THORNHILL, B.A., *Ex-Scholar, Trinity College, Dublin.* Crown 8vo.

DUBLIN : HODGES, FIGGIS, AND CO.

LONDON : LONGMANS, GREEN, AND CO.

A CATALOGUE OF
WORKS IN GENERAL LITERATURE & SCIENCE
PUBLISHED BY
MESSRS. LONGMANS, GREEN, & CO.
39 PATERNOSTER ROW, LONDON, E.C.

Classified Index.

A

A Catalogue of Works

PUBLISHED BY

MESSRS. LONGMANS, GREEN, & CO.

39 PATERNOSTER ROW, LONDON, E.C.

ABBOTT. — *THE ELEMENTS OF LOGIC.* By T. K. ABBOTT, B.D. 12mo. 2s. 6d. sewed, or 3s. cloth.

ACTON. — *MODERN COOKERY FOR PRIVATE FAMILIES,* reduced to a System of Easy Practice in a Series of carefully tested Receipts. By ELIZA ACTON. With upwards of 150 Woodcuts. Fcp. 8vo. 4s. 6d.

ÆSCHYLUS. — *THE EUMENIDES OF ÆSCHYLUS:* a Critical Edition, with Metrical English Translation. By JOHN F. DAVIES, M.A. Univ. Dub. Lit. D. Q.U.I. F.R.U.I. Professor of Latin in the Queen's College, Galway. 8vo. 7s.

A. K. H. B. — *THE ESSAYS AND CONTRIBUTIONS OF A. K. H. B.* — Uniform Cabinet Editions in crown 8vo.

Autumn Holidays of a Country Parson, 3s. 6d.

Changed Aspects of Unchanged Truths, 3s. 6d.

Commonplace Philosopher, 3s. 6d.

Counsel and Comfort from a City Pulpit, 3s. 6d.

Critical Essays of a Country Parson, 3s. 6d.

Graver Thoughts of a Country Parson. Three Series, 3s. 6d. each.

Landscapes, Churches, and Moralities, 3s. 6d.

Leisure Hours in Town, 3s. 6d.

Lessons of Middle Age, 3s. 6d.

Our Little Life. Two Series, 3s. 6d. each.

Present Day Thoughts, 3s. 6d.

Recreations of a Country Parson. Three Series, 3s. 6d. each.

Seaside Musings, 3s. 6d.

Sunday Afternoons in the Parish Church of a University City, 3s. 6d.

ALDRIDGE. — *RANCH NOTES IN KANSAS, COLORADO, THE INDIAN TERRITORY AND NORTHERN TEXAS.* By REGINALD ALDRIDGE. Crown 8vo. with 4 Illustrations engraved on Wood by G. Pearson, 5s.

ALLEN. — *FLOWERS AND THEIR PEDIGREES.* By GRANT ALLEN. With 50 Illustrations engraved on Wood. Crown 8vo. 7s. 6d.

ALPINE CLUB (The). — *GUIDES AND MAPS.*

THE ALPINE GUIDE. By JOHN BALL, M.R.I.A. Post 8vo. with Maps and other Illustrations :—

THE EASTERN ALPS, 10s. 6d.

CENTRAL ALPS, including all the Oberland District, 7s. 6d.

WESTERN ALPS, including Mont Blanc, Monte Rosa, Zermatt, &c. 6s. 6d.

THE ALPINE CLUB MAP OF SWITZERLAND, on the Scale of Four Miles to an Inch. Edited by R. C. NICHOLS, F.R.G.S. 4 Sheets in Portfolio, 42s. coloured, or 34s. uncoloured.

ENLARGED ALPINE CLUB MAP OF THE SWISS AND ITALIAN ALPS, on the Scale of Three English Statute Miles to One Inch, in 8 Sheets, price 1s. 6d. each.

ON ALPINE TRAVELLING AND THE GEOLOGY OF THE ALPS. Price 1s. Either of the Three Volumes or Parts of the 'Alpine Guide' may be had with this Introduction prefixed, 1s. extra.

AMOS. — *WORKS BY SHELDON AMOS, M.A.*

A PRIMER OF THE ENGLISH CONSTITUTION AND GOVERNMENT. Crown 8vo. 6s.

A SYSTEMATIC VIEW OF THE SCIENCE OF JURISPRUDENCE. 8vo. 18s.

FIFTY YEARS OF THE ENGLISH CONSTITUTION, 1830–1880. Crown 8vo. 10s. 6d.

ANSTEY.—*THE BLACK POODLE*, and other Stories. By F. ANSTEY, Author of 'Vice Versâ.' With Frontispiece by G. Du Maurier and Initial Letters by the Author. Crown 8vo. 6*s.*

ANTINOUS.—An Historical Romance of the Roman Empire. By GEORGE TAYLOR (Professor HAUSRATH). Translated from the German by J. D. M. Crown 8vo. 6*s.*

ARISTOPHANES. — *THE ACHARNIANS OF ARISTOPHANES.* Translated into English Verse by ROBERT YELVERTON TYRRELL, M.A. Dublin. Crown 8vo. 2*s.* 6*d.*

ARISTOTLE.—*THE WORKS OF.*

THE POLITICS, G. Bekker's Greek Text of Books I. III. IV. (VII.) with an English Translation by W. E. BOLLAND, M.A. ; and short Introductory Essays by A. LANG, M.A. Crown 8vo. 7*s.* 6*d.*

THE ETHICS ; Greek Text, illustrated with Essays and Notes. By Sir ALEXANDER GRANT, Bart. M.A. LL.D. 2 vols. 8vo. 32*s.*

THE NICOMACHEAN ETHICS, Newly Translated into English. By ROBERT WILLIAMS, Barrister-at-Law. Crown 8vo. 7*s.* 6*d.*

ARNOLD. — *WORKS BY THOMAS ARNOLD, D.D. Late Head-master of Rugby School.*

INTRODUCTORY LECTURES ON MODERN HISTORY, delivered in 1841 and 1842. 8vo. 7*s.* 6*d.*

SERMONS PREACHED MOSTLY IN THE CHAPEL OF RUGBY SCHOOL. 6 vols. crown 8vo. 30*s.* or separately, 5*s.* each.

MISCELLANEOUS WORKS. 8vo. 7*s.* 6*d.*

ARNOLD. — *WORKS BY THOMAS ARNOLD, M.A.*

A MANUAL OF ENGLISH LITERATURE, Historical and Critical. By THOMAS ARNOLD, M.A. Crown 8vo. 7*s.* 6*d.*

ENGLISH POETRY AND PROSE : a Collection of Illustrative Passages from the Writings of English Authors, from the Anglo-Saxon Period to the Present Time. Crown 8vo. 6*s.*

ARNOTT.—*THE ELEMENTS OF PHYSICS OR NATURAL PHILOSOPHY.* By NEIL ARNOTT, M.D. Edited by A. BAIN, LL.D. and A. S. TAYLOR, M.D. F.R.S. Woodcuts. Crown 8vo. 12*s.* 6*d.*

ASHBY. — *NOTES ON PHYSIOLOGY FOR THE USE OF STUDENTS PREPARING FOR EXAMINATION.* With 120 Woodcuts. By HENRY ASHBY, M.D. Lond., Physician to the General Hospital for Sick Children, Manchester. Fcp. 8vo. 5*s.*

AYRE. —*THE TREASURY OF BIBLE KNOWLEDGE ;* being a Dictionary of the Books, Persons, Places, Events, and other matters of which mention is made in Holy Scripture. By the Rev. J. AYRE, M.A. With 5 Maps, 15 Plates, and 300 Woodcuts. Fcp. 8vo. 6*s.*

BACON.—*THE WORKS AND LIFE OF.*

COMPLETE WORKS. Collected and Edited by R. L. ELLIS, M.A. J. SPEDDING, M.A. and D. D. HEATH. 7 vols. 8vo. £3. 13*s.* 6*d.*

LETTERS AND LIFE, INCLUDING ALL HIS OCCASIONAL WORKS. Collected and Edited, with a Commentary, by J. SPEDDING. 7 vols. 8vo. £4. 4*s.*

THE ESSAYS ; with Annotations. By RICHARD WHATELY, D.D., sometime Archbishop of Dublin. 8vo. 10*s.* 6*d.*

THE ESSAYS ; with Introduction, Notes, and Index. By E. A. ABBOTT, D.D. 2 vols. fcp. 8vo. price 6*s.* The Text and Index only, without Introduction and Notes, in 1 vol. fcp. 8vo. price 2*s.* 6*d.*

THE ESSAYS ; with Critical and Illustrative Notes, and other Aids for Students. By the Rev. JOHN HUNTER, M.A. Crown 8vo. 3*s.* 6*d.*

THE PROMUS OF FORMULARIES AND ELEGANCIES, illustrated by Passages from SHAKESPEARE. By Mrs. H. POTT. Preface by E. A. ABBOTT, D.D. 8vo. 16*s.*

BAGEHOT. — *WORKS BY WALTER BAGEHOT, M.A.*

BIOGRAPHICAL STUDIES. 8vo. 12*s.*

ECONOMIC STUDIES. 8vo. 10*s.* 6*d.*

LITERARY STUDIES. 2 vols. 8vo. Portrait. 28*s.*

BAILEY. — *FESTUS, A POEM.* By PHILIP JAMES BAILEY. Crown 8vo. 12*s.* 6*d.*

BAKER.—*WORKS BY SIR SAMUEL W. BAKER, M.A.*

EIGHT YEARS IN CEYLON. Crown 8vo. Woodcuts. 5*s.*

THE RIFLE AND THE HOUND IN CEYLON. Crown 8vo. Woodcuts. 5*s.*

BAIN. — *WORKS BY ALEXANDER BAIN, LL.D.*

MENTAL AND MORAL SCIENCE; a Compendium of Psychology and Ethics. Crown 8vo. 10s. 6d.

THE SENSES AND THE INTELLECT. 8vo. 15s.

THE EMOTIONS AND THE WILL. 8vo. 15s.

PRACTICAL ESSAYS. Crown 8vo. 4s. 6d.

LOGIC, DEDUCTIVE AND INDUCTIVE. PART I. *Deduction,* 4s. PART II. *Induction,* 6s. 6d.

JAMES MILL; a Biography. Crown 8vo. 5s.

JOHN STUART MILL; a Criticism, with Personal Recollections. Crown 8vo. 2s. 6d.

⁎⁎⁎ For other works, see p. 25.

BEACONSFIELD. — *WORKS BY THE EARL OF BEACONSFIELD, K.G.*

NOVELS AND TALES. The Hughenden Edition. With 2 Portraits and 11 Vignettes. 11 vols. Crown 8vo. 42s.

Endymion.

Lothair.	Henrietta Temple.
Coningsby.	Contarini Fleming, &c.
Sybil.	Alroy, Ixion, &c.
Tancred	The Young Duke, &c.
Venetia.	Vivian Grey, &c.

NOVELS AND TALES. Modern Novelist's Library Edition, complete in 11 vols. Crown 8vo. 22s. boards, or 27s. 6d. cloth.

SELECTED SPEECHES. With Introduction and Notes, by T. E. KEBBEL, M.A. 2 vols. 8vo. Portrait, 32s.

THE WIT AND WISDOM OF BENJAMIN DISRAELI, EARL OF BEACONSFIELD. Crown 8vo. 3s. 6d.

THE BEACONSFIELD BIRTHDAY-BOOK: Selected from the Writings and Speeches of the Right Hon. the Earl of Beaconsfield, K.G. With 2 Portraits and 11 Views of Hughenden Manor and its Surroundings. 18mo. 2s. 6d. cloth, gilt; 4s. 6d. bound.

BECKER. — *WORKS BY PROFESSOR BECKER, translated from the German by the Rev. F. METCALF.*

GALLUS; or, Roman Scenes in the Time of Augustus. Post 8vo. 7s. 6d.

CHARICLES; or, Illustrations of the Private Life of the Ancient Greeks. Post 8vo. 7s. 6d.

BENT. — *THE CYCLADES;* or, Life among the Insular Greeks. By J. THEODORE BENT, B.A. Oxon; with Map. Crown 8vo. 12s. 6d.

BLACKLEY & FRIEDLÄNDER. — *A PRACTICAL DICTIONARY OF THE GERMAN AND ENGLISH LANGUAGES:* By the Rev. W. L. BLACKLEY, M.A. and C. M. FRIEDLÄNDER, Ph.D. Post 8vo. 3s. 6d.

BOULTBEE. — *WORKS BY THE REV. T. P. BOULTBEE, LL.D.*

A COMMENTARY ON THE 39 ARTICLES of the Church of England. Crown 8vo. 6s.

A HISTORY OF THE CHURCH OF ENGLAND; Pre-Reformation Period. 8vo. 15s.

BOURNE. — *WORKS BY JOHN BOURNE, C.E.*

A TREATISE ON THE STEAM ENGINE, in its application to Mines, Mills, Steam Navigation, Railways, and Agriculture. With 37 Plates and 546 Woodcuts. 4to. 42s.

CATECHISM OF THE STEAM ENGINE, in its various Applications to Mines, Mills, Steam Navigation, Railways, and Agriculture. With 89 Woodcuts. Crown 8vo. 7s. 6d.

HANDBOOK OF THE STEAM ENGINE, a Key to the Author's Catechism of the Steam Engine. With 67 Woodcuts. Fcp. 8vo. 9s.

RECENT IMPROVEMENTS IN THE STEAM ENGINE. With 124 Woodcuts. Fcp. 8vo. 6s.

EXAMPLES OF STEAM AND GAS ENGINES, with 54 Plates and 356 Woodcuts. 4to. 70s.

BRAMSTON & LEROY. — *HISTORIC WINCHESTER;* England's First Capital. By A. R. BRAMSTON and A. C. LEROY. Cr. 8vo. 6s.

BRANDE'S *DICTIONARY OF SCIENCE, LITERATURE, AND ART.* Re-edited by the Rev. Sir G. W. COX, Bart., M.A. 3 vols. medium 8vo. 63s.

BRASSEY. — *WORKS BY LADY BRASSEY.*

A VOYAGE IN THE 'SUNBEAM,' OUR HOME ON THE OCEAN FOR ELEVEN MONTHS. By Lady BRASSEY. With Map and 65 Wood Engravings. Library Edition, 8vo. 21s. Cabinet Edition, crown 8vo. 7s. 6d. School Edition, fcp. 2s. Popular Edition, 4to. 6d.

[Continued on next page.

BRASSEY. — *Works by Lady Brassey*—continued.

Sunshine and Storm in the East; or, Cruises to Cyprus and Constantinople. With 2 Maps and 114 Illustrations engraved on Wood. Library Edition, 8vo. 21s. Cabinet Edition, cr. 8vo. 7s. 6d.

In the Trades, the Tropics, and the 'Roaring Forties'; or, Fourteen Thousand Miles in the *Sunbeam* in 1883. By Lady Brassey. With 292 Illustrations engraved on Wood from drawings by R. T. Pritchett, and Eight Maps and Charts. Edition de Luxe, imperial 8vo. £3. 13s. 6d. Library Edition, 8vo. 21s.

BRAY.—*Phases of Opinion and Experience during a Long Life:* an Autobiography. By Charles Bray, Author of 'The Philosophy of Necessity' &c. Crown 8vo. 3s. 6d.

BROWNE.—*An Exposition of the 39 Articles,* Historical and Doctrinal. By E. H. Browne, D.D., Bishop of Winchester. 8vo. 16s.

BUCKLE.—*History of Civilisation in England and France, Spain and Scotland.* By Henry Thomas Buckle. 3 vols. crown 8vo. 24s.

BUCKTON.—*Works by Mrs. C. M. Buckton.*

Food and Home Cookery; a Course of Instruction in Practical Cookery and Cleaning. With 11 Woodcuts. Crown 8vo. 2s. 6d.

Health in the House: Twenty-five Lectures on Elementary Physiology. With 41 Woodcuts and Diagrams. Crown 8vo. 2s.

Our Dwellings: Healthy and Unhealthy. With 39 Illustrations. Crown 8vo. 3s. 6d.

BULL.—*Works by Thomas Bull, M.D.*

Hints to Mothers on the Management of their Health during the Period of Pregnancy and in the Lying-in Room. Fcp. 8vo. 1s. 6d.

The Maternal Management of Children in Health and Disease. Fcp. 8vo. 1s. 6d.

CABINET LAWYER, The; a Popular Digest of the Laws of England, Civil, Criminal, and Constitutional. Fcp. 8vo. 9s.

CALVERT.—*The Wife's Manual;* or Prayers, Thoughts, and Songs on Several Occasions of a Matron's Life. By the late W. Calvert, Minor Canon of St. Paul's. Crown 8vo. 6s.

CARLYLE. — *Thomas and Jane Welsh Carlyle.*

Thomas Carlyle, a History of the first Forty Years of his Life, 1795–1835 By J. A. Froude, M.A. With 2 Portraits and 4 Illustrations, 2 vols. 8vo. 32s.

Thomas Carlyle, a History of his Life in London : from 1834 to his death in 1881. By James A. Froude, M.A., with Portrait engraved on steel. 2 vols. 8vo. 32s.

Letters and Memorials of Jane Welsh Carlyle. Prepared for publication by Thomas Carlyle, and edited by J. A. Froude, M.A. 3 vols. 8vo. 36s.

CATES. — *A Dictionary of General Biography.* Fourth Edition, with Supplement brought down to the end of 1884. By W. L. R. Cates. 8vo. 28s. cloth ; 35s. half-bound russia. The Supplement, 1881-4, 2s. 6d.

CHESNEY.—*Waterloo Lectures;* a Study of the Campaign of 1815. By Col. C. C. Chesney, R.E. 8vo. 10s. 6d.

CICERO.—*The Correspondence of Cicero:* a revised Text, with Notes and Prolegomena.—Vol. I., The Letters to the end of Cicero's Exile. By Robert Y. Tyrrell, M.A., Fellow of Trinity College, Dublin, 12s.

COATS.—*A Manual of Pathology.* By Joseph Coats, M.D. Pathologist to the Western Infirmary and the Sick Children's Hospital, Glasgow. With 339 Illustrations engraved on Wood. 8vo. 31s. 6d.

COLENSO.—*The Pentateuch and Book of Joshua Critically Examined.* By J. W. Colenso, D.D., late Bishop of Natal. Crown 8vo. 6s.

CONDER.—*A Handbook to the Bible,* or Guide to the Study of the Holy Scriptures derived from Ancient Monuments and Modern Exploration. By F. R. Conder, and Lieut. C. R. Conder, R.E. Post 8vo. 7s. 6d.

CONINGTON. — *Works by John Conington, M.A.*

The Æneid of Virgil. Translated into English Verse. Crown 8vo. 9s.

The Poems of Virgil. Translated into English Prose. Crown 8vo. 9s.

CONTANSEAU.—*Works by Professor Léon Contanseau.*

A Practical Dictionary of the French and English Languages. Post 8vo. 3s. 6d.

A Pocket Dictionary of the French and English Languages; being a careful Abridgment of the Author's 'Practical French and English Dictionary.' Square 18mo. 1s. 6d.

CONYBEARE & HOWSON.—*The Life and Epistles of St. Paul.* By the Rev. W. J. Conybeare, M.A., and the Very Rev. J. S. Howson, D.D. Dean of Chester.

Library Edition, with all the Original Illustrations, Maps, Landscapes on Steel, Woodcuts, &c. 2 vols. 4to. 42s.

Intermediate Edition, with a Selection of Maps, Plates, and Wood cuts. 2 vols. square crown 8vo. 21s.

Student's Edition, revised and condensed, with 46 Illustrations and Maps. 1 vol. crown 8vo. 7s. 6d.

COOKE.—*Tablets of Anatomy.* By Thomas Cooke, F.R.C.S. Eng. B.A. B.Sc. M.D. Paris, Senior Assistant Surgeon to the Westminster Hospital, and Lecturer at the School of Anatomy, Physiology, and Surgery. Being a Synopsis of Demonstrations given in the Westminster Hospital Medical School in the years 1871-75. Fourth Edition, being a selection of the Tablets believed to be most useful to Students generally. Post 4to. 7s. 6d.

COX.—*Works by the Rev. Sir G. W. Cox, Bart., M.A.*

A General History of Greece: from the Earliest Period to the Death of Alexander the Great; with a Sketch of the Subsequent History to the Present Time. With 11 Maps and Plans. Crown 8vo. 7s. 6d.

Lives of Greek Statesmen. Solon-Themistocles. Fcp. 8vo. 2s. 6d.

CRAWFORD.—*Across the Pampas and the Andes.* By Robert Crawford, M.A. With Map and 7 Illustrations. Crown 8vo. 7s. 6d.

CREIGHTON.—*History of the Papacy During the Reformation.* By the Rev. M. Creighton, M.A. Vols. I. and II. 8vo. 32s.

CROZIER.—*Civilization and Progress;* being the Outline of a New System of Political, Religious, and Social Philosophy. By J. Beattie Crozier. 8vo. 14s.

CULLEY.—*Handbook of Practical Telegraphy.* By R. S. Culley, M. Inst. C.E. Plates and Woodcuts. 8vo. 16s.

DANTE.—*The Divine Comedy of Dante Alighieri.* Translated verse for verse from the Original into Terza Rima. By James Innes Minchin. Cr. 8vo. 15s.

DAVIDSON.—*An Introduction to the Study of the New Testament* Critical, Exegetical, and Theological. By the Rev. S. Davidson, D.D. LL.D. Revised Edition. 2 vols. 8vo. 30s.

DAVIDSON.—*The Logic of Definition Explained and Applied.* By William L. Davidson, M.A. Crown 8vo. 6s.

DEAD SHOT, The, *or Sportsman's Complete Guide;* a Treatise on the Use of the Gun, with Lessons in the Art of Shooting Game of all kinds, and Wild-Fowl, also Pigeon-Shooting, and Dog-Breaking. By Marksman. With 13 Illustrations. Crown 8vo. 10s. 6d.

DECAISNE & LE MAOUT.—*A General System of Botany.* Translated from the French of E. Le Maout M.D., and J. Decaisne, by Lady Hooker; with Additions by Sir J. D. Hooker, C.B. F.R.S. Imp. 8vo. with 5,500 Woodcuts. 31s. 6d.

DENT.—*Above the Snow Line.* Mountaineering Sketches between 1870 and 1880. By Clinton Dent, Vice President of the Alpine Club. With Two Engravings by Edward Whymper and an Illustration by Percy Macquoid. Crown 8vo. 7s. 6d.

D'EON DE BEAUMONT.—*The Strange Career of the Chevalier D'Eon de Beaumont,* Minister Plenipotentiary from France to Great Britain in 1763. By Captain J. Buchan Telfer, R.N. F.S.A. F.R.G.S. With 3 Portraits. 8vo. 12s.

DE TOCQUEVILLE.—*Democracy in America.* By Alexis de Tocqueville. Translated by H. Reeve, C.B. 2 vols. crown 8vo. 16s.

DEWES.—*The Life and Letters of St. Paul.* By Alfred Dewes, M.A. LL.D. D.D. Vicar of St. Augustine's, Pendlebury. With 4 Maps. 8vo. 7s. 6d.

DICKINSON. — *ON RENAL AND URINARY AFFECTIONS.* By W. HOWSHIP DICKINSON, M.D. Cantab. F.R.C.P. &c. With 12 Plates and 122 Woodcuts. 3 vols. 8vo. £3. 4s. 6d.

*** The Three Parts may be had separately: PART I.—*Diabetes*, 10s. 6d. sewed, 12s. cloth. PART II. *Albuminuria*, 20s. sewed, 21s. cloth. PART III.—*Miscellaneous Affections of the Kidneys and Urine*, 30s. sewed, 31s. 6d. cloth.

DIXON.—*RURAL BIRD LIFE;* Essays on Ornithology, with Instructions for Preserving Objects relating to that Science. By CHARLES DIXON. With 45 Woodcuts. Crown 8vo. 5s.

DOWELL.—*A HISTORY OF TAXATION AND TAXES IN ENGLAND, FROM THE EARLIEST TIMES TO THE PRESENT DAY.* By STEPHEN DOWELL, Assistant Solicitor of Inland Revenue. 4 vols. 8vo. 48s.

DOYLE.—*THE ENGLISH IN AMERICA;* Virginia, Maryland, and the Carolinas. By J. A. DOYLE, Fellow of All Souls' College, Oxford. 8vo. Map, 18s.

DRESSER.—*JAPAN; ITS ARCHITECTURE, ART, AND ART MANUFACTURES.* By CHRISTOPHER DRESSER, Ph.D. F.L.S. &c. With 202 Illustrations. Square crown 8vo. 31s. 6d.

DUNSTER. — *HOW TO MAKE THE LAND PAY;* or, Profitable Industries connected with the Land, and suitable to all Occupations, Large or Small. By HENRY P. DUNSTER, M.A. Vicar of Wood-Bastwick, Norfolk. Crown 8vo. 5s.

EASTLAKE.—*FIVE GREAT PAINTERS;* Essays on Leonardo da Vinci, Michael Angelo, Titian, Raphael, Albert Dürer. By LADY EASTLAKE. 2 vols. Crown 8vo. 16s.

EASTLAKE.—*WORKS BY C. L. EASTLAKE, F.R.S. B.A.*

HINTS ON HOUSEHOLD TASTE IN FURNITURE, UPHOLSTERY, &c. With 100 Illustrations. Square crown 8vo. 14s.

NOTES ON FOREIGN PICTURE GALLERIES. Crown 8vo.

The Louvre Gallery, *Paris*, with 114 Illustrations, 7s. 6d.
The Brera Gallery, *Milan*, with 55 Illustrations, 5s.
The Old Pinakothek, *Munich*, with 107 Illustrations, 7s. 6d.

EDERSHEIM.—*WORKS BY THE REV. ALFRED EDERSHEIM, D.D.*

THE LIFE AND TIMES OF JESUS THE MESSIAH. 2 vols. 8vo. 42s.

PROPHECY AND HISTORY IN RELATION TO THE MESSIAH: the Warburton Lectures, delivered at Lincoln's Inn Chapel, 1880-1884. 8vo. 12s.

EDWARDS.—*OUR SEAMARKS.* By E. PRICE EDWARDS. With numerous Illustrations of Lighthouses, &c. engraved on Wood by G. H. Ford. Crown 8vo. 8s. 6d.

ELLICOTT. — *WORKS BY C. J. ELLICOTT, D.D.,* Bishop of Gloucester and Bristol.

A CRITICAL AND GRAMMATICAL COMMENTARY ON ST. PAUL'S EPISTLES. 8vo. Galatians, 8s. 6d. Ephesians, 8s. 6d. Pastoral Epistles, 10s. 6d. Philippians, Colossians, and Philemon, 10s. 6d. Thessalonians, 7s. 6d. I. Corinthians. [*Nearly ready.*

HISTORICAL LECTURES ON THE LIFE OF OUR LORD JESUS CHRIST. 8vo. 12s.

EPOCHS OF ANCIENT HISTORY.
Edited by the Rev. Sir G. W. Cox, Bart. M.A. and C. SANKEY, M.A.
Beesly's Gracchi, Marius and Sulla, 2s. 6d.
Capes's Age of the Antonines, 2s. 6d.
———— Early Roman Empire, 2s. 6d.
Cox's Athenian Empire, 2s. 6d.
———— Greeks and Persians, 2s. 6d.
Curteis's Macedonian Empire, 2s. 6d.
Ihne's Rome to its Capture by the Gauls, 2s. 6d.
Merivale's Roman Triumvirates, 2s. 6d.
Sankey's Spartan and Theban Supremacies, 2s. 6d.
Smith's Rome and Carthage, 2s. 6d.

EPOCHS OF MODERN HISTORY.
Edited by C. COLBECK, M.A.
Church's Beginning of the Middle Ages, 2s. 6d.
Cox's Crusades, 2s. 6d.
Creighton's Age of Elizabeth, 2s. 6d.
Gairdner's Lancaster and York, 2s. 6d.
Gardiner's Puritan Revolution, 2s. 6d.
———— Thirty Years' War, 2s. 6d.
———— (Mrs.) French Revolution, 2s. 6d.
Hale's Fall of the Stuarts, 2s. 6d.
Johnson's Normans in Europe, 2s. 6d.
Longman's Frederick the Great, 2s. 6d.
Ludlow's War of American Independence, 2s. 6d.
M'Carthy's Epoch of Reform, 1830-1850, 2s. 6d.
Morris's Age of Anne, 2s. 6d.
Seebohm's Protestant Revolution, 2s. 6d.
Stubbs' Early Plantagenets, 2s. 6d.
Warburton's Edward III, 2s. 6d.

ERICHSEN.—*WORKS BY JOHN ERIC ERICHSEN, F.R.S.*

THE SCIENCE AND ART OF SURGERY: Being a Treatise on Surgical Injuries, Diseases, and Operations. Illustrated by Engravings on Wood. 2 vols. 8vo. 42s. ; or bound in half-russia, 60s.

ON CONCUSSION OF THE SPINE, NERVOUS SHOCKS, and other Obscure Injuries of the Nervous System in their Clinical and Medico-Legal Aspects. Crown 8vo, 10s. 6d.

EVANS.—*THE BRONZE IMPLEMENTS, ARMS, AND ORNAMENTS OF GREAT BRITAIN AND IRELAND.* By JOHN EVANS, D.C.L. LL.D. F.R.S. With 540 Illustrations. 8vo. 25s.

EWALD.—*WORKS BY PROFESSOR HEINRICH EWALD, of Göttingen.*

THE ANTIQUITIES OF ISRAEL. Translated from the German by H. S. SOLLY, M.A. 8vo. 12s. 6d.

THE HISTORY OF ISRAEL. Translated from the German. Vols. I.–V. 8vo. 63s. Vol. VI. *Christ and his Times,* 8vo. 16s. Vol. VII. *The Apostolic Age,* 8vo. 21s.

FAIRBAIRN.—*WORKS BY SIR W. FAIRBAIRN, BART, C.E.*

A TREATISE ON MILLS AND MILLWORK, with 18 Plates and 333 Woodcuts. 1 vol. 8vo, 25s.

USEFUL INFORMATION FOR ENGINEERS. With many Plates and Woodcuts. 3 vols. crown 8vo. 31s. 6d.

FARRAR.—*LANGUAGE AND LANGUAGES.* A Revised Edition of *Chapters on Language and Families of Speech.* By F. W FARRAR, D.D. Crown 8vo, 6s.

FITZWYGRAM. — *HORSES AND STABLES.* By Major-General Sir F. FITZWYGRAM, Bart. With 39 pages of Illustrations. 8vo. 10s. 6d.

FOX.—*THE EARLY HISTORY OF CHARLES JAMES FOX.* By the Right Hon. G. O. TREVELYAN, M.P. Library Edition, 8vo. 18s. Cabinet Edition, cr. 8vo, 6s.

FRANCIS.—*A BOOK ON ANGLING ;* or, Treatise on the Art of Fishing in every branch ; including full Illustrated Lists of Salmon Flies. By FRANCIS FRANCIS. Post 8vo. Portrait and Plates, 15s.

FREEMAN.—*THE HISTORICAL GEOGRAPHY OF EUROPE.* By E. A. FREEMAN, D.C.L. With 65 Maps. 2 vols. 8vo. 31s. 6d.

FRENCH. — *NINETEEN CENTURIES OF DRINK IN ENGLAND,* a History. By RICHARD VALPY FRENCH, D.C.L. LL.D. F.S.A. ; Author of ' The History of Toasting ' &c. Crown 8vo, 10s. 6d.

FROUDE.—*WORKS BY JAMES A. FROUDE, M.A.*

THE HISTORY OF ENGLAND, from the Fall of Wolsey to the Defeat of the Spanish Armada.
Cabinet Edition, 12 vols. cr. 8vo. £3. 12s.
Popular Edition, 12 vols. cr. 8vo. £2. 2s.

SHORT STUDIES ON GREAT SUBJECTS. 4 vols. crown 8vo, 24s.

THE ENGLISH IN IRELAND IN THE EIGHTEENTH CENTURY. 3 vols. crown 8vo, 18s.

THOMAS CARLYLE, a History of the first Forty Years of his Life, 1795 to 1835. 2 vols. 8vo, 32s.

THOMAS CARLYLE, a History of His Life in London from 1834 to his death in 1881. By JAMES A. FROUDE, M.A. with Portrait engraved on steel. 2 vols. 8vo, 32s.

GANOT.—*WORKS BY PROFESSOR GANOT.* Translated by E. ATKINSON, Ph.D. F.C.S.

ELEMENTARY TREATISE ON PHYSICS, for the use of Colleges and Schools. With 5 Coloured Plates and 898 Woodcuts. Large crown 8vo, 15s.

NATURAL PHILOSOPHY FOR GENERAL READERS AND YOUNG PERSONS. With 2 Plates and 471 Woodcuts. Crown 8vo, 7s. 6d.

GARDINER.—*WORKS BY SAMUEL RAWSON GARDINER, LL.D.*

HISTORY OF ENGLAND, from the Accession of James I. to the Outbreak of the Civil War, 1603–1642. Cabinet Edition, thoroughly revised. 10 vols. crown 8vo, price 6s. each.

OUTLINE OF ENGLISH HISTORY, B.C. 55–A.D. 1880. With 96 Woodcuts. fcp. 8vo. 2s. 6d.

** For Professor Gardiner's other Works, see ' Epochs of Modern History,' p. 9.

GARROD. — *WORKS BY ALFRED BARING GARROD, M.D. F.R.S.*

A TREATISE ON GOUT AND RHEU-MATIC GOUT (*RHEUMATOID ARTHRITIS*). With 6 Plates, comprising 21 Figures (14 Coloured), and 27 Illustrations engraved on Wood   8vo. 21s.

THE ESSENTIALS OF MATERIA MEDICA AND THERAPEUTICS. Revised and edited, under the supervision of the Author, by E. B. BAXTER, M.D, F.R.C.P. Professor of Materia Medica and Therapeutics in King's College, London. Crown 8vo. 12s. 6d.

GOETHE.—*FAUST.* Translated by T. E. WEBB, LL.D. Reg. Prof. of Laws and Public Orator in the Univ. of Dublin. 8vo. 12s. 6d.

FAUST. A New Translation, chiefly in Blank Verse ; with a complete Introduction and Copious Notes. By JAMES ADEY BIRDS, B.A. F.G.S. Large crown 8vo. 12s. 6d.

FAUST. The German Text, with an English Introduction and Notes for Students. By ALBERT M. SELSS, M.A. Ph.D. Crown 8vo. 5s.

GOODEVE.— *WORKS BY T. M. GOODEVE, M.A.*

PRINCIPLES OF MECHANICS. With 253 Woodcuts. Crown 8vo. 6s.

THE ELEMENTS OF MECHANISM. With 342 Woodcuts. Crown 8vo. 6s.

GRANT.— *WORKS BY SIR ALEXANDER GRANT, BART. LL.D. D.C.L. &c.*

THE STORY OF THE UNIVERSITY OF EDINBURGH during its First Three Hundred Years. With numerous Illustrations. 2 vols. 8vo. 36s.

THE ETHICS OF ARISTOTLE. The Greek Text illustrated by Essays and Notes. 2 vols. 8vo. 32s.

GRAY. — *ANATOMY, DESCRIPTIVE AND SURGICAL.* By HENRY GRAY, F.R.S. late Lecturer on Anatomy at St. George's Hospital. With 557 large Woodcut Illustrations. Re-edited by T. PICKERING PICK, Surgeon to St. George's Hospital. Royal 8vo. 30s.

GREEN.—*THE WORKS OF THOMAS HILL GREEN,* late Fellow of Balliol College, and Whyte's Professor of Moral Philosophy in the University of Oxford. Edited by R. L. NETTLESHIP, Fellow of Balliol College, Oxford. In 3 vols. Vol. I.—Philosophical Works, 8vo. 16s.

GREVILLE. — *JOURNAL OF THE REIGNS OF KING GEORGE IV. AND KING WILLIAM IV.* By the late C. C. F. GREVILLE. Edited by H. REEVE, C.B. 3 vols. 8vo. 36s.

GRIMSTON.—*THE HON. ROBERT GRIMSTON:* a Sketch of his Life. By FREDERICK GALE. With Portrait. Crown 8vo. 10s. 6d.

GWILT.—*AN ENCYCLOPÆDIA OF ARCHITECTURE,* Historical, Theoretical, and Practical. By JOSEPH GWILT, F.S.A. Illustrated with more than 1,100 Engravings on Wood. Revised, with Alterations and Considerable Additions, by WYATT PAPWORTH. Additionally illustrated with nearly 400 Wood Engravings by O. JEWITT, and nearly 200 other Woodcuts. 8vo. 52s. 6d.

GROVE.—*THE CORRELATION OF PHYSICAL FORCES.* By the Hon. Sir W. R. GROVE, F.R.S. &c. 8vo. 15s.

HALLIWELL-PHILLIPPS. — *OUTLINES OF THE LIFE OF SHAKESPEARE.* By J. O. HALLIWELL-PHILLIPPS, F.R.S. Royal 8vo. 7s. 6d.

HAMILTON.—*LIFE OF SIR WILLIAM R. HAMILTON,* Kt. LL.D. D.C.L. M.R.I.A. &c. Including Selections from his Poems, Correspondence, and Miscellaneous Writings. By the Rev. R. P. GRAVES, M.A. (3 vols.) Vols. I. and II. 8vo. 15s. each.

HARTWIG.— *WORKS BY DR. G. HARTWIG.*

THE SEA AND ITS LIVING WONDERS. 8vo. with many Illustrations, 10s. 6d.

THE TROPICAL WORLD. With about 200 Illustrations. 8vo. 10s. 6d.

THE POLAR WORLD ; a Description of Man and Nature in the Arctic and Antarctic Regions of the Globe. Maps, Plates, and Woodcuts. 8vo. 10s. 6d.

THE ARCTIC REGIONS (extracted from the 'Polar World '). 4to. 6d. sewed.

THE SUBTERRANEAN WORLD. With Maps and Woodcuts. 8vo. 10s. 6d.

THE AERIAL WORLD ; a Popular Account of the Phenomena and Life of the Atmosphere. Map, Plates, Woodcuts. 8vo. 10s. 6d.

HARTE.— *WORKS BY BRET HARTE.*
IN THE CARQUINEZ WOODS. Fcp.
8vo. 2s. boards; 2s. 6d. cloth.
ON THE FRONTIER. Three Stories.
16mo. 1s.
BY SHORE AND SEDGE. Three
Stories. 16mo. 1s.

HASSALL. — *WORKS BY ARTHUR
HILL HASSALL, M.D.*
*THE INHALATION TREATMENT OF
DISEASES OF THE ORGANS OF RESPIRA-
TION,* including Consumption; with 19
Illustrations of Apparatus. Cr. 8vo. 12s. 6d.
SAN REMO, climatically and medically
considered. With 30 Illustrations. Crown
8vo. 5s.

HAUGHTON. — *SIX LECTURES ON
PHYSICAL GEOGRAPHY,* delivered in 1876,
with some Additions. By the Rev. SAMUEL
HAUGHTON, F.R.S. M.D. D.C.L. With
23 Diagrams. 8vo. 15s.

HAVELOCK. — *MEMOIRS OF SIR
HENRY HAVELOCK, K.C.B.* By JOHN
CLARK MARSHMAN. Crown 8vo. 3s. 6d.

HAWARD.— *A TREATISE ON OR-
THOPÆDIC SURGERY.* By J. WARRING-
TON HAWARD, F.R.C.S. Surgeon to St.
George's Hospital. With 30 Illustrations
engraved on Wood. 8vo. 12s. 6d.

HELMHOLTZ.— *WORKS BY PRO-
FESSOR HELMHOLTZ.*
*POPULAR LECTURES ON SCIENTIFIC
SUBJECTS.* Translated and edited by
EDMUND ATKINSON, Ph.D. F.C.S.
With a Preface by Professor TYNDALL,
F.R.S. and 68 Woodcuts. 2 vols.
Crown 8vo. 15s. or separately, 7s. 6d. each.
*ON THE SENSATIONS OF TONE AS A
PHYSIOLOGICAL BASIS FOR THE THEORY
OF MUSIC.* Translated by A. J. ELLIS,
F.R.S. Second English Edition. Royal
8vo. 28s.

HERSCHEL.— *OUTLINES OF ASTRO-
NOMY.* By Sir J. F. W. HERSCHEL,
Bart. M.A. With Plates and Diagrams.
Square crown 8vo. 12s.

HEWITT. — *WORKS BY GRAILY
HEWITT, M.D.*
*THE DIAGNOSIS AND TREATMENT
OF DISEASES OF WOMEN, INCLUDING
THE DIAGNOSIS OF PREGNANCY.* New
Edition, in great part re-written and
much enlarged, with 211 Engravings on
Wood, of which 79 are new in this Edi-
tion. 8vo. 24s.
*THE MECHANICAL SYSTEM OF UTE-
RINE PATHOLOGY.* With 31 Life-size
Illustrations prepared expressly for this
Work. Crown 4to. 7s. 6d.

HICKSON. — *IRELAND IN THE
SEVENTEENTH CENTURY;* or, The Irish
Massacres of 1641-2, their Causes and
Results. By MARY HICKSON. With a
Preface by J. A. Froude, M.A. 2 vols.
8vo. 28s.

HOBART.— *THE MEDICAL LANGUAGE
OF ST. LUKE:* a Proof from Internal
Evidence that St. Luke's Gospel and the
Acts were written by the same person,
and that the writer was a Medical Man.
By the Rev. W. K. HOBART, LL.D.
8vo. 16s.

HOLMES.— *A SYSTEM OF SURGERY*
Theoretical and Practical, in Treatises by
various Authors. Edited by TIMOTHY
HOLMES, M.A. Surgeon to St. George's
Hospital; and J. W. HULKE, F.R.S.
Surgeon to the Middlesex Hospital. In
3 Volumes, with Coloured Plates and
Illustrations on Wood. 3 vols. royal 8vo.
£4. 4s.

HOMER.— *THE ILIAD OF HOMER*
Homometrically translated by C. B. CAY-
LEY. 8vo. 12s. 6d.
THE ILIAD OF HOMER. The Greek
Text, with a Verse Translation, by W. C.
GREEN, M.A. Vol. I. Books I.-XII.
Crown 8vo. 6s.

HOPKINS.— *CHRIST THE CONSOLER*
a Book of Comfort for the Sick. By
ELLICE HOPKINS. Fcp. 8vo. 2s. 6d.

HORSES AND ROADS; or How to
Keep a Horse Sound on His Legs. By
FREE-LANCE. Crown 8vo. 6s.

HORT.— *THE NEW PANTHEON,* or an
Introduction to the Mythology of the
Ancients. By W. J. HORT. 18mo.
2s. 6d.

HOWITT.— *VISITS TO REMARKABLE
PLACES,* Old Halls, Battle-Fields, Scenes
illustrative of Striking Passages in English
History and Poetry. By WILLIAM
HOWITT. With 80 Illustrations engraved
on Wood. Crown 8vo. 7s. 6d.

HULLAH.— *WORKS BY JOHN HUL-
LAH, LL.D.*
*COURSE OF LECTURES ON THE HIS-
TORY OF MODERN MUSIC.* 8vo. 8s. 6d.
*COURSE OF LECTURES ON THE TRAN-
SITION PERIOD OF MUSICAL HISTORY.*
8vo. 10s. 6d.

HUME.—*THE PHILOSOPHICAL WORKS OF DAVID HUME.* Edited by T. H. GREEN, M.A. and the Rev. T. H. GROSE, M.A. 4 vols. 8vo. 56*s.* Or separately, Essays, 2 vols. 28*s.* Treatise on Human Nature. 2 vols. 28*s.*

HUSBAND. — *EXAMINATION QUESTIONS IN ANATOMY, PHYSIOLOGY, BOTANY, MATERIA MEDICA, SURGERY, MEDICINE, MIDWIFERY, AND STATE-MEDICINE.* Arranged by H. A. HUSBAND, M.B. M.C. M.R.C.S. L.S.A. &c. 32mo. 4*s.* 6*d.*

INGELOW. —*POETICAL WORKS OF JEAN INGELOW.* Vols. 1 and 2. Fcp. 8vo. 12*s.* Vol. 3. Fcp. 8vo. 5*s.*

IN THE OLDEN TIME.—A Novel. By the Author of 'Mademoiselle Mori.' Crown 8vo. 6*s.*

JACKSON.—*AID TO ENGINEERING SOLUTION.* By LOWIS D'A. JACKSON, C.E. With 111 Diagrams and 5 Woodcut Illustrations. 8vo. 21*s.*

JAMESON.— *WORKS BY MRS. JAMESON.*

LEGENDS OF THE SAINTS AND MARTYRS. With 19 Etchings and 187 Woodcuts. 2 vols. 31*s.* 6*d.*

LEGENDS OF THE MADONNA, the Virgin Mary as represented in Sacred and Legendary Art. With 27 Etchings and 165 Woodcuts. 1 vol. 21*s.*

LEGENDS OF THE MONASTIC ORDERS. With 11 Etchings and 88 Woodcuts. 1 vol. 21*s.*

HISTORY OF THE SAVIOUR, His Types and Precursors. Completed by Lady EASTLAKE. With 13 Etchings and 281 Woodcuts. 2 vols. 42*s.*

JEFFERIES. — *RED DEER.* By RICHARD JEFFERIES. Crown 8vo. 4*s.* 6*d.*

JOHNSON.—*THE PATENTEE'S MANUAL ;* a Treatise on the Law and Practice of Letters Patent, for the use of Patentees and Inventors. By J. JOHNSON and J. H. JOHNSON. 8vo. 10*s.* 6*d.*

JOHNSTON.—*A GENERAL DICTIONARY OF GEOGRAPHY,* Descriptive, Physical, Statistical, and Historical ; a complete Gazetteer of the World. By KEITH JOHNSTON. Medium 8vo. 42*s.*

JONES. — *THE HEALTH OF THE SENSES: SIGHT, HEARING, VOICE, SMELL AND TASTE, SKIN ;* with Hints on Health, Diet, Education, Health Resorts of Europe, &c. By H. MACNAUGHTON JONES, M.D. Crown 8vo. 3*s.* 6*d.*

JUKES.— *WORKS BY THE REV. ANDREW JUKES.*

THE NEW MAN AND THE ETERNAL LIFE. Crown 8vo. 6*s.*

THE TYPES OF GENESIS. Crown 8vo. 7*s.* 6*d.*

THE SECOND DEATH AND THE RESTITUTION OF ALL THINGS. Crown 8vo. 3*s.* 6*d.*

THE MYSTERY OF THE KINGDOM. Crown 8vo. 2*s.* 6*d.*

JUSTINIAN.—*THE INSTITUTES OF JUSTINIAN ;* Latin Text, chiefly that of Huschke, with English Introduction, Translation, Notes, and Summary. By THOMAS C. SANDARS, M.A. Barrister-at-Law. 8vo. 18*s.*

KALISCH. — *WORKS BY M. M. KALISCH, M.A.*

BIBLE STUDIES. Part I. The Prophecies of Balaam. 8vo. 10*s.* 6*d.* Part II. The Book of Jonah. 8vo. 10*s.* 6*d.*

COMMENTARY ON THE OLD TESTAMENT ; with a New Translation. Vol. I. Genesis, 8vo. 18*s.* or adapted for the General Reader, 12*s.* Vol. II. Exodus, 15*s.* or adapted for the General Reader, 12*s.* Vol. III. Leviticus, Part I. 15*s.* or adapted for the General Reader, 8*s.* Vol. IV. Leviticus, Part II. 15*s.* or adapted for the General Reader, 8*s.*

HEBREW GRAMMAR. With Exercises. Part I. 8vo. 12*s.* 6*d.* Key, 5*s.* Part II. 12*s.* 6*d.*

KANT. — *CRITIQUE OF PRACTICAL REASON.* By EMMANUEL KANT. Translated by Thomas Kingsmill Abbott, B.D. 8vo. 12*s.* 6*d.*

KERL.—*A PRACTICAL TREATISE ON METALLURGY.* By Professor KERL. Adapted from the last German Edition by W. Crookes, F.R.S. &c. and E. Röhrig, Ph.D. 3 vols. 8vo. with 625 Woodcuts, £4. 19*s.*

KILLICK.—*HANDBOOK TO MILL'S SYSTEM OF LOGIC.* By the Rev. A. H. KILLICK, M.A. Crown 8vo. 3*s.* 6*d.*

KOLBE.—*A SHORT TEXT-BOOK OF INORGANIC CHEMISTRY.* By Dr. HERMANN KOLBE. Translated from the German by T. S. HUMPIDGE, Ph.D. With a Coloured Table of Spectra and 66 Illustrations. Crown 8vo. 7*s.* 6*d.*

LANG.— *WORKS BY ANDREW LANG, late Fellow of Merton College.*

CUSTOM AND MYTH ; Studies of Early Usage and Belief. With 15 Illustrations. Crown 8vo. 7s. 6d.

THE PRINCESS NOBODY : a Tale of Fairyland. After the Drawings by Richard Doyle, printed in colours by Edmund Evans. Post 4to. 5s. boards.

LATHAM.— *WORKS BY ROBERT G. LATHAM, M.A. M.D.*

A DICTIONARY OF THE ENGLISH LANGUAGE. Founded on the Dictionary of Dr. JOHNSON. Four vols. 4to. £7.

A DICTIONARY OF THE ENGLISH LANGUAGE. Abridged from Dr. Latham's Edition of Johnson's Dictionary. One Volume. Medium 8vo. 14s.

HANDBOOK OF THE ENGLISH LANGUAGE. Crown 8vo. 6s.

LECKY.— *WORKS BY W. E. H. LECKY.*

HISTORY OF ENGLAND IN THE 18TH CENTURY. 4 vols. 8vo. 1700-1784, £3. 12s.

THE HISTORY OF EUROPEAN MORALS FROM AUGUSTUS TO CHARLEMAGNE. 2 vols. crown 8vo. 16s.

HISTORY OF THE RISE AND INFLUENCE OF THE SPIRIT OF RATIONALISM IN EUROPE. 2 vols. crown 8vo. 16s.

LEADERS OF PUBLIC OPINION IN IRELAND. — Swift, Flood, Grattan, O'Connell. Crown 8vo. 7s. 6d.

LEWES.— *THE HISTORY OF PHILOSOPHY,* from Thales to Comte. By GEORGE HENRY LEWES. 2 vols. 8vo. 32s.

LIDDELL & SCOTT.— *A GREEK-ENGLISH LEXICON.* Compiled by HENRY GEORGE LIDDELL, D.D. Dean of Christ Church ; and ROBERT SCOTT, D.D. Dean of Rochester. 4to. 36s.

LINDLEY and MOORE. — *THE TREASURY OF BOTANY,* or Popular Dictionary of the Vegetable Kingdom. Edited by J. LINDLEY, F.R.S. and T. MOORE, F.L.S. With 274 Woodcuts and 20 Steel Plates. Two Parts, fcp. 8vo. 12s.

LIST.— *THE NATIONAL SYSTEM OF POLITICAL ECONOMY.* By FRIEDRICH LIST. Translated from the Original German by SAMPSON S. LLOYD, M.P. 8vo. 10s. 6d.

LITTLE.— *ON IN-KNEE DISTORTION* (Genu Valgum) : Its Varieties and Treatment with and without Surgical Operation. By W. J. LITTLE, M.D. Assisted by MUIRHEAD LITTLE, M.R.C.S. With 40 Illustrations. 8vo. 7s. 6d.

LIVEING.— *WORKS BY ROBERT LIVEING, M.A. and M.D. Cantab.*

HANDBOOK ON DISEASES OF THE SKIN. With especial reference to Diagnosis and Treatment. Fcp. 8vo. 5s.

NOTES ON THE TREATMENT OF SKIN DISEASES. 18mo. 3s.

ELEPHANTIASIS GRÆCORUM, OR TRUE LEPROSY. Crown 8vo. 4s. 6d.

LLOYD.— *A TREATISE ON MAGNETISM,* General and Terrestrial. By H. LLOYD, D.D. D.C.L. 8vo. 10s. 6d.

LLOYD.— *THE SCIENCE OF AGRICULTURE.* By F. J. LLOYD. 8vo. 12s.

LONGMAN.— *WORKS BY WILLIAM LONGMAN, F.S.A.*

LECTURES ON THE HISTORY OF ENGLAND from the Earliest Times to the Death of King Edward II. Maps and Illustrations. 8vo. 15s.

HISTORY OF THE LIFE AND TIMES OF EDWARD III. With 9 Maps, 8 Plates, and 16 Woodcuts. 2 vols. 8vo. 28s.

LONGMAN.— *WORKS BY FREDERICK W. LONGMAN, Balliol College, Oxon.*

CHESS OPENINGS. Fcp. 8vo. 2s. 6d.

FREDERICK THE GREAT AND THE SEVEN YEARS' WAR. With 2 Coloured Maps. 8vo. 2s. 6d.

A NEW POCKET DICTIONARY OF THE GERMAN AND ENGLISH LANGUAGES. Square 18mo. 2s. 6d.

LONGMAN'S MAGAZINE. Published Monthly. Price Sixpence. Vols. 1-5, 8vo. price 5s. each.

LONGMORE.— *GUNSHOT INJURIES* Their History, Characteristic Features, Complications, and General Treatment By Surgeon-General T. LONGMORE, C.B F.R.C.S. With 58 Illustrations. 8vo price 31s. 6d.

LOUDON.— *WORKS BY J. C. LOUDON F.L.S.*

ENCYCLOPÆDIA OF GARDENING the Theory and Practice of Horticulture Floriculture, Arboriculture, and Landscape Gardening. With 1,000 Woodcuts 8vo. 21s.

ENCYCLOPÆDIA OF AGRICULTURE the Laying-out, Improvement, and Management of Landed Property ; the Cultivation and Economy of the Productions of Agriculture. With 1,100 Woodcuts. 8vo. 21s.

ENCYCLOPÆDIA OF PLANTS ; the Specific Character, Description, Culture History, &c. of all Plants found in Great Britain. With 12,000 Woodcuts. 8vo. 42s.

.UBBOCK.—*The Origin of Civili-*
zation and the Primitive Condition
of Man. By Sir J. Lubbock, Bart.
M.P. F.R.S. 8vo. Woodcuts, 18s.

,YRA GERMANICA ; Hymns Translated from the German by Miss C.
Winkworth. Fcp. 8vo. 5s.

IACALISTER.—*An Introduction*
to the Systematic Zoology and
Morphology of Vertebrate Ani-
mals. By A. Macalister, M.D.
With 28 Diagrams. 8vo. 10s. 6d.

IACAULAY. — *W O R K S A N D*
LIFE OF LORD MACAULAY.

HISTORY OF ENGLAND *from*
the Accession of James the Second:
Student's Edition, 2 vols. crown 8vo. 12s.
People's Edition, 4 vols. crown 8vo. 16s.
Cabinet Edition, 8 vols. post 8vo. 48s.
Library Edition, 5 vols. 8vo. £4.

CRITICAL AND HISTORICAL
ESSAYS, with LAYS of
ANCIENT ROME, in 1 volume :
Authorised Edition, crown 8vo. 2s. 6d. or
3s. 6d. gilt edges.
Popular Edition, crown 8vo. 2s. 6d.

CRITICAL AND HISTORICAL
ESSAYS:
Student's Edition, 1 vol. crown 8vo. 6s.
People's Edition, 2 vols. crown 8vo. 8s.
Cabinet Edition, 4 vols. post 8vo. 24s.
Library Edition, 3 vols. 8vo. 36s.

ESSAYS which may be had separ-
ately price 6d. each sewed, 1s. each cloth :
Addison and Walpole.
Frederick the Great.
Croker's Boswell's Johnson.
Hallam's Constitutional History.
Warren Hastings.
The Earl of Chatham (Two Essays).
Ranke and Gladstone.
Milton and Machiavelli.
Lord Bacon.
Lord Clive.
Lord Byron, and The Comic Dramatists of
the Restoration.

¹The Essay on Warren Hastings annotated
by S. Hales, 1s. 6d.
¹The Essay on Lord Clive annotated by
H. Courthope-Bowen, M.A. 2s. 6d.

SPEECHES:
People's Edition, crown 8vo. 3s. 6d.

MISCELLANEOUS WRITINGS
Library Edition, 2 vols. 8vo. Portrait, 21s.
People's Edition, 1 vol. crown 8vo. 4s. 6d.

[*Continued above.*

MACAULAY — *W O R K S A N D*
LIFE OF LORD MACAULAY
—continued.

LAYS OF ANCIENT ROME, &c.
Illustrated by G. Scharf, fcp. 4to. 10s. 6d.
———— Popular Edition,
fcp. 4to. 6d. sewed, 1s. cloth.
Illustrated by J. R. Weguelin, crown 8vo.
3s. 6d. cloth extra, gilt edges.
Cabinet Edition, post 8vo. 3s. 6d.
Annotated Edition, fcp. 8vo. 1s. sewed,
1s. 6d. cloth, or 2s. 6d. cloth extra, gilt
edges.

SELECTIONS FROM THE
Writings of Lord Macaulay. Edited, with Occasional Notes, by the Right
Hon. G. O. Trevelyan, M.P. Crown
8vo. 6s.

MISCELLANEOUS WRITINGS
and Speeches:
Student's Edition, in One Volume, crown
8vo. 6s.
Cabinet Edition, including Indian Penal
Code, Lays of Ancient Rome, and Miscellaneous Poems, 4 vols. post 8vo. 24s.

THE COMPLETE WORKS of
Lord Macaulay. Edited by his Sister,
Lady Trevelyan.
Library Edition, with Portrait, 8 vols.
demy 8vo. £5. 5s.
Cabinet Edition, 16 vols. post 8vo. £4. 16s.

THE LIFE AND LETTERS of
Lord Macaulay. By the Right Hon.
G. O. Trevelyan, M.P.
Popular Edition, 1 vol. crown 8vo. 6s.
Cabinet Edition, 2 vols. post 8vo. 12s.
Library Edition, 2 vols. 8vo. with Portrait,
36s.

MACDONALD,—*Works by George*
Macdonald, LL.D.

UNSPOKEN SERMONS. Second Series.
Crown 8vo. 7s. 6d.

A BOOK OF STRIFE, IN THE FORM
of The Diary of an Old Soul:
Poems. 12mo. 6s.

HAMLET. A Study with the Text of
the Folio of 1623. 8vo. 12s.

MACFARREN.—*Lectures on Har-*
mony, delivered at the Royal Institution.
By Sir G. A. Macfarren. 8vo. 12s.

MACKENZIE.—*On the Use of the*
Laryngoscope in Diseases of the
Throat ; with an Appendix on Rhino-
scopy. By Morell Mackenzie, M.D.
Lond. With 47 Woodcut Illustrations.
8vo. 6s.

MACLEOD.—*WORKS BY HENRY D. MACLEOD, M.A.*

PRINCIPLES OF ECONOMICAL PHILO-SOPHY. In 2 vols. Vol. I. 8vo. 15s. Vol. II. PART I. 12s.

THE ELEMENTS OF ECONOMICS. In 2 vols. Vol. I. crown 8vo. 7s. 6d. Vol. II. crown 8vo.

THE ELEMENTS OF BANKING. Crown 8vo. 5s.

THE THEORY AND PRACTICE OF BANKING. Vol. I. 8vo. 12s. Vol. II.

ELEMENTS OF POLITICAL ECONOMY. 8vo. 16s.

ECONOMICS FOR BEGINNERS. 8vo. 2s. 6d.

LECTURES ON CREDIT AND BANKING. 8vo. 5s.

MACNAMARA. — *HIMALAYAN AND SUB-HIMALAYAN DISTRICTS OF BRITISH INDIA,* their Climate, Medical Topography, and Disease Distribution. By F. N. MACNAMARA, M.D. With Map and Fever Chart. 8vo. 21s.

McCULLOCH. — *THE DICTIONARY OF COMMERCE AND COMMERCIAL NAVI-GATION* of the late J. R. McCULLOCH, of H.M. Stationery Office. Latest Edition, containing the most recent Statistical Information by A. J. WILSON. 1 vol. medium 8vo. with 11 Maps and 30 Charts, price 63s. cloth, or 70s. strongly half-bound in russia.

MAHAFFY.—*A HISTORY OF CLAS-SICAL GREEK LITERATURE.* By the Rev. J. P. MAHAFFY, M.A. Crown 8vo. Vol. I. Poets, 7s. 6d. Vol. II. Prose Writers, 7s. 6d.

MALMESBURY.—*MEMOIRS OF AN EX-MINISTER:* an Autobiography. By the Earl of MALMESBURY, G.C.B. Cheap Edition. Crown 8vo. 7s. 6d.

MANNING.—*THE TEMPORAL MIS-SION OF THE HOLY GHOST;* or, Reason and Revelation. By H. E. MANNING, D.D. Cardinal-Archbishop. Crown 8vo. 8s. 6d.

THE MARITIME ALPS AND THEIR SEABOARD. By the Author of 'Véra,' 'Blue Roses,' &c. With 14 Full-page Illustrations and 15 Woodcuts in the Text. 8vo. 21s.

MARTINEAU.—*WORKS BY JAMES MARTINEAU, D.D.*

HOURS OF THOUGHT ON SACRED THINGS. Two Volumes of Sermons. 2 vols. crown 8vo. 7s. 6d. each.

ENDEAVOURS AFTER THE CHRISTIAN LIFE, Discourses. Crown 8vo. 7s. 6d.

MAUNDER'S TREASURIES.

BIOGRAPHICAL TREASURY. Reco: structed, revised, and brought down the year 1882, by W. L. R. CATI Fcp. 8vo. 6s.

TREASURY OF NATURAL HISTORY or, Popular Dictionary of Zoology. Fc 8vo. with 900 Woodcuts, 6s.

TREASURY OF GEOGRAPHY, Physica Historical, Descriptive, and Politica With 7 Maps and 16 Plates. Fcp. 8vo. (

HISTORICAL TREASURY: Outlines Universal History, Separate Histories all Nations. Revised by the Rev. Sir W. Cox, Bart. M.A. Fcp. 8vo. 6s.

TREASURY OF KNOWLEDGE AI LIBRARY OF REFERENCE. Comprisi an English Dictionary and Gramm: Universal Gazetteer, Classical Dictiona Chronology, Law Dictionary, &c. F 8vo. 6s.

SCIENTIFIC AND LITERARY TRE SURY: a Popular Encyclopædia of Scien Literature, and Art. Fcp. 8vo. 6s.

THE TREASURY OF BIBLE KNO LEDGE; being a Dictionary of the Boo Persons, Places, Events, and other matt of which mention is made in Holy Scr ture. By the Rev. J. AYRE, M.A. W 5 Maps, 15 Plates, and 300 Woodc Fcp. 8vo. 6s.

THE TREASURY OF BOTANY, Popular Dictionary of the Vegeta Kingdom. Edited by J. LINDLEY, F.R and T. MOORE, F.L.S. With 274 Wo cuts and 20 Steel Plates. Two Pa fcp. 8vo. 12s.

MAXWELL.—*DON JOHN OF AU TRIA;* or, Passages from the Histe of the Sixteenth Century, 1547-15. By the late Sir WILLIAM STIRLI MAXWELL, Bart. K.T. With numero Illustrations engraved on Wood. Libra Edition. 2 vols. royal 8vo. 42s.

MAY.—*WORKS BY THE RIGHT HO SIR THOMAS ERSKINE MAY, K.C.*

THE CONSTITUTIONAL HISTORY ENGLAND SINCE THE ACCESSION GEORGE III. 1760-1870. 3 vols. cro 8vo. 18s.

DEMOCRACY IN EUROPE; a Histor 2 vols. 8vo. 32s.

MELVILLE.—*THE NOVELS OF G. WHYTE MELVILLE.* 1s. each, sewe or 1s. 6d. cloth.

The Gladiators.	Holmby House.
The Interpreter.	Kate Coventry.
Good for Nothing.	Digby Grand.
The Queen's Maries.	General Bounce.

MENDELSSOHN.—*THE LETTERS OF FELIX MENDELSSOHN.* Translated by Lady WALLACE. 2 vols. crown 8vo. 10*s.*

MERIVALE.—*WORKS BY THE VERY REV. CHARLES MERIVALE, D.D. Dean of Ely.*
HISTORY OF THE ROMANS UNDER THE EMPIRE. 8 vols. post 8vo. 48*s.*
THE FALL OF THE ROMAN REPUBLIC: a Short History of the Last Century of the Commonwealth. 12mo. 7*s.* 6*d.*
GENERAL HISTORY OF ROME FROM B.C. 753 TO A.D. 476. Crown 8vo. 7*s.* 6*d.*
THE ROMAN TRIUMVIRATES. With Maps. Fcp. 8vo. 2*s.* 6*d.*

MILES. — *WORKS BY WILLIAM MILES.*
THE HORSE'S FOOT, AND HOW TO KEEP IT SOUND. Imp. 8vo. 12*s.* 6*d.*
STABLES AND STABLE FITTINGS. Imp. 8vo. with 13 Plates, 15*s.*
REMARKS ON HORSES' TEETH, addressed to Purchasers. Post 8vo. 1*s.* 6*d.*
PLAIN TREATISE ON HORSE-SHOEING. Post 8vo. Woodcuts, 2*s.* 6*d.*

MILL.—*ANALYSIS OF THE PHENOMENA OF THE HUMAN MIND.* By JAMES MILL. With Notes, Illustrative and Critical. 2 vols. 8vo. 28*s.*

MILL.—*WORKS BY JOHN STUART MILL.*
PRINCIPLES OF POLITICAL ECONOMY.
Library Edition, 2 vols. 8vo. 30*s.*
People's Edition, 1 vol. crown 8vo. 5*s.*
A SYSTEM OF LOGIC, Ratiocinative and Inductive.
Library Edition, 2 vols. 8vo. 25*s.*
People's Edition, crown 8vo. 5*s.*
ON LIBERTY. Crown 8vo. 1*s.* 4*d.*
ON REPRESENTATIVE GOVERNMENT. Crown 8vo. 2*s.*
AUTOBIOGRAPHY, 8vo. 7*s.* 6*d.*
ESSAYS ON SOME UNSETTLED QUESTIONS OF POLITICAL ECONOMY. 8vo. 6*s.* 6*d.*
UTILITARIANISM. 8vo. 5*s.*
THE SUBJECTION OF WOMEN. Crown 8vo. 6*s.*
EXAMINATION OF SIR WILLIAM HAMILTON'S PHILOSOPHY. 8vo. 16*s.*
DISSERTATIONS AND DISCUSSIONS. 4 vols. 8vo. £2. 6*s.* 6*d.*
NATURE, THE UTILITY OF RELIGION, AND THEISM. Three Essays. 8vo. 5*s.*

MILLER.—*WORKS BY W. ALLEN MILLER, M.D. LL.D.*
THE ELEMENTS OF CHEMISTRY, Theoretical and Practical Re-edited, with Additions, by H. MACLEOD, F.C.S. 3 vols. 8vo.
Part I. CHEMICAL PHYSICS, 16*s.*
Part II. INORGANIC CHEMISTY, 24*s.*
Part III. ORGANIC CHEMISTRY, 31*s.* 6*d.*
AN INTRODUCTION TO THE STUDY OF INORGANIC CHEMISTRY. With 71 Woodcuts. Fcp. 8vo. 3*s.* 6*d.*

MILLER. — *READINGS IN SOCIAL ECONOMY.* By Mrs. F. FENWICK MILLER. Crown 8vo. 2*s.*

MITCHELL.—*A MANUAL OF PRACTICAL ASSAYING.* By JOHN MITCHELL, F.C.S. Revised, with the Recent Discoveries incorporated. By W. CROOKES, F.R.S. 8vo. Woodcuts, 31*s.* 6*d.*

MODERN NOVELIST'S LIBRARY (THE). Price 2*s.* each boards, or 2*s.* 6*d.* each cloth :—

By the Earl of BEACONSFIELD, K.G.

Endymion.

Lothair.	Henrietta Temple.
Coningsby.	Contarini Fleming, &c.
Sybil.	Alroy, Ixion, &c.
Tancred.	The Young Duke, &c.
Venetia.	Vivian Grey, &c.

By Mrs. OLIPHANT.
In Trust.

By JAMES PAYN.
Thicker than Water.

By BRET HARTE.
In the Carquinez Woods.

By ANTHONY TROLLOPE.
Barchester Towers.
The Warden.

By VARIOUS WRITERS.
The Atelier du Lys. By the Author of 'Mademoiselle Mori.'
Atherstone Priory. By L. N. Comyn.
The Burgomaster's Family. By E. C. W. Van Walrée.
Elsa and her Vulture. By W. Van Hillern.
Mademoiselle Mori. By the Author of 'The Atelier du Lys.'
The Six Sisters of the Valleys. By Rev. W. Bramley-Moore, M.A.
Unawares. By the Author of 'The Rose-Garden.'

MONSELL.—*SPIRITUAL SONGS FOR THE SUNDAYS AND HOLIDAYS THROUGHOUT THE YEAR.* By J. S. B. MONSELL, LL.D. Fcp. 8vo. 5*s.* 18mo. 2*s.*

MOORE.—*The Works of Thomas Moore.*

Lalla Rookh, Tenniel's Edition, with 68 Woodcut Illustrations. Crown 8vo. 10s. 6d.

Irish Melodies, Maclise's Edition, with 161 Steel Plates. Super-royal 8vo. 21s.

MOREHEAD.—*Clinical Researches on Disease in India.* By Charles Morehead, M.D. Surgeon to the Jamsetjee Jeejeebhoy Hospital. 8vo. 21s.

MOZLEY.—*Works by the Rev. Thomas Mozley, M.A.*

Reminiscences chiefly of Oriel College and the Oxford Movement. 2 vols. crown 8vo. 18s.

Reminiscences chiefly of Towns, Villages, and Schools. 2 vols. crown 8vo. 18s.

MÜLLER. — *Works by F. Max Müller, M.A.*

Biographical Essays. Crown 8vo. 7s. 6d.

Selected Essays on Language, Mythology and Religion. 2 vols. crown 8vo. 16s.

Lectures on the Science of Language. 2 vols. crown 8vo. 16s.

India, What Can it Teach Us? A Course of Lectures delivered before the University of Cambridge. 8vo. 12s. 6d.

Hibbert Lectures on the Origin and Growth of Religion, as illustrated by the Religions of India. Crown 8vo. 7s. 6d.

Introduction to the Science of Religion: Four Lectures delivered at the Royal Institution. Crown 8vo. 7s. 6d.

A Sanskrit Grammar for Beginners, in Devanagari and Roman Letters throughout. Royal 8vo. 7s. 6d.

MURCHISON. — *Works by Charles Murchison, M.D. LL.D. &c.*

A Treatise on the Continued Fevers of Great Britain. Revised by W. Cayley, M.D. Physician to the Middlesex Hospital. 8vo. with numerous Illustrations. 25s.

Clinical Lectures on Diseases of the Liver, Jaundice, and Abdominal Dropsy. Revised by T. Lauder Brunton, M.D. 8vo. with numerous Illustrations, 24s.

NEISON.—*The Moon*, and the Condition and Configurations of its Surface. By E. Neison, F.R.A.S. With 26 Maps and 5 Plates. Medium 8vo. 31s. 6d.

NEVILE.—*Works by George Nevile, M.A.*

Horses and Riding. With 31 Illustrations. Crown 8vo. 6s.

Farms and Farming. With 13 Illustrations. Crown 8vo. 6s.

NEWMAN.—*Works by Cardinal Newman.*

Apologia pro Vita Sua. Crown 8vo. 6s.

The Idea of a University defined and illustrated. Crown 8vo. 7s.

Historical Sketches. 3 vols crown 8vo. 6s. each.

Discussions and Arguments o. Various Subjects. Crown 8vo. 6s.

An Essay on the Development o Christian Doctrine. Crown 8vo. 6

Certain Difficulties felt b Anglicans in Catholic Teachin Considered. Vol. 1, crown 8vo. 7s. 6a Vol. 2, crown 8vo. 5s. 6d.

The Via Media of the Anglica Church, illustrated in Lecturi &c. 2 vols. crown 8vo. 6s. each.

Essays, Critical and Historica. 2 vols. crown 8vo. 12s.

Essays on Biblical and on Eccli siastical Miracles. Crown 8vo. 6s.

An Essay in Aid of a Gramma of Assent. 7s. 6d.

NEW TESTAMENT (THE) of ot Lord and Saviour Jesus Christ. Illu trated with Engravings on Wood aft Paintings by the Early Masters chiefly of th Italian School. New and Cheaper Editio 4to. 21s. cloth extra, or 42s. morocco.

NOBLE.—*The Russian Revolt* its Causes, Condition, and Prospect By Edmund Noble. Fcp. 8vo. 5s.

NORTHCOTT.—*Lathes and Turn ing*, Simple, Mechanical, and Ornamen tal. By W. H. Northcott. With 33 Illustrations. 8vo. 18s.

OLIPHANT. — *Madam.* A Nove By Mrs. Oliphant. Crown 8vo. 3s. 6

OWEN.—*THE COMPARATIVE ANA-TOMY AND PHYSIOLOGY OF THE VERTEBRATE ANIMALS.* By Sir RICHARD OWEN, K.C.B. &c. With 1,472 Woodcuts. 3 vols. 8vo. £3. 13s. 6d.

PAGET.—*WORKS BY SIR JAMES PAGET, BART. F.R.S. D.C.L. &c.*

CLINICAL LECTURES AND ESSAYS. Edited by F. HOWARD MARSH, Assistant-Surgeon to St. Bartholomew's Hospital. 8vo. 15s.

LECTURES ON SURGICAL PATHO-LOGY. Delivered at the Royal College of Surgeons of England. Re-edited by the AUTHOR and W. TURNER, M.B. 8vo. with 131 Woodcuts, 21s.

PASOLINI.—*MEMOIR OF COUNT GIUSEPPE PASOLINI, LATE PRESIDENT OF THE SENATE OF ITALY.* Compiled by his SON. Translated and Abridged by the DOWAGER-COUNTESS OF DAL-HOUSIE. With Portrait. 8vo. 16s.

PASTEUR.—*LOUIS PASTEUR,* his Life and Labours. By his SON-IN-LAW. Translated from the French by Lady CLAUD HAMILTON. Crown 8vo. 7s. 6d.

PEEL.—*A HIGHLAND GATHERING.* By E. LENNOX PEEL. With 31 Illustrations engraved on Wood by E. Whymper from original Drawings by Charles Whymper. Crown 8vo. 10s. 6d.

PENNELL.—'*FROM GRAVE TO GAY*': a Volume of Selections from the complete Poems of H. CHOLMONDELEY-PENNELL, Author of ' Puck on Pegasus ' &c. Fcp. 8vo. 6s.

PEREIRA.—*MATERIA MEDICA AND THERAPEUTICS.* By Dr. PEREIRA. Abridged, and adapted for the use of Medical and Pharmaceutical Practitioners and Students. Edited by Professor R. BENTLEY, M.R.C.S. F.L.S. and by Professor T. REDWOOD, Ph.D. F.C.S. With 126 Woodcuts, 8vo. 25s.

PERRY.—*A POPULAR INTRODUC-TION TO THE HISTORY OF GREEK AND ROMAN SCULPTURE,* designed to Promote the Knowledge and Appreciation of the Remains of Ancient Art. By WALTER C. PERRY. With 268 Illustrations. Square crown 8vo. 31s. 6d.

PIESSE.—*THE ART OF PERFUMERY,* and the Methods of Obtaining the Odours of Plants ; with Instructions for the Manufacture of Perfumes, &c. By G. W. S. PIESSE, Ph.D. F.C.S. With 96 Woodcuts, square crown 8vo. 21s.

POLE.—*THE THEORY OF THE MO-DERN SCIENTIFIC GAME OF WHIST.* By W. POLE, F.R.S. Fcp. 8vo. 2s. 6d.

PROCTOR.—*WORKS BY R. A. PROC-TOR.*

THE SUN; Ruler, Light, Fire, and Life of the Planetary System. With Plates and Woodcuts. Crown 8vo. 14s.

THE ORBS AROUND US ; a Series of Essays on the Moon and Planets, Meteors and Comets. With Chart and Diagrams, crown 8vo. 7s. 6d.

OTHER WORLDS THAN OURS ; The Plurality of Worlds Studied under the Light of Recent Scientific Researches. With 14 Illustrations, crown 8vo. 10s. 6d.

THE MOON; her Motions, Aspects, Scenery, and Physical Condition. With Plates, Charts, Woodcuts, and Lunar Photographs, crown 8vo. 10s. 6d.

UNIVERSE OF STARS; Presenting Researches into and New Views respect-ing the Constitution of the Heavens. With 22 Charts and 22 Diagrams, 8vo. 10s. 6d.

LARGER STAR ATLAS for the Library, in 12 Circular Maps, with Introduction and 2 Index Pages. Folio, 15s. or Maps only, 12s. 6d.

NEW STAR ATLAS for the Library, the School, and the Observatory, in 12 Circular Maps (with 2 Index Plates). Crown 8vo. 5s.

LIGHT SCIENCE FOR LEISURE HOURS; Familiar Essays on Scientific Subjects, Natural Phenomena, &c. 3 vols. crown 8vo. 7s. 6d. each.

STUDIES OF VENUS-TRANSITS ; an Investigation of the Circumstances of the Transits of Venus in 1874 and 1882. With 7 Diagrams and 10 Plates. 8vo. 5s.

TRANSITS OF VENUS. A Popular Account of Past and Coming Transits from the First Observed by Horrocks in 1639 to the Transit of 2012. With 20 Lithographic Plates (12 Coloured) and 38 Illustrations engraved on Wood, 8vo. 8s. 6d.

A TREATISE ON THE CYCLOID AND ON ALL FORMS OF CYCLOIDAL CURVES, and on the use of Cycloidal Curves in dealing with the Motions of Planets, Comets, &c. &c. With 161 Diagrams. Crown 8vo. 10s. 6d.

PLEASANT WAYS IN SCIENCE, with numerous Illustrations. Crown 8vo. 6s

MYTHS AND MARVELS OF ASTRO-NOMY, with numerous Illustrations. Crown 8vo. 6s. [Continued on next page.

PROCTOR—*WORKS BY R. A. PROC-TOR*—continued.

THE 'KNOWLEDGE' LIBRARY. Edited by RICHARD A. PROCTOR.

HOW TO PLAY WHIST: WITH THE LAWS AND ETIQUETTE OF WHIST; Whist Whittlings, and Forty fully-annotated Games. By 'FIVE OF CLUBS' (R. A. Proctor). Crown 8vo. 5*s.*

SCIENCE BYWAYS. A Series of Familiar Dissertations on Life in Other Worlds. By RICHARD A. PROCTOR. Crown 8vo. 6*s.*

THE POETRY OF ASTRONOMY. A Series of Familiar Essays on the Heavenly Bodies. By RICHARD A. PROCTOR. Crown 8vo. 6*s.*

NATURE STUDIES. Reprinted from *Knowledge.* By GRANT ALLEN, ANDREW WILSON, THOMAS FOSTER, EDWARD CLODD, and RICHARD A. PROCTOR. Crown 8vo. 6*s.*

LEISURE READINGS. Reprinted from *Knowledge.* By EDWARD CLODD, ANDREW WILSON, THOMAS FOSTER, A. C. RUNYARD, and RICHARD A. PROCTOR. Crown 8vo. 6*s.*

THE STARS IN THEIR SEASONS. An Easy Guide to a Knowledge of the Star Groups, in Twelve Large Maps. By RICHARD A. PROCTOR. Imperial 8vo. 5*s.*

QUAIN'S ELEMENTS of ANATOMY. The Ninth Edition. Re-edited by ALLEN THOMSON, M.D. LL.D. F.R.S.S. L. & E. EDWARD ALBERT SCHÄFER, F.R.S. and GEORGE DANCER THANE. With upwards of 1,000 Illustrations engraved on Wood, of which many are Coloured. 2 vols. 8vo. 18*s.* each.

QUAIN.—*A DICTIONARY OF MEDICINE.* By Various Writers. Edited by R. QUAIN, M.D. F.R.S. &c. With 138 Woodcuts. Medium 8vo. 31*s.* 6*d.* cloth, or 40*s.* half-russia; to be had also in 2 vols. 34*s.* cloth.

RAWLINSON. — *THE SEVENTH GREAT ORIENTAL MONARCHY;* or, a History of the Sassanians. By G. RAWLINSON, M.A. With Map and 95 Illustrations. 8vo. 28*s.*

READER.—*WORKS BY EMILY E. READER.*

VOICES FROM FLOWER-LAND, in Original Couplets. A Birthday-Book and Language of Flowers. 16mo. 2*s.* 6*d.* limp cloth; 3*s.* 6*d.* roan, gilt edges, or in vegetable vellum, gilt top.

FAIRY PRINCE FOLLOW-MY-LEAD; or, the *MAGIC BRACELET.* Illustrated by WM. READER. Cr. 8vo. 5*s.* gilt edges.

REEVE. — *COOKERY AND HOUSE-KEEPING.* By Mrs. HENRY REEVE. With 8 Coloured Plates and 37 Woodcuts. Crown 8vo. 7*s.* 6*d.*

RICH.—*A DICTIONARY OF ROMAN & GREEK ANTIQUITIES.* With 2,000 Woodcuts. By A. RICH, B.A. Cr. 8vo. 7*s.* 6*d.*

RIVERS. — *WORKS BY THOMAS RIVERS.*

THE ORCHARD-HOUSE. Crown 8vo. with 25 Woodcuts, 5*s.*

THE ROSE AMATEUR'S GUIDE. Fcp. 8vo. 4*s.* 6*d.*

ROGERS.—*WORKS BY HY. ROGERS.*

THE ECLIPSE OF FAITH; or, a Visit to a Religious Sceptic. Fcp. 8vo. 5*s.*

DEFENCE OF THE ECLIPSE OF FAITH. Fcp. 8vo. 3*s.* 6*d.*

ROGET.—*THESAURUS OF ENGLISH WORDS AND PHRASES.* By PETER M ROGET, M.D. Crown 8vo. 10*s.* 6*d.*

RONALDS. — *THE FLY-FISHER'S ENTOMOLOGY.* By ALFRED RONALDS With 20 Coloured Plates. 8vo. 14*s.*

SALTER.—*DENTAL PATHOLOGY AND SURGERY.* By S. J. A. SALTER, M.B F.R.S. With 133 Illustrations. 8vo. 18*s.*

SCHÄFER. — *THE ESSENTIALS OF HISTOLOGY, DESCRIPTIVE AND PRACTICAL.* For the use of Students. By E A. SCHÄFER, F.R.S. With 281 Illustrations. 8vo. 6*s.* or Interleaved with Drawing Paper, 8*s.* 6*d.*

SCHELLEN.—*SPECTRUM ANALYSIS IN ITS APPLICATION TO TERRESTRIAL SUBSTANCES,* and the Physical Constitution of the Heavenly Bodies. Familiarly explained by the late Dr. H. SCHELLEN Translated from the Third Enlarged an Revised German Edition by JANE an CAROLINE LASSELL. Edited, with Notes by Capt. W. DE W. ABNEY, R.E Second Edition. With 14 Plates (including Ångström's and Cornu's Maps) an 291 Woodcuts. 8vo. 31*s.* 6*d.*

SCOTT.—*THE FARM-VALUER.* B JOHN SCOTT. Crown 8vo. 5*s.*

SEEBOHM.—*WORKS BY FREDERIC. SEEBOHM.*

THE OXFORD REFORMERS — JOH. COLET, ERASMUS, AND THOMAS MORE a History of their Fellow-Work. 8vo 14*s.*

THE ENGLISH VILLAGE COMMUNITY Examined in its Relations to the Manoria and Tribal Systems, &c. 13 Maps an Plates. 8vo. 16*s.*

THE ERA OF THE PROTESTANT REVOLUTION. With Map. Fcp. 8vo. 2*s.* 6*d.*

ENNETT.—*THE MARINE STEAM ENGINE;* a Treatise for the use of Engineering Students and Officers of the Royal Navy. By RICHARD SENNETT, Chief Engineer, Royal Navy. With 244 Illustrations. 8vo. 21*s.*

SEWELL.—*WORKS BY ELIZABETH M. SEWELL.*

STORIES AND TALES. Cabinet Edition, in Eleven Volumes, crown 8vo. 3*s.* 6*d.* each, in cloth extra, with gilt edges :—
    Amy Herbert.   Gertrude.
    The Earl's Daughter.
    The Experience of Life.
    A Glimpse of the World.
    Cleve Hall. Ivors.
    Katharine Ashton.
    Margaret Percival.
    Laneton Parsonage. Ursula.

PASSING THOUGHTS ON RELIGION. Fcp. 8vo. 3*s.* 6*d.*

PREPARATION FOR THE HOLY COMMUNION; the Devotions chiefly from the works of JEREMY TAYLOR. 32mo. 3*s.*

NIGHT LESSONS FROM SCRIPTURE. 32mo. 3*s.* 6*d.*

SHAKESPEARE.—*BOWDLER'S FAMILY SHAKESPEARE.* Genuine Edition, in 1 vol. medium 8vo. large type, with 36 Woodcuts, 14*s.* or in 6 vols. fcp. 8vo. 21*s.*

OUTLINES OF THE LIFE OF SHAKESPEARE. By J. O. HALLIWELL-PHILLIPPS, F.R.S. 8vo. 7*s.* 6*d.*

SHORT.—*SKETCH OF THE HISTORY OF THE CHURCH OF ENGLAND TO THE REVOLUTION OF* 1688. By T. V. SHORT, D.D. Crown 8vo. 7*s.* 6*d.*

SIMCOX.—*A HISTORY OF LATIN LITERATURE.* By G. A. SIMCOX, M.A. Fellow of Queen's College, Oxford. 2 vols. 8vo. 32*s.*

SMITH, Rev. SYDNEY.—*THE WIT AND WISDOM OF THE REV. SYDNEY SMITH.* Crown 8vo. 3*s.* 6*d.*

SMITH, R. BOSWORTH. — *CARTHAGE AND THE CARTHAGINIANS.* By R. BOSWORTH SMITH, M.A. Maps, Plans, &c. Crown 8vo. 10*s.* 6*d.*

SMITH, R. A.—*AIR AND RAIN;* the Beginnings of a Chemical Climatology. By R. A. SMITH, F.R.S. 8vo. 24*s.*

SMITH, JAMES.—*THE VOYAGE AND SHIPWRECK OF ST. PAUL.* By JAMES SMITH, of Jordanhill. With Dissertations on the Life and Writings of St. Luke, and the Ships and Navigation of the Ancients. With numerous Illustrations. Crown 8vo. 7*s.* 6*d.*

SMITH, T.—*A MANUAL OF OPERATIVE SURGERY ON THE DEAD BODY.* By THOMAS SMITH, Surgeon to St. Bartholomew's Hospital. A New Edition, re-edited by W. J. WALSHAM. With 46 Illustrations. 8vo. 12*s.*

SMITH, H. F.—*THE HANDBOOK FOR MIDWIVES.* By HENRY FLY SMITH, M.B. Oxon. M.R.C.S. late Assistant-Surgeon at the Hospital for Sick Women, Soho Square. With 41 Woodcuts. Crown 8vo. 5*s.*

SOPHOCLES.—*SOPHOCLIS TRAGŒDIÆ* superstites; recensuit et brevi Annotatione instruxit GULIELMUS LINWOOD, M.A. Ædis Christi apud Oxonienses nuper Alumnus. Editio Quarta, auctior et emendatior. 8vo. 16*s.*

SOUTHEY.—*THE POETICAL WORKS OF ROBERT SOUTHEY,* with the Author's last Corrections and Additions. Medium 8vo. with Portrait, 14*s.*

STANLEY.—*A FAMILIAR HISTORY OF BIRDS.* By E. STANLEY, D.D. Revised and enlarged, with 160 Woodcuts. Crown 8vo. 6*s.*

STEEL.—*A TREATISE ON THE DISEASES OF THE OX;* being a Manual of Bovine Pathology specially adapted for the use of Veterinary Practitioners and Students. By J. H. STEEL, M.R.C.V.S. F.Z.S. With 2 Plates and 116 Woodcuts. 8vo. 15*s.*

STEPHEN.—*ESSAYS IN ECCLESIASTICAL BIOGRAPHY.* By the Right Hon. Sir J. STEPHEN, LL.D. Crown 8vo. 7*s.* 6*d.*

STEVENSON.—*WORKS BY ROBERT LOUIS STEVENSON.*

A CHILD'S GARDEN OF VERSES. Small fcp. 8vo. 5*s.*

THE DYNAMITER. Fcp. 8vo. 1*s.* swd. 1*s.* 6*d.* cloth.

'STONEHENGE.'—*THE DOG IN HEALTH AND DISEASE.* By 'STONEHENGE.' With 78 Wood Engravings. Square crown 8vo. 7*s.* 6*d.*

THE GREYHOUND. By 'STONEHENGE.' With 25 Portraits of Greyhounds, &c. Square crown 8vo. 15*s.*

STURGIS.—*MY FRIENDS AND I.* By JULIAN STURGIS. With Frontispiece. Crown 8vo. 5*s.*

SULLY.—*OUTLINES OF PSYCHOLOGY,* with Special Reference to the Theory of Education. By JAMES SULLY, M.A. 8vo. 12*s.* 6*d.*

SUPERNATURAL RELIGION; an Inquiry into the Reality of Divine Revelation. Complete Edition, thoroughly revised. 3 vols. 8vo. 36s.

SWINBURNE.—*PICTURE LOGIC;* an Attempt to Popularise the Science of Reasoning. By A. J. SWINBURNE, B.A. Post 8vo. 5s.

SWINTON.—*THE PRINCIPLES AND PRACTICE OF ELECTRIC LIGHTING.* By ALAN A. CAMPBELL SWINTON. With 54 Illustrations engraved on Wood Crown 8vo. 5s.

TAYLOR.—*AUTOBIOGRAPHY OF SIR HENRY TAYLOR,* K.C.M.G. 2 vols. 8vo. 32s.

TAYLOR.—*STUDENT'S MANUAL OF THE HISTORY OF INDIA,* from the Earliest Period to the Present Time. By Colonel MEADOWS TAYLOR, C.S.I. Crown 8vo. 7s. 6d.

TEXT-BOOKS OF SCIENCE: a Series of Elementary Works on Science, adapted for the use of Students in Public and Science Schools. Fcp. 8vo. fully illustrated with Woodcuts.
Abney's Photography, 3s. 6d.
Anderson's Strength of Materials, 3s. 6d.
Armstrong's Organic Chemistry, 3s. 6d.
Ball's Elements of Astronomy, 6s.
Barry's Railway Appliances, 3s. 6d.
Bauerman's Systematic Mineralogy, 6s.
———— Descriptive Mineralogy, 6s.
Bloxam and Huntington's Metals, 5s.
Glazebrook's Physical Optics, 6s.
Glazebrook and Shaw's Practical Physics, 6s.
Gore's Electro-Metallurgy, 6s.
Griffin's Algebra and Trigonometry, 3s. 6d.
Jenkin's Electricity and Magnetism, 3s. 6d.
Maxwell's Theory of Heat, 3s. 6d.
Merrifield's Technical Arithmetic, 3s. 6d.
Miller's Inorganic Chemistry, 3s. 6d.
Preece and Sivewright's Telegraphy, 5s.
Rutley's Petrology, or Study of Rocks, 4s. 6d.
Shelley's Workshop Appliances, 4s. 6d.
Thomé's Structural and Physiological Botany, 6s.
Thorpe's Quantitative Analysis, 4s. 6d.
Thorpe and Muir's Qualitative Analysis, 3s. 6d.
Tilden's Chemical Philosophy, 3s. 6d. With Answers to Problems, 4s. 6d.
Unwin's Machine Design, 6s.
Watson's Plane and Solid Geometry, 3s. 6d.

TAYLOR.—*THE COMPLETE WORKS OF BISHOP JEREMY TAYLOR.* With Life by Bishop Heber. Revised and corrected by the Rev. C. P. EDEN. 10 vols. £5. 5s.

TAYLOR.—*AN AGRICULTURAL NOTE BOOK,* to assist Candidates in Preparing for the Science and Art and other Examinations in Agriculture. By W. C TAYLOR, Principal of the Agriculture College, Aspatria, Carlisle. Crown 8vo 2s. 6d.

THOMSON.—*AN OUTLINE OF TH NECESSARY LAWS OF THOUGHT;* Treatise on Pure and Applied Logic. B W. THOMSON, D.D. Archbishop York. Crown 8vo. 6s.

THOMSON'S CONSPECTU *ADAPTED TO THE BRITIS. PHARMACOPŒIA.* By EDMUN LLOYD BIRKETT, M.D. &c. 18mo. 6

THOMPSON.—*A SYSTEM OF PS1 CHOLOGY.* By DANIEL GREENLEA THOMPSON. 2 vols. 8vo. 36s.

THREE IN NORWAY. By Two THEM. With a Map and 59 Illustrations on Wood from Sketches by tl Authors. Crown 8vo. 6s.

TREVELYAN. — *WORKS BY TH RIGHT HON. G. O. TREVELYAN M.P.*
THE LIFE AND LETTERS OF LOR MACAULAY. By the Right Hon. G. C TREVELYAN, M.P.
    LIBRARY EDITION, 2 vols. 8vo. 36s.
    CABINET EDITION, 2 vols. crown 8v 12s.
    POPULAR EDITION, 1 vol. crown 8v 6s.
THE EARLY HISTORY OF CHARLI JAMES FOX. Library Edition, 8vo. 18 Cabinet Edition, crown 8vo. 6s.

TWISS.—*WORKS BY SIR TRAVEK TWISS.*
THE RIGHTS AND DUTIES OF N TIONS, considered as Independent Con munities in Time of War. 8vo. 21s.
THE RIGHTS AND DUTIES C NATIONS IN TIME OF PEACE. 8v 15s.

TYNDALL.—*WORKS BY JOHN TY DALL, F.R.S. &c.*
FRAGMENTS OF SCIENCE. 2 vol crown 8vo. 16s.
HEAT A MODE OF MOTION. Crow 8vo. 12s.
SOUND. With 204 Woodcut Crown 8vo. 10s. 6d.
ESSAYS ON THE FLOATING-MATTE OF THE AIR in relation to Putrefactio and Infection. With 24 Woodcut Crown 8vo. 7s. 6d.

[Continued on next page.

NDALL.—*WORKS BY JOHN TYN-DALL. F.R.S. &c.*—continued.

LECTURES ON LIGHT, delivered in America in 1872 and 1873. With Portrait, Plate, and Diagrams. Crown 8vo. 7s. 6d.

LESSONS IN ELECTRICITY AT THE ROYAL INSTITUTION, 1875-76. With 58 Woodcuts. Crown 8vo. 2s. 6d.

NOTES OF A COURSE OF SEVEN LECTURES ON ELECTRICAL PHENO-MENA AND THEORIES, delivered at the Royal Institution. Crown 8vo. 1s. sewed, 1s. 6d. cloth.

NOTES OF A COURSE OF NINE LEC-TURES ON LIGHT, delivered at the Royal Institution. Crown 8vo. 1s. sewed, 1s. 6d. cloth.

FARADAY AS A DISCOVERER. Fcp. 8vo. 3s. 6d.

RE.—*A DICTIONARY OF ARTS, MANUFACTURES, AND MINES.* By Dr. URE. Seventh Edition, re-written and enlarged by R. HUNT, F.R.S. With 2,064 Woodcuts. 4 vols. medium 8vo. £7. 7s.

VERNEY.—*CHESS ECCENTRICITIES.* Including Four-handed Chess, Chess for Three, Six, or Eight Players, Round Chess for Two, Three, or Four Players, and several different ways of Playing Chess for Two Players. By Major GEORGE HOPE VERNEY. Crown 8vo. 10s. 6d.

VERNEY. — *PEASANT PROPERTIES,* and other Selected Essays. By LADY VERNEY. 2 vols. crown 8vo. 16s.

VILLE.—*ON ARTIFICIAL MANURES,* their Chemical Selection and Scientific Application to Agriculture. By GEORGES VILLE. Translated and edited by W. CROOKES, F.R.S. With 31 Plates. 8vo. 21s.

VIRGIL.—*PUBLI VERGILI MARONIS BUCOLICA, GEORGICA, ÆNEIS;* the Works of VIRGIL, Latin Text, with English Commentary and Index. By B. H. KENNEDY, D.D. Crown 8vo. 10s. 6d.

THE ÆNEID OF VIRGIL. Translated into English Verse. By J. CONINGTON, M.A. Crown 8vo. 9s.

THE POEMS OF VIRGIL. Translated into English Prose. By JOHN CONING-TON, M.A. Crown 8vo. 9s.

WALKER.—*THE CORRECT CARD;* or, How to Play at Whist; a Whist Catechism. By Major A. CAMPBELL-WALKER, F.R.G.S. Fcp. 8vo. 2s. 6d.

WALPOLE.—*HISTORY OF ENGLAND FROM THE CONCLUSION OF THE GREAT WAR IN 1815 TO THE YEAR 1841.* By SPENCER WALPOLE. 3 vols. 8vo. £2. 14s.

WATSON.—*LECTURES ON THE PRIN-CIPLES AND PRACTICE OF PHYSIC,* delivered at King's College, London, by Sir THOMAS WATSON, Bart. M.D. With Two Plates. 2 vols. 8vo. 36s.

WATTS.—*A DICTIONARY OF CHEMIS-TRY AND THE ALLIED BRANCHES OF OTHER SCIENCES.* Edited by HENRY WATTS, F.R.S. 9 vols. medium 8vo. £15. 2s. 6d.

WEBB.— *WORKS BY THE REV. T. W. WEBB.*

CELESTIAL OBJECTS FOR COMMON TELESCOPES. Map, Plate, Woodcuts. Crown 8vo. 9s.

WEBB. — *THE VEIL OF ISIS:* a Series of Essays on Idealism. By THOMAS W. WEBB, LL.D. 8vo. 10s. 6d.

WELLINGTON.—*LIFE OF THE DUKE OF WELLINGTON.* By the Rev. G. R. GLEIG, M.A. Crown 8vo. Portrait, 6s. M.D. &c. Founder of, and formerly Physician to, the Hospital for Sick Children.

WEST.— *WORKS BY CHARLES WEST, M.D.*

LECTURES ON THE DISEASES OF IN-FANCY AND CHILDHOOD. 8vo. 18s.

THE MOTHER'S MANUAL OF CHIL-DREN'S DISEASES. Fcp. 8vo. 2s. 6d.

WHATELY. — *ENGLISH SYNONYMS.* By E. JANE WHATELY. Edited by her Father, R. WHATELY, D.D. Fcp. 8vo. 3s.

WHATELY.—*WORKS BY R. WHATELY, D.D.*

ELEMENTS OF LOGIC. Crown 8vo. 4s. 6d.

ELEMENTS OF RHETORIC. Crown 8vo. 4s. 6d.

LESSONS ON REASONING. Fcp. 8vo. 1s. 6d.

BACON'S ESSAYS, with Annotations. 8vo. 10s. 6d.

WHITE.—*A CONCISE LATIN-ENG-LISH DICTIONARY,* for the Use of Ad-vanced Scholars and University Students. By the Rev. J. T. WHITE, D.D. Royal 8vo. 12s.

WHITE & RIDDLE.—*A LATIN-ENG-LISH DICTIONARY.* By J. T. WHITE, D.D. Oxon. and J. J. E. RIDDLE, M.A. Oxon. Founded on the larger Dictionary of Freund. Royal 8vo. 21s.

WILCOCKS.—*THE SEA FISHERMAN.* Comprising the Chief Methods of Hook and Line Fishing in the British and other Seas, and Remarks on Nets, Boats, and Boating. By J. C. WILCOCKS. Profusely Illustrated. New and Cheaper Edition, much enlarged, crown 8vo. 6s.

WILLICH.—*POPULAR TABLES* for giving Information for ascertaining the value of Lifehold, Leasehold, and Church Property, the Public Funds, &c. By CHARLES M. WILLICH. Edited by MONTAGU MARRIOTT. Crown 8vo. 10s.

WILSON.—*A MANUAL OF HEALTH-SCIENCE.* Adapted for Use in Schools and Colleges, and suited to the Requirements of Students preparing for the Examinations in Hygiene of the Science and Art Department, &c. By ANDREW WILSON, F.R.S.E. F.L.S. &c. With 74 Illustrations. Crown 8vo. 2s. 6d.

WITT.—*WORKS BY PROF. WITT,* Head Master of the Alstadt Gymnasium, Königsberg. Translated from the German by FRANCES YOUNGHUSBAND.

THE TROJAN WAR. With a Preface by the Rev. W. G. RUTHERFORD, M.A. Head-Master of Westminster School. Crown 8vo. 2s.

MYTHS OF HELLAS; or, Greek Tales. Crown 8vo. 3s. 6d.

THE WANDERINGS OF ULYSSES. Crown 8vo. 3s. 6d.

WOOD.—*WORKS BY REV. J. G. WOOD.*

HOMES WITHOUT HANDS; a Description of the Habitations of Animals, classed according to the Principle of Construction. With about 140 Vignettes on Wood. 8vo. 10s. 6d.

INSECTS AT HOME; a Popular Account of British Insects, their Structure, Habits, and Transformations. 8vo. Woodcuts, 10s. 6d.

INSECTS ABROAD; a Popular Account of Foreign Insects, their Structure, Habits, and Transformations. 8vo. Woodcuts, 10s. 6d.

BIBLE ANIMALS; a Description of every Living Creature mentioned in the Scriptures. With 112 Vignettes. 8vo. 10s. 6d.

STRANGE DWELLINGS; a Description of the Habitations of Animals, abridged from 'Homes without Hands.' With Frontispiece and 60 Woodcuts. Crown 8vo. 5s. Popular Edition, 4to. 6d.
[Continued above.

WOOD. — *WORKS BY REV. J. WOOD*—continued.

OUT OF DOORS; a Selection Original Articles on Practical Natural History. With 6 Illustrations. Crown 8vo. 5s.

COMMON BRITISH INSECTS: BEETLES, MOTHS, AND BUTTERFLIES. Crown 8vo. with 130 Woodcuts, 3s. 6d.

PETLAND REVISITED. With numerous Illustrations, drawn specially Miss Margery May, engraved on W by G. Pearson. Crown 8vo. 7s. 6d.

WYLIE.—*HISTORY OF ENGLAND UNDER HENRY THE FOURTH.* By JA HAMILTON WYLIE, M.A. one of Majesty's Inspectors of Schools. (2 v Vol. 1, crown 8vo. 10s. 6d.

WYLIE.—*LABOUR, LEISURE, LUXURY;* a Contribution to Pre Practical Political Economy. ALEXANDER WYLIE, of Glasgow. Cr 8vo. 6s.

YONGE.—*THE NEW ENGLISH-GR LEXICON,* containing all the Greek w used by Writers of good authority. CHARLES DUKE YONGE, M.A. 4to.

YOUATT. — *WORKS BY WILL YOUATT.*

THE HORSE. Revised and enlar by W. WATSON, M.R.C.V.S. Woodcuts, 7s. 6d.

THE DOG. Revised and enlar 8vo. Woodcuts. 6s.

ZELLER. — *WORKS BY DR. ZELLER.*

HISTORY OF ECLECTICISM IN GR PHILOSOPHY. Translated by S. F. ALLEYNE. Crown 8vo. 10s. (

THE STOICS, EPICUREANS, SCEPTICS. Translated by the Re J. REICHEL, M.A. Crown 8vo. 15

SOCRATES AND THE SOCR SCHOOLS. Translated by the Rev. REICHEL, M.A. Crown 8vo. 10s.

PLATO AND THE OLDER ACAD Translated by S. FRANCES ALLEYN ALFRED GOODWIN, B.A. Crow 18s.

THE PRE-SOCRATIC SCHOOLS; a tory of Greek Philosophy from the E Period to the time of Socrates. lated by SARAH F. ALLEYNE. crown 8vo. 30s.